About the Authors

Roan Parrish lives in Philadelphia, where she's gradually attempting to write love stories in every genre. When not writing, she can be found cutting her friends' hair, meandering through the city while listening to torch songs and melodic death metal, or cooking overly elaborate meals. She loves bonfires, winter beaches, minor chord harmonies, and self-tattooing. One time she may or may not have baked a six-layer chocolate cake and then thrown it out the window in a fit of pique.

Cursed with a poor sense of direction and a propensity to read, **Annie Claydon** spent much of her childhood lost in books. A degree in English Literature followed by a career in computing didn't lead directly to her perfect job – writing romance for Mills & Boon – but she has no regrets in taking the scenic route. She lives in London: a city where getting lost can be a joy.

Louisa Heaton: I'm a married mother of four (including a set of twins) and I live on an island in Hampshire. When not wrangling my children, husband or countless animals, I can often be found walking my dogs along the beach muttering to myself, as I work out plot points. In my spare time, I read a lot, or crochet. Usually when I ought to be doing something else!

GW00360868

One Christmas Moment

ROAN PARRISH

ANNIE CLAYDON

LOUISA HEATON

MILLS & BOON

First Published in Great Britain 2022
By Mills & Boon, an imprint of HarperCollins*Publishers* Ltd
1 London Bridge Street, London, SE1 9GF
www.harpercollins.co.uk

HarperCollins*Publishers*
1st Floor, Watermarque Building,
Ringsend Road, Dublin 4, Ireland

ONE CHRISTMAS MOMENT © 2022 Harlequin Enterprises ULC

The Lights on Knockbridge Lane © 2022 Roan Parrish
Festive Fling with the Single Dad © 2019 Annie Claydon
Christmas with the Single Dad © 2016 Louisa Heaton

ISBN: 978-0-263-31789-3

MIX
Paper | Supporting
responsible forestry
FSC™ C007454
www.fsc.org

This book is produced from independently certified FSC™ paper to ensure responsible forest management.

For more information visit: www.harpercollins.co.uk/green

Printed and Bound in Spain using 100% Renewable electricity at CPI Black Print, Barcelona

THE LIGHTS ON
KNOCKBRIDGE LANE

ROAN PARRISH

For my wonderful, supportive parents.

Chapter One

Adam

Everyone on Knockbridge Lane had a different theory about Westley Mobray. It was the first thing Adam Mills heard about as he introduced himself around last week, when he and August moved in.

The eight-year-old McKinnon twins next door said he was a vampire. Their parents, Darren and Rose McKinnon, scoffed at that, but said he could be a witch. Marisol Gutierrez three doors down insisted she'd seen him skulking around the neighborhood at night, hunting for animals to sacrifice to the devil. A teenager at the end of the street reported that anyone who looked him in the eyes would be hypnotized, and anyone who touched him would turn to stone. Mr. Montgomery on the corner just said *freak*.

Westley Mobray was never seen before sunset, though mysterious packages arrived on his doorstep often. He never spoke to anyone and never waved hello. And late at night, the windows of his run-down house glowed an eerie green.

At least, that's what they told Adam.

So when he saw the man in question through the

twilit haze of his own front window—with his daughter in tow—he was understandably startled. Especially since he'd thought she was playing quietly in her room.

He'd slammed two coffees to prevent it, but he'd been asleep. The kind of light, unsatisfying sleep he often fell into when he had a moment of quiet. Which was something that didn't happen that often as the newly single parent of an eight-year-old.

His insomnia had been pretty bad since the divorce, and worse since they moved back to Garnet Run, where he was the only one responsible for Gus.

The knock at the door jerked him out of that strange sleep, and he scrambled for the door, stubbing his toe in the process, so that when he yanked it open he was biting back the kind of words that he tried with varying degrees of success not to say in front of Gus.

He focused on Gus first. She was all in one piece and was even smiling. It was her *I did something bad and delightful* smile, but a smile was good—at least when on a child who seemed to have been forcibly dragged home by an irate stranger.

"Where is your coat?" is what came out of Adam's mouth.

Sometimes he tried to remember what it was like when he talked about things like the composition of his next shot, which restaurant's tiramisu he preferred, or the latest cozy mystery he was reading.

Now he said things like "Where is your coat" and "Don't take that apart" and "If you don't stop making that sound I might have to throttle you." Okay, he didn't say the last one so much as think it. Often.

"It's not that cold," his wonderful, brilliant daughter said, her lips only vaguely blue.

Adam counseled himself to breathe.

Once he'd determined that Gus was all in one piece and frostbite wasn't imminent, he turned his attention to the man who'd brought her home.

"Um," he said intelligently.

Westley Mobray was tall and severe, with shaved dark hair and strong dark eyebrows over piercing blue eyes. Those eyes were narrowed slightly, either in anger or—if the neighborhood rumors were to be believed—because he never went outside when there was the slightest bit of light still in the sky, as it would, of course, burn him to ash.

"She broke into my house," he said. His voice was low and rough with disuse.

"She's eight."

Mobray cocked his head as if unsure what that might have to do with Gus' felonious misdeeds.

Adam sighed.

"Gus, did you break into our neighbor's house?"

She squinted and screwed up her face in a way that said she absolutely had. Adam and Gus had a strict No Lying policy, which had resulted in Gus developing a keen sense of words and their exact meanings.

"I didn't break anything," she settled on finally.

Adam offered up a silent prayer to the universe that his daughter not end up in prison.

"Did you enter without being invited?" he clarified.

And the vampire hits just kept coming.

She bit her lip and nodded.

"You can't do that, baby. It's not safe for you and it's not okay to intrude on other people's privacy."

She looked down at her toes, the very image of contrition. Then she peeked up at him with a glint in her big blue eyes.

"But he has lizards," she said softly.

"Okay, let's get you inside," Adam said quickly. Once Gus got going on something that fascinated her—and lizards were the most recent addition to that list—she tended to forget any reason why she shouldn't abandon all sense (or rules) to pursue it.

Adam passed her behind him and looked up at Westley Mobray.

"I'm really sorry about that," he said.

"She climbed in through my basement window."

Adam winced. Gus really was remarkably resourceful. And limber.

"I'm so sorry. I'll talk to her. She just, uh, *really* likes lizards. It started as a dinosaur thing and now… Anyway. Eight-year-olds."

The mysterious neighbor didn't say anything, just continued to look at Adam with a keen, curious gaze.

"I don't think I'm hypnotized," Adam muttered. Would you know if you were hypnotized, or was that part of hypnosis?

"Excuse me?" Westley Mobray said.

"Uh, nothing. Thanks for bringing her home. I'm Adam Mills, by the way." He stuck out his hand.

"We just moved here. That's Gus. August. But she likes Gus."

Mobray didn't shake Adam's hand—so Adam wouldn't feel his preternatural chill?—so he shoved it in his pocket. But at least there was no chance he'd turn to stone.

"Wes," said the man who was probably not a vampire or a witch or a Medusa. Freak? Well, the jury was out. But Adam tended to like freaks.

Then he turned and walked away, broad shoulders blocking the last of the day's light.

Inside, Gus had helped herself to a glass of apple juice and she held up the bottle to Adam angelically, to ask if he wanted some.

He nodded and she poured him some juice. He rummaged around in the disordered cabinets, looking for something to fix for dinner.

"Gus," he began, assuming the lecture would flow naturally once he opened his mouth.

"Daddy, he has the *best* basement," Gus gushed. "*Four* lizards. One has orange and black on its back and one is red and the other two are brown and he has a *snake*—I don't know what kind—and he showed me a huge, hairy spider!"

Adam choked on his juice.

He did not, historically, care for spiders.

"A, um, spider?" he squeaked.

"A turanyulla," she confirmed.

"Tarantula," he corrected automatically. "You saw this when you climbed in the window?"

"He showed me the tarantula." She said the word slowly and carefully. "He put it right in my face!"

Said face was lit with joy. Adam's stomach dropped. "He *what*?"

"I'm sorry I climbed in. It was just *so interesting*."

Interesting was Gus' buzzword. She had discovered, rightfully, that Adam liked when she was interested in things. Now she used it like a shovel to dig herself out of every mess she got in.

"So the, er, tarantula was placed near your, um, face?" His voice broke at the end.

"He thought it would scare me." She grinned hugely. "But it was *so* cool."

"Come," he wheezed. He grabbed her hand, burst through the door and stalked to the last house on the street. Damn, it *was* cold.

Wes Mobray's house certainly did nothing to discourage rumors of his supernatural being. It was a two-story Craftsman cottage, like the one he and Gus were renting. But unlike theirs, which was painted in cheery white and blue, it wore a peeling coat of brown, and every window but two—one that must have been Gus' basement ingress, and one small upstairs window—was covered from the inside with brown paper.

The whole thing gave the house the look of a crumpled paper bag. A crumpled gothic paper bag.

Adam felt a momentary pang of pity for Wes Mobray. Maligned and gossiped about by neighbors, living in this depressing paper bag of a house… But then he remembered what had brought him over here and he steeled himself to ring the doorbell.

It took ages, but after several more rings and some angry knocking, the door creaked open and Wes Mobray peered out, looking very confused.

"You!" Adam accused with a practiced pointer finger to Wes' face. "Put a *tarantula* in my daughter's *face*?!"

"She broke into my house," he said simply.

"I don't care. You do *not* shove *poisonous, terrifying*—" Adam shuddered "—*creepy* spiders in children's faces!"

"You're scared of spiders."

The man's infuriatingly handsome face quirked with the hint of a smile. Adam felt parts of himself turn just the tiniest bit to stone. He squared his shoulders and drew himself up to his full (admittedly not terribly imposing) height.

He looked Westley Mobray dead in his rather beautiful eyes and said firmly and with utter conviction: "Yes. I am terrified of them."

Chapter Two

Adam

Adam's younger sibling, River, was a literal angel.

"You," Adam told them, "are a literal angel."

They rolled their eyes but looked pleased.

Adam had grown up in Garnet Run, but left for Boulder, Colorado as soon as he turned eighteen. He left partly to escape his parents and partly because Garnet Run felt small and isolated and conservative, and yeah, okay, partly because he met the new boy in town and followed him, thinking they'd be together forever, like in the swoony old Hollywood romances that his grandmother favored.

And they were together, for a while.

But when he and Mason divorced, there was no way Adam could stay in Boulder. No way he could take care of Gus by himself on a freelance photographer's salary, and no way he could work a full-time job without childcare, which, of course, he couldn't afford.

River was the main reason he'd decided to move back. They loved Gus and when Adam called them to tell them it was over with Mason, the first thing they said—even before *Sorry*—was *I'm here to help*.

It had made Adam cry then and it still made him a little misty now. River was only twenty, but already a lifesaver. It helped that Gus adored them right back.

River had gotten Adam a job at a local hardware store through their friend Rye. And every day, they picked Gus up from school and stayed with her for an hour until Adam got home from work.

He'd tried to pay them the first three days and they'd turned him down flat. Yesterday, they'd told him to stop offering. Today, before he could open his mouth, they clapped their hand over it, and said, "Shh."

Seriously: angel.

"How's the kitten biz?" Adam asked.

River's eyes lit up. They worked as the manager of The Dirt Road Cat Shelter. River'd always loved animals so it was a dream job.

Before Adam knew it, they'd pushed their phone into his hand and were scrolling through pictures and videos of utterly adorable kittens and cats, introducing them to him and describing their antics.

"I should bring Gus by someday to see all the kitties," he mused.

"You can," River said. "But I don't think she's that interested in cats."

The child in question came into the kitchen then, wearing her hangry face, and Adam jumped up to start dinner.

"You staying?" he asked River.

They shook their head and kissed him on the cheek. "Gotta run."

"Thank you!" Adam called after them, putting water on to boil.

Gus pouted and slumped against the counter dramatically.

"What's up, baby?"

"Nothing," she sighed.

"How's school?"

"Stupid."

"You know I don't like that word," he told her gently. "Can you be more specific?"

"I already did this science lesson at home," she said dejectedly.

Adam winced. *Home* meant back in Boulder.

"And everyone is boring."

He wanted so badly to tell her it wasn't true. That there were kids here who could be her best friends if she'd let them.

But he remembered too well being the odd one out in elementary school. (Not to mention middle school and high school.) He remembered how lonely it felt when other kids weren't interested in the same things. When they thought you were weird.

"Maybe if you talk to them about things you're interested in, you'll make them interested too," he offered.

Gus thought about that.

"Maybe," she reluctantly allowed. After a minute, her eyes lit with excitement in a way that warmed Adam's heart—and then made him suspicious. "Be back," she murmured, and ran to her room.

* * *

"I need to put this in Mr. Wes' mailbox," Gus informed Adam the next morning as they left for school.

She held up a construction paper packet sealed with so many stickers they were overlapping like tape. It said *IMPORTANT* on it in all caps red marker.

Adam opened the mailbox so she could shove the sticky package inside, wondering if he should've asked to know what it was first. But since he was certain it wasn't a bomb or anything dangerous— okay, like, ninety-nine percent certain—he let Gus have her privacy.

Well, ninety-five percent.

"What was that, baby?" he asked casually.

"Secret," she said.

"It isn't, um, anything he won't like, is it?" *Or anything on the FBI watch list?*

"No," she said with certainty. "He will definitely like it."

Gus was sulking when Adam got home from work.

"What happened?" he asked River.

They shrugged. "She looked in the mailbox like five times but wouldn't say what she was looking for."

At dinner, Gus picked at her food.

"He didn't write back," she said finally, looking dejected.

"Wes?"

She nodded and Adam's heart broke. He wanted to strangle their neighbor. He wanted to punch the hell out of him for causing his kid one second of pain. Obviously, he would do neither, since it was totally reasonable not to immediately respond to a strange kid within twelve hours of receiving a mysterious marker-scrawled missive.

"Maybe he didn't check his mail yet," he offered. "Not everyone checks quite as often as you do." *Especially if they only go out at night and are busy hunting for animals to sacrifice to the devil.* Adam amused himself.

Gus cheered up.

"Oh, yeah!" she said. "Probably we should ring his doorbell and give it to him in person."

"Listen, kiddo. I know you want to see those lizards and the—" He swallowed hard. "Tarantula again. But Wes is a stranger. He seems like he enjoys being left alone. You know how sometimes you want to be alone in your room?"

She rolled her eyes and nodded.

"Wes feels that way about his house. So it's okay to put a letter in the mailbox. But we can't bother him at home."

She sighed the sigh of injustice, but nodded again.

After a few unenthusiastic bites of macaroni, she said, "Papa doesn't want to be bothered either."

And Adam's heart broke all over again. Because Wes Mobray might not have had any responsibility toward Gus. But Mason? Mason absolutely did.

Mason had said he would call the night they arrived in Garnet Run, and hadn't. Gus had called him instead. Mason had said she could call him anytime she wanted. When she FaceTimed, he usually didn't pick up the phone.

"Papa loves you, Gus. But he's not the best at doing everything he says he will. It's not you."

A tear ran down her cheek to salt the macaroni.

"He got rid of us."

She said it so fiercely and with such certainty that it startled Adam. And it was true, in its way. From the moment he got River's call about their sister, Marina, Adam had burned with purpose. Marina couldn't take care of Gus, but he could. He *wanted* to. And he'd assumed that Mason would want to as well. It had been a mistake—a genuine one, but a mistake nonetheless, and as much as he wished he could blame Mason for that, it was undeniably reasonable for a young man who'd never thought about kids to be less than enthusiastic about suddenly having one.

No, it wasn't Mason's ambivalence that Adam resented. It was that for a few years, he'd seemed committed. After his initial shock, he'd simply said, "We'll make it work." And for a little while, it had.

Mason's uneven attention and affection had been enough—just enough, but enough—for Gus to want more. Just enough to honor the letter of the agreement he and Adam had struck. For every dinner he ate out and play time he worked through, Mason was there with a few minutes of attention so intense that it seemed like it had lasted far longer; a gift that came at just the right moment.

It would have been better, Adam thought, if Mason had said from the beginning that he had no interest in this life. Better if Gus had never had to experience the singular cruelty of parental rejection. His blood boiled.

He grabbed Gus and pulled her into his arms.

He started to tell her no. To tell her it wasn't like that.

But Gus put her small, slightly sticky hands on his cheeks and looked directly into his eyes.

"No lying," she said, voice flinty and far too adult. "Not ever."

"Okay, no lying."

Adam squared his shoulders and looked right back into her eyes. His sister Marina's eyes. There was no point in explaining that, yes, Mason had gotten rid of them, bit by bit, over the years, but that it had been Adam, finally, who gave the ultimatum: I choose Gus over you, so either choose Gus over all the rest of it, or we're gone. No need to give Gus one more reason to feel like this was because of her. Besides, it was just as likely she would end up angry at him for taking her papa away.

So he told the only truth he was absolutely sure of.

"We're going to have the best time just the two of us. It's going to be Christmas soon, and we're going to have so much fun. I love you to the moon and back, and nothing will ever change that."

There was a flicker in her eyes at *Christmas*.

"What kind of fun?" she asked, not yet convinced.

Unprepared for the question, Adam said vaguely, "Oh, all kinds."

"Can you be more specific?" she demanded, echoing his own words back to him, curse her.

"What would be the most fun for you? If you could do one special thing."

Gus thought hard. She put her elbows on the table and her chin in her hands. And then she looked at Adam, eyes glistening with her earlier emotion, and made a somber declaration.

"I want our house to have the most Christmas lights of any house in the world."

Adam swallowed hard. *It could have been so much worse!* he told himself. She could have wished to turn her bedroom into an entomology laboratory or learn to ride a motorcycle. This was fine.

Adam's mission was clear: in order to convince his daughter that they could still have a wonderful Christmas despite leaving Mason, their home, and all their friends far behind them, he just had to find a way to procure the most Christmas lights in the whole world.

What could possibly go wrong?

Chapter Three

Wes

As the sun set outside his house on Knockbridge Lane, Wes Mobray came alive.

He'd always preferred going out at night. Not because—as his neighbors believed—he was a vampire or a witch or whatever the rumor of the moment was. But because nighttime was peaceful, quiet, and blissfully free of human interaction.

No doorbells ringing or neighbors shouting; no telemarketers or music blasting; no smiling, chatting, questioning, *people*. No one looking at him.

Just peaceful, calm darkness in which to wander in the woods, collect dirt samples, or source small rodents.

Wes' doorbell rang.

He froze.

It couldn't be James with the compost; he knew better than to ring the bell. There must be a new delivery person on his route; all the regulars knew to simply leave his packages outside the front door. But winter was tricky: it got dark early enough that people thought it was still okay to intrude. When whoever it was realized he wasn't going to answer, surely they'd go away.

Wes turned his attention to chopping his food waste from the previous day to add to the biogas generator.

The doorbell rang again.

Wes stalked to the front door and threw it open, ready to inform the new FedEx employee of the agreement he had that his packages simply be left outside without disturbing him.

But it wasn't a delivery person. It was the new kid from across the street who'd crawled through his basement window.

She stood on his front stoop, arms crossed and face twisted in a scowl.

"You didn't write me back," she said, and her voice was softer than her posture, like perhaps anger was a cover for disappointment. Sadness. Wes was familiar.

"What?"

"Didn't you get my letter?"

Wes glanced at the mailbox he never checked. Anything he cared about came through via email.

"No."

"Oh. That's what Daddy said."

As if conjured by his title, the father in question came running across the street.

Wes had watched Adam Mills move in the week before through the periscope mounted on the side of his house. He might not have wanted anyone to look at him, but he certainly watched them.

Adam and his daughter had arrived in a medium

moving van, and Adam had unloaded his belongings himself, with the help of one other person. He had introduced himself to every single neighbor that happened past.

Only of course they hadn't *happened* past—they had coordinated trips to the mailbox and the grocery store with times when Adam was outside, so they could scope out the new addition to Knockbridge Lane.

Wes had lived here for four years. He knew the routine. They'd tried it on him too. And they'd failed. But Adam was friendly. Talkative.

Normal.

"Gus, Jesus, you scared the sh— You scared me," he said.

Adam Mills jogged up the steps and glared at his daughter.

"What did I tell you?" he demanded.

"I know, Daddy, but I just *had* to," Gus said.

Father and daughter seemed to be having an intense conversation made of looks and facial expressions.

Wes cleared his throat.

"I'm really sorry," Adam told him, and slid a hand around Gus' small shoulder.

"It's in your mailbox," Gus said. "Write me back, okay?"

She looked so intent that for a moment Wes considered that perhaps this was a cry for help. But then she pouted at him and spoke sweetly.

"Couldn't we *please* see your taranula again? Just for a second?"

"Tarantula," Wes corrected. He shot a glance at Adam, who had gone pale and shrunk backward, hand that had been on Gus' shoulder hanging in the empty air.

"No, no," Adam said desperately. "We can't bother Mr. Mobray."

Gus put her hands together and bounced in place, mouthing *please* over and over.

Wes was just about to close the door in her wide-eyed little face. Then, inside the house, something exploded.

Wes bolted inside and ran to the room that housed the biogas generator.

He'd had a problem with a leaky valve between the slurry and gas storage before, but that shouldn't have been explosive.

As he rounded the corner, the scene before him came into focus: one splodge of wet compost goo on the floor and a splatter on the wall, one tube that should have been connected flapping free, and one hognose snake hanging from the chandelier, hissing at the raccoon below.

"Oh, dear god—" came Adam's voice behind him, while at the same time Gus said, "A snake! Can I touch it!?"

Wes wheeled around and glared at them. Who just waltzed into other people's houses?

"Sorry!" Adam said, putting his hands up. "We wanted to make sure you didn't blow up."

"I wanted to see the tarantula," Gus confessed.

Wes found himself in an octagon of things out of place. Agitated and flustered as he was, though, he couldn't resist the clarion call of a kid who was fascinated by snakes and spiders like he had always been.

"Her name's Bettie," Wes said grudgingly. "She's sleeping right now."

"Who's that?" Gus pointed.

"Milford," Wes said shortly. But her interest didn't waver, so he grudgingly elaborated. "She's a *Heterodon platirhinos*—a hognose snake, about thirty-six inches long."

"Is that perhaps a...raccoon?" Adam asked. While Gus had come closer with each word, Adam had retreated to the farthest corner of the room and fitted himself into it.

"Janice."

"Oh, sure," Adam murmured weakly. "She's tame, then?"

Wes shrugged. Humans' estimation of tameness was variable and useless.

"Is that what exploded?" Gus asked, gazing raptly at the biogas generator.

Wes nodded.

Gus screwed up her face. "What is it?"

"It's a biogas generator," Wes said. When she crept closer to it, Wes found himself helpless in the face of her curiosity. "It converts food and herbaceous waste into methane that I can use for power."

Gus blinked, cocked her head, and said politely, "Can you use other words?"

"She's eight," Adam said.

Gus was looking up at him, all big-eyed attention, and Wes realized she actually was interested.

"As things decompose—rot—like in the trash, gasses form. One of those gasses is methane. I keep my rotting, uh, stuff, in this container and when the gas is produced, it inflates this rubber thing here, and creates pressure. That pressure can bring that gas to the stove or a light—whatever I want."

"From trash?" Gus said in wonder.

"Yeah. It's basically like a giant stomach. Just like food breaks down in your stomach and creates gas, which expands your stomach, and the pressure makes you...um."

He wasn't sure what the proper word was for a kid.

She giggled. "Fart?! That's why people fart?" She whirled around. "Daddy, that's why people fart!?"

"I...to be honest, I didn't know that, sweetie." Adam looked to Wes. "Do you run your stove off this generator?"

"No, not the stove. That was just an example. I could. But this is an experiment."

"Experiment in what?" Adam asked as Gus, apparently having lost interest in the biogas generator, said, "Can I hold that spider now, please?"

"Oops, we gotta go now," Adam said instantly.

"Daddy's very scared of spiders," Gus whispered completely audibly. "But can I?"

Bettie was a sweet, shy creature who liked to crawl slowly around the perimeter of the house as if she were keeping watch. She didn't like sudden movement or loud noises, and a child seemed a guarantor of both. Wes didn't want to let Gus hold her.

But most children—most people—thought of tarantulas as terrifying, dangerous threats. The fact that Gus was interested in her rather than scared made him happy.

"If I let you hold her, you have to be very, very still," Wes said seriously. "It tickles when she crawls, but you can't jerk your hand back or scream or throw her."

His heart began to pound at the idea of his sweet baby being squished or thrown by a careless hand.

"Maybe it's not a good idea," he said, reconsidering.

"I won't," Gus said solemnly. "I promise."

Wes took a moment to plan precisely how he would swoop in and rescue Bettie at the first sign of trouble.

"Gosh, um," Adam said weakly from the corner. "I'll just…"

He began to edge toward the front door, shoulder blades glued to the wall. That was the typical response.

Wes went into the kitchen where he'd last seen Bettie. She was on the windowsill, looking regal in repose.

"Hi, baby," he said softly, running a finger down her back. "You okay?"

Bettie crawled onto his hand, her body a velvet weight in his palm.

In the other room, Adam was almost to the front door. Even though Wes thought tarantulas were amazing and beautiful creatures, he did understand the fear of them was significant, and he didn't want to upset Adam. He seemed like a sweet man. A caring, kind man. Even if he had pushed his way into Wes' house.

So instead of holding his hand palm-up so Adam couldn't help but see Bettie crawl, Wes angled his body between Adam and his lightly cupped hand.

"Oh, god," Adam wheezed. "I'm so sorry, I just... *ugh*."

"Oh, Daddy," Gus said absently. Then, "Ooh, she's so cool."

The sound of a slamming door echoed through the house.

"Put your hand down on the table," Wes said.

Gus put her hand down, palm-up, and Wes deposited Bettie a few inches away.

Bettie crept close, then felt Gus' finger with her front legs. Gus' eyes got wide.

"How old is she?"

"I'm not exactly sure. I've had her for about ten years. Females can live to be thirty or so, though."

"Why's her name Bettie?"

"Why is your name Gus?"

"It's short for August."

"It's short for Elizabeth," he retorted, which wasn't true.

"But *why*?"

Wes stared and Gus stared right back. But she still didn't move her hand, which Bettie was crawling onto.

Wes scrubbed a hand over his shorn hair. He didn't

care to untangle the serpentine path his brain had
taken to associate the tarantula with Bettie Page, especially since an eight-year-old would surely have no
idea who she was.

"She just," he said slowly. "She looked like a Bettie."

Gus nodded, accepting that answer.

For a while she observed Bettie closely, not seeming to see anything else.

"My mom named me August," she said finally,
stroking Bettie with a gentle finger. "Cuz I was born
in August."

"Your mom doesn't live with you guys?" Wes
heard himself ask.

He made it a habit not to initiate conversations,
but the kid was already in his house, and he found
himself oddly curious about Gus and Adam Mills.

Gus shook her head.

"I never lived with her. Daddy took me right after
I was born. My mom is Daddy's sister, but we're not
friends. She lives in Cheyenne, but I don't see her.
I'm friends with River, though. River's Daddy's other
sibling. Daddy says River's a literal angel. They watch
me after school now that we don't live at home anymore."

Wes smiled at *literal angel*.

"Where's home?"

"Where we used to live in Colorado. With Daddy
and Papa."

She frowned and got quiet.

Wes didn't know what made him ask the next question. As a rule, he didn't ask personal questions of

strangers. People tended to take them as an invitation to ask questions of their own.

"Your dad's gay?"

Gus' eyes shot to his, her expression utterly fierce, though the hand holding Bettie remained completely still.

"Yeah. You gotta problem with that?"

If looks could maim, he'd've been on the floor right now. Wes admired her protectiveness.

"No. No."

In fact, his heart was beating faster for quite the opposite reason.

"You better not be mean to my daddy," Gus said, still vivisecting him with her stare.

And Wes found himself in the strange position of wishing he had someone as fierce as this tiny eight-year-old to have his back.

"I won't," Wes said. "I promise."

That seemed to placate Gus.

"Speaking of which, you should probably go make sure he's okay."

She sighed.

"Yeah. Poor Daddy. He was *so* scared."

She grinned at him conspiratorially. Wes was surprised to find himself smiling back at her.

"He really was."

Very slowly and carefully, Gus stood up and deposited Bettie in Wes' outstretched hand.

"Thanks for letting me hold her," Gus said, and headed for the front door.

With her hand on the knob, she turned back to look at him.

"Can I come back sometime? Hold her again?"

Wes saw the hope in her eyes and even though it went against every instinct of privacy and self-preservation he'd cultivated in the four years since leaving LA for Garnet Run, Wyoming, he said, "Yeah, okay."

Chapter Four

Adam

It was absolutely essential that Adam distract Gus from her burgeoning obsession with Wes Mobray, and, by extension, her obsession with—Adam gulped at the thought—tarantulas. And honoring her Christmas wish was just the way to do it.

"Hey, Charlie," Adam asked his new boss. "Do we have more Christmas lights?"

"More than the ones on display?" he asked patiently, gesturing to the charmingly lumberjack-esque holiday display at the front of the store. It was only the beginning of November, but people were already decorating.

Matheson's Hardware had been around for as long as Adam could remember, but he'd never set foot inside it until River got him an interview with owner Charlie Matheson last week.

Charlie was a big bear of a guy who was helpful and kind to every customer and then turned around and was equally helpful and kind to everyone else. It was pretty endearing. Especially when that extended to giving Adam a job even though what he knew about hardware could fit on the head of a nail. A penny nail. (See, he learned that lingo on his first day at work.)

Charlie's partner, Rye, had started The Dirt Road Cat Shelter, which River managed, and River spoke of him in reverent tones. It seemed it was Rye Adam was replacing, as he didn't have time to work at Matheson's anymore, given how well the shelter was doing.

Rye was heavily tattooed, with long, messy dark hair and eyes the uncanny gray of a morning storm. He tended to glare a lot, seemingly without ire, but he'd grinned wryly when he met Adam.

"It's perfect," Rye had told him. "I didn't know shit about the hardware biz. Now that I'm leaving, of course Charlie should hire someone else who doesn't know shit."

Whatever Charlie's reasons—and Adam was pretty sure it was wanting to help out River as much as to give a job to another queer person—Adam was supremely grateful and was doing his level best never to give Charlie reason to regret it.

The holiday display did indeed feature Christmas lights, as well as a beautiful wooden cutout of a log cabin, painted in full color, on which a string of lights was draped. Whenever anyone commented on it, Charlie proudly informed them that his brother, Jack, had painted it.

"Yeah, I guess I was wondering if there might be a way to get them cheaper if I order some directly from the distributor. If that's not overstepping," Adam added. He *had* only been working there for a week.

"I'm really sorry, Adam." Charlie looked genuinely disappointed. "I pretty much sell these at cost. Around the holidays they're a sure sell, so I use them to get people in the door, but I don't mark them up."

"Oh. That's okay. I'll just buy some of these, then."

He bought ten boxes of lights with his employee discount. There went the day's pay, but he couldn't wait to see the smile on Gus' face when he brought them home.

The scent of snow was in the air when Adam pulled up to his house. Inside, lights glowed warmly, but he found himself glancing across the street at Wes' house, which stood dark and still.

For all that he wanted Gus to forget the lure of Wes' unusual critters, Adam couldn't forget the way Wes had cradled his pet so gently in his large hand. The way he'd explained his…whatever that thing had been to Gus patiently and as if she could understand everything he was saying.

Mason had not been patient. Not with Gus and definitely not with Adam.

"Hey," Adam called as he unlocked the door. "Where's my little monster?"

A giggle, then the rush of footsteps, and Adam turned around to see not Gus, but River, with their arms outflung like a child.

Adam grinned and Gus peeked from around the corner, hand over her mouth to muffle her laughter.

"There you are!" Adam cried, playing along. "Come here, my little monster."

He threw his arms around River and hugged them tight. River tensed for a moment and Adam started to let go, but then they relaxed into his arms. Adam squeezed his younger sibling tight for a few more seconds, then let them go with a ruffle of their hair. He hadn't had the chance to do that much in their lives spent mostly apart, and spared a moment of gratitude that he now had the chance.

"No, me!" Gus yelled, running straight at Adam and plastering herself to him.

"Here's my other little monster."

She nodded and he swung her around until they were both dizzy.

"What's that?" Gus asked, recovering quickly, pointing at the large brown paper bag with Matheson's Hardware stamped on it.

"Look inside."

She poked her nose inside and grinned.

"Lights for me!"

"Lights for us," Adam said.

"Lights for us," Gus echoed politely. Then, to River she said, "I'm gonna make our house have the most Christmas lights in history."

"Whoa," River said. "That sounds beautiful!" They turned to Adam and added under their breath, "And expensive."

Adam grimaced. He hadn't quite realized the expense when he'd agreed to this project.

"Can we put them up?"

Gus was already tearing open the boxes.

"Sure. You wanna help?" Adam asked River.

"Nah, I'm gonna take off. Gotta check on Hydra."

"I hope that's a cat?"

River flushed. "Yeah. Bye."

"Bye, River!" Gus yelled without looking up from her task.

Lights freed from their boxes, they went outside. Immediately, Adam realized their first problem: he didn't have a ladder.

"Shoot, sorry, sweetheart. I'll get one from work tomorrow."

Adam quickly budgeted for that and wondered if Charlie would lend him one, just for the weekend.

"Maybe Wes has one," Gus suggested slyly.

"Er, maybe one of our other neighbors—"

"I'll ask!"

And with that she ran off. Gus knew he should stop her, but he couldn't deny that mysterious, reclusive, frankly weird Wes Mobray had gotten under his skin.

Instead, Adam followed his daughter to Wes' front door. It opened faster this time, and Wes looked less confused to find them there.

"Hi," he said, his frown only at twenty-five percent this time.

One of the neighbors Adam hadn't met yet—a woman who lived with her daughter at the end of Knockbridge Lane—drove past and craned her neck to look at them.

Adam raised a hand in greeting, and she snapped her eyes front. Wes took a step back into the shadows of the house.

"We're hanging Christmas lights," Gus announced. "Wanna help?"

"Oh, honey, that's not— We don't— I thought— Um, we were wondering if you had a ladder we could borrow. You don't have to— That is, you can if you want, but—"

Adam physically forced his lips together to prevent more gibberish from leaking out. Wes was looking at him intently. Then he glanced at Gus. She was vibrating in place like a whippet in a snowstorm, eyes huge and hopeful.

"Um. Okay," Wes said.

Adam gaped.

"Yay! Yes! Yay!" Gus cried, and darted inside. "Can I see Bettie?"

Adam and Wes looked at each other and Adam felt like Wes could see right through him.

"You don't have to," Adam said. "I just. I accidentally promised Gus the biggest Christmas light display in the world and, uh."

Every time he said it out loud it sounded more unrealistic than the last.

Wes raised an eyebrow but said nothing. He kept looking at Adam like there was a mystery he was trying to solve.

"Wes!" Gus' voice sounded more distant. "Can I touch this snake?!"

"Oh god, I'm sorry," Adam said. Then the words registered, and panic ripped through him. "Wait, snake?"

"She's not poisonous, don't worry."

That was actually *not* what Adam's reaction had been in response to, but he made himself nod calmly.

"Good, good."

"Are you coming in, or?"

"Oh, nah, I'll just wait here," Adam said extremely casually. "Don't mind me. Yep. Fresh air. I'll just. Uh-huh, here's great."

Wes smiled for the first time and it was like nothing Adam had ever seen.

His face lit with tender humor, eyes crinkling at the corners and full lips parting to reveal charmingly crooked teeth. *Damn*, he was beautiful.

"Wes, Wes!" Gus ran up behind him and skidded to a halt inches before she would've slammed into him. "Can I?"

"You can touch her while I get the ladder," Wes said.

Gus turned to Adam.

"Daddy, do you wanna touch the snake? She's *so* cool."

Adam's skin crawled.

"Nope, you go ahead."

Adam sank down to sit at the top step and wait. The sun was setting, and it painted the expanse of Knockbridge Lane in muted pinks and purples. The mountains rose to the west, and to the north and east were trees. A Cooper's hawk glided in a wide arc high above the tallest branches.

It was beautiful here, there was no denying. Adam hadn't left all those years ago because it wasn't a beautiful place to live. But no amount of natural beauty could make up for living with parents like his.

The door opened and Gus barreled out.

"Oh my god, Daddy. She sat around my neck like a scarf!"

Gus' eyes were bright as stars, so Adam swallowed down his nausea and smiled right back.

"That's so cool!" he said weakly.

"So. Cool." Gus shivered with delight. "You know how everyone said Wes was a vampire and a witch and stuff?"

"You know better than to believe everything people say, don't you?" Adam admonished.

"I know." Gus waved him away. "I was gonna say, I think he's more like a superhero. He has all these sidekicks, and he knows how to do *everything*."

Gus pulled the door shut and skipped toward the garage. Adam trailed along in her wake. He was embarrassed to admit it, but he was just the tiniest bit jealous of his daughter's worship of Wes.

Wes came out carrying a ladder, a hammer, and some nails.

"Penny nails," Adam said absently.

When they'd lugged the ladder across the street and stood in front of their house, Adam said, "Okay, Gus, your call. Where are they going?"

"Can I go on the ladder?" she asked excitedly, eyes wide.

"Er, no, baby. Sorry, it's too dangerous." She pouted but shrugged. "Because I might have a heart attack," he muttered.

"Let me guess," Wes said. "You don't like heights?"

Adam rounded on him, instantly defensive.

"Why would you say that?"

His whole life people had looked at his small stature and his sexual orientation and his sensitivity and assumed he was weak and scared.

And yeah, okay, he *was* afraid of some things. But it was natural to be afraid. There was nothing wrong with it. Tarantulas and snakes could be *poisonous*. It was self-preservation to fear them. He wasn't upset that he was afraid of things; he was upset that people thought being afraid meant being weak.

And Adam Mills was definitely not weak.

Wes looked taken aback. "You just seemed really worried about Gus going up, so I thought… I don't know. Sorry."

Adam internally cringed at himself for being so defensive.

"Oh. Right. Um, no problem. That's just because she's, you know, a very small child."

Wes nodded.

"I don't really know much about children."

"Surely you at least were one?" Adam said, trying to lighten the mood he'd cast in darkness.

Wes just blinked. "Not this kind."

"What kind?"

He shrugged, and walked onto the porch, then around the side of the house.

"Here's your outlet," he said.

Gus pointed to the front of the house. "Let's put them there, like an outline of light."

Adam nodded and gathered the lights under his arm. Then he began to ascend the ladder.

The truth? Was that Adam *was* afraid of heights. But he would be goddamned if he was going to admit that in front of Wes now.

"Are you okay, Daddy?"

Gus sounded concerned and Adam realized he'd stopped four rungs up the ladder.

"Uh-huh, fine." His voice broke but he made himself keep climbing.

From the top of the ladder, Adam surveyed the neighborhood below him.

This, it turned out, was a huge mistake.

"Oh god, oh god, ohgod, ohgodohgod. It's tall. This is tall. High. Up here. This is *dangerous*! How many people die each year in routine Christmas decorating accidents?!"

"Careful, Daddy," Gus said.

Wes said, "Three hundred ladder-related fatalities annually in the US. Hmm, I would've thought it'd be higher."

Adam squeezed his eyes shut and forced himself to unclench the claw of his fist from around the lights enough to find the end of the strand.

"Here's ten years of Christmas-related injuries." Wes scrolled on his phone. "Wow, 134,281 people were sent to the ER with holiday decoration–related injuries from 2008 to 2017. God, who knew."

Adam's whole body was rigid, and he heard himself make a tiny whimpering sound that he hoped didn't reach the ground.

"They're not straight, Daddy," Gus called helpfully from the ground.

Adam, who was at the moment trying to figure out how on earth it was humanly possible to lift a string of lights, unpocket a nail, hammer in said nail, string the lights on the nail, and move the ladder to another position without falling to his death, just said, "Thank you, baby."

After a great deal of ladder moving (because no, thank you, Wes, Adam did not want to simply climb onto the roof), thumb hammering, and light adjusting, Adam got all ten strands of lights hung.

He climbed down the ladder slowly, feeling extremely pleased with himself. Triumphant, even!

He let out a pleased sigh, slung his arm around Gus' shoulders, and looked up at what he'd just accomplished.

And looked.

And tilted his head and looked some more.

"Huh," he said.

"Hmm," Wes echoed.

The ten strands of lights barely outlined the front triangle of the roof, and even though they twinkled merrily in the darkness, the lights looked sparse against the clear sky full of stars.

"That," Gus declared, "is *not* the most lights in the world."

Which, frankly, was what they were all thinking.

"We'll get more, sweetie," Adam said, wanting to cling to the sense of triumph he'd felt only seconds before. "This is just a start."

Gus nodded seriously.

"Okay," she said.

The *okay* got him. Gus trusted that if he said something would happen, it *would* happen. He treasured her trust more even than her love. It was something he would never betray.

Which just meant he needed to figure out a way to acquire more lights. Lots more. So many more that whenever Gus looked at them, she would stop thinking about Boulder and their house there. She would stop thinking about the friends she'd left behind. And most of all, she'd stop thinking about Mason, her papa who, when Adam's ultimatum came—be a part of their family or have no say in it—chose a life of freedom over being a father.

So many more that Gus would gaze at them and think only about how beautiful it was here, and how cozy their little house was. What a great holiday they would have together. And how very, very much Adam loved her.

Now if he could just figure out how to do that without bankrupting them—or becoming the 301st ladder-related fatality of the year—in the process.

Chapter Five

Adam

Adam hadn't posted anything on his Instagram account for a month. He hadn't thought much about it, since he hadn't done a photo shoot since before they'd left Boulder.

No, that was a lie. He had thought about it. In the wee hours of the night, when he couldn't sleep, when he put on the glamorous films from the forties and fifties that his grandmother had loved, and watched the way the light flickered on the living room wall more than he watched the films themselves, he thought about it.

He thought about what it felt like to see the world through the lens of his camera. How he could write or rewrite the story of any scene just by what he focused on and where he cropped the image.

How he could document the way a feeling or certain fall of light changed a person's face entirely.

He missed it so much it made his chest tight and his stomach hurt.

But he couldn't let himself think about it in the light of day, because if he did he'd question every choice he had made.

Now, he opened his account, ignored the notifications of friends and followers asking where he was, considered looking at Mason's account and instantly rejected the idea, then uploaded a picture of the tangle of Christmas lights he'd taken before ascending the ladder, and posted a call for help.

Hello, friends! I've been busy moving house with my daughter, but here I am, and I'd love your help. If anyone is in the Garnet Run, Wyoming area and has fairy lights to spare—any type—I could really use them. My daughter and I are working on a Christmas project. I'll post pics when it's done!

Four days later, life having driven the post completely from his mind, he arrived home from work to what appeared to be a bag of trash in his driveway. Irritated at whatever neighbor had decided to dump their garbage here, he got out of the car, muttering loudly, picked up the trash bag between two fingers, and moved to deposit it on the curb.

Then he saw the note taped to the side of the bag.

Hi, Adam. Big fan of your work. My mom had these in her garage and hasn't used them for years but they still work. Good luck with your Christmas project, and welcome to Wyoming!
—Matt

Tears filled Adam's eyes. The bag had four neatly coiled strands of lights that, to be fair, did look as though they'd spent more than a few years in a garage. Still, they were lights and Gus wanted lights, and Adam couldn't believe that someone he'd never met had taken the time to drop them off for him.

"Are you okay?"

Adam started. Wes stood in the shadows to his left, hands shoved in his pockets. Adam hadn't even noticed him approach.

"Hi. Yeah. You scared me."

"You were standing outside, clutching a garbage bag, and crying. I got concerned."

There was a time in Adam's life when he would have tried to hide his tears; would've protested, *I wasn't crying.*

The world wasn't kind to the sensitive. Adam had learned that long ago. For years he'd believed that his feelings were too big, too deep, too trip wire reactive.

It hadn't helped that his father had fed him poison his whole childhood. Beliefs about boys and tears that were designed to shame him and change him, but had had the curious effect, in adulthood, of making him treasure his tears. Treat them as proof that he was a different man than his father was.

Adam opened the bag so Wes could look inside.

"Good. Thought it might be a severed head or something."

Adam looked at him in horror.

"Does that…happen?"

Wes blinked and shoved his hands in the pockets of his jeans.

"No. I… Bad joke. Sorry."

"Oh."

They stood in silence for a moment and Adam realized it was the first time he'd seen Wes outside in
the daylight—well, twilight, and he *was* lurking in
the shadows. Adam said, "Do you want to help me
put them up?" at the same time as Wes said, "Guess
I better get home."

Then they both said "Oh" in unison.

Before Wes could turn away, though, Gus burst
out the front door, River close on her heels.

"Wes, Wes!" she shouted, and threw herself at him.

"Oof," Wes said, but caught her handily.

He didn't seem to know what to do with her,
though, so he held her in the air for a moment, then
set her down on the ground and patted the top of her
head, like a friendly monster in an animated film.

"What's that?" she asked, and dove into the trash
bag.

"Good thing it *wasn't* a severed head," Adam said
under his breath.

Wes snorted.

"Oh, this is my sibling, River," Adam said.

River had a way of standing so still and quiet that
you could forget they were there. Adam had no doubt
it was a survival tool, but he felt guilty every time it
worked on him.

"River, this is Wes. He lives over there."

Wes and River shook hands and nodded at each
other—two quiet, self-contained people reaching out
of their containment to make reluctant contact.

Gus pulled lights out of the bag and tugged on
Wes' jacket.

"Can we please go borrow your ladder to hang the lights?"

"Ladder's still here from last time." Wes pointed at it leaning against the side of the house.

"Oh." Gus sounded disappointed, but then she rallied and asked with perfect innocence, "Well then can we please go to your house to borrow something else?"

Adam snorted and River quirked a smile—Adam had filled them in on Gus' fascination with Wes' house. Wes just cocked his head and said, "What do you want to borrow?"

Gus thought about that, but honesty won out and she sighed.

"Nothing. I just wanna look at everything."

And Wes, whether because he was desperate to get back inside or because he honestly was a saint who didn't mind Gus' intrusion, said, "Okay."

The minute they got inside, Gus made a beeline for the basement and Adam bolted after her before she accidentally pulled bottles of chemicals down on her head or something.

The basement glowed with an eerie green light and for a moment, everything the neighbors had said about Wes echoed through his mind.

Gus had frozen in her tracks and was staring at the far wall of the basement, where glass jars on staggered shelves, with tubes protruding from them, contained the glow. Jars full of fireflies was all Adam could compare it to. He remembered that long ago summer when Marina had trapped them in her hands and put them in jars she'd carry around like night-lights against the coming dark.

Adam had thought it was the most beautiful thing he'd ever seen—like stars brought down to earth—until he realized that with the lid on the fireflies died, their beautiful glow darkened forever.

He'd cried when he found the first jar. Marina had been flippant. There would be more that night and they could just collect another jar. His father had been scornful. But Adam had never intentionally killed another thing again.

"What is it?" Gus asked, awed.

"I don't know."

"They're bacteria with luciferase enzyme and lu-ciferin substrate," Wes said from behind them. "Fed on methane. It mimics naturally occurring biolumi-nescence."

"Whoa," Gus said worshipfully. She got quite close, then turned to Wes. "Can I touch it?"

"You can touch the jar."

She put her hand on it, then held her hand behind it so the glow traveled up her arm.

"Can you make anything glow?" she asked.

"Theoretically, yes," Wes said.

The basement was set up like a laboratory and Adam peered at Wes in the dim, virid light, imag-ining him as a Victor Frankenstein type, all moody eyes, sharp cheekbones, and ill-fated passion for cre-ating life.

Ill-fated or no, Wes looked much more at ease in

his house than he had outside. His hands were out of his pockets, his anxious, darting glance had been replaced by an intent focus, and his words seemed to come easier.

"What are these?"

Gus moved to pick up a nonglowing jar on the table, and Wes and Adam both lurched toward her.

"Honey, don't touch things without asking," Adam said, taking the jar from her before she could drop it by accident.

However, when something inside it *moved*, Adam very nearly dropped it himself.

"Oh, god, what *are* they?"

Wes took the jar from him and cradled it to his chest protectively.

"Leeches."

Adam's stomach lurched.

"Like, uh, blood-sucking…bugs, leeches?"

"Leeches aren't bugs. They're in the worm family," Wes said matter-of-factly.

"Do they really suck blood?" Gus asked with fascinated glee. "Like vampires?"

"Well, not like vampires," Wes said mildly. "Because vampires aren't real."

Gus considered him. "You know everyone says *you're* a vampire."

"I know. And a werewolf."

He winked at her, then howled.

Adam started, but Gus laughed and then joined in the howls.

"Darren and Rose McKinnon said witch," Adam added.

Wes nodded sagely.

"Yeah, that too. I'm a vampire-werewolf hybrid who practices witchcraft and worships Satan. I'm extremely busy."

Adam laughed.

"Okay, but seriously. What's up with the snakes and spiders and leeches?"

Wes carefully set the jar of leeches down with a little pat, like the one he'd given Gus earlier.

"I like them," he said simply. "I've always liked them. They're fascinating."

He trailed a finger over an aquarium that Adam now saw contained several lizards.

"Everyone likes fuzzy things like dogs and cats. No one asks them why. But tarantulas are fuzzy and people find them terrifying. They love butterflies but they think leeches are disgusting. People kill totally harmless snakes all the time because they're scared of them."

He reached into the aquarium and one of the lizards—a small black one with an orange back—scampered up on his hand.

"But if people spent as much time with lizards and snakes as they did with dogs and cats, they'd realize how amazing they are. They have personalities too. All animals do."

Adam edged closer to Wes. The lizard was very beautiful. It flicked its tiny tongue out like it was tasting Wes' thumb.

He could acknowledge the beauty of the lizards, but the thought of that tarantula still filled him with utter horror.

"I don't mean to be scared of them," Adam said softly. "But isn't it, like, human nature?"

"No," Wes said. "Wolves are a threat to humans too, and anyone confronted with them would be afraid of them, but we don't naturally jump back from dogs because of it. We learn to fear snakes and spiders because we only encounter them in threatening contexts. By surprise in nature, or as villains in kids' movies. The way they move is unfamiliar, so we find it creepy."

He was watching the lizard fondly.

"But if we grew up in a culture where everyone had snakes and tarantulas as pets, we would be much less afraid of them. It's considered strange to have a pet rat, but normal to have a pet hamster. They're both in the Cricetidae family. But we think one is cute and one is horrible."

"Let me guess," Adam said. "You think rats are cute."

"Not especially. But I acknowledge that it's merely convention that makes people think they're less cute than hamsters."

He looked at the jar on the table.

"Leeches are much cuter than hamsters," he said.

Adam laughed, until it was clear Wes wasn't kidding.

"Can I hold a leech?" Gus asked.

Wes said, "If you do, it'll bite you and suck your blood a little. Are you okay with that?"

Adam gaped.

Gus asked, "Will it hurt?"

"Not really."

Gus shrugged. "Okay."

"Um, sorry, *not* okay. I would really prefer my daughter doesn't hold anything guaranteed to *suck her blood*."

"Well, I suppose it's not guaranteed—" Wes began.

"No. Nope. Thanks, but no."

"We have plenty to spare," Wes said mildly. Then, "You can hold Ludwig. He doesn't suck blood."

Wes held up the lizard that had scampered up his arm and onto his shoulder.

Gus nodded and held out her hand. She stroked the small lizard's back and giggled with delight when it ran onto her wrist.

"Gus isn't scared of them," Adam said.

"No." Wes cast a fond, respectful look at Gus.

"Wes, what do you *do*?" Adam asked. "Besides being a vampire-werewolf hybrid who practices witchcraft and worships Satan, of course."

Wes' blue eyes were intense as he spoke.

"I'm working to create a viable sustainable natural alternative to electric light," he said intently. "It's a huge problem, both in terms of unnecessary energy output and lack of access to necessary energy. Lighting accounts for twenty percent of worldwide energy used every year, so a natural alternative would cut down on our general energy usage. Electric light pollution spoils rural areas and scares animal populations out of their natural habitats, which can change entire ecosystems over time, so a natural alternative would be less disruptive. And urban neighborhoods that are primarily lower-earning people of color are severely underserved by cities' infrastructures, so they have a lack of electric streetlights, which makes the areas less safe and more susceptible to crime. A natural alternative to electric light could be more accessible for neighborhoods of that sort. If I can find a way to create this bioluminescent light, it could be used everywhere. Anywhere."

His eyes glowed with purpose.

"Holy crap," Adam said. "You really are a superhero."

Chapter Six

Wes

Adam Mills arrived at Wes' doorstep looking harassed.

Since Adam had called him a superhero two nights before, Wes had carried around a feeling he didn't recognize. A spacious, fizzy sensation that made his head feel a bit light and the corners of his mouth turn up.

"I need to ask you a huge favor," Adam said, grimacing. "It's Gus' turn to do a show-and-tell at school, and all she'll talk about is wanting to bring, er, Bettie."

Adam shuddered when he uttered the tarantula's name, but Wes was touched. If Gus brought Bettie in to school and talked about why she was interested in her, she could convince a whole classroom of kids that tarantulas were lovely, fascinating creatures, and nothing to be afraid of.

"So," Adam said, "I need you to talk her out of it."

"Huh?"

"Yeah, just tell her Bettie doesn't like to ride in cars or something, maybe. Whatever you want. I can bring her by, or you could pop over. Whatever's easiest for you. I'm really sorry."

He ran a hand through his silky dark blond hair, and it settled in a messy fall around his face.

"It's just, when Gus gets fixated on something, it's nearly impossible to get her off it. You really have to replace it with another fixation instead." He seemed to be half talking to himself. "Anyway, I'm sorry to put you on the spot, but can you?"

"Can I talk her out of it?"

"Yeah."

"Or she could just take Bettie to school," Wes offered.

He had Adam's full attention now.

"Oh, no. No, no, that's not necessary. Nope. No worries."

Adam swallowed hard when he was scared, and his eyes darted around.

Wes couldn't believe what he was about to offer. But with each passing day he thought about Adam Mills more.

"I could go. With her. If she wants."

Adam blinked up at him. His eyes were a bluish-grayish color that reminded Wes of the Pacific Ocean on smoggy days.

"Can you *do* that?" He immediately flushed. "Oops, sorry. I didn't mean. Um."

There was a childish wonder to Adam that delighted Wes. He imagined it was probably where Gus got her own sense of wonder and curiosity, even if hers was for different topics.

"Will the sun burn me to a crisp, you mean?"

Adam laughed nervously, but he bit his lip and

looked up at Wes like he really would like to know the answer.

Wes leaned closer. Usually, Adam was energy in motion—one eye on Gus, the other on the ground in front of him to make sure he didn't trip.

But now Wes had his full attention. He looked into Adam's stormy eyes and took in the way his pupils dilated and his lashes swept downward. The way his mouth softened and parted slightly.

And he said, very seriously, "I'm willing to chance it."

Adam snorted and then looked sheepish.

"Sorry," he muttered.

"I'm not a vampire," Wes said mildly. Then, in his best Bela Lugosi voice, "I am a daywalker."

Adam's eyes got wide and Wes relented.

"Do you believe in vampires?" he asked.

"No!" Adam said very quickly. Too quickly. "Not really." He scuffed the stoop with the toe of his worn sneaker. "I don't know. It's just as possible as anything else, isn't it? No, no, never mind. Forget I said that."

He rolled his eyes at himself.

Wes thought about it. Adam's statement seemed absurd on the face of it, yes. But Wes hadn't gotten where he was today by dismissing ideas without thinking about them just because they sounded impossible.

"Leeches and lampreys feed on blood. So do some bats. Mosquitoes and fleas do too, and bedbugs. The oxpecker is a bird that eats bugs off oxen, then drinks blood from the wounds they created. Oh, and there's a finch that lives in the Galápagos that drinks blood from the booby bird. So, the blood-drinking part isn't unreasonable. It's really the immortality that's the sticking point. And the transforming others into a different creature through their bite. But I suppose those things could just be part of the mythos, not the biology."

Adam was watching him with a strange look. Usually, Wes hated being looked at. But Adam's attention didn't make him squirm.

"You're very open-minded," Adam said.

Wes shrugged. "It's just science."

Adam regarded him in silence, like he'd forgotten why he'd come.

"So, show-and-tell," Wes prompted. "When is it?"

"Huh? Oh, Friday. We leave at 8:30."

"In the morning," Wes said.

"Yeah."

Adam just looked at him. Wes had been trying to make a joke, but it had fallen flat.

"Okay," he said, and moved to shut the door, embarrassed.

"Thank you!" Adam called.

Wes watched him walk across the street, arms wrapped around himself against the cold.

He watched him and wondered what Adam would think if he knew Wes had just offered to leave Knockbridge Lane in the daylight for the first time in four years.

Early Friday morning, the ancient alarm clock that Wes had found in the basement and plugged in for the first time jerked him awake with violent beeps.

Banana chirped with displeasure at the unusual interruption, shoved her face under the blanket, and curled back up with Janice, looking more like a grouchy cat than a raccoon.

Wes wished he could curl back up with them. His nocturnal schedule was usually aligned with the raccoons', but today Wes dragged himself out of bed and into the shower. He couldn't remember the last time he'd gotten up before 2:00 p.m.

But that disruption to his schedule paled in comparison to the larger disruption. Westley Mobray was about to leave his house and go to a school full of people—full of *children*, no less—in the daylight, where anyone could look at him.

The mind reeled.

Wes wasn't agoraphobic. He didn't get panic attacks in crowded places, nor was it precisely fear he felt at the prospect of going to them. What he absolutely, positively hated was being looked at. Feeling as though he was being observed.

And because of that, he had a habit of trying to make himself invisible in scenarios when people would observe him. This resulted in a sensation of being alienated from his own body. Little by little as he stood there, pieces of him would begin to feel wrong. The arm closest to people would go all strange—like it had no function. Then perhaps the legs he stood on. Then a shoulder.

Until, after a while, he felt like a mass of whirling energy trapped in a strange and clumsy form that became a prison. When people looked at the prison, or needed it to function, it became bigger and clumsier and less effectual.

And then, all Wes wanted was to disappear.

It had begun the year he was fifteen. The year the whole world had seemed to be observing him. And it had never gone away. For the next three years he'd been forced to capitulate to social conventions because he was living in his parents' home. But once he moved out, he had the freedom to eschew those conventions and avoid people as he pleased.

With each passing year of doing so, he'd found it increasingly unpleasant to attend the social functions that other people seemed to navigate with ease.

Now, with no one to dictate his schedule or police his habits, Wes was free to avoid the places and situations that made him feel distant from himself.

He had everything delivered, from groceries to laboratory equipment. During the day, when sensory stimulation and chance encounters with people were at their height, Wes slept. In the quiet, private darkness, he lived his life. He found places to do experiments and caught rodents for the snakes. He socialized online or via video chat; and conducted his meetings and conference appearances in the same way.

Wes had cultivated precisely the life he wanted.

And now he was breaking every barrier he'd put in place to take a tarantula to a little girl's school.

Chapter Seven

Adam

Adam had spent the previous evening trying to temper Gus' excitement by reminding her that it was possible Wes might not show up.

"He will, Daddy. I know he will," Gus insisted, and Adam's heart clenched at the faith she already had in Wes—and at the knowledge that Wes might betray it.

He cursed himself one hundred times for not getting Wes' number so he could text to remind him.

By 7:00 a.m., he was a mess of nerves, gulping coffee and peering out the kitchen window at Wes' house, trying to see if he could spot a light or a TV on that might indicate his mysterious neighbor was awake.

It was impossible because of the paper covering all the windows.

"God, he's so weird," Adam muttered to himself as he poured another cup of coffee. "And hot," he added, regrettably honest with himself when he'd had very little sleep—which he had, the night before, waking at 2:00 a.m. convinced Wes would be a no-show, then watching a loop in his mind of all the times Mason had disappointed him or let Gus down.

"Why do I think he's so hot?"

Wes Mobray was strange and awkward and lived in a hellscape of a haunted house crawling with things that Adam didn't even wish to think about.

He was also kind and generous and obviously brilliant. He took Gus' interests seriously and didn't treat her like a kid. He loved animals that most people thought were creepy and was gentle with them. His blue eyes were warm and honest and when he smiled it made Adam want to smile.

"Welp, I guess that's why."

"Why what, Daddy?"

Gus wandered into the kitchen rubbing her eyes, wearing jeans, one sock, and her pajama top.

"Why you're the greatest kid in the world."

Gus rolled her eyes, but smiled a little, and Adam brushed her soft blond hair back from her face. She had a spot at the back of her head that was always knotted from sleeping on it and his heart swelled with tenderness whenever he saw it.

"Can I have waffles?" she asked, leaning into his touch.

"Yeah. I'll make them while you go put on a shirt and another sock."

She trudged out of the kitchen and Adam popped a frozen waffle into the toaster.

Absently, he added *Learn how to cook* to his ever-expanding list of things to do.

When the waffle popped up and Gus wasn't back yet, Adam nibbled on it absently and put another one in for her.

Adam was combing Gus' hair as she ate her waffle when the doorbell rang.

"He's here; he's here!" she shouted, and jumped up, knocking over the syrup jug.

Adam dove for it and got a handful of syrup for his trouble, but did save the jug from rolling to the floor.

He heard Gus open the door and Wes' quiet voice, but couldn't make out what he said.

"Hi," Adam called from the kitchen. "Be right there."

He washed his hands, cast a glance at the table and decided to leave the dishes for later, and went to greet Wes.

He had forgotten that for the duration of this outing, Wes equaled Wes and Bettie. He caught one glance of the tarantula in her carrier and decided that actually the dishes absolutely needed to be cleared from the table this very instant.

Adam deposited sticky dishes into the sink one at a time, taking deep breaths and saying to himself over and over again, *It's in a box; it can't hurt you.*

When he couldn't stall a moment longer, he steeled himself and went into the foyer. Wes stood there by himself, staring into space.

"Gus went to get something," he said when Adam approached. "I put a covering on her."

He held up the carrier that held Bettie, now draped with a pillowcase.

"Oh god, thank you," Adam said. "I'm so sorry. I know she's just a spider being a spider, but I'm terrified of her."

"I understand," Wes said simply.

He was wearing brown corduroy pants and a rust-colored wool sweater under a navy wool peacoat. He looked warm and touchable (tarantula aside), and Adam found himself wondering what it would feel like to run his hand up Wes' back. Feel his warmth through the softness of the fabric.

Gus skidded into the hallway holding her favorite accessories: a khaki explorer-style jacket that was a million times too big for her and a beekeeping hat with a veil of netting that covered her face.

She stuffed them in her backpack and announced, "Ready!"

Adam smiled. "My little naturalist."

Gus rolled her eyes because she thought *naturalist* sounded tame, but it was Adam's joke with himself, as when Gus was younger, she'd refused to wear any clothing, running around the house naked, and he'd called her his little naturist.

Adam buckled his seat belt and Wes slid in beside him, Bettie on his lap. Adam gulped.

"Um. Any chance Bettie can sit in the back seat, because if she gets out in the car, I will crash and kill us all."

Gus giggled, but Wes must've heard the mounting tension in his voice because he solemnly placed Bettie on the back seat and then rested his elbow on the armrest between their seats, blocking any potential spider entry point.

Adam silently melted.

They got to school without incident—spider or

vehicular—and Gus ran over to Abel, whom she'd described as having friend potential.

Adam turned to Wes to thank him again for going to all the trouble of coming here today, but Wes wasn't walking with him. He was standing, pressed to the side of the car, eyes wild.

"Hey. You okay?" Adam said softly, approaching on the non-tarantula side.

"Yes," Wes said, though he clearly was not. Then, "I don't go many places."

Adam almost made a flippant, unthinking comment, like *Me neither, since I had a kid* or *Not many places to go around here anyway.* But he quashed the knee-jerk impulse to defuse the awkwardness he felt and really looked at Wes.

Wes wasn't being flippant. Wes didn't seem to ever be anything but completely genuine, in fact, except on the rare occasions he attempted a joke. He was holding himself completely still and his eyes looked like he was elsewhere.

Adam touched him very lightly on the shoulder. When he didn't recoil, Adam let his hand rest there.

"How come?" he asked.

Wes looked down at him, his blue eyes unsure.

"I don't like people looking at me. It makes me feel very...strange."

Adam waited for more but no more was forthcoming and there wasn't really time now to ask all the questions he wanted to.

Instead, he squeezed Wes' shoulder and said,

"Well, there are at least two people here who think your brand of strange is pretty awesome."

Wes blinked at him.

"Uh, me and Gus, I meant," Adam clarified, feeling very corny.

"I knew who you meant," Wes said softly. "Thanks."

Gus ran over to them and bounced in place. Adam wondered, for the four-thousandth time, if he had ever in his life possessed that much energy.

"Come on, come on!"

Gus grabbed Adam's left hand and Wes' right hand and tugged them toward the school. Wes looked startled, but let himself be led.

Adam caught his eye as they were dragged, like a vee of geese, into the flock of children entering the building. He raised his eyebrows in question and Wes gave him a slight nod.

As they made their way down the hallway to Gus' second grade classroom, Adam was struck with the memory of walking Gus into her first day of kindergarten. She'd held his and Mason's hands just this way, but had been so tiny she practically dangled between them.

Mason had been flustered, wanting to find the right room and wondering aloud about the school, while Adam had worked hard to hold back tears at the thought of his baby going to school like such a big kid.

Gus had looked up at Mason and smiled and he'd been too distracted to notice. Then she'd looked at Adam and he'd smiled at her big enough for both her parents. She had grinned, showing the gap where one of her front teeth had fallen out the week before, and Adam had felt a physical jolt of love so strong he couldn't believe he could function after.

How was a parent to survive feelings of such enormity? How could he go about his daily life when another person held his heart in her tiny hand?

It had never gone away, that feeling, though Adam now fancied himself a bit better at functioning despite it.

Now, as if she shared his memory, Gus looked up at him and grinned just as she had that day more than two years ago. Adam smiled back at her and winked.

Then, Gus turned her head and looked up at Wes.

As if he felt her eyes on him, Wes looked down at her and smiled.

Adam's eyes filled with tears he quickly blinked away. Wes was practically a stranger—at most, a neighbor. Adam had no business expecting anything from him, no matter how damn wonderful he was being. Expecting things from people was how you ended up disappointed, foolish, and heartbroken.

Gus pulled them into her classroom and over to her teacher.

"Ms. Washington, Ms. Washington, this is my dad, and this is Wes, and that's Bettie. She's my show-and-tell."

She pointed to the covered cage Wes held.

"That's great, August," she said brightly, bending down. "Is Bettie a hamster? A guinea pig?"

Gus reached out and before she could unceremoniously whip the pillowcase off, surprising Ms. Washington with a tarantula in the face, Adam grabbed Gus and threw an affectionate arm around her.

He gestured Ms. Washington away slightly and made a crawling spider with his fingers. Her eyes got very wide and she raised one elegant eyebrow. Adam inclined his head. *I'm afraid so*, his gesture said.

Without missing a beat, Ms. Washington said, "Why don't you sit down, August, and your dads can wait in the back with—er—Bettie?"

Gus skipped off to her desk without correcting Ms. Washington.

From the back of the room, Adam could see how small Gus was compared to the other kids. He'd been small for his age too.

She was nearly bouncing in her seat, and she kept looking over her shoulder at them. She waved at Wes and he waved back—a tiny movement of his hand at his side.

Wes leaned in. "They're so…little," he mused.

"Yeah, isn't it weird? You don't feel little as a kid. You're always the biggest you've ever been."

Adam wanted to ask Wes what he'd been like as a child. Had he been an amateur scientist, fascinated by dinosaurs and insects, as Adam imagined him? Had he always been so quiet, so self-contained? Or had that happened later—the result of his interactions with the world rather than the cause of them?

When it was time for Gus' show-and-tell, she ran to the front of the room, pulling on her explorer jacket and beekeeping hat as she went.

"My show-and-tell is named Bettie. She's a tarantula!"

Gus was grinning, her eyes wide with excitement. This was the moment Adam had been dreading. Not all of her classmates were going to be pleased with this addition to their number, and he didn't want to see the light in Gus' eyes dim with their rejection.

A few of the kids exchanged scared looks, but many leaned forward, interested.

"Should I go up?" Wes murmured.

"I think so."

Wes strode through the aisles of desks, looking like a giant in a land of Lilliputians. He stood next to Gus, awaiting her command.

Gus told the class a few tarantula facts that she'd read about in the insect compendium Adam had brought home from the thrift store, and more that Wes had clearly told her. Wes softly corrected her pronunciation of *arthropod*, and then it was time.

Adam pinched his arm, telling himself that Bettie was all the way across the room. She'd have to get past twenty second-graders to make it to him. Still, he let his eyes unfocus as the pillowcase came off Bettie's cage.

It did help a little to think of her as Bettie, rather than a spider. Bettie lived with Wes. Wes held her in his hand. That meant it was all okay.

Adam was concerned that his brain had begun to equate *Wes* with *Everything is okay*.

Wes held Bettie's cage up so everyone could see. Then he told them he would take her out, but they had to be very quiet and very still. His voice was low and soft, and not a child moved or made a sound as he opened the Plexiglas door and gently picked up Bettie.

He cooed to her and she stayed in his cupped palm. Adam focused on Wes' face, pretending his hand didn't even exist.

From across the room, as if he could feel Adam's gaze on his face, Wes' eyes snapped to his.

Wes' expression was subtler than Gus', but Adam saw in his clean, rough features the same joy, the same excitement, and the same desire to share that fascination with others.

It was beautiful. He was beautiful.

The children asked questions and Wes answered every one. He told them what Bettie ate, when she slept, and if she spun webs. When he told them that tarantulas shot silk from their feet, one of the boys called, "She's like Spiderman!" and Wes said, "Spiderman's like her." The boy looked like his mind had been blown.

For all their fascination with Bettie, the kids were clearly nervous when Wes asked if anyone wanted to touch or hold Bettie. No one raised their hand. Gus held out her cupped palms and Wes placed Bettie into them.

Once they'd seen Gus touch Bettie and live to tell the tale, another girl's hand went up, and Gus put the tarantula into her palm very carefully. "Don't move, even when she moves," Gus told her seriously, as Wes had once told her.

Once everyone who wanted to had held or touched

Bettie, under Gus' watchful eye, Ms. Washington called an end to show-and-tell. The class applauded and Gus stood, grinning from ear to ear.

As Wes and Adam walked out of the classroom and through the empty hallways, Adam touched Wes' arm, the wool of his sweater as soft as he'd imagined.

"Thank you," Adam said. "Thank you so much for doing this. It meant the world to Gus. And to me."

Wes looked down at Adam and seemed at a loss for words. Clearly the experience in the classroom had meant something to him.

"They weren't scared of her," he said.

"Kids are brave. They mostly haven't learned to be afraid of things yet."

The lucky ones, anyway. The ones who didn't have fear fed to them at home, where fear should never be.

"Like you said. I think we learn to be scared and then once we're scared we hate the things we fear because it's easier than working on our fear."

Wes glanced at Bettie's cage, once more covered with the pillowcase.

Adam reached over and very slowly, breathing deeply to ground himself, pulled the fabric away.

He felt his heart start to beat faster, Bettie's movements triggering a long-held disgust deep within him. He let his eyes go a bit unfocused so he could see her through a haze. This was Bettie. Wes' beloved pet. She was an animal, like a cat or a squirrel.

He watched her for a few moments, and thought neutral thoughts about her. He didn't even notice he'd stepped back until Wes moved to put the pillowcase back over the cage.

Wes' blue eyes were warm and soft and he stepped toward Adam.

Adam's heart was beating fast now for an entirely un-spider-related reason. Wes' mouth looked lush and soft and his shaved hair looked like velvet.

Wes pressed one broad shoulder into Adam's and said solemnly, "Thank you."

Chapter Eight

Wes

"**Y**ou did what?!" His friend's voice was at least an octave higher than usual. Wes had just told Zachary about Gus' show-and-tell. "But you mean an actual, human child?"

"Yes, a *Homo sapiens* child."

Zachary snorted. His friend was one of the only people who could tell when he was joking.

Zachary only lived four miles away, but they mostly spoke on the phone or via chat. Once in a while, Zachary would FaceTime him to show him something, but he didn't seem to mind that Wes preferred they never meet in person.

"How did the Halloween decorating go?" Wes asked, realizing Halloween had come and gone without his notice.

"Excellent. I won. Obviously."

Zachary lived on Casper Road, and every year the residents competed in a neighborhood Halloween decorating contest. Kids from all around the county went there and trick-or-treated. Zachary took it extremely seriously, not caring about the children or the neighborhood—only about the trophy that was bestowed on the house with the best decorations.

He'd won every year he had lived on Casper Road and approached the Halloween season with all the planning and dedication with which he approached his architectural blueprints—if a bit more of a competitive spirit.

"Congratulations. I'm sure you terrified the human children."

"Oh, to be sure." Wes could hear the smile in his voice. "And I'm already planning for next year. It's going to be truly epic."

"I can do lighting," Wes offered absently.

In the past he'd created some eerily glowing effects for Zachary's windows.

"Definitely."

Zachary began to outline his plans for the next year's decorations, and Wes tuned out as he checked the biogas generator. It was an accepted tenet of their friendship that both of them had free rein to wax enthusiastic about their niche pursuits, and either of them were welcome to stop listening when they lost interest. It worked for them.

When he finished with the biogas generator and went into the basement to feed the lizards, Zachary was describing something made of wire and silicone that sounded like it might be a skeleton.

His phone beeped with an incoming call.

"Hang on a sec, Zachary."

Wes looked at his phone. The incoming call was from Adam Mills. Wes' heart sped up at the sight of his name. They'd exchanged phone numbers after Gus' show-and-tell, Adam adorably flustered and making up reasons why it was good for neighbors to have one another's contact information, but Wes hadn't thought anything would come of it.

"Hello?"

"Wes, thank god. I'm so glad you answered. I mean, hi, hello, it's Adam. Mills. From across the street. How are you?"

Though it was the first time he'd heard Adam's voice on the phone, somehow Wes felt as though they did this all the time—Adam calling, enthusiastic or in a hurry; Wes answering, waiting for the infusion of sparkle that Adam's next words might bring.

"What's up?"

"Okay, I'm so damn sorry to ask you for another favor, but I'm at work and my damn car won't start. River's with Gus, but they have to leave in half an hour to meet the vet at the cat shelter so they can't stay with her. Is there any way you would be able to pop over to my house and stay with Gus until I can get home? It shouldn't be more than an hour or so."

"Go over to your house," Wes echoed.

"And hang out with Gus, yeah. Wes, are you there?"

He'd thought he was speaking, but apparently not.

"I don't know what to do?"

"With Gus? No worries, just watch a movie, or you can read a book and tell her to play in her room. Really, it's just so she's not alone."

If he were to stop and think about it, Wes would

realize that Adam and Gus were the first people outside his family to ask him for anything in years.

Once, he had been someone people asked things of. Asked far too much of. But when he pulled into himself, he shed those connections like a snakeskin.

He waited to see if the request would feel suffocating, as requests once had, but all he felt was a warm tingle in his stomach. Excitement at the prospect of seeing Adam again.

"Okay."

"Really?! Oh, god, thank you so much, Wes. You're saving my life, seriously."

"Should I go now?"

"If you don't mind, that would be wonderful."

"Okay."

He hung up and switched over to the other call.

"Zachary, I have to go."

"Oh. Okay."

"I have to go watch a human child."

"The kid from across the street again? You never told me if her dad is attractive. Wes. Westley. Is he hot? Wes, hey!"

"Bye, Zachary."

River answered the door with their coat already on.

"Thanks, Wes," they said. "I'd stay, but the vet is coming by to look at one of the kittens and I have to be there to let her in."

"That's understandable. I hope the kitten is okay."

River smiled. "Me too."

Gus ran at Wes the second he got inside.

"Wes!"

"Hi, Gus. What are you up to?"

Gus shrugged. "Me and River were building a fort, but I'm bored of that. Can we do science?"

"Building a fort is science. It's physics."

Gus cocked her head like she was considering that. "Oh. Well can we do *other* science?"

Wes didn't know much about kids, but as Adam had pointed out the other day, he had *been* one. He could certainly give Gus what he wished someone had given him when he was her age.

"Want to do some chemistry?"

Gus grinned and nodded enthusiastically.

Two and a half hours later, Adam walked into the kitchen looking exhausted. There were circles under his blue eyes, and his clothes were rumpled. Wes had the strongest urge to fold him in his arms. To press his thumbs to those dark circles as if he could erase them simply by noticing.

When Adam saw the state of the kitchen, his eyes widened. Wes had intended to clean things up before Adam returned, but had lost track of time. He'd been having such fun with Gus.

"Whoa."

"Daddy, we're doing science!" Gus announced.

"That's great, sweetheart," Adam said weakly.

"We were looking at some chemical reactions," Wes explained, hoping to distract from the mess.

"We made a volcano that erupted all over the place," Gus said, pointing with a grin and ruining any chance of a distraction. "And we made plastic out of milk!"

Adam raised an eyebrow at that, like he thought it was a child's whimsy.

"Milk contains casein molecules," Wes explained. "Proteins. A chain of casein monomers makes a polymer that can be molded, kind of like plastic."

"Wow, cool."

Adam's blond hair was messier than usual, as if he'd run his hands through it over and over in frustration, and Wes had the strangest urge to push it back from his face.

"You really saved us today," Adam was saying. "Do you wanna stay for dinner? I was just gonna make mac and cheese, but…"

Part of Wes itched to get back home where it was safe and private.

But he also felt a competing pull to stay. Suddenly, he dearly wanted to eat macaroni and cheese with Adam and Gus.

"Okay," he heard himself say to Adam for the second time that day.

"Yay!" Gus shouted and threw her arms around his waist.

Over gloppy orange macaroni and cheese, Gus regaled Adam in greater detail about their science projects and Adam told the harrowing tale of his car breaking down outside Matheson's Hardware. ("Charlie wanted to try and fix it himself and then when he couldn't, insisted on calling his friend to tow it.")

It mostly sounded nice to Wes, but Adam seemed embarrassed to have needed his boss' help.

Gus launched into a monologue about leeches and Adam turned a suspicious eye at Wes. Wes innocently ate another spoonful of macaroni and cheese, impressed that Gus remembered most of what he'd told her, and Adam's face fizzed into a smile.

Wes didn't notice he was staring into Adam's blue eyes until Gus said, *"Hello?!"*

Wes blinked. Adam cleared his throat, flustered, and said, "That's rude, sweetheart."

After dinner, Adam went to tuck Gus into bed and Wes looked around the kitchen at the mess they'd made. He could go home. Adam would understand. His critters were there, and his work. And the darkness, and the solitude.

Instead, Wes cleared the table and began to make order out of the chaos he'd created.

Chapter Nine

Adam

Adam was exhausted by the time Gus fell asleep. She'd been abuzz with excitement about her evening with Wes and had wanted to tell him everything she'd learned. It was sweet and wonderful and he'd wanted to press a mute button on her after about six minutes.

Finally, he trudged back to the kitchen to clean up, and pulled out his phone to send Wes a thank-you text.

But when he got to the kitchen, Wes was still there, and it was the mess that was gone.

The floor and countertops sparkled, and the dishwasher was humming.

Relief and gratitude consumed him. They never told you about this: the part where sometimes after a day of work and car trouble and kid wrangling, not having to do the dishes could bring you to tears.

Wes looked startled and held out a large hand quellingly.

"Hey. Oh. Hey," he stumbled.

"You cleaned up," Adam said, voice shaking.

"Well, yeah. I made the mess."

Adam nodded, because that was logical and also miraculous.

"Listen, I did something," Wes said, shoving a hand in his pocket and looking guilty.

Please don't be anything creepy, Adam begged the universe. *He's so great; please don't make me have to hate him.*

"I organized your dry goods," Wes said.

"My...dry goods."

Wes opened three cabinets, revealing perfectly ordered foodstuffs where once there had been a riot.

"I was cleaning up and it just kind of leaked into the cabinets," he went on. "I guess I lost track of time. I can put them back to the way they were if you want..."

Heat bloomed in Adam's chest. Wes was so damned adorable. This large, strong, recluse of a science genius had organized his pantry storage by... He stared at the cabinets, trying to parse the logic.

"Um. How did you arrange it?"

Wes blinked at him as if it were obvious.

"Alphabetically."

Adam didn't let himself laugh.

"Of course," he murmured.

And so it was, almonds to ziti.

"I'm gonna make a wild guess that you don't cook," Adam said.

"I cook. Quite a bit, actually."

They stared at each other. Adam pictured Wes in his own kitchen, reaching for ingredients filed alphabetically as he cooked a meal for himself and his coterie of critters.

"Thank you for cleaning up. And for, er, rearranging my dry goods."

They stood in awkward silence for a moment. Wes was gorgeous and kind and smart and incredibly weird, but in great ways. Once, Adam would have kissed him. He would have said, *Thanks for cleaning up. I want to kiss you. Whattaya say?*

But Adam's days of risking his heart were behind him. These days, he didn't go around falling for gorgeous, kind, smart, weird-in-great-ways men— especially ones who lived right across the street.

Did he?

Wes reached out a hand and his fingers hovered near Adam's shoulder.

"Your hair looks so soft," he murmured.

"You can touch it," Adam said, breath catching. "If you want."

He expected tentative fingertips, or the gentle *hush* of his hair being swept back.

But at his invitation, Wes slid his large hands into Adam's hair, massaging his scalp with strong fingers. An involuntary groan escaped Adam's lips and he let his head fall forward and rest against Wes' firm chest.

He could hear the steady thump of Wes' heart and closed his eyes. Wes rubbed at his scalp and combed through his hair, stopping here and there to untangle.

"Adam."

"Mmm-hmm."

But he didn't say anything else. Adam tipped his head up to look at Wes. His eyes were burning hot and he was looking down at Adam like he held something precious in his hands.

"Wes," Adam whispered. "Can I kiss you?"

There went the neighborhood.

Wes' hands moved from his hair to his face, gently—so gently—cupping his jaw. He nodded.

Adam stood on his tiptoes and brushed his lips against Wes' softly. Wes let him, so Adam kissed him again. Wes' hands remained gentle, but his breath caught.

Suddenly, Adam wanted him with a hunger he hadn't felt in years. He pressed against Wes, leaning in to deepen the kiss. Wes' mouth was hot, his kiss clumsy with desire, but so damn sincere. Adam lost himself in it.

The kiss burned hotter and hotter and Adam pressed closer, desperate to feel Wes' body. Finally, Wes' arms came around him, clutching him close, tight, exactly as he craved.

Adam felt wild. The desire for Wes coursed through him until he was nearly dizzy with it. It had been so long. So damn long since he'd gotten what he needed.

Even with Mason sex had never been their main compatibility. Mason had been all about experimentation and erotic novelty, where Adam had craved intimacy and intensity. But Adam felt an answering passion in Wes that made him dare to hope that maybe Wes' desires would match his own.

Flushed and so turned-on he could hardly think, Adam wrapped his arms around Wes' neck and gave himself over to the kiss. Wes slid his hands to Adam's ass and gave it a rough squeeze that had Adam's eyes rolling back in his head.

"Yes, yes, yes," he murmured into Wes' mouth.

He pressed Wes against the freshly washed countertop, getting as close as he could. He loved it like this—so entwined that there was no breath that wasn't shared, no movement of his partner's body he couldn't feel.

Wes grabbed him by the ass and picked him up, walking them out the kitchen, through the living room, and up the stairs. Adam pointed to his bedroom at the end of the hall, light-headed with desire.

Wes wasn't making a show of strength, which made it a thousand times hotter. He just wanted Adam in bed, *now*. When they got inside Adam's room, Wes tossed him onto the bed then closed the door.

"Is it okay?" he asked, gesturing down the hallway to where Gus slept.

Adam's heart melted at his concern and he nodded.

"She sleeps with a noise machine, and these are pretty thick walls."

He didn't mention that he'd forced River to test that fact with him when they'd first moved in, making his sibling stand in Gus' room while he made noise in his own. But he'd needed to know.

Wes' gaze heated as he approached the bed, towering over Adam.

"Good."

Adam knew in that moment that Wes was going to be exactly what he wanted. What he craved. The roughness, the intensity, the glorious ability to not have to take care of anything and trust that the other person would take your pleasure in hand.

He also knew in that moment why the neighbors had so many rumors that Wes was a vampire, werewolf, et cetera. Looming over Adam, cheeks flushed with desire, eyes dark with lust, he looked intimidating. Devastating. Potent. And completely focused on Adam in a way that took his breath away.

"Wes, I want you," Adam whispered, and he turned onto his stomach, looking back at Wes pointedly.

"Yeah?"

Wes sat on the edge of the bed and ran a hand up Adam's spine. The heat from his palm was searing.

"Yes! I want—"

But even though he was pretty sure his needs were echoed in Wes, it was hard to say them out loud.

Wes leaned close and spoke in his ear. His voice was a velvet growl.

"Tell me exactly what you want."

Adam whimpered. Shook his head. The words wouldn't come.

"Adam, tell me."

"I want you to have me. Completely. Take me apart."

With the words came the liquid fire of want.

Wes groaned and his hand tightened around the nape of Adam's neck.

"Yeah? Kinda...take charge?"

"Yes," Adam moaned.

"In charge, but not...mean?"

Adam was dizzy with the potency of this understanding. That was exactly what he wanted. Exactly what he needed.

"Yes, yes, please, Wes, yes."

Adam pressed his hips into the bed and shuddered at the contact. He was hard and swollen, exquisitely sensitive.

But Wes caught his hip and flipped him onto his back. He straddled his hips and pressed a hand to his chest, keeping him in place. Adam trembled, loving the warm pressure.

Wes kissed Adam's jaw, then moved to his neck. At the crook where his shoulder and neck met, he sucked, and Adam felt it in his bones. He shuddered and thrashed under Wes' touch.

"Are you sure you aren't secretly a vampire?" he teased, with the last of his wits.

"Maybe I am," Wes murmured against his skin.

Adam giggled and Wes smiled—an easy, warm smile that said *We are in this together. I got you.*

Then he pinched Adam's nipple through his shirt and made him squirm.

"Sensitive," Wes murmured, ghosting a kiss to his flushed cheekbone.

Adam had heard that his whole life, and not only in this context. It was true, either way.

Wes pushed his shirt up slowly, kissing the skin he revealed, until the shirt was around Adam's neck. Then he began to torment his nipples so exquisitely that Adam wondered if he could come from it. But each time he felt the pleasure begin to crest, Wes would switch sides.

Adam was desperate for more and he pulled Wes down on top of him. Wes devoured his mouth and settled into the space between Adam's legs. When their erections came into contact they both gasped.

Breathing each other's exhalations, they slowly began to move. Above him, Wes was fire and steel and laser-focused attention, and Adam threw his head back, overwhelmed by the magnitude of his want.

He didn't even realize he was begging until Wes said, "Okay."

Wes rolled Adam's hips up and ground them together, hard and slow. Adam shuddered as waves of pleasure tore at him. He cried out and Wes swallowed his cry along with his kiss.

Then it was a frenzy. Wes held him and thrust their hips together with perfect force. Adam tossed his head on the pillow helplessly.

"Need you, please," he begged, straining upward.

Wes bore down on him, chest rubbing over his sensitive nipples, and ground against him so perfectly Adam saw stars. The seam of Wes' jeans was catching the spot just beneath the head of his cock that always made him come ribbons, and he threw his head back and let Wes have him.

Wes' thrusts got harder and faster, then just as Adam thought he'd lose it, Wes backed off, leaving Adam panting and desperate.

When he thought he couldn't take it anymore, Wes cupped his cheek and said, "You're so beautiful."

Then he swiveled his hips, twisting and grinding down in a movement that sent sparks shooting up Adam's spine.

"Again," Adam begged.

Wes did it again and again until Adam was a sobbing mess. Only then did Wes kiss his wet cheeks, slide his hands under Adam's ass to lift him up, and press them together perfectly.

The pressure built and built until Adam thought he would scream, then he was coming in wracking waves of pleasure that tore sounds from his throat he didn't recognize.

Just as it began to ebb, Wes pinched his nipple and roared his own orgasm, and Adam tumbled back into pleasure.

The aftershocks left him twitching and gasping on the bed, and when Wes collapsed on top of him, kissing his neck softly, he moaned at the ghosts of pleasure.

"Oh my *god*, Wes," Adam groaned.

He looked over at Wes and saw tenderness in his eyes. A soft connectedness that he'd never seen before.

Wes smiled at him and began to say something, when a yell shattered the silence.

"Daddy! Daddy!"

Chapter Ten

Adam

It had only been a nightmare, but Gus' cries had been enough to disrupt the mood. When Adam got back to bed, Wes was fully clothed and standing at the window, looking out at the moon. Or his own house. Adam couldn't be sure.

"Hey," he said, uncertain of his reception. He imagined the shrieks of an eight-year-old weren't everyone's postcoital cup of tea.

"I should get home," Wes said, confirming his suspicions.

"Sure."

Adam tucked his hair behind his ears and walked out into the living room, looking for Wes' shoes.

"Sorry," Adam offered miserably when Wes stood at the door.

"For what?" Wes seemed genuinely puzzled.

"For...Gus? Interrupting?"

Wes shrugged and shook his head.

"Nightmares suck," was all he said. Then he stepped out into the night.

Adam had nothing to say to that, so he watched Wes give him a wave, then walk away home.

* * *

"We need more, Daddy," Gus lamented, looking up at the house.

Adam thought the Christmas lights they had so far looked good, but he couldn't deny they were still sparse.

"Well, it is Saturday morning," Adam said, waggling his eyebrows.

"Oh, nooo," Gus groaned.

"Come on, it'll be great! There're sure to be lights."

"Okay, but we need a time limit." Gus tapped the black rubber watch she'd worn since before she was old enough to know what time was.

"Aw, you can't put a time limit on treasure hunting," Adam said, but he winked at her. "Fine, thirty minutes per stop."

Gus narrowed eyes the same blue as his own.

"Twenty," she offered.

"Deal."

Adam stuck out his hand and they shook on it.

"I'll grab snacks, you get dressed."

Estate sales were one of Adam's favorite things in the whole world. Mason had tolerated them but didn't have the same enthusiasm Adam did. Gus liked to pretend that it was torture to be dragged along, but Adam knew the truth.

She loved picking through the tangle of trash and treasure the same as he did. It was how she'd gotten her explorer jacket and her beekeeping hat, not to mention all her best wooden blocks and a trash can for her room that had a beetle hand-painted on it.

Adam had found his love for them by accident. Their elderly neighbor next door in Boulder had died, and her children hired a company to run a sale. Adam had gone over to offer his condolences to her daughter and instead found a new passion.

The world of estate sales was as particular as any, and as he went more often he learned the conventions of bargaining, of putting together a lot, of paying cash, of going on the last day of the sale for cut prices.

He also began to recognize many familiar faces at multiple sales. They were mostly, though not exclusively, white women in their fifties and sixties, and white men in their seventies, so he stood out.

But Adam had always stood out, so he was used to it.

Gus came crashing downstairs with several reusable totes on her arm.

"Ready!" she said, forgetting that she'd been feigning a lack of enthusiasm.

She skipped outside to the car and Adam followed her. His eyes were immediately magnetized to Wes' house and he shivered at the memory of his orgasm the night before.

How perfectly firm and gentle Wes had been. Brutal and caring. Adam shuddered again, hoping he wasn't flushing visibly.

"Daddy, let's invite Wes!"

"Oh, honey, Wes sleeps really late. It's only nine."

Gus pouted at Wes' house, and as if it saw her, the paper covering an upstairs window fluttered aside.

"Look, he's awake!" She pointed. "Unless that was one of the snakes," she mused.

"Oh god," Adam muttered.

"Let's ask. Can we please just ask?"

Adam really did want to see Wes. He wasn't proud of letting his kid do the dirty work for him, but he also wasn't above seizing the opportunities presented to him. Sometimes they were all you had.

"Well," he began.

"Yay!" Gus cried, sensing his imminent capitulation.

Then off she ran across the street, after exaggeratedly looking both ways.

Adam sighed and followed her, texting a warning to Wes as he went.

"You didn't ring more than once, did you?" Adam asked as he caught Gus up on the porch.

She blinked up at him. "Well. Twice."

"We've talked about this," Adam began, but before he could remind Gus, the door opened.

Wes was dressed and he was wearing sunglasses. He was holding a book and something that Adam, as a hardware store employee, really should've been able to identify, but could not.

"Hi," Wes said. And even though Adam couldn't see his eyes behind the sunglasses, somehow he knew Wes was looking right at him.

Gus bounced in place.

"Wanna come treasure hunting with us?" She held up the tote bags like they were a map where x marked the spot.

Adam opened his mouth to explain, but Wes said, "Yes."

"You *do*?" Gus sounded as surprised as Adam felt and Wes looked. But unlike him, his daughter knew when not to question a good thing. "Yay, come on!"

And then she grabbed his arm to pull him outside.

"Sweetie, he might need a minute."

Wes held up one finger and disappeared inside.

"Yay!" Gus crowed again, and hugged Adam.

Adam squeezed her tight and stroked her soft hair and tried to pinpoint why his heart was racing.

Excitement at spending time with this intriguing, lovely man? Yes.

But also…fear. In the space of two weeks, Gus already admired him. Already automatically included him in their plans.

And Adam—well, Adam knew what it was to fall fast and hard. He knew what it was to have a heart that gave itself away. And he knew what it was to have that heart treated without care.

You slept together one time! Don't turn a hot night into a lifelong commitment.

But then Wes came outside, navy blue peacoat perfectly showcasing his broad shoulders, mouth looking like sweet temptation, and all Adam could do was cross his fingers that this didn't end in devastation.

The first estate sale was a bust, but the second was gold. A farmhouse full of Western antiques and a two-story barn that was a picker's paradise. Or, in their case, paradise for an eight-year-old who fancied herself a scientist and an *actual* scientist who seemed to see possibility in everything.

Adam left them to rummaging through the tools, screws, and bits of twisted metal in the abandoned barn and wandered back into the house.

The joy of estate sale-ing for Adam didn't lie in buying. It lay in seeing someone's life laid out before you in objects and their arrangement. Imagining, as you ran reverent fingers over their belongings, the months, years, decades that assembled this collection in this configuration.

Each one was the museum of a life, and Adam was a happy tourist.

Though he wasn't a big buyer, there was one thing he always looked for: Royal China Jeanette ceramic pie plates printed with recipes. His grandmother had once had a whole set of them: apple pie, strawberry pie, rhubarb pie, pumpkin pie—each with a picture and recipe painted on them.

He didn't know what had happened to them when she died—for all he knew, the plates he'd once eaten cherry pie off of in her cozy kitchen had found their way into this very house.

He didn't find any, but he did find a French press for three dollars that he bought before going to find Gus and Wes in the barn.

"Daddy, Daddy, look!"

Gus ran toward him, her green Boulder Farmer's Market tote bulging.

She was holding a small aquarium with one pane of glass missing and her smile was radiant.

"Cool," he said, hoping it was the right response.

"Yeah, Wes says he has a piece of glass that will fit, and we can pox it."

"Epoxy," Adam murmured.

"And then I can fill it with whatever I want," she concluded triumphantly.

"Sounds great." The thing looked cheap enough, and he was always glad for Gus to have projects. "Let me just find the person to pay for it."

"Wes already gave me money and I bought it. And this stuff."

She opened her bag to reveal... Adam couldn't really tell what. A jumble of bits and pieces that no doubt made sense to his daughter. He'd just go through it later and make sure nothing was sharp.

"Well that was really generous of him. Did you say thank you?"

"Yes!"

Gus looked offended. Adam held up his hand and she gave him a high five.

"Where is Wes?"

Her eyes lit once more, and she pulled him to the barn entrance.

Wes was in the process of unearthing some kind of very rusty piece of equipment.

"Do you know what that is?" Adam asked.

Gus nodded sagely, ever delighted to be in the know.

"A trough."

"Like...for animal feed?"

"Wes said it's for algae," she explained graciously. Paused. Then said, "What's algae?"

With each passing year—no, month—Gus' questions challenged him more and more. Revealed all the things he didn't know. It was disturbing how often she asked him something that he'd lived his whole life not questioning, only to realize he wasn't sure enough of it to explain it to his kid.

"Algae's...um...a little plant that lives in the water? I think?"

Gus nodded. "We can google it."

Adam's heart swelled. This was what he always told her when he wasn't sure. Then they looked it up together. Some of his favorite moments with Gus were standing in the middle of wherever they were—the farmer's market, the drug store, a park—huddled over his phone, satisfying her curiosity and his desire to give her accurate information.

It had irked Mason. *She's three*, he'd say. *She doesn't need to know the genus and species. Just tell her it's a damn turtle.* Or, *She's five. You can tell her the sun revolves around the earth for all she'll care or remember.*

He hadn't meant it cruelly. He'd thought it was burdensome for Gus and a waste of time for Adam. He never understood that Adam was devoted to delivering the world to Gus in the most accurate way he could imagine. He'd never understood a lot of things about Adam.

But Adam *was* devoted to it. Because it was the right thing to do.

And because his own parents had given to him a world so warped by their own prejudices, beliefs, and convictions that he had spent a decade untangling it.

He would spend as long as it took googling every single goddamned thing in the world if it meant he never did that to Gus.

Wes made a triumphant noise, and the trough was free. When he looked up and saw Adam standing there, Wes smiled at him. A smile so automatic and sweet and happy at Adam's presence that it took Adam's breath away.

"What'd you find?"

Wes ran a palm over his shaved head the way he sometimes did when he explained things. It thrilled Adam that he knew that.

"Bioluminescence occurs naturally in microorganisms like dinoflagellates. I've been working with bacteria and methane gas, as you know."

Adam nodded, remembering the glowing green bottles.

"But I've been curious about the viability of individuals farming their own bioluminescent dinoflagellates. Pyrocystis fusiformis, probably."

Adam had understood only a few of the words that had just been spoken.

"You mean, um, you're gonna see if people can grow the bioluminescent algae themselves to, like, light their houses and stuff?"

"Oh, no," Wes said, smiling. "Algae are far too temporary a measure for replacing light sources. They only remain viable for a few weeks and then they need to be replaced or divided. This would just be an experiment for me. Just for fun."

"Sure, fun," Adam echoed. "Er, what is algae, precisely?"

"Photosynthetic, mainly aquatic eukaryotic organisms ranging from microscopic single-celled forms to multicellular forms one hundred feet or more long. They lack the true roots, stems, and leaves that other plants have, as well as nonreproductive cells in their reproductive structures. But there is dissent about the exact definition, because the word describes such a large and diverse group."

Adam blinked.

"And in layman's terms that would mean...?"

Wes cocked his head. "Oh. They're organisms that live in the water and can be as tiny as one cell or as big as kelp and seaweed."

"Nailed it," Adam congratulated himself. "Uh, is that gonna fit in the car?"

Wes seemed not to have considered that.

It turned out that the trough did fit, with some aggressive reorganizing of the seats and their body parts. Wes drove so that Gus could sit on Adam's lap, squeezed into one corner of the back seat, the trough sitting diagonally across most of the back seat and the front passenger seat.

Adam attempted not to feel one hundred years old as his knees were crunched to his chest. Gus was in her glory, rubbing at the trough and smelling her fingers, declaring that it smelled "fresh and dirty."

At the next estate sale they hit the Christmas lights

jackpot, thank god, because Adam didn't think he could spend much more time scrunched around the trough.

The house was prim and unappealing, with chintzy drapes swaddling every window and pastel wallpapers in every room. But it had clearly belonged to a family that celebrated Christmas with serious ceremony because an entire upstairs bedroom was packed with decorations. Everything from a faux gingerbread dollhouse to boxes of carefully packed collectible glass ornaments lined the walls.

Adam didn't care about any of that. He was perfectly happy with their ornaments made of pine cones and bits of ribbon and Gus' handprints in various sizes of salt dough over the years. But he snatched up the two paper bags of tangled lights and began plugging them in to see if any worked. A few didn't, but most did.

Gus' face lit up and Adam decided that actually, he could remain crunched in the car forever if it meant they found more lights and could make her vision come to life.

Wes had chosen to stay in the car, so while Gus poked at a train set, Adam quickly popped into the kitchen and opened the cabinets. There, at the bottom of a stack of Corningware, was a single Jeanette pie plate.

It was pumpkin pie, which Adam didn't have, and he held it to his chest gleefully.

"Found another one, Grandma," he whispered, feeling instantly embarrassed but not really caring.

His grandmother had been a source of warmth and caring in a childhood that severely lacked both, and Adam resolved once again that he would learn to make pie in her honor.

Riding high on their success, they decided to hit one more sale, but there were no lights to be found, and they headed home.

Back on Knockbridge Lane, they freed the trough from the car and wrestled it down the stairs to Wes' basement. Adam kept his eyes on Wes to ensure he didn't accidentally come face-to-face with Bettie or one of the snakes or god knew what else that Wes had crawling around in there.

"Can we please hang the lights now?" Gus asked, the required *please* doing little to temper her impatience.

Adam smiled and nodded and tamped down the squirmy feeling in his stomach that signaled his impending separation from Wes.

Chapter Eleven

Wes

Wes didn't want Adam to leave. It was a strange sensation for someone who generally craved solitude, but the evidence was right there, and Wes couldn't discount evidence.

So when Gus said, "Do you wanna help?" Wes said yes with the same speed as he'd accepted her invitation this morning. Of course, he hadn't realized when she'd offered treasure hunting that it would involve going to people's houses, which contained, well, people. He'd assumed they would be going to the woods or something. Still, he'd made it work by sticking to outbuildings and waiting in the car.

At this assent, he saw Adam's eyes widen but he thought it was simple surprise, not dislike. In fact, Adam moved a little closer to him.

Of course, that could simply have been his fear of spiders.

In Adam's driveway, they discovered that a few of the strands of lights they'd found at the estate sale were able to be linked together, so Gus decided those should run from one side of the house around the front door and over to the other side.

It gave the impression of a gingerbread house, door outlined in light.

Some of the other strands were so short that once plugged in they barely reached the roof. Wes suspected this would be a persistent issue with older lights, and lights clearly designed for indoor use.

There was a better way. A more organized way that would take advantage of the shape of the roof, and Wes began mapping out how they could balance out the splash of illumination on the side of the house where the outlet was.

Then he stopped himself. This wasn't an experiment. This was a little kid's vision, and he didn't want to ruin it.

Wes had never cared for Christmas. Growing up, it had been an excuse for his father to glad-hand and show off, and Wes had been one of the things on offer. As an adult, it became just one more occasion for large gatherings, small talk, idleness, and non-consensual touching.

But the joy on Gus' face as she watched the house become illuminated almost made Wes reconsider. He started to wonder if maybe, this Christmas, things might be different…

"I wanna go make inventions," Gus announced after they'd hung the final strand of lights and stood admiring their work.

She had told him in the barn that she planned to use her findings to "invent things." He had been impressed. It was how he had started himself, monkeying with bits and pieces of broken things, seeing how they might fit together. Seeing what they might create.

She reminded Wes of himself in a lot of ways: her intense interest in science and invention, her love of misunderstood creatures, her single-minded curiosity about the world.

In other ways, though, she was everything he'd never gotten the chance to be as a child: naive, trusting, friendly, carefree.

He admired more than he could say the fact that Gus could have her intense curiosities and never lose touch with people she cared about. That was Adam's doing, he imagined. Adam who seemed to care about everything.

"Do you know how to make pie?" Adam asked him as they went inside.

"I assume you don't mean of the 3.14159 variety?"

Adam bumped him with his shoulder and smiled.

"No, I don't."

Adam began to wash the tall-sided plate he'd bought.

"My grandma used to have a whole set of these, and she'd make pies in them. See?"

He held it up to reveal a painted slice of pumpkin pie and a recipe painted on the plate. "I've never made a pie but it kinda seems like I'm supposed to since I found this, right?"

Wes wasn't a fatalist, so he didn't believe the two were related, but he knew what Adam meant: finding the plate was an encouragement to do something he wanted to do anyway.

"I can help, if you want?" he found himself offering.

Adam's whole face lit up, just as Gus' had when she looked at the illuminated house.

Wes placed this picture of Adam—sweet and excited and open—next to another picture in his head: one of Adam from the night before. Desperate and needy and so turned-on he could hardly breathe.

Both were gorgeous. Both were appealing. And together they made Wes' heart pound.

"What?"

"I said do you want to cut up this butter?"

Adam was peering at his phone and holding out two sticks of butter.

"This says it should stay very cold."

Wes stood next to Adam and looked at the recipe. He could feel the heat of Adam's body. He *knew* how perfectly they fit together and the temptation to pull Adam flush to his side was overwhelming.

"Do you have a food processor?" he asked, scanning the recipe.

"Huh? Oh. No." He squinted at the phone. "My grandma always did it with two forks."

"What if I make the filling and you make the crust," Wes offered, not wanting to tread on memories of Adam's grandmother.

"Great." Adam grinned at him.

"What kind of pie are we making?"

"Oh, right." Adam opened the refrigerator and the cabinets. "Apple, looks like. I don't have anything else. Do you know what to do?"

Wes didn't, but he had eaten apple pies before. How hard could it be?

"Sure."

He set about chunking the apples, mind drifting back to the night before. He'd floated home in a haze of pleasure, wonder, and—frankly—confusion. All these feelings for Adam were coming faster and more intensely than he'd ever experienced.

He'd wanted to know what Adam was doing, what he was thinking—make sure he was okay.

"I was watching you this morning," Wes blurted. "Through the upstairs window." And that had come out creepier than he'd intended.

Adam's blue eyes were curious, though.

"I was surprised you were awake," he said. "I thought you usually slept until afternoon."

"Usually. I couldn't sleep."

Their eyes were locked, and he saw Adam's pupils dilate.

"I can't sleep sometimes," Adam said.

"I know. I see the light come on downstairs. I see the flicker of the TV."

"I had insomnia in high school," Adam said. "It went away when I left town. I thought it was gone forever but it came back when Mason and I split up. Being alone, I guess?"

"What happened?"

Adam began smushing butter and flour together on the counter with two forks. It looked extremely unappetizing.

"I met Mason our last year of high school. He'd just moved here. He was cute and moody and smart, and I couldn't believe he was into me. I wasn't exactly popular in high school."

Wes bet high school Adam was a sweetheart.

"My parents…well, my father especially, was not good. We didn't get along. He's cruel and—" Adam broke off, shaking his head.

"Just, the opposite of what a dad should be. After high school, Mason was going to college in Boulder, so I went with him. It was great at first. He loved school and I loved not being anywhere near my parents. Or here."

Wes put the apple chunks in a bowl and poured sugar and cinnamon on them. That seemed to be what apple pie tasted like.

"One semester Mason took this photography class. He wasn't that interested in it, but I fell in love. At first I was just taking pictures of friends and random things I'd see around town. But then one of my friends asked me to shoot their wedding, and after that I started doing portraiture. It was awesome."

Adam looked lost in his memories, pie crust forgotten on the counter.

"River called me one day to tell me that our sister had had a baby. Hell, I didn't even know she was pregnant. River was just a kid. Marina tried with Gus for a little while, but she—"

He looked around to make sure Gus wasn't around, and lowered his voice.

"She loved Gus so much, but she never wanted to be a parent. Even if she had wanted to, she was working full-time to support herself and her boyfriend, and they couldn't afford any daycare. She said she'd rather die than let our parents have anything to do with Gus. So I...I offered to take her."

Adam blinked, remembering, and his face got the softest expression Wes had ever seen.

"I always wanted kids. Mason... Well, I should've discussed it with him first. I know that. I just thought... He was so great and Gus was so great, it *had* to work."

Wes cringed. "What happened?"

"He was furious. Said he was supposed to be focusing on finals, not on raising a kid. I told him I'd do all the work. I'd get up with her and feed her and change her diaper. I knew it was a lot to ask, but I thought maybe with a compromise..."

"You wanted her more than you wanted him."

Adam's eyes got wide. Had that been too harsh a phrasing?

"I guess...yeah. She was nonnegotiable. The thing is, when she started talking and walking around, Mason was more interested in her. He liked showing her off, liked playing with her sometimes. He wasn't a horrible father."

In comparison with Adam's own father, perhaps. And Wes'.

"But when she turned five, Mason started asking how long this was going to last. Like, like, like he thought we were gonna give her *back*. At first I figured he was just letting off steam. He'd started working at this tech company and he had really long days. He was tired, stressed, and of course having a kid doesn't exactly make it easy to come home at the end of the day and put your feet up.

"But we had a great babysitter who watched her while I was out on jobs, and she could've taken on more hours. It wasn't the hours, though. It turned out he just…wasn't willing to give anything up to be a father."

Adam started in on the butter mush again, wielding the forks like twin weapons.

"And Gus…there was Gus now. Gus was…she was everything. And I just knew. I was a dad now, and that was the most important thing. Maybe we could've found some kind of compromise eventually, I don't know. But I didn't want to compromise. I wanted a life with Gus.

"For the last year and a half or so we stayed living together but we weren't a couple anymore. We dated other people sometimes. Well, Mason did. I went on like three dates and all I could think the whole time was that I'd rather be hanging out with Gus or watching a movie. Or sitting quietly by myself not dealing with another person's ego. So that didn't go great."

"Did you tell Gus?"

"We didn't tell her while we were still living together. It was complicated enough without adding another variable. But it could only ever be a temporary situation. Eventually, something would change. And it did. Mason met someone he wanted to actually date. I thought…it would be hard for Gus, but we'd work it out. People do this all the time."

Adam trailed off and peered at the recipe on his

phone again. He sprinkled more flour onto the mush and started making it into a ball.

"I started looking for an apartment, but there was nowhere near Mason's place that I could afford working as a photographer. Not with any kind of money to pay for the help I'd need when Gus wasn't in school. Then it turned out, Mason didn't care if we stayed near him. Because he didn't want to be Gus' father anymore."

Adam's voice broke and Wes knew his grief was for Gus and not for himself. He took out a water glass and started rolling the ball of dough into a disk. When it tore, he smushed it together again. What he ended up with was a Frankenstein of ragged pieces of floury dough that he pressed into the pie plate.

"Should I put the filling in?" Wes asked.

"I think so?"

Wes poured the mixture of apples, sugar, and cinnamon into the crust and Adam put the other half of the pie crust on top of it, pinching the top and bottom together.

"My grandma used to do this cool, like, pinch and twist thing that made it look—nope, not like that. Oh, well."

He shrugged, put the pie into the oven, turned it on, and set a timer. They sat at the kitchen table.

"So you came here?"

"Yeah. Once it was clear Mason wasn't going to be part of our lives, it didn't make sense to stay. I just couldn't afford it. I was talking to River one day about six months ago. They were telling me all about how great the cat shelter was doing and how they had this whole group of queer friends now. How things were changing here. And they said they wished they could be a part of Gus' life. They were only a kid when she was born, so they'd hardly spent any time together. That clinched it.

"I felt horrible making Gus leave her friends, but coming here just made sense. Rent is affordable and River was excited to watch her sometimes. It seemed like a good solution."

"Could I see your pictures?"

"My photography?" Adam looked surprised. "Yeah, if you want."

"You said you loved it."

"Well, yeah."

Wes wanted to see what it looked like for Adam Mills to love something.

"Hang on a sec."

Adam returned with a beat-up laptop.

"This is some of my stuff."

The website was called *Adam Mills Photography* and its aesthetic was a combination of rustic mountain charm and elegance.

Adam scrolled through his portfolio and talked about the shots. He used words like *composition*, *balance*, and *focus*, but all Wes saw was how every single one of Adam's photographs looked happy.

Some were of people, and even those who weren't smiling had an air of lightness about them; of ease. The pictures of nature looked peaceful and joyous.

Even a shot of a general store at sunset managed to convey a sense of cheer.

"They're lovely," Wes said, then amended, "I don't know anything about photography. But they make me happy."

"Yeah?"

Adam's voice was soft and he was smiling.

"Yup."

Gus wandered into the kitchen then, hands and face smudged with gray streaks of grease.

Wes snorted to hide a laugh and watched Adam's eyes go wide.

"Daddy, can I have a snack?"

"Your timing is perfect," Adam said excitedly. "I just made apple pie."

"You did?"

Gus did not sound optimistic.

"Yeah. My grandmother used to make it in these special dishes, and I wanted to make it for you. That's your great-grandmother. You never met her..."

Adam kept talking while he scrubbed at Gus' hands and face. He asked her about what she invented, and she said it was a secret. Adam's eyes sparkled at Wes when she said that, and Wes got the idea that *secret* might be code for *nothing much*.

"Okay, sit down and get ready to have your mind blown with deliciousness!" Adam said.

Wes worried Adam might be overselling this a bit.

The timer went off just as Gus sat down and Adam grinned as if this were another sign of the fated perfection of this pie.

He opened the oven door and paused.

"Hmm. Um. Well? Hmm."

"Everything okay in there?"

"Oh, yeah. Well. I mean. Sure."

Wes and Gus exchanged a look and the second their eyes met, Gus raised an eyebrow conspiratorially and shook her head slowly, then put her hands to her throat and made a face like she was choking.

"Do you bake often?" Wes asked.

"Oh, sometimes," Adam said breezily. "I made cookies for Gus' class."

Gus made a crossed-eyes death face.

"And I always make her birthday cakes."

Gus shook her head rapidly in warning.

Adam turned to the table with the pie and Gus just smiled. When he turned away to get silverware, though, she caught Wes' eye again and shook her head deliberately, eyes wide.

A plate was placed before each of them, and Adam regarded the pie.

"Well, it doesn't look quite like what my grandma's used to look like. But I'm sure all pies are different?"

He cocked his head like perhaps looking at it aslant would change it from hideously misshapen to appetizing. After all, he had just spent ten minutes telling Wes about how changing perspective could change any photograph.

Adam shrugged. "Let's dig in!"

He cut into the pie and liquid bubbled up in the incision. With extensive wiggling, sawing, and scooping, he managed to excavate three pieces of watery pie.

Pieces was perhaps an overstatement. Globs? Piles.

Wes was not a picky eater. Food was just calories and calories were just energy and every human needed energy to get through the day. He took a bite of the pie.

It turned out *pie* was rather an overstatement as well.

"Mmm," Wes said, trying to swallow the bite very quickly to avoid tasting any more of it and also not swallow it because the filling was very hot and felt like it might scorch a path directly through his esophagus.

He blinked rapidly. His body's attempt to rid itself of this unholy abomination, or just a side effect of burning himself, he couldn't tell.

Gus was watching him, wide-eyed with shock, and he realized that she had been right to warn him off.

"Um," he gasped. "It's..."

Adam was watching him eagerly, fork poised over his own sluice of pie.

Gus was leaning back, arms crossed over her chest, looking at them like they were both fools.

Adam took a bite, and Wes saw the exact moment his hopes for a pie that was an homage to his beloved grandmother crumbled, unlike the gluey crust.

He looked horrified, lurched upright, and spat the pie into the sink.

He whisked Gus' plate away before she could touch it—though she'd clearly had no intention of so doing.

"Oh my god," he said. "I'm... I don't know what happened."

"You can't bake is what happened," Gus said, and Wes started to laugh.

It was so damn charming that Adam Mills, never having made a pie in his life, would decide that this pie would be perfection. It was so optimistic, so sweet, and so utterly unrealistic. But what the hell was reality anyway?

"It wasn't all his fault," Wes told Gus, to be fair. "I made the filling."

Gus shook her head slowly, looking worldlier than an eight-year-old had any business being.

"You should stick to your strengths," she told them both.

Chapter Twelve

Adam

It was three in the morning so of course, Adam was awake.

He rolled out of bed, sighing. This had been going on long enough that he knew there was no utility to lying there and trying to fall back asleep. It never worked, just left him irritable.

He'd been making his way through *Fanny and Alexander* the last few weeks, so he settled on the couch and cued it up to where he'd left off, three and a half hours in.

The movie was endless and beautiful and Adam let his mind wander along with the camera for a while.

The Christmas decorations in the 1907 Ekdahl house in *Fanny and Alexander* were grand and gorgeous—the kind of breathtaking drama that Gus must've hoped for when she said she wanted them to have the most Christmas lights ever.

eBay had provided a few more boxes of cheap lights, but Adam was quickly reaching the edge of the budget he could reasonably spend on this project and still have money left to get Gus anything for Christmas.

Biting his lip, he opened his Instagram again. There were a number of comments on his previous call to action—people saying they wished they could help, people offering to mail him lights, and people expressing how happy they were that he hadn't disappeared forever.

It had always given Adam a thrill to see the response to his photographs.

Maybe…

He paused Bergman and pulled on wool socks and a heavy sweater over his pajamas. After a quick peek to check that Gus was sleeping peacefully, he went outside, camera in hand.

He'd been minutes away from selling the camera before they moved. Gus was the one who stopped him, and now he was grateful she had.

Adam plugged in the lights and the house flared to life. Every other window was dark this late at night, so the lights blazed like fire in the night.

Adam backed down his driveway, considering his angles. At first, he shot it to make the lights look lush and luminous. Shot that way, it looked like an ordinary house with cheery Christmas lights—a well-composed shot, but still ordinary.

When he ditched the camera and shot with his phone from the other side, though, the image that emerged was of a bleak house and sparse lights that hardly stretched to cover it, all precariously plugged in to an overburdened power strip. It looked sad and pathetic.

It was unlike any other photo Adam had ever posted. But Adam wasn't a photographer anymore. He was just a single dad, working at a hardware store whose merchandise he knew nothing about, trying to make his daughter's Christmas wish come true.

Adam posted the picture.

Hello, everyone! he wrote in the caption. *I promised to show you my newest project, and...here it is. It's not my usual subject matter, but when your kid tells you that the one thing that would really make her happy for Christmas in a new town is to have "the most Christmas lights ever," well, what's a dad to do except try and make it happen?*

As you can see, it's not going so well -__- So here I am, asking for your help again. I would be so grateful if you wanted to help me make Gus' dream come true! You can mail any lights to me here, and I'll keep posting pics of our progress. My deepest thanks for anything you want to send, and I hope you're all having a happy December 1st!

"Adam?"

Adam wheeled around, clutching his chest, and dropped his phone.

Wes put his hands up. "Sorry, sorry, I didn't mean to scare you."

"Jesus. Hey."

Adam scooped up his phone, incredibly glad he'd put his camera down when he had, or it would've been in pieces.

"Sorry," Wes said again, looking sheepish. "I saw you from my basement window and I thought I'd… Anyway, hi."

He sketched a wave that was so awkward and geeky that Adam wanted to pull him into his arms and squeeze him tight.

Maybe it was residual daring from asking strangers for help on the internet after posting a *very* off-brand photo, or maybe it was the accumulated sleepless nights. Whatever it was, Adam followed his desire. He slowly stepped closer to Wes, giving him time to retreat, and when he didn't, he wrapped his arms around him.

They stood in the cold night air, before the blaze of lights. They held on to each other for a long time.

Adam breathed deeply, trying to figure out what Wes smelled like. It was something very green, like moss or wild grass, combined with something smoky, like…well, smoke.

Whatever it was, it clung to his sweater and Adam nuzzled closer, chasing it and Wes' warmth and running his hands up and down Wes' broad back.

"Hi," Adam said after a while. It was just an empty thing to say that meant *I'm here*, and Wes murmured back, "Hi."

Wes made no move to let go.

Was this happening? Were they doing this?

"Are we doing this?" Adam accidentally said out loud.

"Hugging in the middle of the night, in the middle

of the street, in the middle of the winter, when we both have perfectly good houses ten steps away? Yes."

"*One* of us has a perfectly good house," Adam retorted. "The other has a house of horrors, filled with spiders and snakes and bags of gas."

For a moment he thought he'd gone too far. Then Wes chuckled into his hair.

"Spiders and snakes need love too," Wes said placidly.

And Adam supposed that was true.

"The lights look..." Wes began, then cut himself off.

"Pathetic. I know. I was just trying to get some more."

Wes nodded.

"Can't sleep?" he asked softly, brushing Adam's hair back.

"Nope. I was watching *Fanny and Alexander.* I've been trying to get in the Christmas spirit for Gus' sake."

"What's *Fanny and Alexander*?"

"A really long movie by Ingmar Bergman about a Swedish family's Christmas in 1907."

Wes just blinked at him. "I guess that would probably help put anyone to sleep?"

"I like it," Adam clarified. "It's beautiful."

"Oh."

Wes looked nonplussed.

"You know, really long movies by Ingmar Bergman about Swedish families' Christmases in 1907 need love too," Adam said.

Wes grinned. "Fair."

"Do you want to come in?"

Wes darted a look back at his house where, Adam noticed for the first time, the basement windows glowed green.

"I was working," he said regretfully.

"Do you want to take a break?"

"A break."

Wes said it like it was as mysterious a thing as *Fanny and Alexander.*

"Cup of tea and a cookie?" Adam offered. "I didn't make the cookies, I swear."

Wes smiled.

"Okay."

Inside, Adam brought mint tea and gingersnaps into the living room. Wes was sitting on the couch looking pensive.

"When you said *this*, you did mean us, right?" Wes said before Adam even sat down.

"Huh? Oh, yeah. I meant…" Adam put the tea and cookies on the coffee table. "I mean, I like you. You're lovely. And hot. And smart."

And my kid worships you, he added silently. But that was way too much pressure.

Wes was watching and listening intently. Adam had never been the subject of such intense focus. He thought he could really get used to it.

"I just like you," Adam concluded simply.

"I like you too," Wes replied, still very intent.

Adam's heart stuttered.

"Cool," he said, mortifyingly.

Wes smiled. "Cool."

* * *

What Adam needed in his life was a best friend. Someone he could talk to about his burgeoning relationship. Someone to whom he could send texts like, Made out w W in middle of street. Are we boyfriends now?!?!?! And Dating yr neighbor who might be a vampire—Y/N???

Unfortunately, most of his friends had faded away when Gus entered the picture, and the rest had revealed themselves more Mason's friends than his when they split. He and River were close, but Adam wasn't sure if they were on romantic-talk terms quite yet.

So, lacking an actual best friend, Adam turned to what he did have: coworkers.

Bright and early Monday morning, Adam posed the question to Charlie and Marie.

"What would you think about dating your neighbor?"

He said it neutrally, casually, as if he didn't have his entire heart wrapped up in their answers.

Marie didn't talk much, but her facial expressions spoke volumes, and this one said beyond a shadow of a doubt *That is the worst idea I have ever heard and if you do that you will suffer.*

Or maybe he was just projecting.

Charlie was one of the fairest people Adam had ever met. He thought things through from all sides and he didn't jump to conclusions.

So when even Charlie hesitated, Adam felt his stomach fall.

"Yeah, okay," he said.

Hot tears pricked his eyes and he blinked them away and ducked behind the counter, pretending to pick up his pen.

Charlie turned away and pulled out his phone, and Adam considered the conversation over.

But a few minutes later, Rye, Charlie's partner, breezed through the door, dark hair flowing around his shoulders, kohl-rimmed gray eyes snapping.

"I received a bat signal?" he said.

Charlie cleared his throat.

"Oh," Rye said, and grinned. "I mean, oh, look, I've shown up here completely coincidentally and for no particular reason whatsoever."

Adam laughed.

Charlie shook his head and pulled Rye into his side with a fond expression. Rye patted his chest placatingly and smiled up at him.

"Tell us the whole story," Charlie said.

Adam blinked at him, overwhelmed by the generosity he was offering, and at work, no less.

For a moment, he couldn't speak for fear of crying again. Rye hummed absently and waved to an older man in the paint aisle.

"Keeping out of trouble, son?" the man asked.

"Never," Rye said with a grin. "You?"

"Naturally," he said, but winked at Rye with a twinkle that made Adam wonder.

"Okay, hit me," Rye told Adam.

Charlie swatted him playfully on the ass and Rye turned a wolfish look up at him, raising one eyebrow.

This. This was what Adam wanted. A partner. Someone he had rapport with. Someone he could joke around with, depend on, call and know he would show up.

"I'm falling for my neighbor and I'm scared it's gonna be a total disaster," Adam blurted, then clapped his hand over his mouth.

Falling for him? Oh, shit, I am falling for him, Adam thought.

"Back up," Charlie said.

Adam blew out a breath and told them the whole story.

"He's incredible," he said. "And Gus already worships him. And that's what I'm afraid of. What if things don't work out and she gets attached and then we're living right across from this man who she loved and now he doesn't want anything to do with her? I can't do that to her again. Not after Mason," he added under his breath.

Charlie and Rye were telegraphing over Adam's head, and even Marie's expression had softened. Less *Your choices will wreak ruin and misery* now, and more *Oh, you poor fool of love; I pity you and your daughter.*

"Ah, at the risk of overstepping," Charlie began, then seemed to reconsider, and didn't finish his sentence.

Rye rolled his eyes.

"You're not talking about Gus; you're talking about yourself," Rye asserted.

Adam froze.

"Yeah. I mean, it's true about Gus too. I get it. But this is definitely about you."

Marie gave the tiniest nod, and it was like a judgment from on high.

Adam looked to Charlie, who seemed like someone who'd never been afraid of anything.

Charlie said, "I know you're worried about your daughter. You'd never want to set her up to be hurt. But part of being a parent is trusting that you've raised a person who can handle negative emotions, not be drowned by them. And you'll be there to support her if she's upset. I agree, the real issue is you."

The Real Issue Is You: The Adam Mills Story.

Adam sighed, but wasn't Charlie right? Wasn't Gus already hurting from everything with Mason, and wasn't she dealing with it beautifully? He was helping her, and she was doing great. He was the one who couldn't sleep, had abandoned his passion, and was attempting to make pie.

Rye chimed in, "I don't know shit about kids, but I bet your daughter would want you to be happy, wouldn't she?"

Adam *knew* that was true. It was Gus, after all, who'd stopped him from selling his camera in Colorado; Gus who'd told him he loved taking pictures, so he had to keep it. It was Gus who, River had confided in Adam, had confided in River that she was worried Adam was sad because he'd left his friends behind.

His daughter was a sweet, empathetic person. She would absolutely want him to be happy.

Rye leaned in, expression mischievous.

"You're welcome. Also. Have you f—"

"Rye!" Charlie barked.

Rye grinned and shrugged. Then winked at Adam.

"Okay, but how was it, though?"

Adam let a slow, appreciative smile spread across his face.

Chapter Thirteen

Adam

"Daddy, don't be mad, but…"

Adam opened his eyes. Apparently he'd managed to sleep through the night, which was wonderful.

The beginning of that sentence, however…

He was instantly awake.

"Are you okay? What's wrong? What happened?"

"I'm fine," she said instantly. "It's just… It's Bettie…"

Panic struck Adam.

The night before, in the spirit of facing his fears, being bold, and living expansively, he had said yes when Gus asked him if Bettie could have a sleepover with her, even though the idea of the tarantula in the house horrified him.

He'd instructed Gus explicitly on being responsible with Wes' pet—and, fine, had taken Wes aside to say, "Are you absolutely, positively *sure* you want an eight-year-old in charge of Bettie?" in the hopes that he would see reason and change his mind.

He had not.

Adam had spent the last several days worrying about starting a relationship with Wes. But if Gus had hurt or killed Bettie, he could stop worrying about that, because Wes would probably want nothing more to do with them.

When he spoke, his voice was choked and high.

"What happened to Bettie?"

Gus' eyes went wide.

"Oh, nothing. She's fine."

Relief flooded Adam, and he closed his eyes.

"Good, good."

"It's just… I can't…exactly…find her."

"What!"

Adam jumped up, skin acrawl.

"I just took her out for a few minutes," Gus explained. "Wes *said* it was okay. And she was so sweet, crawling on my arm, and then I guess I must've fallen asleep for just a *minute*—"

"Okay, okay, okay," Adam said, trying to tamp down his horror and panic in front of Gus. "No problem, we'll just look for her. Okay."

But although his brain sent the message *Get off the bed and go look for the huge tarantula crawling around your house*, his body didn't seem able to carry it out.

"Daddy. Are you getting down?"

"Hmm? Ohmm, sure, yep."

Adam did not get down.

"Daddy?"

Adam nodded fervently, trying to figure out what to do.

"Uh, just hand me my phone, would you, sweetie?"

Gus did, and he dialed with shaking fingers. It was

morning, so he doubted Wes would be awake, but it was all he could think of to do.

A groggy-sounding Wes answered, and relief rushed through Adam.

"Wes, Wes, can you come over? Please!"

Wes was instantly alert. "Are you okay? Should I call someone?"

"No, no, I'm fine. I…it's…"

Gus took the phone from him.

"Hi, Wes. It's Gus. Can you help me look for Bettie? She's crawling around somewhere and Daddy's *too* scared. Okay, bye."

She tossed the phone on the bed and bounced cheerily out the door.

"I'll let him in," she called.

Adam did some deep breathing with his eyes closed, then realized that with his eyes closed, Bettie could crawl onto him and he'd never know. So he opened his eyes.

To find Wes standing in the doorway of his bedroom, looking at him with a strange expression. Amusement? Scorn?

No. Fondness.

Wes looked under the bed, in the closet, and all around the room, then came to the edge of the bed and held out his hand.

"I'm *so* sorry about all this," Adam said, taking his hand. *All this* encompassed approximately forty things at this point.

"It's okay," Wes said simply.

Adam let himself be soothed, and Wes tugged him into his arms, lifting him easily to the floor.

"I'll just make some coffee," Adam said. Coffee would make everything better.

Wes didn't let go of his hand but reeled him in and tipped his face up.

"Are you okay?" he asked.

"Um, it's honestly not the best wakeup call I've ever received, but I'll be fine. Once you find her," he added with a grimace and a little push.

Wes nodded, letting himself be pushed. Then he doubled back and caught Adam in a kiss.

Adam didn't have time to think about how he hadn't brushed his teeth yet or Gus could walk in at any moment. All he could do was be joyfully, gloriously kissed.

Thoroughly melted and in much better spirits, Adam made his way down to the kitchen, put the kettle on, and collapsed into a chair. It was only eight o'clock in the morning and already he was exhausted.

He got the box of pancake mix down from the cupboard—filed under *P* for pancake; god, Wes was so damn cute—put on the new Rhys Nykamp album, and lost himself in daydreams about more kisses from Wes as he made pancakes.

When he heard Gus' triumphant, "Bettie!" he felt a wash of relief.

"Pancakes!" he called, and Gus came galloping down the stairs, Wes following with a discreetly draped box under his arm that he placed near the front door before coming into the kitchen.

"Where was she?" Adam asked trepidatiously.

"The shower," Gus chirped gleefully, shoving pancakes into her mouth.

Adam pushed that image as far from his mind as possible, in the interest of ever cleaning himself again.

Wes sat down at the third plate Adam had set and took a sip of coffee.

"Don't worry," Gus told Wes with her mouth full. "They come from a mix."

Adam snorted. "I think what you meant to say was, 'Thank you for breakfast, and all the other meals you make for me so I don't starve to death.'"

Gus grinned. "Thank you for breakfast and all the other meals you make for me so I don't starve to death."

"That's what I thought."

Gus giggled.

"Gus and I are going to The Dirt Road Cat Shelter, where River works, to visit them and play with some cats. Wanna come with us?"

Adam said it casually, but he dearly wanted Wes to say yes. Of course, he had likely woken the man up just hours after he went to bed, and scared him into thinking his beloved pet was lost.

"I mean, I know cats aren't your animal of choice…" Adam gave him an easy out. "But no one will be there except River."

"I like cats," Wes corrected. "I just don't like them more than snakes and lizards."

"Yeah, come!" Gus said. "River showed me a video

of this cat they have there who always walks backward."

Wes' and Adam's eyes met, and Adam raised an eyebrow, and after a moment, Wes nodded.

"Okay."

"Yay!"

The Dirt Road Cat Shelter had begun its life as a house Rye Janssen inherited from a grandfather he'd never known. Over the course of the last two years, with a lot of help from River and many other residents of Garnet Run, Rye had built it into a first-rate shelter, with a huge social media following, adoption events, and, recently, a line of bespoke cat treats.

The outside of the shelter had retained the cabin shape, but the inside was nothing like one. The entrance was a set of two consecutive doors to keep cats from getting out, because inside, rather than being contained in pens, the cats had free rein of a complex network of cat ramps, tunnels, and obstacles that ran along the upper half of all the walls and led to a back room that was completely openwork metal mesh backed with Plexiglas that looked outside, so the cats had a panoramic view of the trees behind the shelter.

River grinned when they walked through the door, their blue eyes, usually wary, lit up with excitement.

"River!"

Gus ran at them and grabbed them around the waist, and River tweaked Gus' unruly ponytail.

"Hey, Bug. You wanna see some cats?"

"I wanna see the one that goes backward."

River smiled.

"Hey, Adam. Hi, Wes."

Adam hugged River and Wes shook their hand.

There was no one else in the shelter, so River led them to the room full of toys and beds where most of the cats spent their days. Many of them snoozed in puddles of sun. Others batted at toys, scratched the posts in the corners, and tumbled around with one another.

"This is Archimedes," River said, leading them to a large black cat with long whiskers and owlish yellow eyes.

Gus plopped down beside the cat and peered at it.

"Come here, Archimedes," River said, and threw a felt fish.

The cat scrambled toward the toy, but did so backward, with its head turned around to watch where it was going. When he got there, he tossed it himself and ran forward. Then got it and ran backward again.

"Whoa!" Gus exclaimed.

Wes leaned close to Adam.

"You really think that cat's cuter than Bettie?"

To be fair, the cat's movements had given Adam a bit of an *Exorcist* vibe, but he still thought it was adorable.

"Yes, because *cats*."

"It's just because certain animals are socially constructed as cute and others as scary," Wes grumbled.

Adam knew it was true. He made a silent promise to himself that he wouldn't say anything negative about Wes' pets again. Even if he was scared of them, it was no reason to rain on Wes' slimy parade.

River introduced them to some of the other cats and one of them took a liking to Wes. It was a small orange cat named Shirley and it kept pouncing Wes' legs whenever he walked past.

"You looking to adopt a cat by any chance?" River asked.

Wes scooped Shirley up and looked at her.

"I don't know if she'd get along with Janice and Banana."

"His raccoons," Gus explained to River.

River raised their eyebrows and nodded, the picture of diplomacy.

"Well, if you decide you want a cat, she definitely likes you."

"I'll think about it," Wes said. "Thanks."

He gave Shirley a pat on her little head and deposited her onto the nearest cat ramp.

Rye and Charlie walked through the front door, waving hello, and Adam had a sneaking suspicion that River might have texted Rye to tell him Wes was here. He narrowed his eyes at Rye, but Rye just winked.

"Hey, Adam," Charlie said. "And this must be Gus."

He held his hand out to Gus somberly, and she shook it just the same.

"You're Daddy's boss," she said, sizing him up. And his size was about thirteen times hers.

"That's right."

"You should be really nice to him because he's the best," Gus instructed Charlie very seriously.

"I will certainly try my hardest," Charlie pledged.

"This is Wes," Adam said, before his daughter could negotiate a raise or stock options on his behalf. "Wes, this is Charlie—he owns and runs Matheson's Hardware—and his partner, Rye, who created this place."

"Nice to meet you," Wes said. His voice sounded choked and he immediately retreated to the cat playroom. Gus and River followed, leaving Rye to grin at Adam and bump his shoulder, and Charlie to look on benevolently.

"That's him, huh?"

Adam nodded.

Rye opened his mouth to say something, but stopped and regarded Adam. At whatever he saw in Adam's face, he simply said, "Good for you."

Turning back onto Knockbridge Lane, Adam saw a pile of packages on the driveway. He spared a moment of irritation for the delivery person who hadn't put them on the front stoop, but it was quickly erased when he saw that there were more packages crowding the stoop.

"What the hell?"

Gus burst out of the car the second it stopped, and ran to the pile of boxes.

"Daddy, this one's for me!"

"Christmas presents?" Wes asked.

"Not from me," Adam said.

He had a brief swell of hope that maybe Mason had decided to shower Gus with gifts to make up for being an absolute failure, but he knew in his heart it wasn't the case. Mason wasn't the bother-with-the-post-office type any more than he was the amends-making type.

Adam insisted on opening one of the packages addressed to him first, in case this was a prank. He slit the first box open with his house keys and pulled out two boxes of Christmas lights.

"Oh!" Gus' mouth fell open.

"I'll be damned," Adam said. "The Instagram post worked."

Darren and Rose McKinnon, the Mills' next-door neighbors, picked that moment to come outside with their sons who were the same age as Gus—Dustin and Derek, or Donny and Derek, or Dennis and Dunstan; Adam could never remember.

Wes retreated to the side of the house.

"Looks like Santa came early this year, huh, sweetheart?" Darren McKinnon called to Gus.

"Oh, there's no such thing as Santa," Gus called back.

The McKinnons looked scandalized and Rose clapped her hands around either Derek or Dunstan's ears to try and shield them, but she was too late and had only the two hands.

"Of course there's a Santa Claus," she called, eagle eyes trained on Adam. It was clear she expected him to correct Gus. He smiled back at her, no intention whatsoever of doing so.

Gus laughed, then she waved. "Hi, Drake, hi, Dakota."

They ignored her.

Adam stopped bothering trying to remember their names.

Darren and Rose shepherded their kids to the car and drove off without another word.

"I don't think you're supposed to tell other kids that Santa doesn't exist, sweetie."

Gus shrugged.

"Santa's stupid. If Drake and Dakota want to think some old man is climbing down their chimney that's their problem."

Wes emerged from the shadows, nodding like this was a perfectly reasonable stance. Adam bit his fist to avoid laughing.

Having had the final word in the Santa Claus discussion, Gus turned to ripping open the rest of the boxes, eyes glowing with delight. All told, Adam's fans had sent him twenty-nine strands of lights: twenty-one white, five multicolored, and one package of three strands of bright pink lights, which Gus declared "Weird, but cool."

Many of the packages had notes with them, wishing Adam and Gus a happy Christmas and good luck with their project. A couple were from people Adam had worked with, and those had more personal messages.

One card was from a woman named Claire whom he'd shot a few years before, coincidentally on Gus' fourth birthday. During the shoot, he'd started crying thinking about how big she was getting and how much he loved her. He'd been mortified at his lack of professional veneer, but Claire had been lovely and hugged him, and told him that feeling never went away.

Her note was to Gus.

"Sweetie, this one's to you. It's from a friend of mine in Boulder. 'Dear Gus, I'm not surprised that your dad is doing something to make your dreams come true because that's the kind of father he is.'"

Wes put his arm around Adam's shoulders and squeezed.

When Gus had turned four, Adam had been overcome by the feeling of her growing up. The knowledge that his baby was gone and a small person was there in her place. Now, he looked at the strong, smart wiseass Gus had become, and his heart swelled with pride.

"'He loves you so much and I hope you never forget all the wonderful times you spend together. All my best, Claire.'"

"Thanks, Daddy," Gus said quietly, and fit herself to his other side.

With the man he was falling for on one side of him and the daughter he loved more than anything on the other side, Adam Mills felt utterly and completely at peace.

Chapter Fourteen

Wes

With the lights that Adam's Instagram followers had sent him, the Mills' house was beginning to look more like the competition for Most Lights Ever that Gus wanted.

Of course, they would never actually achieve that. Wes had looked it up the first time she mentioned it to find that the Guinness record for most Christmas lights ever on a residential property was held by the Gay family in Lagrangeville, New York, with 641,695 lights.

With each passing day, more and more lights were delivered. Adam had Wes take a picture of him and Gus standing in front of their newly illuminated house that he posted to his Instagram account, thanking everyone who had sent lights and announcing that they were still looking for more if anyone had them.

The Mills house was no Lagrangeville, but at least now when Gus got home from school and flipped the power switch, the lights no longer looked depressing.

In fact, this evening it looked downright inviting. The lights cast a glow around the house, every window downstairs was lit, and Wes imagined he could hear laughter and chatter coming from inside. He'd been glorying in the versatility of algae for hours now, but he couldn't help getting up every ten minutes or so, going to the periscope, and peeking at the Mills' house.

Don't do this, he cautioned himself. *Don't put yourself in this position. It won't end well.*

Sighing, Wes settled in front of his tub of algae once more, forced himself to stay seated, and tried to remember what his nice, private life was like before Adam and Gus had arrived on Knockbridge Lane, bringing with them the chaos that is a functioning heart.

"It's his sixtieth birthday," his sister said.

"I know."

"I'll pay for your flight," she went on. "Just come for Christmas."

"It's not about the money, Lana."

It had never, ever been about money, though his mother and sister refused to believe that.

"Then what?"

Wes could hear her begin to move around her house, doing other things. As always, his sister wasn't interested in any explanations other than her own.

"You know what. I can't spend time with Dad."

"You *won't* spend time with him. It's not like it'd kill you."

Also as always, Lana managed to say the exact thing that sent rage sizzling through him. She was the only one who made him feel this way. Even with his father, it wasn't rage. It was a gut full of guilt, pity, and a slow-burning resentment that would reach rage if allowed to kindle.

But Wes hadn't allowed it to kindle since he was fifteen. And he'd keep it tucked away inside him as long as he didn't have to spend time with his father.

Wes bit back the torrent of fury he wanted to unleash on Lana. It wouldn't do any good and would leave him with the bitter taste of guilt in his mouth for days to come.

"Yeah, you're right, Lana. It wouldn't kill me. I choose not to spend time with Dad. I'm hanging up now."

She didn't try to stop him. She never did. Because if he was the absent child, the child who didn't call on birthdays or come visit for holidays, who wasn't in publicity pictures with their father, who didn't send gifts, then she got to be the good child. The one who was there, who cared.

The one who had followed their father's plan for both of them, after Wes had torn it to pieces and flung it in his face.

Not that that had been his intention.

Wes jumped up and shook out his hands, needing to discharge all this energy. It wasn't late enough to go for a run yet—there might still be neighbors about—so he settled for doing pushups until his arms and back trembled and he couldn't hold himself up any longer.

He buzzed his hair as he did every week, turned

the shower as hot as he could stand it and ran a handful of soap over his shorn hair. Once, that hair had
been a feature people recognized. Wes made sure no
one would ever recognize it again.

He walked around the rooms upstairs, air-drying,
still irritated.

What would happen if he did go back to Los Ange-
les? If he set the record straight in front of everyone.

He got as far as picking up his phone, when it rang
in his hand.

Adam.

Just the sight of his name was like a cool breeze,
dispelling the lingering heat.

"Hello?" he said, despite knowing it was Adam,
the habit of learning to answer the phone that way
unshakeable.

"Do you wanna come over and get drunk with
me?"

Adam pitched his voice jovially, but it was clear
he wasn't happy.

"Are you okay?"

"Yeah. I mean, I will be. Just a bad day." He
sighed. "I've got boxed mac and cheese?" he offered,
as if that was tempting.

"Okay."

"Yeah? Yay! Okay, come on over."

Wes stared at his reflection in the bathroom mirror after Adam disconnected the call.

It was the only mirror in the house, half fogged
over from his shower.

Once, he had looked in every mirror he passed,

searching their reflections for what it was that made people care about his face. Whatever it was, he didn't see it. After things had imploded at home, an unexpected glimpse in the mirror was enough to fold him over with a clawing pain in his stomach.

He'd started training himself to look straight ahead so he didn't see himself in shop windows; to look at the water swirling down the drain so he didn't see himself in bathroom mirrors; to unfocus his eyes when speaking to people wearing mirrored sunglasses, so he didn't see his talking head in their reflection.

Dark eyebrows, intense blue eyes, a rather large nose, a mouth, a chin. Ears. Cheekbones. Stubble.

They were neutral in his mind. Clean of line, perhaps, and that seemed to be a thing people responded to aesthetically, but other than that…just features like any others.

Now, though, he found himself wondering what Adam thought of them. Might they appeal to Adam the way they once had to people he didn't care about?

Wes blinked and the man in the mirror blinked. Wes imagined it was Adam—beautiful, sweet Adam—looking back at him and he watched the man in the mirror's features become something hopeful, something tender, something yearning.

"Adam," Wes whispered, and the man in the mirror whispered it too.

Wes touched his lips to the lips in the mirror, wanting to see what Adam had seen when their lips met, but it was just a blur.

Scoffing at himself, Wes swiped at the mirror with the heel of his hand and went to get dressed.

Adam opened the door brandishing a bottle of gin and already-flushed cheeks. He smiled when he saw Wes and Wes felt as if he were the man in the mirror, looking out at the living, breathing world as if through a pane of glass.

Adam's expression dimmed at whatever he saw on Wes' face, and Wes saw exhaustion in the shadows beneath Adam's smiling eyes.

"What's wrong?" they said simultaneously.

"Jinx," Adam said, and gestured him inside.

Wes kicked off his boots and followed Adam into the kitchen.

"You like gin?" Adam asked.

"It's okay."

"You want some mac and cheese?"

"Okay."

"You wanna sit?"

"Okay."

"Have you recently been stricken with a curse that only allows you to say the word *okay*?"

Wes smiled.

"Okay," he teased, and Adam grinned.

"Oh, good. Then, uh, do you want to help me hang approximately one million strands of lights tomorrow that people have sent?"

"Okay," Wes said.

Adam rolled his eyes. "I was just joking."

"I know. But I'll help. You're a menace on the ladder. Can't have Gus orphaned, can we?"

He'd been going for levity but swore at himself internally when Adam's face fell.

"I'm sorry," Wes said instantly. *Not* the thing to say about a kid whose mother hadn't been able to care for her and whose other father had abandoned her. "I didn't mean…"

Adam shook his head.

"It's not that. I got home from work today and all Gus wanted to talk about was why Mason wasn't going to be with us for Christmas. And I don't want him here, but I'm so furious that he won't be here. For Gus, I mean. River told me she called him today while they were here and left a message on his voice mail and he never called back."

Wes felt his earlier anger flare back to life, only now it was directed at Adam's ex.

Adam put a bowl of macaroni and cheese in front of Wes. Clearly he'd been spending more time with Adam and Gus than he even knew, because the first bite of neon orange goo tasted familiar and homey.

"Here's to dad problems," Wes said, toasting Adam with another spoonful.

"Oh my god, *you* have a father?" Adam's blue eyes got comically large. "Tell me everything. I assumed you had sprung fully-formed from the head of Zeus or something, from the amount you talk about yourself."

"Nah, that's my sister, Athena."

Adam laughed, then said, "Wait, you don't really have a sister named Athena do you?"

"No. Lana."

"Okay, just checking."

Adam poured something into cups with the gin and handed one to Wes.

"Gin and mac and cheese. Parenthood classic."

"Cheese," Wes said, and clinked his bowl with Adam's.

Adam smiled but his brows wrinkled.

"You're in a weird mood. Or is this normal for you once you get comfortable with people?"

Wes tried to remember the last time he got comfortable with people. Only Zachary came to mind.

"Weird how?" Wes asked.

"Funny."

"I'm hilarious," Wes said seriously.

Adam smirked at him.

"It's cute you think I'm gonna be distracted from your dad problems."

Wes shoved more mac and cheese in his mouth and gave Adam an innocent look.

"Here, take this." Adam picked up the drinks and his bowl and gestured for Wes to bring his. "And come sit down."

They settled on the couch in the living room, farthest from Gus' room. Adam turned on the TV where a video of a wood fire played.

"Until I can have a real one," Adam said.

The fire crackled cozily, and Adam pulled a quilt over them. The first sip of the cocktail—make that *concoction*, Wes revised as the taste registered—cooled his lips and warmed his stomach. The second tasted slightly less weird.

"What is this?"

"Gin and apple juice. I don't make cocktails much anymore," he said sheepishly.

It wasn't precisely disgusting, so Wes knocked it back and chased it with the last bite of his mac and cheese. Then he took a deep breath and began to tell Adam Mills a story he hadn't told in fifteen years.

"My dad's an actor in LA. That's where I'm from. When I was little he landed a pretty good role on a soap. So he had steady work my whole childhood."

"Whoa, what soap?" Adam asked excitedly. "Sorry, never mind." He mimed locking his mouth and throwing away the key.

"When I was twelve, he decided it was time to make the leap to film. It was all he talked about."

Every night at dinner—when he was home for dinner—and every morning at breakfast, his father detailed each line of his resume that would make him appealing and unappealing. He monologued about his looks, his ability with different accents, his charisma.

Lana, three years younger than Wes, hung on their father's every word. But Wes' mind would wander. He thought about the way the tree at the corner of their street grew at an odd angle. He thought about the lizard he'd seen snoozing in the sun on their deck. He thought about the way the air smelled electric before a storm.

"Was he good?" Adam asked.

"He was okay, I think. Good enough for soaps, but nothing special."

And that was the part that had really killed his father. He yearned for the kind of acclaim that came from uniqueness, never satisfied to be part of an ensemble. He wanted to be a star.

"I don't exactly know how it all went down. But around that time, my dad started telling me there was a role for me on the soap. I wasn't interested and I told him so. He thought I was just playing it cool, but I really had no interest. It sounded so boring. Standing around all day, waiting for your scene to come, and then saying some fake words? What was appealing about it?"

Adam smiled and took his hand, tracing his palm under the blanket with warm fingers.

"You would think that." He said it fondly.

"When I told him I really, truly had no interest, he told me that he'd made a deal with his agent to get me as her client. She wanted me. I don't know why. But the way my dad put it to me was that either I did the show and he got to be a movie star, or I said no and flushed his dreams down the toilet."

"That's horrible," Adam murmured, squeezing his hand.

"Yeah. Now I know it was nonsense. My dad probably wanted the publicity that would come from having a father and son both in the business. Something like that. But at the time, I honestly thought if I didn't do it I'd be wrecking my dad's career."

"Lemme guess. You did it?"

Wes nodded.

"When I told my dad I would do it…it's…"

The look on his father's face had been—he realized now—relief. But at the time, he'd thought it was joy. Joy that Wes was causing. And it was the first time he felt like his dad was glad to have him around.

"Usually he just thought I was weird. He never understood my interest in science or why I wanted to take things apart and learn how they worked. He wanted me to be interested in Hollywood and publicity. Or at least sports. Something he could talk to me about. Something I could discuss at parties. So when I said I would do it, it was like I finally did something he could understand. Something he approved of."

That night at dinner, Wes' dad spoke about work as if it included Wes; as if they were embarking on a journey together. It felt good.

Six months later, when Wes started rehearsing, his father walked him onto the set with a hand on his shoulder, proud to show him off to everyone.

This is my son, he'd say with a wink. *He'll be playing Crawford Magnusson.* People on set thought that was just precious: Wes playing his real father's son on the show.

"It was supposed to just be a short subplot," Wes explained. "My character showed up and revealed that my dad had a son he never knew about. Then I was supposed to die in a bank robbery. But when it started airing, something weird happened."

Adam frowned and squeezed his hand harder.

"They didn't want to kill my character off anymore. They kept writing more scenes for him."

"You must've been really good," Adam said.

Wes shook his head.

"My character was a slimeball. I don't know. But my dad got weird. Weirder. He talked about how great it was. What a success to have a role expanded. But he was clearly upset."

"Jealous," Adam murmured.

"Maybe."

"Did you stay on the show?"

Wes bit his lip, afraid Adam would respond the way his family and friends had at the time. The way his father told him every normal person would respond: with scorn at his ingratitude.

"The thing is…" Wes noticed he was rubbing his shaved head over and over with the hand not holding Adam's, and he forced himself to stop. "People started to look at me. To *notice* me."

Nausea crept through Wes' stomach and burned in his throat.

"They would talk to me. Yell at me from across the street. *Touch* me. The first time it happened I tried to do what I'd seen my dad do. I smiled and said hi. But I didn't know what they wanted. After a little while I… just needed to get away. I was with my dad, going into the studio, and a girl tried to cut a piece of my hair."

The nausea swelled and Wes regretted every bite of macaroni and cheese.

"I freaked out," Wes made himself say. "It wasn't about my hair. Not really. It was… I hated the attention. I hated people seeing me. People paying attention to what I ordered in a cafe or what shirt I chose to wear."

Adam's eyes were wide. "That sounds horrible."

Wes nodded. Something had happened to him, then. Something confusing and insidious. The more visible he became on the outside, the more he became invisible to himself. Every worry about being seen, every thought spent on the perceptions of those who might see him, stripped away the part of himself that engaged with the world on his own terms. That wondered what would happen if he put the coffee machine together backward, or how a plant could grow through concrete.

The inner peace he'd always possessed when tinkering, experimenting, observing, had been obliterated by the threat of constant observation.

Wes couldn't stand it. Without his questions, without his experimentation, he didn't know who he was. And worse, he didn't care.

"I quit. I told my dad I wouldn't do it anymore. It didn't go over well. My dad told me I was making a huge mistake. That I was an idiot to throw away something that anyone would kill for."

"But *you* wouldn't," Adam said fiercely. "You didn't want it."

Wes shook his head.

He would never forget the look in his father's eyes when he'd told him. A furious disgust that had burned as hot as his approval had when Wes agreed to do the show.

You'll change your mind, his father had said at first. *Sleep on it. I know, fame can be a lot of pressure.* Adam had slept on it, knowing his mind was made up, and the next morning he'd tried again. The mild mentor was gone, then, and his father's judgment had rained down—falling like acid rain on their tenuous connection until it was eaten away to nothing but holes.

"I was foolish to think I could just walk away and it would be over," Wes said. "The publicity machine runs on speculation, and my privacy was the chaff that got spit out in the process."

Where In the World is Crawford Magnusson?!, *Soap Digest* had asked on its front cover as Wes tried to go to school, go to the store, hang out with his friends. People seemed to recognize him more than ever. They would bombard him with questions about when he was returning to the show.

After a group of tourists surrounded him when he was coming out of a bookstore, Wes shut himself in his bedroom, staring at himself in the mirror. His hair had been shoulder-length, then. A fall of shiny, tight curls that bounced as he walked. It was distinctive. Noticeable.

Wes shaved his head with his father's electric razor and dumped his curls in the garbage can. He'd kept his head shaved ever since. It had worked, mostly. Little by little, the longer he stayed out of the spotlight, the public lost interest. Eventually, they left him alone.

And so, it turned out, did his father.

For the year after Wes quit, his father hounded him, guilted him, berated him for his choice and his selfishness. But when it became clear Wes would not return, his father was simply done with him. Wes served no purpose for his career, so Wes was of no interest any longer. He only had one thing to say, and he'd said it with utter conviction: "You will regret this."

Then Lana turned thirteen and told their father that she wanted to be an actor, and a new alliance was made.

"So what's the deal now? Do you have a relationship with your dad?"

"I text him on his birthday. Sometimes he responds."

Thank you with a period at the end was usually the response, when there was one. Once, a few years ago, the text had come through late at night. Wes had been up, as was his habit, but his father was clearly drunk and alone, likely on the couch in Wes' childhood home, staring at the picture of himself that hung over the television: standing on the red carpet in a tux and shiny shoes, young and vibrant, laughing at something just out of frame.

We really could've been something, son, that text had said. It all could've been different.

Wes hadn't responded.

"My sister called earlier. My dad's birthday is right before Christmas. She wanted me to come home. It's his sixtieth."

"Are you gonna go?"

"Hell no. Lana doesn't actually want me to come. She just wants to be able to tell my parents she tried to get me to."

"Do you get along with your sister?"

Wes could remember her as she used to be, when

she'd sit quietly in the corner as he tinkered, knowing she'd get kicked out if she made a sound but wanting to be near him.

"We never had much in common, but we got along fine. She went into acting after I quit. My dad helped her get started."

Adam was silent for a moment, then looked up with narrowed eyes.

"I'm sorry, I *have* to know who your dad and sister are. I'm too curious."

Wes chuckled. He'd heard Gus say that too: *I'm too curious*.

Wes pulled out his phone and showed Adam their IMDb pages.

"You changed your name?" Adam asked.

"It's my mom's last name."

"I don't think I've seen anything they're in, but they definitely look familiar." He made a picture of them at the Emmys bigger and brought the phone closer.

"You look a bit like your dad, I guess. But not like your sister."

Wes nodded. Adam's finger hovered over the screen.

"You can look," Wes said, resigned.

"Huh?" Adam looked at him innocently.

"Go ahead, it's fine."

Adam bit his lip, then clicked the link on his dad's profile that led to Westley Brennan.

Wes gazed at the flickering fire on Adam's television.

"Oh my god, your hair," Adam murmured. "Wow."

Then he passed Wes back the phone. "You were pretty cute," he said.

Then he swung over Wes' lap and put his hands on Wes' shoulders.

"But you're absolutely stunning now."

Wes shrugged. He knew Adam meant well, but he still didn't like to have his looks commented on.

"I won't say it again if you don't want," Adam said, perceptive as ever. "There's so many more important things about you that are also stunning."

Wes' heart fluttered.

"Yeah?" he asked, and heard the roughness in his voice. He couldn't quite bring himself to ask what they were, but he desperately wanted Adam to tell him.

"Oh, yeah."

Wes swallowed hard. Adam's blue eyes were luminous and tender.

"You're very kind," Adam said.

Wes closed his eyes. His family would certainly disagree with that. A soft kiss was dropped on one eyelid, then the other.

"You're incredibly smart."

A kiss on each cheek.

"You're kinda funny, turns out."

Wes snorted and got a kiss on his forehead.

"You're generous."

A kiss on his chin.

"And you're very, very sexy."

Adam caught his mouth in a sweet kiss that deepened into searching tongues and the hot crush of lips.

Wes' body came alive with desire for the sweet, sexy man in his lap.

"Adam," he breathed between kisses.

"Wes, god. I like you so much," Adam said.

Heat bloomed in Wes' stomach. Not the heady fever of lust but the steady, banked heat of care. Of something you want to keep burning.

"I like you too," Wes said. Then added, "So much," because it paled in comparison to what he felt.

The expression of joy on Adam's face was something Wes would carry with him for a long time. Adam's fingertips traced his face.

"I was thinking of you. Earlier," Wes continued, the confessions seeming to spill out of him tonight. "I couldn't concentrate. Kept wondering what you and Gus were doing. How you were."

He brushed Adam's blond hair back from his face, the fine strands catching on his roughened palms.

"I was thinking about you too," Adam said with a giddy smile. "I didn't want to bug you."

"I like bugs," Wes murmured, and Adam giggled, then shushed him with a kiss.

Adam ground his hips against Wes' thickening erection and Wes threw his head back.

"C'mon," Adam said, standing and tugging at his hand. His eyes were heavy lidded, lips swollen. He was irresistible.

Wes allowed himself to be led down the hall to Adam's bedroom, but the second the door was locked behind them, he grabbed Adam and threw him onto the bed.

Adam moaned, looking up at Wes and biting his lip. *Yes*, he mouthed.

Wes stripped him and pressed his shoulders to the mattress, licking at his pert nipples. Adam writhed beneath him, trembling at each swipe of Wes' tongue and gasping at each nibble of his teeth.

Adam fumbled in the bedside table, coming up with a bottle of lube and a condom and dropping them on the bed. His pupils were blown.

"Want you," he said. "Please?"

Soles of his feet on the bed, Adam let his knees fall apart, baring creamy thighs, dark blond hair, and a ruddy erection already leaking for Wes.

"Damn." The scent of skin and desire was heady.

Wes bent to kiss the pale skin of Adam's inner thighs. He rubbed his cheek on the soft flesh and Adam gasped. Wes rubbed harder, and the skin turned pink. Adam's hands fisted the sheets.

"What else do you have in there?" Wes murmured, eyeing the drawer that had produced lube and condoms.

Adam flushed, but grinned. He twisted just enough to pull open the drawer, and Wes was treated to a colorful glimpse of toys. Adam pulled out a small black toy that fit over two fingers. He pressed a button and it began to vibrate.

Adam raised an eyebrow and moved to put it away and grab something else, but Wes stopped him.

"Show me the rest later," he said, and took the small vibrating ring.

Wes undressed slowly, watching Adam's flush

move down to his neck, then his chest. He was so pale Wes could trace the veins from his throat to his groin.

"God you're gorgeous," Adam groaned as Wes bared himself. Then he clapped a hand over his mouth. "Sorry. Said I wouldn't mention your looks."

Wes was moved.

"It's okay. Feels different in this context. Thanks, I mean," he added when his brain caught up to him. "You're beautiful, Adam. Truly."

Adam smiled and drew him down for a kiss. Their erections caught and Wes pressed them together, groaning at the contact.

They rocked together as they kissed, and Wes let the heat grow between them. He could feel Adam leaking against his hip and drew back to put the condom on.

Adam handed him the lube, and Wes coated two fingers. He lifted Adam's hips.

"Okay?" he murmured, pressing gently inside.

Adam groaned and nodded quickly.

Wes slid his fingers deeper into the inferno of Adam's body. There was the initial resistance, then it gave way, and he was a part of Adam. Part of his silky, clenching heat.

"Oh, god," Adam moaned. "Yes, yes, yes, that's so good."

Wes kissed his belly and found his prostate, rubbing it with the pads of his fingers.

Adam's eyes rolled back in his head and he went stiff. Then, when Wes rubbed harder, he let out a groan and melted around Wes' questing fingers.

"Oh my god that feels so good, unnghh."

Wes fingered him slowly, made sure his body was relaxed, then slid his fingers out, treasuring Adam's disappointed gasp.

He stroked lube onto his erection quickly, suddenly desperate to be buried deep inside his lover.

"Adam," Wes whispered. "I want you."

"Yes, please," Adam moaned.

Wes pressed the tip of his erection into Adam, relishing the slick heat. He made himself go as slowly as he could, gritting his teeth with restraint. But Adam gasped, grabbed at his shoulders, and pulled him closer.

Liquid heat shot up Wes' spine as he felt himself slide deep inside Adam. He was rocked by wave after wave of pleasure, and it took every ounce of restraint he possessed to pause and wait until Adam's body relaxed.

"Oh my god, Wes," Adam groaned after a few moments. "Yes."

Wes nodded, unable to summon a single word. He kissed Adam instead, put Adam's feet on his shoulders, and began to move inside him.

He angled his hips so his strokes would caress Adam's prostate and Adam opened his mouth in a silent scream.

Wes felt himself coming unspooled. The heat of Adam's flushed cheeks, the tender flesh of his thighs, the silk of his rose petal lips, and the hot clench of his body were so potent that Wes heard the groans spilling from his lips and felt his stomach tighten with lust.

Adam was moaning and clutching at him, the flush pinking his cheeks obscenely.

Wes slid the vibrating toy onto his fingers and flicked the tiny button to turn on the vibrations.

Adam's eyes got wide. Then one corner of his mouth lifted in a lusty smile and he nodded.

God, he was perfect.

Wes slid the vibrating toy over the tip of Adam's erection and felt every muscle in his body clench.

Adam swore and panted and Wes felt peace descend over him that he usually only felt in the lab. But here, all he wanted was to make Adam feel better than he had ever felt in his life.

"Oh god, oh god, ohgod, ohgod, ohgodohgodohgod," Adam chanted, coherence losing out to his body's needs.

"Yes, baby," Wes purred.

He thrust faster, seeking an explosion of the pleasure that mounted higher and higher. As he drove deeper inside Adam, he kept the vibrator tight to the ultrasensitive tip of his erection. Adam keened, throwing his head back.

"Wes, Wes, Wes, Wessss."

Adam's mouth fell open and every muscle clenched. Then he was gone, shuddering around a silent scream.

It was the hottest thing Wes had ever seen. Adam was spread out before him, writhing in ecstasy, and it was the last straw. Wes drove deep inside Adam and felt the burning pressure erupt out of him in wave after wave of perfect pleasure.

He shuddered with the intensity of it as he came down. Then Adam clenched around him and tendrils of pleasure grabbed him again, sending aftershocks juddering through him.

"Jesus Christ," Wes groaned, and collapsed on top of Adam. He buried his face in Adam's throat, breathing in the scent of his skin, glazed with clean sweat.

"Oh my god," Adam said, letting a hand fall heavily on Wes' back. "What the hell did you just do to me."

But it wasn't a question, and Wes hummed. The vibrator, buried in the covers now, buzzed its agreement, and Wes fumbled for it and turned it off.

"C'mere," Adam murmured. Wes slowly slid out of Adam and they both hissed with the loss. Wes took care of the condom then settled in next to Adam, gathering him in his arms.

"That was…outrageous," Adam said, and kissed his shoulder before snuggling closer. "In a great way," he clarified, and Wes chuckled.

He loved the weight of Adam against his chest and side, loved the feel of him wiggling closer under the covers, loved the scent of their combined pleasure lingering heavily in the air, and the sound of Adam murmuring sweet, sleepy things against his skin.

"I agree," Wes said, and Adam gave him a squeeze.

"Will you stay?" he asked.

He wanted to. He wanted to kiss Adam back to slumber if he couldn't sleep, and wake up to him, heavy and soft in the morning light.

"Is it okay? With Gus, I mean?"

"Mmm-hmm."

"Okay."

"Yay," Adam said happily, and cuddled closer.

Wes usually didn't go to bed for hours yet, so he knew he wouldn't fall asleep. But it didn't matter. If he got to hold Adam then he was exactly where he wanted to be.

Chapter Fifteen

Adam

Adam surfaced from sleep slowly, gradually becoming aware that he was held in strong arms and that a warm, muscular form was behind him.

Wes.

Adam felt his entire body flush with heat as memories from the night before came flooding back. It had been the best sex of his life. Wes had felt perfect inside him, gloriously nailing his prostate on every stroke. When he'd added the stimulation of the vibrator Adam had been done for.

And he couldn't wait to do it all over again.

Wes made a sleepy sound behind him and pressed his face into the crook of Adam's neck. It made Adam's stomach go gooey.

"Morning," Adam said softly.

"Mmng," was the sleepy response into his hair, and Wes' arm gathered him closer.

"You can keep sleeping," Adam said, "but I should—"

But he didn't get any further than that because that was the moment that Gus opened the door.

Only the door was locked, so she just banged on it.

"Daddy!" she said in a singsong voice far too peppy for early on a Saturday morning. "Daddy, I'm awake now!"

"Yeah, I can hear that, sweetheart. Why don't you go watch TV for a few minutes and I'll meet you in the living room."

"'Kay. Can I get juice?"

"Yeah."

Wes had buried his head under the pillow when Gus had started yelling, whether out of embarrassment or simply to muffle the skull-rattling noise Adam wasn't sure.

"Um. You okay under there?"

"Mmm-hmm."

"You sure?"

Adam pushed the pillow aside and Wes' arms came up and grabbed him, pulling him down on top of Wes.

Adam couldn't help the small *yeep* that squeaked out of him. He kissed Wes, and Wes kissed back, squeezing him tight.

It felt like home.

"So, do you want me to climb out the window and down the drainpipe or what?" Wes asked.

Adam's stomach fell.

"Oh. I…if you want."

"I don't think anyone ever really *wants* to climb down a drainpipe," Wes said.

But Adam wasn't in the mood to joke. He wanted to walk out of his bedroom with Wes as if it were normal. To make coffee and eat waffles with Gus, and…

What? Be a family?

The words were said in a nasty voice in his head, and it wasn't his voice. It was Mason's.

But Adam had let Mason ruin enough of his days when they were together; he'd be goddamned if he'd let him do it now that they were over.

"Yes, actually," he told Mason's sneering voice in his head.

"Oh," Wes said. "Well, I was kind of kidding, but if you really want me to…"

"Huh?"

"Climb out the window."

"No, no. Oh. No, I don't want that."

Wes lay in his bed, gloriously naked, blankets pooled around his waist. With his shaved hair, he didn't even look morning mussed. He just looked like Wes all the time.

Adam wanted to see Wes in every conceivable scenario: getting out of the shower, covered in sweat, sleepy, grouchy, stuffing his face with spaghetti. He wanted to *know* Wes. He wanted to be with Wes.

"Aw, hell," Adam muttered. He'd been trying to cut the f-word out of his vocabulary so he didn't say it around Gus and it had resulted in some awkward phrasing.

"Hey," Wes said. "You wanna fill me in? I really will sneak out if you want. Although…" He eyed the window seriously, and Adam could practically see the calculations he was doing. "I don't think the drain-pipe will actually hold my weight."

He was making light of things. Giving Adam a

chance to collect himself. And it filled Adam with a fizzy sense of possibility.

Slowly, Adam leaned in and kissed Wes. His breath was a little sour and his lips were soft, and Adam kissed him again.

"Do you wanna come have some breakfast?"

"You sure?"

Adam nodded. "If you're okay with Gus making some assumptions."

"Would her assumptions be, um, correct?"

Wes' blue eyes were warm and searching, and Adam saw something vulnerable and nervous in them.

He cupped Wes' face, thinking about young Wes who'd experienced love as conditional. Whose family hadn't cared about his desires. Hadn't accepted him for who he was but only for how they could use him.

"If her assumptions are that we're dating," Adam said, "then I'd be okay with that being correct." He bit his lip. "Would you?"

Wes' smile was soft and peaceful.

"Yeah, I could deal with that hypothesis panning out."

"Such a nerd." Adam kissed him again.

"Such a romantic," Wes said, returning the kiss.

They dressed and went to find Gus. Just before they descended the final step into the living room, Adam grabbed Wes' hand. His heart felt like a hummingbird's in his chest, suddenly, at the thought of his daughter not approving of him and Wes.

Gus was lying on the couch, her head hanging over

the side, watching TV upside down. She claimed it was more interesting that way.

She smiled when she saw them, and then her eyes tracked down (well, up, for Gus) to their joined hands and her eyes went wide. Her mouth opened in a perfect O and she flipped right side up.

She bounced on the couch and clapped a hand over her mouth, something Adam had taught her to do when she had something she was about to say but wasn't sure if it was appropriate.

"It's okay, sweetie," Adam said.

"You! Are you? You're!" She bounced with each word.

"We're dating," Adam said.

He walked over to the couch and Gus stopped bouncing. Standing on the cushions she was almost as tall as him. Her expression was serious as she said to Adam what he'd said to her many times: "You made a *very* smart choice."

Adam burst into laughter that turned, in an instant, to tears. He grabbed Gus in a hug and squeezed her tight. Before becoming a parent he never could have imagined the singularly exquisite feeling of his daughter being proud of him. He cried happy tears into her messy blond hair.

"Thanks, sweetie," he gulped.

"Are you okay?" Wes looked concerned.

"He's fine," Gus said, unconcernedly patting Adam's head. "Daddy gets very emotional sometimes."

Her nonjudgmental explanation just made Adam cry harder.

He felt Wes' strong arms come around them both, holding them tight.

When Adam's tears dried and Gus got bored of hugging, they went to the kitchen and Adam put waffles in the toaster as Wes made coffee. Gus set the table and began a long, enthusiastically detailed description of the book she was reading about a girl who discovers alien life on Mars.

"Mars is not the most likely planet to play host to life forms," Wes said seriously.

"It's fiction," Adam said.

"Still!"

And Wes began an equally long and enthusiastically detailed explanation of the meteorological and chemical environment of Mars as compared with other planets.

Adam tuned them both out and watched as if it were a movie. He felt so utterly joyful—so full up with warmth and happiness—that it seemed his skin could hardly contain it.

"Be right back," he murmured, though Gus and Wes were too focused on aliens to notice.

In the bathroom, Adam stared at himself. His eyes looked shockingly blue against the redness left over from crying, and that almost got him started again. He'd always cried easily, but sometimes the tears felt so close to the surface that they just welled over.

He looked in the mirror and let his chin wobble and his lips tremble and his eyes fill with tears. He smiled at himself and said firmly, "It's brave to take risks. It's okay if things don't work out. It's still worth trying. Love is always worth trying for."

Love, love, love.

It was what he'd never felt from his parents. It was what he'd wanted so desperately with Mason, and realized wasn't there. He'd learned what love was from Gus, and now that he knew, he would never accept anything less.

"It's not silly to want love. It's not foolish to admit you want it."

"Daddy?"

Gus' voice came from the other side of the door.

"Be out in a sec, sweetie."

"Is your tummy not feeling good?"

Adam grinned.

"Nope, I'm fine. Be out in a minute."

"Okay."

Just when he thought she'd surely left, she said. "I ate your waffle."

Adam laughed, hand over his mouth. At his silence, Gus said, "I can make you another one."

"That'd be nice. Get Wes' help if it's still hot, though."

He heard her walk away and sank down on the toilet seat, scrubbing the tears off his face.

His daughter was a goddamned jewel. The amazing man he was quickly falling for liked him back. It was almost Christmas, his favorite time of the year.

Nothing could ruin Adam's perfect happiness.

Chapter Sixteen

Wes

Wes was on fire. He hadn't felt this alive since he walked into the lab his first semester at Caltech and saw the equipment that would enable him to carry out all the experiments he had in his head.

It was the buzz and pop of possibility, the tingle of potential.

It was happiness. He'd just never had a name for it before.

Telling Adam about his family, his past—putting it into words for the first time in years—had clarified it for him. His father had been wrong. Wes hadn't realized how muddy he'd allowed that to get in his mind after all this time. How much the guilt of choosing not to have a relationship with the man had complicated the story.

Now, though, eating waffles at Adam and Gus' kitchen table, seeing how everything Adam did was in service of showing Gus fairness, exposing her to honesty, both in fact and feeling, and giving her space to be herself, it was very, very clear. His parents hadn't been like that. They hadn't been like that at all.

"Hey, what's up?" Adam asked.

"Huh? Nothing. Just thinking."

"Anything good?" Adam said lightly, with a soft smile that said they could talk about it later if he wanted.

"You're an exceptional parent," Wes said. "That's all."

Adam's eyes went wide, then filled with tears.

Gus patted Adam's hand, then shoved another bite of waffle in her mouth.

"Thank you," Adam said thickly. "I...wow, thank you."

"What are we doing today?" Gus asked.

"Well, I thought we could hang some more lights. Wes said he could help."

"Can I climb the ladder?" Gus hedged.

"A little bit," Adam said. "And I get to stand right underneath you in case you fall."

Gus rolled her eyes but agreed, and it gave Wes an idea.

"Do you like the woods?" he asked Gus.

She nodded excitedly.

"Maybe after we hang lights we could go on a little adventure."

Gus immediately turned to Adam. "Can we?"

"What does *little* mean in this instance? Also *adventure*?"

Wes laughed.

"Just a little hike. In the woods. To a clearing that I want to check out."

"That doesn't sound at all like you're going to murder us," Adam mumbled. "Okay, sure. Lights, then being led to a mysterious spot in the woods."

"Yay!" Gus said, then ran to get dressed.

"I'm gonna run home and change," Wes said. "Feed the animals. Meet you back here in an hour or so?"

"Okay." Adam was gazing at him. "Can I have a kiss before you go?" he asked tentatively.

Wes didn't want him to ever feel tentative about asking for that. He stood and drew Adam into his arms. When their lips met, everything else melted away, and it was just them and this moment. Wes cupped Adam's cheek and kissed him again, light and sweet. Adam's eyelashes fluttered.

"Okay, bye," Wes said.

Adam smiled and gave a little wave.

When Wes closed the front door behind him, he felt a little tug in the region of his heart, as if with each step he took away from Adam he was leaving behind something essential.

It had only been twelve hours, but his own house felt dark and oppressive after being in Adam's cozy, airy home.

He made the rounds, feeding everyone, cleaning up, kissing lizard heads, scratching raccoon backs, and letting snakes slither their way around his neck.

After a shower and a change of clothes, Wes texted Zachary.

I really like him. Then, as he pulled on his shoes, I don't want to screw it up.

Good plan, Zachary texted back. I wish I had some advice, but I've been told I screw up every relationship I have. So maybe just do the opposite of what I'd do?

Well what would you do?

If I knew what I did wrong I'd stop! Zachary wrote. Then, after a minute, Probably. Another minute. I mean I'd try.

Wes snorted.

Kay going over there now. Later.

During the day?! It must be true love! Zachary wrote, then flooded Wes' screen with pink hearts.

Wes had hiked out to this spot once a week for the last six months, but he'd always gone at night. After all, you could only tell if lights were bright enough in the dark. And it had the added bonus of never bringing him in contact with people.

But seeing it in the daylight was a treat. They'd hung the fairy lights on Adam and Gus' house, and all agreed that it was almost to the point where they looked like they had the most lights in the whole world.

(Wes was glad he'd decided not to tell Gus about the Gay family of Lagrangeville, New York.)

In fact, Mr. Martinelli from next door commented on how glaringly bright the lights were as he stepped out to get his mail.

"Thank you!" Gus had called back.

Adam and Wes had snickered behind her back. Mr. Martinelli had narrowed his eyes at Wes and a flicker of unease had licked at Wes' stomach. It felt the same now as it had then, being observed. Anxious, vulnerable, squirmy.

"So, where's this clearing, then?" Adam asked after they'd walked for twenty minutes.

Gus had turned out to be an enthusiastic hiker after Wes' own heart, delighted by the footprints of animals and the bits of nature she kicked up as she walked, and prone to touching and smelling everything.

"About five more minutes," Wes told him.

"And how do you know this place?"

"I found it last year. I was looking for a spot where I could test out various bioluminescent apparatuses. But I needed somewhere far enough off the path that things wouldn't get disturbed, and someplace dark enough that there would be no light pollution. I checked out a lot of spots and this one was the best."

"What's light pollution?" Gus asked.

"It's when ambient light—light from the environment—reaches a spot. Like, light from people's houses or streetlights or buildings."

"You're trying to see if your bioluminescence will work to light this clearing?" Adam asked.

"Yes, basically. I'm trying to see how far each different illumination casts to understand how much of the biome would be required per square foot to light it."

They reached the clearing and Adam stopped short. Gus ran to examine things.

"What *is* this!?" she asked.

With a gentle finger, she traced the needles of the largest of the saplings Wes had planted.

"That's a Sunburst pine. That one is a Douglas fir. Those are blue spruce." He pointed to the ground in front of them. "These are Spartan junipers."

"They look weird," Gus said, screwing up her face and peering at them.

"Well, it's hard to see in the daylight. But they glow. If you cup your hand around a part of the plant, you can see it."

Wes used his larger hands to create enough darkness around Gus' eyes so she could see.

"Whoa! Did you do that?"

Wes nodded and Adam put a hand on his back.

"Can I see?"

Wes shaded Adam's eyes, too, and used the excuse to brush back his soft hair.

"Oh my god," Adam breathed. "You *made* trees glow? How?"

Satisfaction coursed through Wes. This was a project he'd begun at home, but he could quickly see that the laboratory setting, though generally useful for iterative experiments, wouldn't tell him if the glowing plants could survive in nature as well as in a hothouse. So he'd moved them out here in the spring, hoping the summer months would let them establish themselves sturdily enough in the environment that they'd survive the winter. He'd mulched them aggressively against the cold and so far they were doing well.

"In lay terms, if you can," Adam said.

Wes nodded. He was beginning to enjoy this new challenge of taking the complex processes he knew backward and forward and reimagining them in the simplest terms possible.

"You know how fireflies and algae glow?" Adam and Gus nodded. "I took the chemical that makes them glow and injected it into plants to see if they could make it part of themselves."

It had been eighteen months of painstaking experimentation, but that truly was the crux of it.

Adam was looking at him with a strange expression and Wes wondered if he hadn't simplified things enough.

"You're amazing." Adam shook his head. "That's amazing."

Wes ducked his head, self-conscious. "Thanks."

"Can I have a glowing tree?" Gus asked, eyes wide.

"Sweetie, this is Wes' research."

"I know," she said. "But maybe just a little one?"

Wes smiled. He'd thought she would be intrigued by his strange glowing trees.

"Maybe you can come over sometime and we can make you a glowing indoor plant, since it's winter."

"Really?!"

"Sure."

"I'm gonna have a glowing plant!" Gus sang to the trees around them. Then she plopped down beneath a nonglowing tree and began picking apart a pine cone.

"That's very sweet of you," Adam said, sliding his arm through Wes'. "You don't have to."

Wes knew he didn't have to. In fact, he'd spent the

last fifteen years of his life proving to himself over and over again that he didn't have to do a single goddamned thing he didn't want to do. Not anymore.

But he wanted to. Since he'd met Adam and Gus, he wanted to do something for someone else—reach outside the world of his home and connect with people for the first time in a long time.

"I want to," Wes said. "Maybe she'll get into plants because of it and give you a break with the spiders."

"Oh, bless you," Adam said, looking up at him with those mesmerizing blue eyes. "That would be a true Christmas miracle."

Chapter Seventeen

Adam

Adam had been forced to order several industrial power strips to accommodate all the lights they'd been sent for the house. Their electrical bill would be astronomical this month, but it didn't matter, because Gus' eyes lit up as bright as the house whenever she saw it.

Several people on Instagram had reposted his pictures and they'd gotten even more lights in the mail. Last night, when he put Gus to bed, instead of one of the stories he usually told her, she'd asked for the story of the magic lights.

"What do you mean, sweetie? Why don't you tell me the story?"

Gus snuggled into bed and told him the story.

"I wanted the most lights in the world, so you got tons of people to send us lights. We needed help with hanging them, and Wes helped us, and now you and Wes are gonna fall in love and he's gonna be with us all the time. So the lights have to be magic."

She'd been half asleep by the time she got to the end of the story, but that had heightened its impact

rather than lessened it. Gus had never attributed anything to magic before. She'd always been exceedingly
scientific—weirdly scientific for a child, truth be told.
To hear her attribute Wes' presence in their life to
magic showed Adam how very much she wanted a
family Christmas.

And yes, Adam knew the two of them *were* a family, but clearly Gus wanted more.

It was a week until Gus' winter break started, ten
days until Christmas, and Adam still had no present
for her, and no idea if Mason would deign to even
wish her a merry Christmas. He had considered texting Mason to ask, but couldn't even draft a message
that wasn't razor-sharp.

Adam closed Gus' door and settled in front of *Meet
Me in St. Louis* to brainstorm gift ideas for Gus.

"A video game console?" Charlie suggested at
work the next day. "Kids like video games, right?"

"A bike?" Rye suggested. "I always wanted one
when I was Gus' age."

"What presents would you have liked when you
were eight, Marie?" Adam asked his mysterious co-
worker.

Marie's expression turned instantly mischievous
and fond, but she just said mildly, "Does she like to
read?"

"Could I put together a little laboratory for her or
something?" Adam asked Wes that night after Gus
was asleep.

Wes had come over for dinner and made lasagna about which Gus proclaimed, "Oh, weird, it's really good."

Adam gave her a look and she revised her sentiment.

"Sorry, I just meant, I didn't think you'd be able to cook but this is really good."

"Sweetie, it's not very nice to say that you assumed someone couldn't cook."

Gus cocked her head.

"Why?"

"Because making assumptions about people means that you are judging them based on what you believe, not what's true."

"Oh." She thought about that for a minute. "It's not bad to not be able to cook. You can't cook and you're awesome."

Adam smiled.

"Assumptions aren't necessarily bad. But what would you think if someone said they assumed you weren't good at science?"

"Why would someone think that? I'm great at science!" Gus said angrily.

"I know. It doesn't feel very good, huh?"

"Sorry, Wes," Gus said. "I didn't mean to make you feel bad."

"Thanks," Wes said. "Why *did* you assume I couldn't cook?"

Gus ate a huge bite of lasagna and chewed thoughtfully. Adam had worked very hard to teach her to be open to questions and not get defensive. He watched proudly as she really considered the question.

"I guess cuz your house is full of weird stuff and cooking's such a normal thing. I thought you maybe wouldn't care about it."

Wes nodded. "That makes a lot of sense. Good lesson that a real scientist can't extrapolate too much."

"What's that?"

"It means a scientist can't take one piece of data they know and make the mistake of thinking it also means another piece of data they don't know."

"I want to be a real scientist," Gus said softly.

"Well, now you know one way to be an even better one," Wes said, and held up his hand.

Gus high-fived it.

"Thanks," she told him, like he'd given her a gift. Then she shoved more lasagna in her mouth.

Adam looked at Wes, his heart so full he could hardly stand it. Wes winked at him and pressed his knee to Adam's under the table.

Now, after cleaning up the kitchen, they were in the living room, fire once again crackling merrily on the television screen.

"A laboratory…" Wes mused. "Maybe. Depends what you mean. My eight-year-old self would kill me for saying so, but I think she's probably too young for an actual chemistry set with, you know, chemicals."

Adam's heart lurched, imagining his baby getting burned with acid or spattered in…something else corrosive.

"Yeah, no chemicals, definitely not. Um. What else is in a laboratory?"

"Fire."

Adam blanched.

"Just kidding," Wes said. "I mean, there *is* fire, but—"

"Yeah, yeah, yeah, I get it, a laboratory is basically a death trap. Never mind."

Adam deflated.

"I just. I know it's silly. I know the perfect holiday gift won't really…make Gus forget stuff with Mason or leaving Boulder. I just want this Christmas to be great. I want Gus to be happy and see that this is a good move for us and that we're gonna be okay and, and, and…"

He gestured broadly, like he could pluck the words out of the air.

Wes caught his hands and brought them to his lips, kissing the knuckles of each. His eyes were warm and intense and Adam wanted to let himself drown in them.

"You're already doing everything to help Gus feel that way," he said, soft and sure. "You're thinking about what is best for her. You've practically buried your house alive in lights because she asked for it. And most important, you're here. You're spending time with her. That's what makes it feel like a holiday. That's what makes it special."

Wes' eyes grew shadowed.

"At least, I assume so."

"Your family didn't spend time together at the holidays?"

Wes snorted.

"The holidays were just an excuse for my dad to throw huge, lavish cocktail parties for all the people he wanted to impress. He and my mom would spend months planning every detail of the food, the drinks, the music, their outfits, and then they'd spend the entire party pretending it was effortless. Lana and I had to be there, dressed to the nines, so they could show us off like ornaments on a tree. But when the guests were gone and the music was turned off, all we had for Christmas was a fridge full of leftover hors d'oeuvres and a pile of fancy, impersonal gifts from strangers."

Wes shrugged, his eyes flat.

"And now?" Adam asked.

"Now?"

"Yeah, now that you can do whatever you want, how do you celebrate?"

"Oh. I don't, really. At all. Anything."

"How come?"

Wes traced Adam's cheek absently, and when he spoke his voice was husky and low.

"I guess I never felt like I had much to celebrate."

Adam felt the words like they'd been thrown at him, and they hurt.

Wes—beautiful, brilliant, sweet, generous, weird-in-a-great-way Wes—didn't feel like he had anything to celebrate.

Adam's mission was clear: he had to celebrate the hell out of Westley Mobray.

"Well that's settled, then," Adam said, forgetting he hadn't said any of that out loud.

"What's settled?"

"You should have Christmas with us!"

For a moment, Adam thought Wes didn't like the idea. Maybe it was too soon? Mason had always told him he got too invested, too enthusiastic, jumped the gun. But it felt *right* to Adam—so right. And when things felt right, he wanted more of them.

Then Adam realized that Wes had turned away and was clenching his fists because he didn't want Adam to see the emotion in his face.

"Come here," Adam said. He tugged Wes back to him. "Look at me."

Wes raised his eyes to Adam's. His nostrils flared and he licked his lips, and Adam could see the years of solitude and isolation crumble like a cliff face into the sea.

"I— If you— Really?"

Adam's heart swelled with affection for Wes. He wanted to pull him so tight against his chest that he could feel Wes' heartbeat and the movement of each breath. He wanted to kiss him and kiss him until all they could taste was each other. He wanted to sleep and wake and sleep and wake with Wes' arms around him and his arms around Wes, and *shit*, Adam knew what that meant.

He knew what it meant and he knew it was too soon and *Adam, gah, don't say it out loud!* he screamed at himself. But even if he didn't say it, he knew: he was falling for Wes Mobray. Seriously, deeply, no joke falling in love with him.

Love. *Shit*.

Chapter Eighteen

Wes

Adam Mills had invited him for Christmas.

It was such an ordinary sentence, but it set Wes' blood on fire with joy and possibility.

His senior year of high school had been the last time he'd attended his parents' annual holiday cocktail party. He'd made the obligatory appearance, endured the endless comments about his stint on *The Edge of Day*, and ducked every offer from an agent or casting director to get him back in the spotlight. The spotlight was, he explained, exactly what he wanted to escape.

The next year, he'd stayed at Caltech through winter break, making excuses about needing to monitor his experiments in the lab, and he did so for the next three years too, until he graduated. When he started back at Caltech as a grad student, he stopped going home to visit altogether. The invitations became perfunctory, then. More an excuse for his parents and Lana to express their disappointment and hurt than any genuine desire to see him (or so Wes believed).

Every now and then over the years someone in his

cohort would drag him to a holiday party. They were a relief of cheap drinks and frozen hors d'oeuvres and white elephant gifts with budgets of ten dollars or less. But although they were less stressful, he didn't enjoy them. Just like his parents' parties, they reminded him that he didn't belong; just in a different way.

One year, he was dating Lyle seriously enough that he agreed to accompany him home for the holidays. It had been an exercise in torment because Lyle had told his parents about Wes' family and they took advantage of any downtime by asking him to tell them stories of Hollywood and what it was like to be on a film set. He looked at Lyle differently after that. He'd been the first person in grad school that Wes had confided in about his family and he'd thought Lyle understood how reticent he was to be connected with them. After all, he'd enrolled in grad school under his mother's last name precisely to distance himself from his past, his father, and now his sister, because Lana's star was also on the rise.

Lyle had blinked wide eyes and apologized, but said he thought his family would be so interested that he'd been sure Wes wouldn't mind slaking their curiosity.

Wes hadn't left in the middle of the trip because he abhorred drama of all kinds. But he'd quietly ended the relationship in his mind right then and there, and ended it out loud a week later when they returned to Pasadena.

He hadn't celebrated a holiday since.

Occasionally on his birthday, he'd buy himself some piece of gear he'd wanted for his work, but he did that not on his birthday as well. And he never, ever, ever acknowledged Christmas (although he enjoyed Zachary's seasonal texts repurposing cheesy Christmas memes into Chanukah ones).

But this year...

This year, he wouldn't be alone.

This year, Christmas wouldn't pass unnoticed and unacknowledged.

This year, he had two people to share it with. Two people who gleamed like bright stars in the darkness.

Wes stroked Bettie's back as he began to dream up the gift he would give to Adam and Gus. It wasn't impossible, but it would be a time crunch. He decided to put on another pot of coffee and get down to business.

"Daddy says you're having Christmas with us—is it true!?"

Wes had opened the door at Gus' enthusiastic bell ringing, and found her cheeks flushed and Adam waving from across the street.

"Come on in," Wes said, saluting Adam and giving him a wink over Gus' head.

She was there, as agreed, to create her glowing plant.

"But is it true, Wes?!"

She bounced inside and shoved her hands in her pockets, something Adam had taught her to do when she got so excited she wanted to tug on people to get their attention.

Wes grinned. She was so freaking cute.

"Yeah, it's true. That okay with you?"

"It's perfection!" Gus trilled, spinning around, and Wes couldn't help agreeing with her.

"Cool."

"Cool," she echoed. "Cool, cool, cool!"

She was practically vibrating with excitement as she skipped after him to the living room where he'd laid out everything they would need.

He was going to be showing Gus how to flood the plant with the luciferase enzyme instead of splicing it into the plant's DNA as Wes had done with the trees he planted in the clearing. He had a feeling Gus was far more interested in quick results than long-lasting ones.

He had packaged luciferase, luciferin, and coenzyme A in nanoparticles to help each one get to the right part of the plant, and suspended them in a solution.

"Okay, so we're going to take your plant and put it in this tube. The tube is full of a solution I made that is what will make the plant glow."

Gus nodded, eyes wide.

"Do you know what kind of plant this is?" Wes asked her.

She shook her head.

"It's kale."

She wrinkled her nose. "Do you eat that?"

"Yeah. It's a very hardy plant that can grow in lots of different environments. If you put it in your window, even in the winter, the cold won't bother it."

She nodded.

"This is an autoclave. It's gonna pressurize the solution, which will allow the particles that hold the glowing agent to enter tiny pores in the plants, called stomata."

He tapped his own face.

"Pores are like what we have in our skin. They let our skin breathe. It's the same with plants. Basically. Once the particles have entered the stomata, it will begin to glow."

Gus' eyes were huge.

He showed her how to put the kale plant into the solution, then turned on the autoclave, and they watched the plant slowly darken as the solution was pushed in through the stomata.

"Whoa," Gus breathed.

"It'll take a bit before it starts glowing," Wes said, not wanting her to be disappointed.

"Okay. Can we take it to my house so Daddy can see it too?"

"Sure."

She was so excited about the soon-to-be-glowing plant that she only called hello and goodbye to Bettie and the other animals, before grabbing Wes' hand and pulling him to the door.

"Just grab my coat," he said, managing to snag it with one hand before he was encouraged out the door.

"Sorry." Gus grimaced and waited impatiently as he pulled it on.

She shielded the kale plant inside her own jacket for the walk across the street, hugging it to her chest against the cold.

She reminded Wes so much of himself sometimes.

"Daddy!" she yelled as they got inside. "I made a plant glow!" She paused and looked back at Wes. "Wes helped," she added, and Wes smiled.

Adam came out of the kitchen with an adorable smear of flour on his cheek.

Wes' eyes got wide.

"Oh, no. Daddy. Are you baking?" She asked it with the horror usually reserved for questions like "Was it malignant?" or "Is it contagious?"

Adam laughed.

"Never fear. It's slice and bake cookies. I just used a little flour to roll out the dough. I got Christmas cookie cutters. Wanna help?"

Plant instantly abandoned in Wes' hands, Gus made a beeline for the kitchen.

"Hi," Adam said. "How'd it go?"

"Good. I'll just put this in her room, if that's okay?"

"Sure." Adam studied it. "Is it really going to glow?"

"It should."

Adam shook his head.

"Jesus. You're seriously unbelievable, do you know that?"

The word had been levied at Wes before, yes, but never in the extremely fond, slightly awed tone that infused Adam's voice.

Wes caught his elbow and drew him close. Adam smelled of sugar and Wes wanted to see if he tasted like it too. He leaned in and kissed Adam's soft lips. They tasted as sweet as he smelled and Wes sank into Adam's warmth.

Kissing Adam felt like home.

"Daddy, can I make a Christmas monster!?" Gus called from the kitchen.

"Sure, sweetie."

Adam kissed Wes one more time.

"I'll meet you in the kitchen," Wes said, running his fingers through the hair at Adam's nape.

Wes settled the kale on Gus' windowsill, adjusting the blinds to make sure it would get enough sun. It was a western-facing window, but maybe he'd bring a clip-on plant light over tomorrow if it didn't seem like the winter sun was enough.

Gus' room was a tornado of bits and pieces of things she'd clearly taken apart, or found, or taken off of other appliances. She had a screwdriver, a pair of needle-nose pliers, and a spool of floral wire next to a pile of rivets in a drawer, and everywhere were books, flopped open on their spines and flagged with bits of torn paper as bookmarks. Wes felt like he'd wandered back in time to his own childhood bedroom—although that had been ruthlessly ordered once a week by the cleaning lady his parents employed. In between, though, Wes collected piles of this and that to experiment with, and consulted books for guidance.

He truly didn't mean to snoop. He was just curious if he could get a sense of what she might be making.

On her desk lay an unfinished letter, written in Gus' chaotic scrawl.

I know you don't exist, it said, *but just in case you do, will you make Wes stay? Daddy and me are so happy now and I want us to be a family.*

The letter was addressed to *Nicholas Santa Claus*.

Wes froze, awash in conflicting emotions. First and most superficial: fear. The fear that someone needing him would end up the way it had the last time, when his father had needed him. With their relationship in tatters and Wes guilty and miserable.

But when he dug a little deeper there was also hope. That maybe this time, being needed didn't mean doing something he didn't want, but participating in something he did. He adored Gus. And his feelings for Adam grew stronger every hour they spent together.

He took deep breaths through his nose and blew them out his mouth, and slowly, the fear dissipated. He reread the letter and focused on the hope.

Daddy and me are so happy now. So happy.

So was Wes. And if Gus and Adam were happy and so was he...then...

Wes walked into the kitchen where Gus and Adam stood at the kitchen table. Backs to Wes, their blond hair similarly messy, they had their arms around each other and were concentrating on something on the table.

Wes was filled with such overwhelming affection that he felt his nose tickle and his eyes prick with tears. He put a hand on each of their shoulders and peered over their heads. On the table was...something made out of dough.

"Is that, um...what is that?"

"It's a Christmas monster!" Gus said gleefully.

Adam smiled up at him.

"It eats Christmas lights and then it glows, just like my plant. See?"

She pointed and Wes could vaguely make out a blob that might've been fairy lights around what might've been the midsection of the creature.

"Got it," Wes said.

"It'll be better when I frost it," Gus assured him.

Over the next two hours they cut out dozens of shapes—Gus had eschewed the cookie cutters immediately, claiming that snowflakes and reindeer were boring, and Wes was inclined to agree with her. They made monsters that ate Christmas trees and Christmas trees that ate monsters. Santa Clauses that were half lizard and half human and tarantula elves. (Adam shuddered at them even in dough form.)

As the cookies baked, they tinted frosting with food coloring and Adam spooned it into plastic bags he cut the tips off of to make piping bags. "I saw it on Pinterest," he explained, and Gus started chatting before Wes could ask what Pinterest was.

To get them the colors they wanted, the frosting ended up a bit runny, so when Wes tried to use green frosting to outline the tree his monster was eating, it mixed with the red frosting he'd used to frost the monster, resulting in a gloppy brown mess that looked less like a monster and more like what you might do if you saw one.

Adam's and Gus' didn't look much better—in fact, truth be told, Adam's looked much worse—but no one cared. Adam had put on Christmas music and while outside the snow was coming down in freezing gusts, the kitchen was oven warm and cheery, all of them laughing as Gus launched a monster attack where one of her tree-eating monsters became a tree-eating-monster eater and demolished Wes' tree-eating monster, smashing both to a sugary paste that she scooped up and ate with her fingers.

"Monsters are so yummy," she said an hour later, tongue, teeth, and lips an unearthly blue-green color from the dye in the frosting. She was tired and crashing from the sugar, so Adam got a peanut butter sandwich in her and then put her to bed, claiming that the food coloring would come off on its own eventually.

Wes cleaned up the kitchen while Adam settled Gus in, getting blue-and-red fingertips for his trouble, and made some mint tea.

When Adam came back in the kitchen he draped himself over Wes' shoulders and squeezed him.

"You angel," he murmured, and kissed his neck. "Thank you for cleaning up. You really didn't have to."

"'S okay," Wes murmured.

Christmas music still issued faintly from Adam's phone, a tinkly song Wes recognized but couldn't name. He stood and pulled Adam against him, rocking to the rhythm of the song. With Adam's cheek on his chest and his arms around him, Wes felt perfectly at peace.

The wind whistled outside, but Adam was warm and smelled so good. They were half dancing, half swaying, and went on that way for a song and a half, until the music cut out and Adam swore.

"Phone died," he muttered.

"Doesn't matter," Wes said.

They settled in the living room with their tea.

"Guess what," Adam said.

"Hmm?"

"The plant was glowing just a bit when I turned the light off."

"Oh, good. I was worried it might not work and she'd be disappointed."

"She was really excited. She wanted to come back out and show you but I made her go to bed."

Wes hummed with quiet satisfaction.

"Can I ask you something?"

"Mmm-hmm, anything."

"I don't know how to say it exactly, so forgive me, but, do you do things with what you create? Like, do you sell them to someone? Are you employed by someone?"

"I'm still in the experimentation phase, mainly," Wes said carefully.

Adam's question had been gentle, if clumsy, but Adam was not the first one to point out that Wes hadn't actually *done* anything yet.

"I didn't mean to be mean about it," Adam said, putting a hand on his arm and sounding so much like Gus that Wes smiled.

He shook his head.

"Not mean. I…I know it's weird that I just work out of my house. I, um. I had a job offer a few years ago, but it wasn't a good fit."

He'd had many over the years, in fact, all contingent on compromising his research in order to rush to sale.

"I got a big grant in my last year of grad school and that's what I used to initially fund most of my research. But since then, I've used the money I had in the bank from *Edge of Day*. I didn't like to use it, but all the companies that are interested in biolumi-nescence want me to design a product for them to sell rather than just funding research. There's a lot of money in green marketing. A lot of people who will pay handsomely for alternative energy and feel like they're offsetting their carbon footprint or whatever."

Wes rolled his eyes.

"But I'm not interested in selling it. Not like that, anyway. My goal isn't to make glow-in-the-dark nightlight plants for Pasadena kindergarteners. This science could rewrite the way we use energy, period. Did you know lighting accounts for twenty percent of worldwide energy consumption? Sorry, did I already tell you that? Anyway, it's huge."

Adam nodded.

"And that usage is public as well as private. And on the public side of things, there are huge discrepancies in where lighting is used. There are neighborhoods in LA where you could read a book in the middle of the night—rich, heavily surveilled neighborhoods. Then there are ones where the streetlights got smashed or burned out years ago and were never replaced. Or where the city just stopped routing electricity to lights altogether. It's the same in every city in the country. Poor neighborhoods, neighborhoods the city government considers dangerous or unimportant, they don't get the same budget for lighting, which makes them *more* dangerous, less desirable. And on and on."

"I saw it in Boulder too," Adam agreed.

"Or rural areas where houses are too far apart for the county to want to light the road—they have so many collisions with animals or other cars. But imagine if we could light those neighborhoods the cities underserve, or those rural roads the county has dismissed, with something that is self-sustaining and doesn't require any fabricated energy source, like trees. It could revolutionize the way people experience their environments."

Adam threw himself into Wes' lap and kissed him.

"You're so damn hot," Adam said. "Seriously, you're just amazing."

"I...thank you," Wes stammered, not knowing what to say to that.

"Would you ever want to— Never mind."

"What?"

Wes cupped Adam's face.

"Nah, you just said you wanted to revolutionize the world. This isn't that."

"Tell me."

"Well, it's really small, but... I was talking with one of the other parents at Gus' school the other day when I dropped her off, and in the winter, the bus stop for her daughter is dark because the sun rises so late. So she waits with her because it's kind of scary in the dark. I guess I was thinking maybe there was a way to light them. Never mind," he said again.

"Hmm."

Wes immediately began parsing what would and would not work, filing away the former and rejecting the latter, narrowing to a plan.

Adam said, "Wes? Are you mad?"

"Huh? No, course not."

"Oh. You're frowning."

"Sorry, just thinking," Wes said. "Where is the bus stop?"

"I'm not sure what road, exactly, but I can ask Caroline next time I see her."

Wes nodded, already miles ahead.

"Maybe I can get a map of the bus stops from the school district. If I overlay a map of the lighting grid from the Department of Energy, I can see which stops would be in darkness starting on which day of the year, given sunrise times, then I could—"

Adam cut him off with his mouth, kissing him passionately.

Wes laughed and kissed him back.

"Too much detail?" he asked.

Adam nodded. "You're amazing. Now shut up and kiss me."

Wes was happy to oblige.

Chapter Nineteen

Adam

The day had started out perfectly. Adam had woken in Wes' arms with Wes nuzzling his neck, then Wes had slid beneath the covers, pressed kisses to the sensitive skin of his inner thighs, and then brought Adam to transcendent orgasm, light bursting behind his eyes and shock waves of pleasure rolling over his whole body.

Matheson's Hardware was cheerily busy all day, customers buying tools and fixings to hang decorations and searching for the perfect aid for their last-minute holiday projects.

Rye had even come in to help out for the day, though he mostly seemed to swear at the cash register as it jammed or spat out long scrolls of tape. During one lunchtime lull, he regaled Adam and a customer with the tale of his own failed DIY, which he'd meant to be a laptop desk for Charlie, but which had turned out a hunched and mangled hunk of wood so covered in glue that Charlie deemed it unsafe even to burn in effigy.

Adam was laughing at this when Charlie came

out of the office and gave him a questioning look. Rye simply said mournfully, "Laptop desk. RIP," and Charlie snorted and pulled Rye against his side in a tight hug.

As he drove home, Adam got a text from Wes that said, You're so lovely. Thanks for liking me, and was moved to tears. How very like Wes to thank him for that.

At a stoplight he texted back a string of heart emojis, and sighed happily, turning the radio to a station playing Christmas music. He'd even had an idea for Gus' Christmas gift. His heart was very, very full.

He was trying (and failing for the thousandth time) to whistle a Christmas carol as he walked in the front door, planning what to make for dinner and wondering if Wes would want to come over again tonight.

Shoes off, Adam paused. The house was oddly silent. Usually when he got home from work, the television was on or Gus was laughing or River was talking. But now, nothing.

"Hello?"

River came into the living room, looking drawn, and Adam's heart felt like it leapt to his throat.

"What is it, what's wrong, what happened?"

River squeezed his arm.

"She's fine," they said immediately. "She's just… uhh."

Adam pulled River down on the couch, his entire being desperate to hear what had happened.

If one of those little shits hurt my baby I will rend them limb from limb!

But before River could explain, Adam's phone rang. It was Gus' school. He showed the screen to River, whose eyes went wide.

"Yeah, yeah, get it. I'll see you later."

They waved and were out the door.

Adam answered the phone, a pit forming in his stomach as he listened to the principal.

"Mr. Mills, August is a delightful child. She's engaged and curious, and quite an, er, critical thinker. It's the last of these that I need to talk with you about. I've had multiple calls from parents about an incident that transpired today with August. It would seem she made an announcement on the playground during recess that Santa Claus does not exist."

Oh, Gus.

"She was *quite* insistent about it, even after it clearly upset several of the other children. Now," Mrs. Gordon said gently, "Of course it is up to each family what they teach their children, but as I'm sure you're aware, the timing of the Santa-isn't-real discussion is something that most parents want to choose for themselves."

Adam pinched the bridge of his nose, feeling a headache threatening.

"Gosh, I'm really sorry. I get that, of course. I'm not sure what I can do, though," he said honestly.

The loud sigh on the other end of the call rather suggested that Mrs. Gordon also didn't know what there was to be done.

"Perhaps a conversation with August about which are at-home conversations and which are at-school conversations."

Adam rubbed deeply into the spot between his eyebrows.

"Yeah, I can do that," he said. "But Gus is eight. Eight-year-olds are gonna say what they're gonna say, and there really doesn't seem to be a power on earth that can stop them. I've tried. I'm sure there were plenty of kids saying that Santa *does* exist. So..."

He shrugged even though she couldn't see him.

"There were *tears*, Mr. Mills. *Phone calls.*"

Adam sighed.

"Yeah, I get it. My kid made your life harder by being a kid. But Gus isn't who your problem is with. It's with the parents who are bothering you. It is up to all of them what they tell their kids and when. But it's not up to Gus—an *eight-year-old*—to manage that for them. Part of living in the world is that people are different and believe different things. It's not bad for those kids to learn that lesson, even if their parents apparently haven't."

"Mr. Mills," she began, placatingly. "If August could just tell the other children that she was joking—"

Sometimes Adam forgot, because he was an adult now, and in charge of his life, but he was back in Garnet Run. Back in the town that he'd spent eighteen years of his life in. Back in the town where his classmates had tormented him for being different, for being sensitive, for having the gall to want a life beyond its borders. He knew this place, even if it had been over a decade since he'd left. And there was no way he was having his child go through what he had.

"I'm sorry, but no. I grew up in Garnet Run. I know

what it's like. But you are a *public* school. Those kids' parents can teach them whatever they want at home, but so can I. I'm sorry that you're having to deal with these parents, but I imagine if it wasn't about Gus, they'd be calling you about something else. I am absolutely not going to ask my daughter to lie. Period. I don't see this conversation bringing about any more useful solutions, so I'm going to end it."

Adam hung up the phone, wishing his cell phone was a landline so he could've slammed it for emphasis.

"Small-minded piece of shit conservative fu—"

Adam cut himself off when he saw Gus standing wide-eyed in the doorway. Her face was blotchy and tear streaked.

"Am I in trouble?" she asked timidly, and crept into the living room.

"No way," Adam said fiercely. "But we did talk about how it's unkind to tell other kids that Santa isn't real if they're still enjoying the magic of him. I know we say no lying. But make believe isn't the same as lying. And sometimes we choose to believe things because they bring us joy or comfort."

Gus hung her head.

"The truth is important. But kindness is important too. And taking away someone's joy or comfort isn't kind."

"I know."

"Why'd you do it, then?"

Gus sulked her way to the couch.

"Tommy VanderHaag said Santa was bringing him a new mom for Christmas cuz his dad's getting married. I told him that wasn't Santa, that was a wedding. And he said…" She scowled. "He said, what did I know cuz I didn't even have a mom."

Adam's heart broke for her, but Gus went on.

"So I said, of *course* I have a mom, I just live with my dad and what did *he* know because Santa didn't even exist. It just slipped out! And then a lot of other kids came over and they started saying Santa *was* real and I got mad, so I told them the evidence."

Adam surreptitiously rubbed at his temples where the headache had spread.

Just then, a text came from Wes: You guys okay over there?

Adam's eyes went wide.

How'd you know something was up?

What's wrong?! Do you need help??

Then Wes added, It's the first day Gus hasn't turned the lights on the second she got home from school.

Tears stung Adam's eyes. Wes paid attention. Wes cared.

It's okay. Gus just had a hard day, Adam wrote. She got in trouble at school and it's UNJUST.

Wes sent a quizzical face emoji. I'm here if you need me.

Adam sent a heart and wrote, I'll tell you everything in a bit.

"Is that Wes?"

"Yeah."

"Wes would agree with me."

"That Santa isn't real? I'm sure he would." Gus looked triumphant. "The thing is, sweetie… Here, come in the kitchen while I make dinner."

Adam rubbed his head harder, trying to think of how to say this.

"There's science-y real and then there's the other kind of real. A story can be real, even a fantasy story, because it lets you understand things that strictly real reality doesn't."

"Like what?" Gus asked, of course, because Adam didn't have an answer.

"Um, like…like what happens after we die. No one really knows. But stories that explore different possibilities can be useful and comforting, even if they're just things to think about."

Adam rummaged through the cabinets trying to find where Wes had filed the rice, because it wasn't under *R*. He found it under *B*, for basmati.

"The point is that sometimes there are things that aren't true, but truth isn't the point of them. And Santa Claus is one of those things. It's like a…a collective story that we participate in because it can be fun and magical. Like, what makes Christmas so great? The feeling, right? It feels cozy and exciting and special because it's about family and love. When we give someone a gift, it shows we're thinking about them and what they would like. When we share a special meal or a ritual, it's creating something that's just for our family or friends. Something that brings us closer together. That feels good." Gus nodded reluctantly. "Sometimes," Adam said, tipping her chin up and kissing her forehead, "feeling cozy and loved and together is more important than scientific truth."

The doorbell rang after dinner and Wes ducked inside, shaking snow off his hat.

"Wes!" Gus cried, spirit undampened.

"Hey, Gus. I heard you had a rough day so I brought someone to spend the night with you. She's, uh, in the entryway."

Wes winked at Gus and her eyes got wide.

"I'll keep her in the box this time," she whispered completely audibly.

Wes had texted Adam earlier to see if he could stand having Bettie in the house and Adam had told him he'd feel a lot better if he had Bettie *and* Wes. Wes had replied with a heart emoji.

As Gus ran for the entryway, Wes held up a bag to Adam.

"I also brought ice cream, for those less excited about Bettie."

Adam smiled and Wes crossed to him and pulled him into his arms.

"You okay?" Wes asked. He stroked Adam's hair.

"Yeah. Thanks."

"What kind did you bring?" Gus asked, face bright. Bettie seemed to have revived her completely.

Wes put the bag on the table. "Check it out."

Gus' eyes got wider and wider as she pulled six different kinds of ice cream out of the bag.

"Wow," she breathed worshipfully.

Adam shook his head but squeezed Wes' hand.

"I wasn't sure what you liked," Wes said.

Gus seemed to be trying to hold all the containers at once.

"One bowl," Adam said, perusing the selection himself.

Gus considered each flavor seriously and then said, "One bowl or one flavor?"

"Go to town, kid," Adam said, and Gus did a little dance of excitement. She then proceeded to put some of every flavor in the bowl.

Adam helped himself to some mint chocolate chip. Wes took the salted caramel. They settled in the living room and Adam put the fire on.

"Oh, Dad," Gus said, like this amused her.

"Oh, Gus," Adam replied. "How's that combination of lemon sorbet and peanut butter cup treating you?"

Gus took a big bite and mushed it around in her mouth a little.

Adam cringed.

Gus swallowed and grinned.

"Pretty good," she declared.

Wes shuddered.

"Ah, to be young and unburdened by taste," Adam said.

Gus ate her Frankenstein ice cream happily for a while and then turned her attention to Wes.

"Why aren't you having Christmas with your family?" she asked.

Wes put his bowl down and addressed her seriously.

"Well, because I don't get along with my parents or my sister. I haven't seen them in years. You're supposed to spend time with people who make you happy. But my family makes me feel bad. So I don't spend time with them."

Gus wrinkled her brow.

"Did they leave?"

"No. I left. I choose not to spend time with them."

Gus' mouth formed an O, like she didn't know you could do that.

"Are you sad?" she asked.

"Nope. I'm happier not seeing them."

"Oh."

She thought about that for a while.

"I bet they're sad."

Wes' face did something complicated.

"Why do you say that?"

Gus shrugged like it was obvious.

"You're awesome. Too bad for them that they made you stay away."

Wes blinked and Gus dropped her spoon into her empty bowl with a sigh.

"Well, I'm tired," she announced, stretching dramatically. "Guess I'll go to bed early."

It was one minute before her bedtime so the pronouncement had less impact than she might have intended.

"Hey, thanks, Gus," Wes said. He looked a little dazed.

She smiled.

"Night."

* * *

Adam woke to eighty-three mentions on Instagram. Even when he'd used Instagram to try and drum up attention for his work he'd never woken to eighty-three mentions.

Wes had kissed him goodbye and gone home a few minutes earlier because Adam thought it would be good for Gus to have a low-key morning, given the events of the day before.

Blearily, Adam tapped the screen.

His most recent shot of himself and Gus in front of their lit-up house had apparently been shared under the hashtag WinterInWyoming and then landed in several people's stories. One of them, an account with a million followers that comprised images of cozy cabins with roaring fires, mugs of cocoa cupped by mittened hands, and winter trees glazed with icicle lights, had shared the picture along with hands making a heart and a string of lights gif, commenting, "Dad and daughter Xmas goals. Adorable!!"

That account seemed to be the source of most of the shares. He liked the posts and reposted the stories, thrilled to show Gus.

He took his phone into her room and gently stroked her hair to wake her up.

"Morning, baby. Wanna see something cool?"

Gus nodded, instantly awake. She could never resist a line like that.

Adam showed her the reposted photograph and she flipped through the mentions expertly.

"Oh my god," she breathed. "Are we famous?"

Adam laughed.

"Nah, but people seem to think we're kinda cool."

He winked at her in an aggressively uncool way and she laughed.

"Wish I had a phone so I could show people at school," she said innocently.

Adam took a moment to bask in his utter relief that Gus did not have a phone, because he could only imagine the things she would show her classmates in the interest of scientific rigor.

"Listen, about the kids at school."

Adam had spent a long time thinking about the situation the night before and had come to a conclusion that satisfied him. Somehow, snugged tight in Wes' arms, everything had seemed less galling. In fact, when Adam told Wes the whole story, complete with Gus' Martin Luther nailing the ninety-five theses of Why Santa Obviously Doesn't Exist to the door, Wes cracked up.

"I want you to let them believe whatever they believe about Santa. No, wait. Listen," he said as she started to open her mouth. "You don't know what everyone's situation is, or what they do at home. Some kids like to believe in magic and Santa Claus and the Tooth Fairy because it makes them happy, just like science and truth make you happy. It's not okay for you to force your beliefs on anyone—period."

Gus wrinkled her brows.

"Yes, baby, some people think science is a belief.

So if there are kids who want to talk about it with you and they're okay with Santa not existing, then fine. But it's not your place to try and convince anyone if they want to believe. This is really important. I need you to promise me. You won't try and force your beliefs on anyone."

"Okay," Gus sighed. "I won't."

Adam had extracted one more promise from Gus when he dropped her off at school—this one a pinkie promise, that most sacred of vows—not to argue about Santa. And he considered it a good sign that he didn't get any phone calls during the day, either from irate parents or from Gus' principal.

Just before he finished work, though, River texted, *NBD but text me when you can.*

At Adam's expression, Marie waved for him to go, so Adam called them back as he tidied up the shelves in aisle two.

"Is something wrong? Is Gus okay?"

"Dude, we need a code word that I'll use if something is actually wrong. You raise my blood pressure every time you do this."

"Sorry, sorry," Adam said. "What's up?"

"Just, there are a *lot* of packages on your driveway. Gus wanted to open them when we got home. She said you guys are famous now? I didn't want her to, in case… I dunno. In case there was something weird in any of them. I just wanted to let you know."

"Have I told you lately that you're the best sibling in the whole world and that I appreciate you so much?" Adam said.

River made a predictably dismissive sound.

"Seriously, River. I could not be here without you."

"Aw," River said. They sounded pleased.

Suddenly Adam realized how close it was to Christmas and that he hadn't discussed it with River yet.

"Do you need to be with the cats on Christmas, or can you come over?" Adam asked.

There was a pause, then River said, "Yeah? Really?"

Crushing guilt lodged in Adam's stomach. He'd been so concerned about Gus and himself that he'd forgotten to invite River until now.

"Of course! I'm so sorry I didn't ask you before now. I've been a little…"

He made a scattered gesture that River couldn't see.

"No worries."

"No, seriously. You've been here for me and I've been really self-involved. I'm sorry. I'm gonna do better. But of course I want you to come. And Gus would love it. Also, um, you know Wes…from across the street? He might come too."

"For real?" They dropped their voice. "So it's going well?"

Adam grinned into a tub of hex bolts. "So damn well."

River's voice was tender.

"I'm really happy for you."

"Thanks. So you'll come, then?"

"Yeah, okay."

Adam hung up the phone with a solemn vow that he would be better about making sure he was there for River just as they'd been there for him.

Chapter Twenty

Adam

It had taken Adam and Wes hours yesterday, under Gus' watchful directorship, but they had finally hung all the lights that had been dropped off.

"Can't believe you put your home address on Instagram," Wes had muttered halfway through.

Adam had agreed. Originally he'd thought maybe two or three people might drop off lights. He hadn't been worried about his privacy—this was Garnet Run, Wyoming, population five thousand on a populous day, where people left each other alone.

With people sharing the post, though… He'd opened his original post and edited it to remove his address.

It was five days until Christmas. Adam figured people had better things to do than concern themselves with his lights.

"Daddy!"

"In the kitchen! Do you want oatmeal or waffles?"

"Daddy, look!"

Adam took a slug of his coffee and wiped eyes bleary from another late night with Wes. *Totally worth it.*

Adam followed Gus' voice to the front door and found her face pressed to the window.

Outside, their neighbor Mr. Montgomery was pointing at their house and talking to two strangers, bundled up against the cold. One of them raised her phone and snapped a picture of the house.

"Stay here," Adam instructed.

He pulled on a coat and stepped into his boots.

"Can I help you?" he asked.

"Hi! I'm sorry," the woman who'd taken the picture said, smiling. "I saw your picture on Instagram and I wanted to see the lights you and your little girl hung. It's such a sweet story. Guess it was silly to come during the day."

She looked sheepish.

Adam could imagine what Wes would say if he were here. He'd mutter, "Well, certainly don't come prowling around my house at *night*."

But Adam wasn't Wes, and the idea that a real-life person had been moved by Gus' wish for the most lights in the world filled him with warmth.

"That's okay. Hi, I'm Adam."

"I'm Naomi," the woman said. "That's my brother, Jordan." She pointed to the guy getting something out of their car. "We brought you these."

Jordan gave a self-conscious wave as he turned around. He was holding two coils of lights.

"Hey," he said. "Thought maybe you all could use some more."

He held out the lights and Adam swallowed a lump in his throat.

"Wow," he breathed.

"We know it's a little weird that we came here," Naomi said. "It's just, um. Our parents used to get really into Christmas. Tons of lights and decorations and all. Our mom died a few years ago and last year our dad had a heart attack. He can't really be climbing on ladders to hang lights anymore. When I saw your post it just reminded me so much of when we were kids."

Naomi gave a sad smile and Jordan squeezed her hand.

"It's really cool, you doing this for your daughter," he said.

Adam was desperately holding back tears, not wanting to make these kind strangers uncomfortable.

"Thank you," he choked out. "That's really so kind of you. And I'm sorry about your parents. I wish—"

He broke off, tears too close to the surface.

"Ignore me," he said, waving a hand in front of his face as if that might disappear the tears.

"Daddy!" Gus came running up behind him and wrapped her skinny arms around his waist the way she often did when he was having feelings. "What'd you do to him?" she accused Jordan and Naomi.

"It's okay, sweetie," Adam managed. "They didn't do anything."

"Did he get emotional?" she asked knowingly.

"I suppose so," Jordan said.

Gus nodded sagely.

"You like my lights?" she asked brightly, accusations forgotten.

"They're great," the siblings chorused.

"They brought us some more," Adam said, holding them out to Gus.

"Thank you!" Gus said. She pointed to the house. "Wanna see them on?"

Adam watched Naomi's face turn hopeful for a split second, then politeness overtook hope.

"Oh, that's okay. We didn't want to intrude. Just snap a quick picture and drop these off."

"That's okay, right, Daddy?"

Adam smiled.

"Yeah, it's fine. You gonna do it?"

She grinned and ran for the side of the house. She'd become quite an expert at toggling the various power strips on over the last few weeks.

The house lit up and Naomi gasped. Adam hoped it was a happy gasp, although in his opinion the house was looking very overburdened: more light than structure.

"Wow," she said, and Jordan nodded. "It's beautiful."

Gus came skipping back to them, seemingly impervious to the cold.

"It's not the most lights *ever*," she said. "I looked it up. There's a family called the Gay family. Like you, Daddy. Anyway, they have way more, but theirs is a whole huge thing. But it's pretty good!"

Adam clamped his lips together and nodded.

"It looks amazing, honey," Naomi said. Then to Adam, "Do you mind if I take a picture?"

"Go for it. If you post it anywhere, though, will you not put our address? When I originally put out the call, I didn't think more than a few people would see it."

"Of course," she said. She took a few pictures, slid her phone in her pocket, and said, "I'll tag you." She was clearly stalling. Finally she turned to Gus and said, "You've got a great dad, you know?"

Gus grinned and nodded. "I know."

Adam saw Naomi's eyes fill with tears before she turned away. She and Jordan waved from the car as they drove off down Knockbridge Lane.

True to her word, a few hours later Naomi posted the picture with their address blurred out and tagged Adam. She wrote, *Nothing is as important as family. So lucky to see this labor of love by a father to make his daughter's dreams come true. #LitByLove.*

By the time he left work that day, Naomi's post had been shared enough times that Adam was getting follows and tags every few minutes. He couldn't wait to show Gus, who'd talked excitedly about Naomi and Jordan's visit the whole drive to school that morning.

When he turned onto Knockbridge Lane, something felt different. It looked brighter. For a moment, Adam thought it was all the lights on their house gleaming up the darkness. But as he rounded the bend, he saw the cars. Six or seven cars lined the street between their house and Wes', and people stood on the sidewalk, looking at the house, lights ablaze.

Adam parked in the driveway and got out, waving at them.

"Uh, hey, everyone."

A chorus of *Hey*s and *Sorry*s and *Awkward*s greeted him, and one woman approached him haltingly.

"This is super weird, probably, sorry," she said.

"It's okay. It's nice that people are interested," Adam said. "I'm surprised anyone would trek up here. Are you from around here?"

"My parents live down in Douglas and I'm visiting for Christmas." She shrugged. "Not much to do, so…"

Adam nodded. "I grew up here, so I know what you mean."

She grinned. "Cool if we take a picture?"

"It's fine. Just don't post my address if you share it, okay?"

"Sure thing, thanks. And Merry Christmas!" she called as he walked to the front door.

"Merry Christmas," Adam called back with a wave.

Adam was trying and failing to whistle "Joy to the World" as he walked in the door.

"I'm home!" he called to River and Gus, but it was Wes who stepped out of the kitchen.

"Hey," he said. "Hope you don't mind—"

Adam shut him up with a kiss to show him exactly how little he minded.

But whereas Wes usually wrapped his arms around Adam and kissed him deeply, now Wes was tense, his shoulders rigid.

"What's wrong?" Adam asked. "Is Gus okay? Where's River?"

Chapter Twenty-One

Wes

When Wes had seen the first car pull up while Gus was at school and Adam was at work, the first person get out to take a picture, he'd been mildly charmed. He knew Gus would get a kick out of it.

When the second car came, he felt his jaw clenching, teeth grinding.

When the third car came, his heart started to pound.

Through the window, he watched River and Gus get home, watched Gus flip the power strips on with glee. River took a selfie of them in front of the house, presumably to send to Adam, and they went inside.

When the fourth car came, Gus came outside and waved, and River peeked shyly through the window. Wes got the sense that River didn't appreciate the attention any more than Wes did, though likely for different reasons.

Gus went back inside, River pulled the curtains, and Knockbridge Lane went back to its usual sleepy quiet.

Wes relaxed. Some weirdos with nothing better to do than take pictures of Christmas lights wasn't a big deal. At least, that's what he told his clenched jaw, his grinding teeth, and his pounding heart. He stroked Bettie's back and recorded the results of his recent light readings as the sun set.

Then a camera flash bloomed in his periphery and Wes found himself sitting on the floor below window level, even though he was in the basement. He couldn't even be positive he'd *seen* the camera flash. But they were out there, just the way they used to be.

All Wes could think about then was Gus. He'd only been a little younger than her when he'd realized that his dad was famous. And a little older when he'd realized his dad wasn't nearly as famous as he wished he was. Gus might think this was fun at first—attention for a project that excited her.

But what about when she wanted to hang more lights and she and Adam couldn't go outside without people taking her picture and she didn't know how to get them to stop and she didn't want to be mean but she really, really needed to feel like a person instead of like something other people controlled like a puppet or a paper doll or a trading card and by then it was too late and she couldn't get out of it.

What about that?

Wes pulled on a hooded sweatshirt and heavy jacket and a hat and put the hood up over the hat and snuck out his own back door. He snuck down the road and around to the side of the Mills' house, and then walked to the front door with his back to the three people taking pictures.

Gus opened the door with a happy smile and pulled him inside.

"River, Wes is here!" she called happily.

River waved and then snuck a nervous glance outside.

"Those people still there?"

"Three of them."

"I wish this place had a back door," River muttered.

Wes fervently agreed.

They stood there awkwardly for a moment, River chewing their lip and Wes trying very hard to come up with a normal reason he'd come over that he could proffer to River. A reason that wasn't *I had a famous dad and I was famous for a second and it ruined my life and I'm FREAKING out right now.* Because River was Adam's sibling and he wanted to make a good impression.

"I, um, thought I could make dinner before Adam got home?"

It came out sounding like a choked question and River raised an eyebrow, but Gus looked up at him excitedly.

"What are you gonna make?"

Oops.

"Rice?" Wes offered, trying to think of the rest.

"Great. I love rice," Gus said.

She was such a damn gem.

"Okay," River said, clearly catching on that he didn't want to explain. "Maybe I'll take off if you're good to stay with her?"

"Sure."

"Okay, bye, Bug," they said, and hugged Gus.

They eyed the window.

"Here, do you want this?" Wes offered, pulling off his hooded sweatshirt.

River took it gratefully, though it was too big for them.

"Thank you," they said, pulled the hood up, and slipped out the door.

Wes opened the refrigerator and found some cauliflower and carrots that he cut up to stir-fry with the rice. He forced himself to focus only on making even, deliberate cuts, not on what might or might not be going on outside.

Gus chatted while he cooked, telling him about the words on her spelling test and how while red, blue, and yellow were the primary colors, light had its own primary colors, and it was red, blue, and green, did he know?

"And did you know," Gus went on fervently, "that there's no colors when you turn the lights off? They *disappear*! Where do they go? Nowhere! I don't know. No one knows where they go!"

Wes nodded and asked her more questions, but all the while he was thinking about that. He remembered learning it in elementary school—remembered a few people making much of it, existentially, in pondering (and ponderous) middle school poems.

But it was strange that Gus should bring it up now—the day before his father's birthday—because this was his father's problem. He felt like he disappeared when he didn't have the lights on him. And what Wes had chosen all those years ago, by stepping out of the spotlight himself, was to turn off a source of his father's light. His dad felt like Wes had made him disappear. And there was nothing he could do about that. No amount of explaining that he, Wes, felt like *he* disappeared when the lights were *on* him. It had never mattered, he realized, because his father didn't feel he disappeared any less for understanding it.

"Wes. Wes!" Gus was saying.

"Huh?"

"You look really weird. And the cauliflower is burning."

"Shit!"

Wes snatched the pan off the heat.

"Sorry, Gus."

She shrugged. "Why are you weird?"

"Oh, uh."

He knew about Adam and Gus' no lying policy and tried to figure out how to formulate an appropriate truth.

"Remember I told you I don't spend much time with my family?"

"Uh-huh."

"Tomorrow is my dad's birthday, so he's been on my mind. And thinking about stuff with him makes me kind of…stressed-out."

"Oh. Like Daddy feels about money?"

Wes filed that tidbit away.

"Probably something like that, yeah."

He didn't feel the need to disclose that her lights were currently driving him to near panic attack levels of anxiety. One truth was probably enough.

"You could send him an e-card," Gus suggested.

"Oh, yeah?" Wes said absently.

"Yeah. Daddy says that's what you do when you don't really care about someone but you have to keep up appearances." She shrugged. "Appearances of what?"

Wes snorted with amusement and decided then and there never to say anything in front of Gus that he wouldn't want repeated in the worst possible context.

"Thanks for the suggestion."

Wes scraped rice and slightly burned stir-fry into a bowl and put it on the kitchen table. It didn't look very appetizing, but Gus seemed game.

"Daddy will be home in a minute. We should wait for him because of politeness."

Wes high-fived her as the front door opened and Adam arrived.

"Gus is fine," Wes assured Adam. "And River left because I came over. I, uh, made dinner. Kind of."

"Daddy!" Gus threw herself at him. "Wes made rice!"

"Thanks," Adam said, looking at him questioningly. "I'm happy to see you."

"Me too," Wes said. "You too, I mean."

He couldn't quite get himself together. He knew he was behaving strangely but he had that feeling. The feeling he hadn't had much since meeting Adam, but had apparently only lain dormant. The sense of being inside his prison of a body as one by one his limbs began to feel strange and alien.

But Adam just smiled at him and followed Gus back into the kitchen.

Wes forced his prison to walk into the kitchen and get bowls out of the cabinet. He made it scoop rice and vegetables into the bowls. He made it say *Thanks* when Adam got out silverware and asked if he wanted water. He made it bend its legs and sit down at the table and scoop food into its untasting mouth. He made it nod when people talked and made it smile when they smiled.

And all the while, he felt flashbulbs going off in his face as he shrank smaller and smaller inside his panopticon.

After dinner, Adam asked him to stay, but Wes knew that he couldn't keep up the charade once they were one-on-one. And he didn't want the alien prison to touch Adam. It felt like watching someone else touch him.

"Sorry, I can't. I'm…"

"Your dad's birthday's tomorrow, right?" Adam said, knowingly.

"Yeah."

Wes was touched he'd remembered. At least, he would be if he could feel anything except disgust for the prison and the people who looked at it.

"I understand," Adam said. But he didn't, because Wes couldn't tell him. Not right now.

Wes pulled Adam close to the prison, wishing his warmth could penetrate its walls.

"Talk tomorrow, okay?" Adam said, and Wes nodded, desperate to get home so he could sort himself out. He'd text Adam later and apologize for not being as affectionate as he wanted to be. For being strange.

He pulled on his coat and hat, only remembering he'd given his hoodie to River as he closed the front door behind him.

And someone shoved a news camera directly in his face.

Chapter Twenty-Two

Adam

Adam heard indistinct voices outside as he cleaned up the dinner dishes, but paid them no mind until someone shouted. Then, curious, he poked his head out the front door. A woman with a microphone was standing on his driveway speaking into a camera. Was it...the news?

"What the hell?" Adam muttered, stepping into his boots.

"Adam Mills?" the woman said when she saw him.

"Uh, yeah?"

"I'm Tamara Michaelson and we're filming for KCWY. I'd love to interview you about your lights! We're doing feel-good pieces to intro and close out each news broadcast, and the story of your lights is just the thing for us. I tried to call you, but your number isn't listed."

She was blinking at him brightly.

"Oh, um, wow," Adam said. "I can't believe you think this is newsworthy."

"A parent's love for their child is just the kind of *up* story our viewers will love," Tamara Michaelson said.

"Well, sure, then. Cool."

Adam was just sorry Gus had gone to bed already, because she would love this.

"Daddy!" a familiar voice hissed from the front door.

And there was Gus, in pajamas, boots, and a hat, looking excited and guilty.

"Can I please come see?"

Adam smiled and gestured her outside. She'd be a grouch in the morning, but it was the last day of school before vacation anyway.

"Yay!"

She pulled her coat on as she came.

"You must be Gus," Tamara Michaelson said with a smile. "Want to be on TV? If it's all right with your dad, that is."

It's your funeral, Adam thought, but said, "It's fine with me."

Tamara Michaelson and the camera operator set up the shot of the house lit up sky-high, Adam and Gus in front of it. Gus was vibrating with excitement.

"Do you think Wes sees us?" Gus asked, waving at his house.

"I'm in Garnet Run, standing in front of a labor of love. Adam Mills and his daughter, Gus, have been collecting lights to decorate their house all month, and a recent outpouring of support on Instagram has made it a sight to behold. Mr. Mills, can you tell us how this began?"

"Well, I asked Gus what would make her happy this year, and she said she wanted a lot of lights, so—"

"The *most* lights," Gus corrected. "I wanted the most lights *ever*."

"It looks like you've got them!" Tamara Michaelson said cheerily.

"No," said Gus. "I looked it up. The most is by the Gay family, in New York." Tamara Michaelson opened her mouth, but Gus continued. "Daddy wanted me to be happy because we had to move and I was sad."

"Why did you have to move, sweetie?" Michaelson asked, clearly hoping for some viral video tale of a holiday miracle.

"Papa didn't want to be my dad anymore, so Daddy brought us back here, and said we'd have the best time on our own. But we're not on our own anymore," Gus rambled.

"That's right," Michaelson said, trying to regain control of her interview. "You have a lot of people who want to help you."

Gus shook her head. Adam knew what she was about to say: that they had Wes now. But Adam cut her off.

"That's right," he said. "I want to thank everyone who sent or dropped off lights. It was so generous of you, and Gus and I really appreciate it. Right, sweetie?"

"Right!"

Michaelson nodded at him gratefully and turned back to the camera.

"There you have it," she said, voice fixed precisely in human interest timbre. "A community's generosity can make all the difference in a family's life. Good night, and happy holidays."

She turned back to Adam and Gus and held out her hand. Gus shook it, then Adam.

"Thank you," she said. "That was great."

"I hope you can edit," Adam muttered.

She winked at him and gave a warm smile.

"Not necessary."

Back inside, Adam attempted to get Gus back to bed, but she was so hyped up that it took an hour to calm her down. When he'd finally turned out her light, leaving her in the soft glow of her kale plant, Adam collapsed on the sofa, flicked on the TV fire, and took out his phone to fill Wes in on the excitement, in case he hadn't seen it from his window.

A tiny warmth kindled in his stomach when he saw he already had a text from Wes. He opened it excitedly, then his stomach seized.

Wes: I can't do this. I'm sorry. We have to be done.

"Wait," Adam said to no one. "What?"

He read it again because clearly he was missing something.

But no. That's all the text said.

Adam called Wes but he didn't answer.

"What the hell."

He texted: You can't just text me that and then not answer the phone, Wes. PLEASE pick up. Gus is asleep and I can't leave.

He waited a minute, then called again. This time, Wes answered. His voice sounded strange and croaky.

"I'm sorry," he said.

"What's going on? Are you okay? I don't understand. What do you mean we're done?"

Adam could feel the tears flooding his eyes and knew that soon his voice would sound squeaky and emotional. He'd come to terms with being an emotional person a long time ago, but he still resented that when he got angry he cried.

"I'm so sorry," Wes said again. "I just can't. I thought I could be… I thought with you I could… But I just can't. It's too much. I'm… God, I'm so sorry."

Then he hung up.

Furious, Adam called him right back. He picked up but didn't speak.

"Wes, come on. What happened? You can't… We had… What the hell is going on?"

Wes sighed and when he spoke again his voice was choked. Desperate.

"Please," he said. "Please just leave me alone."

The line went dead and Adam let the phone slide from suddenly numb fingers.

Outside, the lights still lit the night cheerily. The fire still crackled merrily on the television. Gus still slumbered sweetly in her bed.

But everything was different now.

Adam was alone again. And this time he didn't even know why.

Chapter Twenty-Three

Adam

Adam woke on the couch, fire still blazing on the TV, neck crooked painfully, with Gus standing over him.

"Can I have waffles with faces?" she asked excitedly, then crowed, "It's almost vacation!"

Adam's eyelids felt like they were made of sand, and his mouth tasted like he'd licked stamps in hell. When he managed to sit up, his skull protested by splitting in two and running in opposite directions away from his cringing brain.

Oh, right. The wine.

After Wes had destroyed him with sentence fragments like shrapnel he'd opened a bottle and attempted to play Sherlock Holmes with his life.

With a physical form that made him long for death and nary a clue to show for his investigations, Adam concluded that there was a reason Sherlock was more into cocaine than white wine.

"Um," he said intelligently.

"Great!" Gus said, and skipped into the kitchen in her red-and-white-striped pajamas, like the world's loudest candy cane.

Adam disagreed with the word on principle at the moment, but if there was one thing he would not do it was ruin Gus' mood with his own heartbreak. There'd be time enough for that later, unfortunately.

So he scraped himself off the couch, instructed his emotions to stay coiled acidly in his stomach, and dragged himself into the kitchen to slice strawberries and arrange them in smiling faces on his daughter's morning waffles.

Work was a nightmare. Adam was not good at keeping his emotions inside. Even customers so oblivious they asked where the hammers were while standing in front of the hammers asked Adam what was wrong. When Marie told him his "Nothing!"s were scaring the customers he switched to, "Oh, just a bad day. Now what can I help you with?"

But it was a losing battle. By the time he left work early to pick up Gus—something he'd planned weeks ago to celebrate the start of her vacation—his eyes were red with unshed (and some shed-in-the-bathroom) tears and his lips bitten red.

He knew what he really needed was a couple of days on his own to cry his heart out and watch old movies while he ate cookie dough from the tube, but he didn't have that luxury.

Instead, he blasted Christmas music on the radio, rolled the windows down, and scream-sang along at the top of his lungs as the freezing wind reddened his whole face to match his eyes. There was a kind of exultant frenzy to it that made Adam feel better enough that he arrived at Gus' school in a state that could easily be misread as pre-vacation sugar high mania, rather than heartbroken despair.

So that was good.

Gus ran to the car with her arms full of papers and her scarf streaming behind her, and immediately began to chatter excitedly about a science project she wanted to talk to Wes about.

That…wasn't.

Adam and Gus lay on the couch, legs interlaced, staring blankly at the marathon of old Christmas movies on TV.

Gus had taken the news that Wes wouldn't be spending Christmas with them hard. At first, she'd asked if he decided to go visit his parents after all, and Adam had dearly wanted to say yes and avoid the entire conversation. Have their Christmas and hide his feelings from Gus until after. But that would only delay the inevitable. Besides, he was terrible at hiding his feelings.

And, most importantly: no lying.

So he'd told her the truth, as gently as he could, and then he'd taken his emotions to the shower and cried them out under a fall of water so hot it was almost painful.

Not as painful as the truth, though.

That this was precisely what Adam had been trying to avoid: bringing another adult into Gus' life that she admired—no, *loved*—and that person abandoning her. He cursed himself for bringing this pain into Gus' life.

But when the water started to lose heat, so did his temper, and he wept a gentler kind of tears—these for himself. Because the truth was that he'd fallen in love with a kind, brilliant, sweet, gorgeous, weird man whom he'd thought might love him too. Might love Gus. Might want to make a family with them.

And he'd been wrong.

So wrong.

The worst kind of wrong. The kind that sucker punched the breath from your lungs and left only emptiness in its place.

Adam had to work the next day and River had been going to hang out with Gus, but Gus was feeling tender and begged to come to work with him instead. She promised that she wouldn't be any trouble and that she'd read in the back, so Adam texted Charlie and got his okay.

It was three days till Christmas.

Gus had cheered a little at the rare opportunity to hang out in Matheson's, but as they pulled out of the driveway, both their eyes went to Wes' house.

The paper, which had come down window by window over the last weeks, almost without Adam's notice, was back, and the whole place had an air of remoteness about it once more.

Adam realized that once he got to know Wes he'd stopped thinking of his house as creepy or sad. It was just the place where Wes did his experiments and had his brilliant ideas. The home of Wes' unusual menagerie that Gus loved.

That Wes hadn't cared about keeping up the landscaping or the exterior paint made sense—he just had other things he cared about.

Unfortunately, Adam wasn't one of them anymore.

The pain hit again and Adam cringed in the driver's seat.

Gus fell silent and fidgeted with the fringe on her scarf.

As they turned onto the main road, snow falling softly, the snowy mountains in the distance glowing against the blue sky, Gus said, "It's the lights."

"What's the lights, sweetie?"

"The lights made Wes go away."

Something more delicate than pain clawed at Adam's guts and he pulled the car over to the side of the road and faced his daughter.

"Baby, no."

"I wanted the most lights to have fun without Papa, and that's what made Wes help us, and then when we got a lot, it made him leave."

Her lip was trembling, and Adam realized that this was what she'd been holding on to since he told her: guilt.

"Listen to me, Gus. Wes didn't leave because of the lights, or anything else because of you. Wes thinks you're great. In fact, we got to know Wes because he thought you were so cool and smart and interesting."

Slash because you broke into his house, Adam added to himself, knowing someday they'd laugh about that. About the time Adam dated the neighbor for a few months because Gus pulled a B&E.

Gus sniffed miserably.

"I think they're magic," she said, like she hadn't heard him at all.

"I didn't think you believed in magic," Adam said gently.

She shook her head and when she looked back up at him it was with his sister's eyes. Eyes far too old for an eight-year-old.

"Maybe you don't have to believe in things for them to be real," she said in a haunted voice. "Just like sometimes you can believe things really a lot, and they never become real."

This was the saddest thing he'd ever heard Gus say.

"Is there something you believed in a lot that didn't become real?" he forced himself to say, dreading her answer.

But Gus just looked at him with those ancient eyes and said, "Never mind, Dad."

She'd never called him Dad before.

True to her word, Gus read in Charlie's office the whole morning. At lunchtime, Charlie showed up with a stack of pizzas for everyone in the store. The waft of hot cheese lured Gus out, and they enjoyed a pleasant hour eating and chatting.

As the pizza boxes were cleared away, Gus turned big eyes on Charlie and said, "Can I please have a job?"

For a moment, Charlie's eyes got as big as Gus' and Adam could see him working out how to let her down easy by citing child labor laws.

"I think she means a job to do for the afternoon," Adam murmured.

"Oh." Charlie looked relieved. "Sure thing. Let me introduce you to the different sizes of nails."

Gus' eyes lit up and she followed Charlie eagerly.

"Thanks, Charlie," Adam said when he returned, Gus happily sorting the bins of nails and humming along with Christmas carols on the radio. "Um. Wes broke up with me. Us. Me."

Charlie frowned, his red-brown eyebrows drawing together.

"I'm real sorry, Adam. That's a hell of a thing to deal with at the holidays." He glanced over at Gus. "Does she know?"

"Yeah. It's been a crappy couple days. That's why I didn't want to leave her alone today. Thanks for letting her come in. I—"

"Shh, don't worry about it," Charlie said, putting a large, warm hand on Adam's shoulder.

A customer approached and Adam rang him up while Charlie inquired after his family.

"Do you know why?" Charlie asked when they'd left.

Adam shook his head.

"He just said he couldn't do it. He thought he could, but he was wrong. And he asked me to leave him alone."

"Huh."

He looked contemplative.

"Huh, what?"

"Well, I know I'm not exactly in the know here, but that sounds like someone who's scared."

"Scared of what?"

Charlie shook his head, expression serious.

"I don't know."

At 3:00 p.m., Charlie flipped the sign on the door to *Closed* and told them all to get out of there. Gus made them all wait another five minutes until she'd perfectly sorted the last nail into its proper container, then collapsed dramatically on the floor, sniffing her metallic fingertips and making Vanna White-esque arm gestures to show off her work.

"Good job," Charlie said. "Come back in ten years and I'll give you a job."

Gus nodded seriously and Adam smiled.

As they trouped out into the parking lot, Charlie pressed an envelope into Adam's hand.

"Merry Christmas," he said.

Adam's face must've expressed his panic at not having anything for Charlie, because the big man chuckled and said, "Holiday bonus. You deserve it."

Then he loped off to his truck, calling, "Have a good one," behind him.

Adam peeked into the envelope and saw a check for five hundred dollars.

"Holy shit," Adam murmured.

"What's that?" Gus asked, skipping up to him.

"Oh, um, Charlie gave me a holiday bonus."

"Like, money?"

"Yeah." Adam chucked her under the chin, smiling. "Like, money."

The snow had stopped falling and it was a beautiful, clear day despite the cold.

"Hey, you wanna go visit River at the cat shelter?"

"Yeah!"

Gus ran to the car and Adam shot River a quick text, and got their enthusiastic response immediately.

On the way, they stopped at Peach's Diner, which had been in Garnet Run as long as Adam could remember, and picked up a pie.

The Dirt Road Cat Shelter looked cheery, with purple, white, and yellow lights in every window.

"Love the color scheme," Adam said.

"Thanks." River smiled. "Rye let me do the decorations."

"River, River, can I do one?"

Gus was standing at the front desk, where crayon drawings of cats who'd been adopted were taped.

"Sure, Bug."

River sat Gus on the chair and set her up with paper and crayons. Adam unboxed the apple pie and they ate it with spoons right from the tin.

Adam had told River about Wes via text that morning in explaining why he was taking Gus to work with him, and Adam could tell River had a million questions.

"You okay here for a minute, sweetie?" Adam said. "I wanna cuddle some cats."

Gus nodded, totally focused on her drawing, and Adam and River went into the large cat playroom.

Adam felt instantly calmed by the cats snoozing on perches and curled up in corners around the room. Two played with something that looked like a felt Pop-Tart on the floor, rolling around together and coming to rest in a single floof of fur and paws, looking up at River.

"Hi, Dancer, hi, Prancer," River said. "Just temporary names," they muttered. "So what the hell happened with Wes?"

River picked up either Dancer or Prancer, cuddling the tabby cat to their chest where it settled and began to purr loudly.

"Uggh." Adam scrubbed his hands over his face. "That's what's killing me. I don't know."

"He seemed pretty tense when he showed up the other day. When all the people were taking pictures. I was too." River kissed the cat between its ears. "He gave me his hoodie when I went to leave, so I could cover my face."

Somehow, despite all its abuse, Adam's heart still soared. That was so kind. So like Wes.

"He did?"

"Yeah. He seemed... I don't know. Spooked, maybe? Is he in witness protection or something?"

"I wish," Adam muttered. Then, realizing how horrible that was, said. "God, no, I don't wish that. I just meant that I wish he had a good reason for breaking up with me."

"What would be a good reason?" River asked curiously.

"I dunno. Like, we fought all the time, or I cheated on him, or, or, or I stole all his money or something."

River looked doubtful.

"You would never do those things."

"I know, I just mean a real reason."

River bit their lip.

"Those just sound like easy reasons. Clear reasons. But I think sometimes it's more likely that the reasons are complicated...subtle."

River's eyes had taken on a faraway look and Adam wondered if they'd been dating someone.

"Anyway, I just think sometimes it's not quite so clear-cut," River concluded. "And by the way, you probably wouldn't know if he was in witness protection. I mean, that's kind of the whole idea."

They said it casually, and half-joking, but it made Adam realize that he actually didn't know that much about Wes. So much of the time they'd spent together had focused on what Adam and Gus needed—hanging the lights, show-and-tell, estate sales, Gus' interest in Wes' critters. And when they'd talked about Wes, it had mostly been about his research and experiments.

Most of what Adam knew about Wes came from observing his behavior. Adam knew he was kind and generous and patient because he'd seen him be all those things. And, of course, funny and smart and hot as hell.

In fact, most of what Adam knew about Wes' past was about the unfortunate experience he'd had with acting and his father.

...And how he absolutely hated attention. The kind of attention that Adam's Instagram posts had brought down on the street.

Oh, no.

Chapter Twenty-Four

Wes

Wes hadn't slept since ending things with Adam.

Since the night before the strangers with their phones and the newscaster with her camera had shattered his conviction that he could be a normal person living a normal life with another person in the world.

He'd plastered the windows with paper and locked the door, and it had still taken hours for him to stop shaking; to realize that the cameras hadn't been there for him. And that likely they wouldn't be back.

With realization came despair.

First it was *What the hell have I done.* Then, when he'd calmed down a bit, it was *How do I fix this.* In that mode, he'd picked up his phone a dozen times, fingers hovering over messages to Adam that said *NEVER MIND I JUST PANICKED I AM SO DAMN SORRY!* Then, seeing the messages he actually had sent to Adam, he'd cringed and moved on to *They're better off without me.* Swift on its heels: *God, I miss them.*

Finally, rage. Rage at himself for still not being over this reaction. Then rage at his father for all of it. By that time, it was the next day—his father's birthday—and Wes picked up and put down his phone all over again.

Janice and Banana had been very happy to have him awake the night before, back to their nocturnal schedule, and had gamboled around, scratching at the piles he'd made for them in their enclosure. But come morning, when they'd crashed, Wes hadn't gone to bed.

And now, hours later, he picked up his phone one more time, and this time, he dialed.

His father answered in the hearty, hail-fellow-well-met voice he used for journalists, producers, and now, it seemed, his son.

"Happy birthday," Wes said, because his mind went blank of every other thing he wanted to say.

"Well, thank you. I'm surprised to hear from you."

"Yeah."

An awkward silence during which Wes could hear the jazzy Christmas music his parents had played during December since he was a child.

Wes walked to the periscope and looked at Adam and Gus' house. The lights were off and all he could see was the flicker that meant the TV was on in the living room. He wondered if Gus' kale plant was still glowing or if the luciferase had worn off.

He wondered what Gus and Adam were watching. He wondered if Adam had told Gus he wouldn't be around anymore.

He wondered a lot of things he'd probably never know the answers to. Not as long as his only access to them was through this damned periscope.

Adam's voice on the phone had been so hurt and confused. Shocked.

"Westley, are you there?" came his father's oil-slick voice.

Wes intended to say, "What are you doing for your birthday this year." But what came out instead was quite different.

"You weren't a very good father."

"Excuse me?" Nigel Brennan said, voice now cold as ice.

It was the voice the public never heard—except for the brief arc where he'd played his own evil twin on *Edge of Day*. That voice had made Wes shudder when his father slid into it in response to Wes' revelation that he was done with show business and it made him shudder now.

He kept his eyes fixed on Adam and Gus' house through the periscope, remembered how it had felt to be up on their roof, with the big sky around him and the cold wind nipping at his ears. When he'd hung lights, he hadn't worried about the neighbors seeing him because he'd been focused on making Gus and Adam happy. He remembered how it felt to speak to Gus' classmates about Bettie. Though he'd been nervous at first, he hadn't worried about them looking at him because none of them found him even one-tenth as interesting as his tarantula.

The newscaster had scared him. Terrified him, in fact. But even she had only cared about what he might have to say about Adam and Gus' lights.

It was the wound of trauma that was reopened

every time someone paid overt attention to him. Now the wound could open at a hair trigger, and those triggers had become phobias. He knew it. He just wasn't quite sure what to do about it.

But he *did* know what to do about his father's disapproving, judgmental, entitled voice.

"You heard me. I didn't know any different at the time. But I know now what it looks like to be a good father. You model best practices for your children. You show them how to make the world a better, more interesting, more loving place. You're honest with them because trust between you matters. You ask them how they feel and why they feel it and you honor those feelings. You don't instrumentalize them for your own gain. And you don't ever, *ever* make them feel responsible for your happiness as a person."

Wes could hear the cold fury in his voice so he knew his father could hear it too.

"I was so terrified of hurting you, of ruining your career, that I did things I hated. Things that hurt me. That are still hurting me now. And you didn't care. You didn't care how I felt or what I needed. You only cared about yourself. I know that now. And I know how selfish that is."

Wes took a deep breath. He felt as if a huge weight had slid off his shoulders, and his heart was pounding with adrenaline.

"I'm sorry to say this on your birthday, but I can't sit with it for one more day. I did something that hurt people I care about yesterday because I was so terrified of being visible in the world. It was a stupid mistake and I regret it, but I don't know if I can ever make it right. But I'm sure as hell gonna try."

He wasn't even talking to his father anymore. He was just saying aloud the things that needed to be said.

Before his father could say anything in response, Wes blurted out, "Happy birthday," and hung up the phone.

He was shaking.

"Holy shit," Wes said. "Holy, holy, holy shit."

He slid down to the floor, back against the wall. His hands were trembling but he felt exultant, like he'd finally beaten an enemy in a game he hadn't even admitted he was playing.

And if he could do that…if he could face his father after all these years and tell him exactly what he thought of him?

Then he could do anything.

He grabbed a piece of cardboard lying near him and a marker near his foot and started to make a plan. He sketched and calculated and plotted and schemed.

Then he picked up his phone and placed one more call.

"Zachary?" he said when his friend picked up. "I'm sorry to bother you, but I need you to help me save Christmas."

Chapter Twenty-Five

Adam

It was the day before Christmas Eve and Adam and Gus were trying to pretend like they were having fun. It was a rather pitiful scene.

Adam kept coming back to his realization about Wes and what might have gone wrong between them, and why. He'd composed and deleted three separate text messages, because if he was wrong...well, it felt too pathetic to text the guy who broke up with you and say, "I think I figured out why you dumped me and I'm sorry and here's how we can fix it" and have him say, "No, actually, I dumped you because I'm just not that into you."

Adam cringed and sternly banished the thought, resolving yet again to be present with Gus. His heartbreak would still be there after Christmas was over.

"Hey, I know," Adam said. "Let's go get a Christmas tree!"

Gus lifted her drooping head at that idea, but then slumped back onto the couch.

"I don't wanna murder a tree," she said.

"We could get a fake tree," Adam offered, but even

as he was saying it he worried they'd be sold out at the few nearby stores.

Gus just sighed and flipped over on the couch so her blond hair streamed to the floor.

Adam tapped around on his phone, then went to sit beside her.

"Look, here. We could get a tree that has the root ball still attached and that way we can plant it again after Christmas."

Gus sat up.

"We don't have any ornaments," she said, but he could tell her interest was piqued.

"We can make them!"

"Hmm." Gus contemplated for a minute, then jumped up. "Okay!"

Adam grabbed her in a hug. She was truly the greatest kid on the planet.

"Thanks for being a sport," he said. "I'm sorry this Christmas hasn't turned out as good as I promised."

"It's not your fault," she sighed.

It was, but Adam chose to accept her absolution in the spirit in which it was given.

The Christmas tree farm was about thirty minutes away and they sang along to Christmas carols the whole way, moods lifting with each mile they got from home. It was good to just *leave* sometimes, Adam realized. To physically distance yourself from your problems so you could get some perspective. It had certainly worked with Mason. Mostly.

"Why's it called a carol?" Gus mused.

"I have no idea. Look it up."

He passed her his phone.

She read, "Middle English, ring, circle of stones, enclosed place for study (see carrel), ring dance with song (hence, song)." Then she trailed off and said, "Do you speak Latin?"

"I don't think anyone really speaks Latin anymore."

"Oh. It says something in Latin and then 'piper for dance.'"

"Cool. So the word for the circle of stones that they danced in became the word for the song."

"Words are neat," Gus said, handing back the phone.

"Have I told you lately that you're the greatest kid in the known universe?"

She grinned. "Nope."

"Well. You're the greatest kid in the known universe."

"What about the unknown universe?"

"I can't be sure. But you're probably the greatest kid there too."

At the farm, they parked in the cordoned-off area and got out to peruse.

"Hey, there," said a man who looked almost comically like a lumberjack. Although Adam supposed if there were any place it was reasonable to find a lumberjack it was around trees. "A last-minute shopper."

"Yeah." Adam snugged his hat down over his ears. "Life, you know?" he said by way of explanation.

The bearded man nodded.

"I do. So what kind of tree can we match you up with?"

"We need one that won't die," Gus said.

"Ah, got it. I have just the thing."

They followed the man's broad, flannel-clad form down a row of trees to ones that were in tubs.

"These have their root balls wrapped in burlap. You can plant them as soon as the ground thaws and until then keep them alive by watering them in the tub."

Gus gave a nod to indicate these trees passed muster, and she went to look around while Adam paid.

"Uh, any chance you know how to attach this tree to my car?" Adam asked, and the lumberjack clapped him on the back and went to get the rope.

"How far you goin?" he asked.

"To Garnet Run."

"Sorry, I'm not familiar. I just moved here last month."

"Oh, where from?"

"Olympia, Washington."

Adam nodded. "Garnet Run's about half an hour away. It's small. No reason you'd know it. Are you living around here?"

"Yeah, I've been subletting from the guy who owns this place while I work it for him. But the job ends—well, now, really. He'll be out of town till summer, and then I'll find another place. I'm Bram, by the way." He held out his hand.

"Adam. Nice to meet you. That's my daughter, Gus."

"She likes trees, huh?"

"Yeah, she said she didn't want to murder a tree for Christmas."

Bram smiled. Although he was quite a large man, he had a free, easy smile.

"I happen to agree with her."

Adam forced himself not to say, *But clearly you fell trees for a living.*

Bram laughed.

"You must be a terrible poker player, cuz I can tell exactly what you're thinking."

Adam flushed, but Bram didn't seem the slightest bit bothered.

"Yeah, well."

"Anyway, let's get this puppy strapped on."

Adam watched as Bram lifted the tree onto the top of his car and secured it. He handed Adam the bucket it came in and took his money with another easy smile.

"Time to go, Gus," Adam called, and she came running, the tip of her nose pink from the cold.

"What was the name of that town, again?" Bram asked.

"Garnet Run."

"Thanks," he said. "I'll get the lay of the land soon enough."

"Thank you," Adam and Gus chorused as they got into the car.

What a nice man, Adam thought. If only he weren't totally smitten with another.

They spent a surprisingly pleasant day making ornaments for the tree and watching the cheesiest romantic comedies they could find. Gus had the idea that they could take some of the bits of metal she'd gotten at the estate sale and repurpose them into ornaments, which is how they ended the day regarding with satisfaction a Christmas tree bedecked with glittered toilet paper roll snowflakes and hunks of metal hung with paper clips.

"They really shine," Adam said of the hunks of metal.

He lifted Gus up so she could place the tree topper, a paper towel roll snowflake covered in red glitter.

They'd snagged a few strings of lights from the side of the house to light the tree. Gus hadn't wanted to turn them on anymore anyway. So now the tree twinkled happily in the corner of the living room.

They ate mac and cheese and leftover Christmas monster cookies in front of *Home Alone*. Gus had never seen it and was overjoyed that there was a tarantula in it. Adam had forgotten about the tarantula and was decidedly underjoyed to see it.

Gus was nodding off before the movie ended, so Adam shut off the TV and the tree lights, and they brushed their teeth and went to bed.

It wasn't the most festive night, but it had definitely ended better than it had begun, so Adam considered it a win.

They spent the day of Christmas Eve sledding down the hill behind The Dirt Road Cat Shelter with River. Midmorning, Charlie and Rye, and Charlie's brother, Jack, and Jack's partner, Simon, showed up and joined them, as did one of River's friends, Tracy.

Adam hadn't been particularly looking forward to a day of sledding—cold and wet and sweaty was not his favorite combination—but it was what Gus had wanted to do, and River had arranged it. It had turned out to be a blast, however. As fun as the actual sledding was, Adam was having an even better time watching a gaggle of grownups attempting to fit on sleds clearly made for children.

Charlie and Rye were especially amusing because Charlie's muscular bulk meant that the sled didn't want to move, so Rye was having him push the sled and then jump on before it crested the hill, leading to several unexpected accelerations and one notable instance when Charlie missed the sled altogether, and Rye rocketed down the hill by himself while Charlie rolled down, ass over elbow for a few feet, then came to an undignified stop in the snow.

They all loved Gus and she was having the time of her life being the center of their attention (not to mention having their assistance carrying her sled back up the hill).

As the sun began to set and the warmth of home and hearth—or in Adam and Gus' case, home and TV fire—beckoned, they went their separate ways.

"We'll see you tomorrow, around eleven?" Adam asked River.

They nodded, cheeks flushed with cold, smiling. "Can't wait." They winked at Adam, indicating that everything was set on their end for Gus' gift.

"Bye, River!" Gus called. Then she practically collapsed into the car, lips chapped, eyes bright, and hair everywhere.

"Have fun, baby?" Adam asked.

"So much fun!"

"Good! What should we do tonight?"

Her smile faded. Adam knew what she was thinking. That they'd planned to spend the evening with Wes.

"Maybe we should try baking more Christmas cookies," Adam suggested brightly, wanting to preserve her previous good mood.

"Maybe," she murmured.

When they turned the corner onto Knockbridge Lane, the first thing Adam saw were the lights. For a moment, he didn't think anything of it—after all, besides the last two days, they'd had the house lit up at night since they'd started collecting lights.

But this wasn't just fairy lights. This was...

"Oh my god," Gus breathed in awe. "The lights are magic."

Their house and the trees and the lawn around it were...glowing.

It was a green familiar to everyone on Knockbridge Lane because every night it emanated from Wes Mobray's basement windows. A green that had led Marcy Pennywhistle and her sister to the conviction that Wes Mobray was a sorcerer.

But no one—Adam included—would ever be able to think of that green as evil again. Because now it was the glowing green of pine trees, holly leaves, and wreaths.

The green of Christmas.

It truly did look magical. Adam stopped the car at the curb to take it all in.

There were more fairy lights filling in the sides of the house where they'd run out. The windows each seemed aglow with candle lights, and the ground sparkled with a net of twinkles, like stars had fallen to earth.

The three large trees in the front and side of the house glowed with a subtle pulsation, just like the trees they'd seen in the clearing in the woods with Wes. On the front door was a large wreath that seemed to be made of antlers woven with boughs of holly.

But although he agreed with Gus that the glowing lights *looked* magic, it was something else entirely that held all the magic for Adam.

Across the front of the house, five words glowed in bioluminescent light: *I love you. I'm sorry.*

And there, on the front step of their house, in full view of all Knockbridge Lane, bundled up against the Wyoming December, sat Wes Mobray.

Chapter Twenty-Six

Wes

When Adam's car had pulled out of the driveway that morning, Wes and Zachary had sprung into action, implementing the plan Wes had spent the night crafting. And bless Zachary for acting like it was no big deal for Wes to call him in a frenzy and request a visit when they'd never met in person before. When he'd opened the door, Zachary had just smiled and said, "My friend." And Wes had known he truly was.

The real trick was controlling the form of the bioluminescence. That and the cold. Zachary had brought some tricks of the trade from his cache of Halloween decorations to help with both.

Wes had taken a deep breath, set his jaw, and walked across the street to the Mills' house in broad daylight, without Adam and Gus there as a buffer.

The guy with the gaggle of yappy poodles walked by, dogs booted and jacketed in different colors. Wes stood very still, as if he could disappear. But the man just walked by.

Mrs. Whatshername from next door came out to get the mail, shielded her eyes from the sun, and

peered over. But she just gave an awkward little sa-
lute, as if the sight of two grown men with armfuls
of lights, wires, and glowing bioluminescent material was perfectly normal. Wes supposed that after the
time Adam and Gus had spent lighting their house
up, it kind of was.

As they worked, Wes composed a speech. The
speech he would give to Adam when he got home. It
was full of heartfelt confessions, fears, and promises.
It was full of explanations and plans.

But when Adam's car turned the corner of Knockbridge Lane, Wes forgot every single word he'd re-
hearsed. The only word he could remember was
home. Because that's what Adam felt like to him.

Adam's lips formed his name and Gus ran to the
middle of the yard to get the full effect of the lights.
Wes tried to wave but his body seemed to have stiff-
ened up as he sat on the stoop. He wasn't sure how
long he'd been there, but he'd watched the dark set in.

Adam approached him slowly, eyes darting warily
from him to Gus to the house that screamed the five
words Wes wanted to say.

Usually, Adam was so full of emotion that it prac-
tically leaked from him. But now, he was oddly calm.
He regarded Wes for a minute, then said, "Come in.
You must be freezing."

Wes staggered to his feet. Still the words wouldn't
come.

He lurched inside and fumbled his jacket and boots
off. Adam guided him into the living room and into

the easy chair, and before he knew it, he was swaddled in a blanket and Adam and Gus were staring at him from the couch—twin blond, blue-eyed angels waiting for him to speak.

Once, his fourth year of graduate school, Wes had stayed in the lab for the whole weekend working on an experiment. When someone entered on Monday morning and asked him a question, Wes had opened his mouth to answer and found words utterly inaccessible.

That was how he felt now. He cleared his throat to buy time and Adam's uncanny calm cracked.

"Are you okay?" he asked, leaning forward. "Do you mean what you wrote on the house? What happened?"

Under the warmth of Adam's care, Wes thawed and felt things begin to work again.

"I'm so sorry," he said. "I panicked and I couldn't explain, but I'm ready to talk now. And…yes." His heart flickered back to life. "I meant it. Completely."

Adam's blue eyes were usually the blue of the sky in a painting of a rural idyll. Now they glowed with a hot longing that warmed Wes deep inside. He wanted to grab Adam to him, pull him into the bed, wrap him in his body and explain everything under the cover of proximate flesh.

Adam, he saw now, would always listen to what he had to say.

But Adam wasn't the one who spoke next.

Gus stood, squared her narrow shoulders, and looked at Wes with the seriousness of someone who knows what it is to lose people.

"I'm so mad at you," she said. "You can't be our friend one day and then be mean to us the next. That's *not* being a good friend. Right?" she asked Adam.

"That's true, sweetie," Adam said, and Wes could tell that was something Adam had told her, likely about a friend of hers.

"You made me and Daddy really sad," Gus went on. "We were very nice to you and you were usually nice but then you ran away and I didn't like it."

Her lip was quivering but she held his gaze and spoke clearly and honestly. At eight years old she was able to do what he had never been able to until the day before: say to someone that they had hurt her and that she deserved better.

Wes was so ashamed. He was so damned proud of her.

"You're right," he said. "You're right, Gus. I was a bad friend. I got scared, and instead of being honest about it, I ran away. I'm not as brave as you and your dad. I guess I still have a lot to learn about how to be a good friend. About how to be…part of a family."

He ventured this last tentatively, hoping Adam would hear it for the offer it was.

Adam blinked back tears.

Gus was unyielding.

"Family shouldn't run away," she said. "That's what Papa did and Daddy said that he didn't want to be our family."

Adam's eyes widened.

"I didn't say that," he said.

"Yes you did," Gus insisted. "To River."

"Thought you were asleep," Adam muttered.

"Well I don't *want* Papa to be my family anyway." She wrinkled her brow in thought. "And I don't wanna call him Papa anymore, either."

She had Adam's full attention now.

"Well…what do you want to call him, baby?" Adam asked.

Gus scrunched up her face with anger.

"A very bad word!"

"Okay, you have permission, just this once."

Gus' cheeks flushed as she worked up to it.

"Butt!" she ejaculated triumphantly.

It took every ounce of self-control that Wes possessed not to laugh, and he could see the same struggle in Adam's face. Adam clearly managed it by the slimmest of margins, nodding seriously and pulling Gus into a hug.

Their eyes met over Gus' head and neither of them looked away. Then Adam smiled, and Wes smiled back at him.

Chapter Twenty-Seven

Adam

"What do you think?" Adam asked Gus as he kissed her good-night.

Her previous severity had been softened by dinner, winning at Uno, and sleepiness. Now she closed her eyes and smiled softly.

"I love Wes," she said. "I think people deserve a second chance."

Adam's heart felt too large to be contained in any human form.

"Me too, baby," he said. "Me too."

In the living room, Wes had put the crackling fire on TV and lit the tree, bathing everything in a warm glow.

He stood, reticently, until Adam gestured him onto the couch and pulled the blanket over both of them.

"If you're too tired to talk, I understand," Wes said.

Adam was tired, but he'd missed Wes so damn much, and been so damn sad without him, that there was no way he was putting this off for even a minute.

"No, I'm ready."

Adam forced himself to sit quietly as Wes sorted

through his words. He forced himself not to forgive Wes before he'd even spoken.

Adam had heard his whole life that he was a pushover. Too quick to forgive; too easy on people.

But the truth was that Adam had never once regretted forgiving someone. Because forgiveness was about him, and not about them at all. He had forgiven his father for being a bad parent, even though he had no interest in ever seeing him again. He'd forgiven his mother for being a coward. He'd forgiven friends for not coming around anymore after he became a father. Forgiven Marina for not being able to take care of Gus. And Mason…well, okay, he wasn't quite there yet with Mason.

He carried a deep well of forgiveness inside him and when he doled it out it gave him peace and never diminished. It was, he believed, the thing that rescued him from the deep damage of other people's failures. That he had the power to forgive, and in forgiving heal his own wounds without needing the instrument of them anymore.

Wes took a deep breath and Adam knew he could see the promise of forgiveness in his eyes.

"The other night, when I left your house. After all those people came? The newscaster stuck a camera in my face. She thought I was you at first, I guess, but I wasn't thinking clearly. It was like I was right back there, people taking my picture and trying to cut off locks of my hair and writing about what I ate for breakfast. I…I just panicked."

Adam nodded. He was relieved to have called it right.

"I kind of realized that's maybe what happened. Those people coming to take pictures… I didn't even think about your past. I guess, if I'm honest, I didn't understand it was as much of a phobia for you as it is."

"It's… I don't mean to react the way I do. But after that time in my life, I never felt normal. People *were* always staring at me, and I hated it so much, and had such a clear strategy of just kind of freezing and being a nonperson. Being the fake person they were taking a picture of instead of myself, so it wasn't me they were seeing."

Adam remembered the way Wes had frozen at the car outside Gus' school the day of her show-and-tell.

"Even years later, every time someone looked at me, I felt that way. So I started hating *anyone* looking at me. And that led to me not wanting to be in public because that was a sure way to avoid being looked at. So when that lady stuck her camera in my face, all I could think was *Shit, they found me*. And even after I got inside and calmed down cuz I realized it wasn't about me, I still…"

He trailed off and Adam got scared.

"I still knew that if I…if I was with you. Part of a family with you and Gus… I couldn't do that. I couldn't hide in my house. I would have to do things like go to parent-teacher night and go to her science fairs and take you out to dinner."

A look of horror passed over Wes' face.

"Sorry, I don't mean those are bad things. I just mean... I never thought I'd do them. Never. I thought if I was just by myself I could be..."

"Safe," Adam supplied.

"Yeah."

Wes took Adam's hand, and the feel of those gentle, rough hands after days without them nearly brought Adam to tears of relief.

"But I don't *want* to be safe like that. Not if it means missing out on this. On you. You and Gus." Wes' eyes burned. "Have I messed it up too much? Have I lost you?"

"No. But Gus was right. I was pretty heartbroken, Wes. I thought you were just done. I thought you'd thrown us away."

"Like Mason did," Wes murmured.

And there was that. But not exactly.

"Different than Mason. Because Mason didn't know what he was getting, and you did. And you seemed to like what you were getting."

"I did! I do. I really, really do."

Adam smiled.

"The thing is, if we're together, it really *is* about me and Gus. It would be serious pretty fast, because I'm not going to have someone in Gus' life that she could lose this easily."

Wes winced. "When she was telling me off earlier, I was so ashamed. This eight-year-old knows how to ask for what she needs and be honest and I don't. Obviously she gets that from you. So maybe...is it too much to ask that maybe you could help show me?"

It was exactly what Adam wanted to hear. Not empty assurances that Wes would never get scared again, or would be perfect from hereon out. But a request for help in becoming the kind of person that Adam needed, of his own volition.

"I could do that."

Wes leaned in. He stroked Adam's hair and Adam felt electricity dance on his skin.

"I missed you so much," he said.

"I missed you too. I um. I told my dad he was a bad, selfish parent. On his birthday. Whoops."

"You did? Whoa."

"Yeah, and I know that's because of you. Seeing the kind of parent you are to Gus showed me that I wasn't delusional about my dad. So really, you've shown me how to be more honest already. Thank you."

Wes pressed his forehead against Adam's. He smelled like home.

"I'm proud of you," Adam said.

He felt Wes shiver, then the arms he'd missed so dreadfully wrapped around him and pulled him close.

"I love you, Adam," Wes said. "I really love you. And Gus. And I'm so damn sorry I was such a coward."

Adam cupped his face.

"You weren't a coward, baby. You got triggered and had a reaction to something you never fully dealt with. If it happens again, hopefully you'll know that you can tell me."

Wes nodded miserably.

"Hey, Wes?"

"Yeah?"

Adam looked into the beautiful, warm eyes of his brilliant, kind, generous, sweet weirdo.

"I love you too."

Wes blinked, and his expression reminded Adam of Gus' when they'd seen the magical glow of lights this evening.

"Thank you," Wes said. "Thank you, thank you."

He squeezed Adam so tight he almost couldn't breathe, and it was the best breathlessness Adam had ever felt.

Held tight and secure in Wes' arms, Adam felt brave.

"Do you wanna know a secret?" he whispered.

"Always," Wes said immediately.

Adam took a deep breath.

"I think I've loved you almost from the start. And I want to be a family with you. Like, now. I just…"

But he didn't have to explain anything, because Wes was holding him so tight and murmuring words of love into his hair.

Wes lifted him up and carried him like something in a swoony old movie, dropping him on the bed and moving over him, all heat and strength and intense care.

"Wes, I missed you so much."

Wes tipped Adam's head back and kissed him, and Adam could feel every bit of love and desire returned.

"Want everything with you," Wes murmured.

With.

It was exactly what Adam wanted to hear, and he opened his arms, welcoming Wes home.

They held each other, snuggled under the covers, and Adam listened to Wes breathe. Listened to his heartbeat. Smelled his skin and his hair. Every now and then, their mouths would find each other in a kiss.

"I love you," Adam said, pressing a kiss to Wes' chin.

"I love you so much I can't believe it," Wes said.

"You can't believe you love me?" Adam asked.

"I can't believe you exist. I can't believe how wonderful you are. And Gus. Can't believe you want me. Can't believe I'm not still hiding in my house. I can't believe any of it."

Adam didn't try and stop the tears from coming this time. He just shrugged and let Wes kiss them away.

"Merry Christmas," he said.

Then he sat up so fast he almost cracked Wes' skull.

"Oh, no!" Adam said.

"What's wrong?" Wes looked alarmed.

"I don't have a present for you cuz you dumped me."

He was genuinely forlorn. Wes snorted.

"I think the second half of that sentence excuses the first."

"Oh. Right. Asshole," he said, jokingly.

"I'm very sorry," Wes said, not joking at all. "If it makes you feel any better, I don't have a present for you either. Or Gus. Wow, great start to this whole being a family thing, huh?"

All joking aside, Adam lay back down next to Wes. "Having you here for Christmas and every day after is the best gift I can possibly imagine."

Wes stroked his hair and relaxed, pulling the covers over them.

They entwined in the perfect configuration and Adam felt himself start to doze off. He was exhausted.

"Oh, I should warn you," he managed to get out just before sleep took him. "Gus wakes up *very* early on Christmas morning."

He thought maybe Wes said something like *That's okay* or *I love you*, but he wasn't sure because relaxed in the arms of his beloved, sleep came easily.

Chapter Twenty-Eight

Adam

Christmas dawned—well, it didn't quite dawn *anything* because before the sun had risen, Adam was pulled from a deep slumber wrapped in Wes' warm arms by the sound of someone bouncing excitedly outside his door while trying very hard not to make noise.

He nuzzled close to Wes, enjoying his smell for a moment, then, knowing what would happen any second, pressed a kiss to his jaw and whispered, "I'm sorry."

As if attuned to Adam even in sleep, Wes mumbled a sleepy, "Whatswrongbaby?"

Adam stroked his hair, then slid out of bed and into pajamas. He got back into bed and made sure the covers were completely covering Wes' gorgeous body.

"Come in, sweetie," Adam called just as Gus' control broke, and she cried, "Daddy, it's Christmasssss!"

Wes jolted awake as Gus flew through the air and landed in the middle of the bed.

"Get up, get up, it's Christmas!" she crowed, throwing her arms around Adam.

Wes rubbed his eyes as if Adam's apology had just registered, and slid his clothes on under the covers.

"I'm up," Adam assured her. "Go into the living room and turn on the tree and we'll be out in a minute."

"Okay!"

She bounced off the bed and down the hall and strains of a tuneless "It's Christmas, it's Christmas" carol grew fainter as she went.

"Um," Adam said by way of apology.

"Hey. C'mere."

Adam let himself be gathered back into Wes' arms.

"Merry Christmas," Wes said. "I love you."

It was absolutely, positively, without a doubt, the best Christmas present Adam had ever gotten.

"I love you," Adam murmured, kissing him.

They dragged themselves out of bed.

"That's not very cozy," Adam said, indicating the heavy jeans and sweater Wes had pulled on from the night before. "You could go home and get pajamas if you want? Pajama Christmas. It's a thing."

Wes smiled, but hesitated, then shook his head.

"Do you not own pajamas or something?"

"Huh? Oh. Well, I don't, actually, but it's not that."

"What, then?"

"It's silly."

Adam tipped Wes' chin up so he could look into his eyes.

"Say it anyway."

"I'm afraid if I leave I'll realize this was a dream

and I never came here and you never forgave me and everything will be back like it was."

"Oh, baby." Adam pulled him into a hug and stroked his back. "It's not a dream."

"Yeah, well, that's what you'd say if it were a dream too," Wes muttered. Adam couldn't refute that.

"Okay, well, do you want to borrow something of mine instead? It'll be a little small but I have sweats and stuff in there."

"Thanks," Wes said, pulling off the jeans.

"I'll see you downstairs."

"For Christmas," Wes said, like he was still processing it.

Adam didn't mind. He'd give Wes every reassurance he needed because Wes had given the same to him.

"Yup, for Christmas with me and Gus and River."

Adam kissed him and gave his ass a friendly squeeze.

The tree was twinkling and the TV fire was blazing and Gus was sitting suspiciously innocently on the couch.

Adam narrowed his eyes and her gaze cut over to the tree, but she just smiled.

"How about pancakes?" he asked, and she nodded.

While he was pouring the first one onto the griddle, Wes came downstairs wearing Adam's clothes.

Adam hadn't previously known that it was possible for someone to look simultaneously hot, adorable, and ridiculous, but it turned out that it was. Wes had chosen some blue pajama pants with gold stars on them and an old, paint-spattered yellow sweatshirt that Adam had bought from a fundraiser at Gus' preschool. It said *Proud Parent of Little Tyke* on it in red.

The pajama pants fit Wes almost like leggings. They were clearly too short, so he'd borrowed some of Adam's wool socks and pulled them up to his calves. The sweatshirt was tight on him and too short in the arms. The whole effect was of a child that had chosen their own outfit.

Only, you know. Hot. Because Wes.

Adam didn't mention the outfit because he didn't want to make Wes uncomfortable—especially knowing his feelings about being looked at. Gus had no such compunction.

"You look so funny!" she said. "Those are Daddy's clothes."

"Pajama Christmas. I was told it's a thing," Wes said.

Gus high-fived him.

They ate pancakes and Adam made a double-strong pot of coffee, knowing they'd need their energy. They played several more rounds of Uno with Christmas movies in the background, and Gus had Wes take her around the outside of the house to show her all the lights he'd added to the house, bioluminescent and otherwise.

After that Wes ran home briefly to feed the animals and, he said, get presents. Adam gave him a funny look because Wes had said he didn't have presents, but he returned with several boxes that he instructed them not to touch.

By the time River arrived at 11:30, Gus had consumed too much sugar and taken to running around the living room pretending to be a lyrebird that they'd just learned about from a David Attenborough special.

"Yay, River!" she shouted when they came in the door. "It's Christmas!"

"It is," River said, catching her in a one-armed hug. The other arm was occupied with several boxes.

"Come in," Adam said, winking at them. "Want me to hold that for a minute?"

River put the medium-sized box down gently on the floor to take their boots and coat off.

"It's okay, actually," they said very quietly. "But I think we should do presents sooner rather than later."

"Got it."

Adam left River to get cozy in the living room, and corralled Gus out of the kitchen, where she was trying to add mini candy canes to the Christmas monster cookies they'd made after breakfast, and into the living room.

"Is it presents, is it presents?"

She was bouncing in place. Adam nodded, wiping icing off her eyebrow with his thumb.

"Yay!"

She rocketed through the living room, and upstairs, then back down, with her arms full of three presents wrapped in grocery bags and covered with marker and stickers.

Adam's heart lurched.

"Can I give mine first?" Gus asked.

Adam looked to River who peeked at their box, then nodded.

"Sure, sweetie."

"Okay this is for you, Daddy." She handed him the largest package. "This is for you." She gave a slightly smaller one to River. "And this is yours," she told Wes. "I was working on it before you went away, so now you're back and you get a present."

She smiled when she said it so Adam knew she was just being honest, not trying to make Wes feel bad. From Wes' smile, he knew it too.

Adam opened his first.

It was… He had no idea what it was. There were washers and twists of wire and what appeared to be part of a chrome hubcap. The entire thing was beautiful in a brutal, abstract way.

"Thank you, Gus, it's beautiful," Adam said, hoping that would satisfy her. "Maybe you can show me where I should put it to best appreciate it."

Adam caught Wes' eye and saw the humor there.

"It's an invention!" Gus said. "Can't you tell?"

"I absolutely can," Adam said. Because yes, he taught his daughter not to lie. But there was room for a little fib in some instances.

River and Wes unwrapped their gifts, revealing similarly constructed objects.

"What a cool invention," River told Gus, and Gus beamed.

Wes examined his from every angle, then pronounced it perfect.

Gus looked ecstatic.

"Okay, now me," she said.

Adam nudged the box that River had brought toward her.

"Merry Christmas, sweetheart."

Gus bent down and lifted the lid off the box. Adam held his breath. Then a small orange head popped out.

"I thought, since you wanted a pet so much, we could adopt her," Adam said.

River added, "Her name is Neon, but you can totally change it."

Gus patted the cat's head in the box.

"It's really cute," she said. "Thanks."

Gus' reception of River's gift of a litter box, cat food, and some cat toys was similarly lukewarm. Neon's enthusiasm for the toys in particular was far greater.

Adam's heart sank. Gus had so clearly wanted a pet, he'd thought this would be the perfect gift. He'd wanted so badly to make her happy.

"Um," Wes said, looking conflicted. "At the risk of overcrowding the house…"

He pushed the box he'd brought from his house toward Gus. She lifted the lid just as she had on Adam's gift. But this time, her eyes got wide and her mouth fell open as she gasped with joy. Exactly the response Adam had been hoping for and didn't get.

Suddenly, Adam got a very bad, creepy feeling. His eyes flew to Wes.

"I swear, it's not a tarantula," Wes said immediately.

Adam could breathe again.

Wes reached into the box and extracted…an orange and brown lizard.

"Oh my god, I love him!" Gus cried, stroking the lizard and cuddling it to her chest.

She turned to Adam with big, pleading eyes.

"Can I keep him?"

Over her head, Wes grimaced the grimace of the non-child-having when they realized too late that they should have checked with a parent before giving something to a kid. Luckily for everyone, Adam was fine with it.

"As long as you promise to take very good care of it and as long as I never have to touch it."

"I will!"

Adam turned to River.

"I guess I have a cat now," he said.

River grinned. "You'll love Neon. She's the best."

Truth be told, Adam was delighted to have Neon. And if Gus was happy because of Wes' present and not his? It didn't matter. The only thing that mattered was that she *was* happy.

Adam and River made hot chocolate while Gus and Wes got the lizard (whose name, it turned out, was Ludwig) settled in her bedroom. He'd brought an aquarium for it and a jar that he hid behind his back and told Adam he didn't want to know when Adam asked what was in it.

"So," River said. "You and Wes are okay now?"

Adam nodded.

"He just got scared. But everyone deserves a second chance."

"I'm so happy for you," they said. "And for Gus. She really loves him."

"I know. The feeling's mutual."

Adam imagined Wes helping Gus with her science projects and tramping through the woods with her looking for mushrooms or spiders or whatever the hell people looked for in the woods.

"He's gonna make a really, really good dad," Adam said.

River's eyes got wide, but they nodded.

"I think so too."

"What about you, sweetie? Are you seeing anyone?" Adam asked.

A dreamy, mysterious look passed over River's face.

"Not quite…maybe…there's kind of someone," they said. They were flushing at the thought.

"I'm glad," Adam said, handing them a mug of cocoa.

River left around four, citing the need to get back and give the cats their dinner, but now that Adam knew they were not quite, maybe, kind of seeing someone, he wondered if River didn't have a second stop to make.

Gus, high on Christmas adrenaline, her new lizard, and a day full of sugar and running around, crashed out hard right after dinner. Adam carried her to bed and tucked her in, all without looking at what was in the jar that now sat next to the newly ensconced lizard aquarium.

"Hi, Ludwig," Adam said as he passed the tank, in the spirit of Christmas.

Back in the living room, Wes had collapsed on the sofa, head lolling languidly against the cushion.

Adam arranged himself within Wes' arms and pressed a kiss to his lips.

"So this is Christmas," Wes said.

"Yeah. What do you think?"

"I give it a solid nine," Wes said. "Bumped up to a ten for the part where you got yourself a cat for Christmas."

"Oh my god, I know, but she's so cute."

As if Neon could hear the praise being heaped upon her, she padded into the room, walked in a circle, then plopped down in the exact middle of the living room floor and proceeded to fall instantly and adorably asleep.

"Is it okay to go outside for a minute?" Wes asked. "I wanna show you something."

Adam was pretty sure Gus was down for the count. So he bundled up and followed Wes outside into the front yard.

Wes took a pair of binoculars from his coat pocket. He stood behind Adam and wrapped his arms around him, putting the binoculars up to Adam's eyes.

Adam looked and saw the moon, nearly full, hanging heavy in the velvet sky. Lines crisscrossed the cratered surface. It looked unreal.

"Wow," Adam said.

"Sometimes I go outside at night," Wes said. "I have a telescope I take to the roof. I look at the stars and the moon. It's the most beautiful, expansive, peaceful thing. Vast and quiet. And... I wonder what it would be like if there was someone up there with me."

Wes' arms tightened around Adam's stomach and he rested his chin on Adam's shoulder.

"I'm sorry I don't have a real gift for you. But I thought you might like this."

Adam swallowed around the lump in his throat. He felt a happiness that seemed so large it could launch itself outside his body and find a home glowing brightest among the stars.

"It's so damn beautiful," Adam said, voice thick. "I don't care about presents. I have everything I want."

Adam and Wes stood, huddled together, in front of a house dripping with lights that had come from as far away as New York and as near as across the street. They stood in front of that house that yelled *I love you!* and watched the stars move over Garnet Run, Wyoming, as Christmas settled into a memory in the houses nearby.

Once, the residents of Knockbridge Lane had told stories of Westley Mobray the vampire, the witch, the Satanist, the freak.

But Adam knew better.

Wes Mobray was a brilliant, kind, generous, sexy, romantic weirdo. And he was going to be a part of Adam and Gus' family.

Adam leaned his head back and claimed a kiss from the lips of the most amazing man he'd ever known.

By next year, the residents of Knockbridge Lane would tell a very different story. The love story of Wes Mobray and Adam Mills.

* * * * *

FESTIVE FLING WITH THE SINGLE DAD

ANNIE CLAYDON

To Charlotte
With grateful thanks

CHAPTER ONE

UP CLOSE, HE looked even more…

More outdoorsy. Taller and blonder and… Just more. A two-day beard covered a square jaw, and his mane of shoulder-length hair was tied at the nape of his neck. His casual shirt and worn jeans gave the impression of an off-duty Norse god, and Flora McNeith resisted the temptation to curtsey. It was slightly over the top as a greeting for a new neighbour.

'Hi. I'm Flora. From next door.' She gestured towards her own cottage, tugging at Dougal's lead in a fruitless attempt to get him to sit down for just one moment. 'Welcome to the village.'

He looked a little taken aback when she thrust the food box, containing half a dozen home-made mince pies into his hands. It might be more than three weeks until Christmas, but the lights of the Christmas tree in the village had already been turned on, and in Flora's book any time after September was a good time for mince pies.

'That's very kind.' His voice was very deep, the kind of tone that befitted the very impressive chest that it came from. And it appeared that whatever kind of deity Aksel Olson was, language and communication weren't part of his remit. He was regarding her silently.

'I work at the Heatherglen Castle Clinic. I hear that your

daughter, Mette, is a patient there.' Maybe if she explained herself a little more, she might get a reaction.

Something flickered in his eyes at the mention of his daughter. Reflective and sparkling, like sunshine over a sheet of ice.

'Are you going to be part of Mette's therapy team?'

Right. That put Flora in her place. Apparently that was the only thing that interested Aksel about her.

'No, I'm a physiotherapist. I gather that your daughter is partially sighted…' Flora bit her tongue. That sounded as if everyone was gossiping about him, which was half-true. The whisper that Mette's father was single had gone around like wildfire amongst the female staff at the clinic. Now that Flora had met Aksel, she understood what the excitement was all about.

'You read the memo, then?' Something like humour flashed in his eyes, and Flora breathed a small sigh of relief. Lyle Sinclair must have told him about the memo.

'Yes. I did.' Every time a new patient was admitted a memo went round, introducing the newest member of the clinic's community and asking every member of staff to welcome them. It was just one of the little things that made the clinic very special.

'Would you like to come in for coffee?' Suddenly he stood back from the door.

'Oh!' Aksel's taciturn manner somehow made the words he did say seem more sincere. 'I shouldn't… Dougal and I are just getting used to each other and I haven't dared take him anywhere for coffee yet. I'm afraid he'll get over-excited and do some damage.'

Aksel squatted down on his heels, in front of the ten-week-old brindle puppy, his face impassive.

'Hi, there, Dougal.'

Dougal was nosing around the porch, his tail wagging

ferociously. At the sound of his name he looked up at Aksel, his odd ears twitching to attention. He circled the porch, to show off his new red fleece dog coat, and Flora stepped over the trailing lead, trying not to get snagged in it. Then Dougal trotted up to Aksel, nosing at his outstretched hand, and decided almost immediately he'd found a new best buddy. Finally, Aksel smiled, stroking the puppy's head.

'I'm sure we'll manage. Why don't you come in?'

Two whole sentences. And the sudden warmth in his eyes was very hard to resist.

'In that case… Thank you.' Flora stepped into the hallway and Dougal tugged on his lead in delight.

He took her coat, looking around the empty hallway as if it was the first time he'd seen it. There was nowhere to hang it and he walked into the kitchen, draping it neatly over the back of one of the chairs that stood around the table. Flipping open a series of empty cupboards, he found some packets of coffee and a small copper kettle, which seemed to be the only provisions he'd brought with him.

Dougal had recovered from his customary two seconds of shyness over being in a new environment and was tugging at the lead again, clearly having seen the young chocolate-coloured Labrador that was sitting watchfully in a dog basket in the far corner of the kitchen. Flora bent down, trying to calm him, and he started to nuzzle at her legs.

'Kari. *Gi labb.*' In response to Aksel's command, the Labrador rose from its bed, trotting towards them, then sitting down and offering her paw to Flora. Flora took it and Kari then started to go through her own *getting-to-know-you* routine with Dougal.

'She's beautiful.' The Labrador was gentle and impressively well trained. 'This is Mette's assistance dog?'

Aksel nodded. 'Kari's staying with me for a while, until Mette settles in. She's not used to having a dog.'

'Part of the programme, up at the clinic, will be getting Mette used to working with Kari. You'll be taking her there when you visit?'

'Yes. I find that the canine therapy centre has some use for me in the mornings, and I'll spend every afternoon with Mette.'

'It's great that you're here to give her all the support she needs.'

He nodded quietly. 'Mette's sight loss is due to an injury in a car accident. Her mother was driving, and she was killed.'

Flora caught her breath. The rumours hadn't included that tragic detail. 'I'm so sorry. It must be incredibly hard for you both.'

'It is for Mette. Lisle and I hadn't been close for some years.'

All the same, he must feel something... But from the finality in his tone and the hint of blue steel in his eyes, Aksel clearly didn't want to talk about it. She should drop the subject.

Kari had somehow managed to calm Dougal's excitement, and Flora bent down to let him off the lead. But as soon as she did so, Dougal bounded over to Aksel, throwing himself at his ankles. Aksel smiled suddenly, bending towards the little dog, his quiet words and his touch calming him.

'Sorry... I've only had him a couple of days, I'm looking after him for Esme Ross-Wylde.' Aksel must know who Esme was if he was working at the canine therapy centre. Charles and Esme Ross-Wylde were a brother and sister team, Charles running the Heatherglen Castle Clinic, and

Esme the canine therapy centre. 'He's a rescue dog and Esme's trying to find him a good home.'

'You can't take him?' Aksel's blue gaze swept up towards her, and Flora almost gasped at its intensity.

'No...no, I'd like to but...' Flora had fallen in love with the puppy almost as soon as she'd seen him. He'd been half-starved and frightened of his own shadow when he'd first been found, but as soon as he'd been given a little care his loving nature had emerged. The strange markings on his shaggy brindle coat and his odd ears had endeared him to Flora even more.

'It wouldn't be fair to leave him alone all day while you were at work.' Aksel's observation was exactly to the point.

'Yes, that's right. I drop him off at the canine therapy centre and they look after him during the day, but that's a temporary arrangement. Dougal's been abandoned once and at the moment he tends to panic whenever he's left alone.'

Aksel nodded. A few quiet words to Kari, that Flora didn't understand, and the Labrador fetched a play ball from her basket, dropping it in front of Dougal. Dougal got the hint and started to push it around the room excitedly, the older dog carefully containing him and helping him play.

Aksel went through the process of searching through the kitchen cupboards again, finding a baking sheet to put the mince pies on and putting them in the oven to warm. The water in the copper kettle had boiled and he took it off the stove, tipping a measure of coffee straight into it. That was new to Flora, and if it fitted exactly with Aksel's aura of a mountain man, it didn't bode too well for the taste of the coffee.

'I hear you're an explorer.' Someone had to do the getting-to-know-you small talk and Flora was pretty sure that wasn't part of Aksel's vocabulary. He raised his eyebrows in reply.

'It said so in the memo.'

'I *used* to be an explorer.' The distinction seemed important to him. 'I'm trained as a vet and that's what I do now.'

'I've never met anyone who *used* to be an explorer before. Where have you been?'

'Most of South America. The Pole….'

Flora shivered. 'The Pole? North or South?'

'Both.'

That explained why she'd seen him setting off from his cottage early this morning, striding across the road and into the snow-dappled countryside beyond, with the air of a man who was just going for a walk. And the way that Aksel seemed quite comfortable in an open-necked shirt when the temperature in the kitchen made Flora feel glad of the warm sweater she was wearing.

'So you're used to the cold.'

Aksel smiled suddenly. 'Let's go into the sitting room.'

He tipped the coffee from the kettle into two mugs, opening the oven to take the mince pies out and leading the way through the hallway to the sitting room. As he opened the door, Flora felt warmth envelop her, along with the scent of pine.

The room was just the same as the kitchen. Comfortable and yet it seemed that Aksel's presence here had made no impact on it. Apart from the mix of wood and pine cones burning in the hearth, it looked as if he'd added nothing of his own to the well-furnished rental cottage.

Kari had picked the dog toy up in her mouth, and Dougal followed her into the room. She lay down on the rug in front of the fire, and the puppy followed suit, his tail thumping on the floor as Kari dropped the toy in front of him.

'He'll be hot in here. I should take his coat off.' Flora couldn't help grimacing as she said the words. Dougal liked the warm dog coat she'd bought for him, and getting him out of it wasn't as easy as it sounded. Perhaps he'd realise that they were in company, and not make so much of a fuss this time.

Sadly not. As soon as he realised Flora's intent, the little dog decided that this was the best of all times for a game of catch-me-if-you-can. When she knelt, trying to persuade him out from under the coffee table, he barked joyously, darting out to take refuge under a chair.

She followed him, shooting Aksel an apologetic glance. His broad grin didn't help. Clearly he found this funny.

'He thinks this is a game. You're just reinforcing that by joining in with him. Come and drink your coffee, he'll come to you soon enough.'

Right. The coffee. Flora had been putting off the moment when good manners dictated that she'd have to take her first sip. But what Aksel said made sense, and he obviously had some experience in the matter. Flora sat down, reaching for her mug.

'This is…nice.' It *was* nice. Slightly sweeter than she was used to and with clear tones of taste and scent. Not what she'd expected at all.

'It's a light roast. This is a traditional Norwegian method of making it.'

'The easiest way when you're travelling as well.' A good cup of coffee that could be made without the need for filters or machines. Flora took another mouthful, and found that it was even more flavoursome than the first.

'That too. Only I don't travel any more.' He seemed to want to make that point very clear, and Flora thought that she heard regret in his tone. She wanted to ask, but Dougal chose that moment to come trotting out from under the chair to nuzzle at Aksel's legs.

He leaned forward, picking the little dog up and talking quietly to him in Norwegian. Dougal seemed to understand the gist of it, although Flora had no idea what the conversation was about, and Aksel had him out of the dog coat with no fuss or resistance.

'That works.' She shot Aksel a smile and he nodded, lifting Dougal down from his lap so that he could join Kari by the fire.

'You're not from Scotland, are you?' He gave a half-smile in response to Flora's querying look. 'Your accent sounds more English.'

He had a good ear. Aksel's English was very good, but not many people could distinguish between accents in a second language.

'My father's a diplomat, and I went to an English school in Italy. But both my parents are Scots, my dad comes from one of the villages a few miles from here. Cluchlochry feels like home.'

He nodded. 'Tell me about the clinic.'

'Surely Dr Sinclair's told you all you need to know…'

'Yes, he has.' Aksel shot her a thoughtful look, and Flora nodded. Of course he wanted to talk about the place that was going to be Mette's home for the next six weeks. Aksel might be nice to look at—strike that, the man was downright gorgeous—but in truth the clinic was about all they had in common.

The first thing that Aksel had noticed about Flora was her red coat, standing out in the feeble light of a cold Saturday morning. The second, third and fourth things had come in rapid and breathtaking succession. Her fair hair, which curled around her face. The warmth in her honey-brown eyes. Her smile. The feeling in the pit of his stomach told him that he liked her smile, very much.

It was more than enough to convince Aksel to keep his distance. He'd always thought that dating a woman should be considered a privilege, and it was one that he'd now lost. Lisle had made it very clear that he wasn't worthy of it, by not even telling him that they'd conceived a child together. And now that he *had* found out about his daughter, Mette was his one and only priority.

But when he'd realised that Flora worked at the clinic, keeping his distance took on a new perspective. He should forget about the insistent craving that her scent awakened, it was just an echo from a past he'd left behind. He'd made up his mind that being a part of the clinic's community was a way to help Mette. And his way into that community had just turned up on his doorstep in the unlikely form of an angel, struggling to control an unruly puppy.

He'd concentrated on making friends with Dougal first, as that was far less challenging than looking into Flora's eyes. And when she'd started to talk about the work of the children's unit of the clinic, he'd concentrated on how that would help his daughter. *His daughter.* Aksel still couldn't even think the words without having to remind himself that he really did have a daughter.

'I've arranged with Dr Sinclair that Mette will be staying at the clinic full time for the first week, to give her a chance to settle in. After that, she'll be spending time at the weekend and several nights a week here, with me.'

'Oh. I see.' Flora's eyebrows shot up in surprise.

Aksel knew that the arrangement was out of the ordinary. Dr Sinclair had explained to him that most residents benefited from the immersive experience that the clinic offered, but he'd listened carefully to Aksel's concerns about being separated from Mette. The sensitive way that the issue had been handled was one of the reasons that Aksel had chosen the Heatherglen Castle Clinic.

Flora was clearly wondering why Mette was being treated differently from other patients, but she didn't ask. Aksel added that to the ever-growing list of things he liked about her. She trusted the people she worked with, and was too professional to second-guess their decisions.

'Mette and I are still working on…things…' *He* was the one who needed to do the work. He was still practically a stranger to Mette, and he had to work to prove that she could trust him, and that he'd always be there for her.

'Well, I'm sure that whatever you and Dr Sinclair have agreed is best.' She drained her cup and set it down on the small table next to her chair. 'I'm going to the clinic to catch up on a few things this afternoon. Would you mind if I dropped in to see her, just to say hello and welcome her?'

'Thank you. That's very kind…' Sudden joy, at the thought of seeing Flora again turned his heartbeat into a reckless, crazy ricochet. 'I'll be going in to see her this afternoon as well.'

'Oh…' Flora shot him an awkward smile, as if she hadn't expected that eventuality. 'Would you like a lift?'

'Thanks, but Kari needs a walk.' Kari raised her head slightly, directing her melting brown gaze at Aksel. Flora appeared to be taking the excuse at face value, but there was no getting past Kari.

He'd explain. On the way to the clinic, he'd tell Kari about yet another dark place in his heart, the one which made it impossible for Aksel to get too close to Flora. He'd confide his regrets and Kari would listen, the way she always did, without comment.

Dougal had been persuaded to say goodbye to his new-found friends and had followed Flora through the gap in the hedge, back to her own front door. When they were inside, she let him off the lead and he made his usual dash into the kitchen and around the sitting room, just to check that nothing had changed while he'd been away.

She leaned back against the door, resisting the temptation to flip the night latch. Locking Aksel out was all she wanted to do at the moment, but it was too late. He was already giving her that strong, silent look of his. Already striding through her imagination as if he owned it. At the moment, he did.

But if Flora knew anything about relationships, she knew that losing the first battle meant nothing. Aksel might have taken her by surprise, and breached her defences, but she was ready for him now.

Not like Tom... Eighteen, and loving the new challenges of being away from home at university. Her first proper boyfriend. So many firsts...

And then, the final, devastating first time. Flora had gone with Tom to visit his family for a week, and found his parents welcoming and keen to know all about her and her family. But when she'd spoken of her beloved brother, they hadn't listened to anything she'd said about Alec's dry humour, his love of books or how proud Flora was of his tenacious determination to live his life to the full. The only two words they'd heard were 'cystic fibrosis'.

Tom's parents had convinced him that his relationship with Flora must end. She had desperately tried to explain. She might carry the defective gene that caused cystic fibrosis, but she might not and if her children developed the condition then it would be a result of her partner also carrying the gene. Tom had listened impassively.

Then Flora had realised. Tom had already understood that, and so had his parents. Pleading with him to change his mind and take her back would have been a betrayal, of both Alec and herself. She'd gone upstairs and packed her bags, leaving without another word.

'What do you think, Dougal?' The puppy had returned to her side, obviously puzzled that she was still here in the hallway, and probably wondering if she was *ever* going to find her way to the jar in the kitchen that held the dog treats.

No answer. Maybe Dougal had that one right. He'd been abandoned too, and he knew the value of a warm hearth and a little kindness. Flora had found a home here, and she needed nothing else but her work.

'We're going to find you a home too, Dougal. Somewhere really nice with people who love you.' Flora walked into the kitchen, opening the jar of dog treats and giving Dougal one, and then reaching for a bar of chocolate for herself.

Chocolate was a great deal more predictable in the gamut of feel-good experiences. Aksel might be blood-meltingly sexy, and far too beautiful for anyone's peace of mind, but the few fleeting affairs she'd had since the break-up with Tom had shown Flora that desire and mistrust were awkward bedfellows. It was as if a switch had been flipped, and her body had lost its ability to respond. Sex had left her unsatisfied, and she'd given up on it.

If you could trust someone enough...

It was far too big an *if*. She'd kept the reason for her break-up with Tom a secret, knowing that it would hurt Alec and her parents beyond belief. They didn't deserve that, and neither did she. It was better to accept that being alone wasn't so bad and to channel all her energies into her work and being a part of the community here in Cluchlochry.

The next time she saw Aksel, she'd be prepared, and think of him only as a new neighbour and the father of one

of the clinic's patients. When it came to thoughtless pleasure, she had chocolate, which made Aksel Olson's smile
officially redundant.

CHAPTER TWO

AKSEL HAD WALKED the two miles to the clinic, with Kari trotting placidly beside him. It had done nothing to clear his head. Flora's smile still seemed to follow him everywhere, like a fine mist of scent that had been mistakenly sprayed in his direction and clung to his clothes. He was unaware of it for minutes on end, and then suddenly it hit him again. Fleeting and ephemeral, and yet enough to make him catch his breath before the illusion was once again lost.

His feet scrunched on the curved gravel drive. Castle Heatherglen Clinic was a real castle, its weathered stone walls and slate roof blending almost organically with the backdrop of rolling countryside and snow-dappled mountains. The Laird, Charles Ross-Wylde had added a new chapter to its long history and transformed his home into a rehabilitation clinic that offered its patients the best medical care, and welcomed them with a warm heart.

The children's unit was a little less grand than the rest of the building, and the sumptuous accommodation and sweeping staircases had been replaced by bright, comfortable rooms arranged around a well-equipped play area. Aksel had come prepared with a list of things that Mette might like to do, and suitable topics of conversation that might please her. But she seemed restless and bored today, not wanting to sit and listen while he read from her story-books, and laying aside the toys he presented to her. Aksel's heart ached for all that his daughter had been through.

The awkward silence was broken by a knock at the door. Mette ignored it, and Aksel called for whoever it was to come in. Maybe it was one of the play specialists, who were on duty every day, and who might help him amuse his daughter.

Mette looked up towards the door, an instinctive reaction, even though she couldn't see anything that wasn't within a few feet of her.

'Hi, Mette. My name's Flora. May I come and visit you for a little while?' Flora glanced at Aksel and he wondered whether his relief at seeing her had shown on his face.

'Flora's our neighbour in the village, Mette.' He volunteered the information in English, and Mette displayed no interest. Flora sat down on the floor next to them, close enough for Mette to be able to see her face.

'I work here, at the clinic. I'm a physiotherapist.' Mette's head tilted enquiringly towards Flora at the sound of a word she didn't know. 'That means that I help people who are hurt to feel well again.'

'Where do they hurt...?' Mette frowned.

'All sorts of places. Their arms might hurt, or their legs. Sometimes it's their backs or their hips.'

Mette nodded sagely. She'd grown used to being surrounded by doctors and various other medical specialists, and while Aksel valued their kindness, it wasn't what he wanted for his daughter.

'Have you come to make me better?'

The question almost tore his heart out. No one could make Mette better, and he wondered how Flora could answer a question that left him lost for words.

'No, sweetie. I'm sorry, but I can't make your eyes better.' Flora pulled a sad face, the look in her eyes seeming to match his own feelings exactly. 'You have a doctor of your own to look after you. Dr Sinclair is very important around here, and he only looks after *very* important people…'

Flora leaned forward, imparting the information almost in a whisper, as if it were some kind of secret. She was making it sound as if Mette was someone special, not just a patient or a child who couldn't be helped.

'*I've* come because I heard that you were here, all the way from Norway. I'd like to be friends with you, if that's all right?'

Maybe it was the smile that did it. Aksel wouldn't be all that surprised, he'd already fallen victim to Flora's smile. Mette moved a little closer to her, reaching out as if to feel the warmth of the sun.

'I have a little something that I thought you might like…' Flora produced a carrier bag from behind her back, giving a little shiver of excitement. Mette was hooked now, and she took the bag.

'What is it?' There was something inside, and Mette pulled out a parcel, wrapped in shiny paper that caught the light.

'Open it up and see.'

Mette didn't want to tear the wrappings and Flora waited patiently, guiding her fingers towards the clear tape that held it down. It peeled off easily, and Mette got the paper off in one piece, laying it carefully to one side, and started to inspect her gift.

A rag doll, with a brightly coloured dress and a wide smile stitched onto her face. Mette smiled, clutching the doll tightly to her chest.

'Why don't you show her to your dad?'

'Papa, look.' Mette held out the doll, and Aksel's heart began to thump in his chest. It wasn't the gift that had made

Mette smile, but the way it had been given. The way it was wrapped so carefully, and the warmth of Flora's manner.

'It's beautiful… Thank you, Flora.'

'*She's* beautiful, Papa,' Mette corrected him.

'Yes, of course. Sorry. What's her name?'

Mette thought for a moment. 'Annette.' His daughter pronounced the name with a Norwegian inflection and Aksel repeated the English version for Flora.

'That's a lovely name. It sounds even better the way you say it…' Flora waited, and Mette responded, saying the name again so that Flora could mimic her.

This was all so easy, suddenly. Mette laughed over the way that Flora struggled to get her tongue around the Norwegian pronunciation, and when Flora stretched out her arms Mette gave her a hug. So simple, so natural, without any of the thought that Aksel put into his hugs. None of the wondering whether he was going too fast, or too slowly.

But, then, Flora didn't have agonised hope to contend with. Or the feeling that he didn't deserve Mette's hugs. Aksel watched as Mette showed Flora her toys, noticing that Flora didn't help Mette as much as he did, and that his daughter responded to that by becoming more animated.

'What's that?' Flora pointed to a box of jumbo-sized dominoes and Mette opened it, tipping the contents onto the floor. 'Oh, dominoes! I *love* dominoes…'

'Would you like to play?' The words slipped out before Aksel could stop them. He wanted to watch her with Mette for just a little longer.

Flora treated the request as if it was an invitation to a tour of the seven wonders of the world. Mette couldn't resist her excited smile and gave an emphatic '*Yes*!'

'Shall we do that thing first…?' Mette took a few uncertain steps towards Flora, clearly wanting to know what *that thing* was. Aksel wanted to know too. 'Where you stand them all up in a row and then knock them down again?'

Flora started to gather the dominoes together, putting them in a pile on the floor. 'It's such fun. Your papa will show you, I can never get them to balance properly.'

That was a ruse to get him involved. But Flora could manipulate him as much as she liked if this was the result. Aksel sat down on the floor, and started to line the dominoes up in a spiral pattern, seeing his own hand shake with emotion as he did so. Flora and Mette were both watching him intently, Mette bending forward to see.

'Spirals, eh? Show-off…' Flora murmured the words and Aksel felt his shoulders relax suddenly. Maybe this wasn't so difficult after all.

When Flora walked out to her car, it was already getting dark. She'd stayed longer than she'd intended with Aksel and Mette, and the work that she'd expected to take an hour had taken two. That might be something to do with the daydreaming. Aksel's bulk and strength and the gentle vulnerability that little blonde-haired, blue-eyed Mette brought out in him were downright mouth-watering.

He was so anxious to please and yet so awkward with his daughter. Aksel watched over Mette's every move, ready to catch her if there was even the smallest likelihood that she might fall. He meant well, but he was smothering her.

Not your business, Flora. Dr Sinclair will deal with it.

Lyle Sinclair had a way of taking patients or their families aside and gently suggesting new ways of looking at things. And Lyle would have the advantage of not feeling quite so hot under the collar at the mere thought of a conversation with Aksel.

'Flora!'

Flora closed her eyes in resignation at the sound of his voice. However hard she tried to escape him… When she turned and saw him striding across the car park towards her, she didn't want to escape him at all.

'I wanted to thank you.'

He'd done that already. More than once, and in as many words as Aksel seemed capable of.

'It was my pleasure. I always bring a little gift for the children, to make them feel welcome.' She'd told him that already, too. They could go on for ever like this, repeating the same things over and over again.

'I…' He spread his hands in a gesture of helplessness. 'You have a way with children.'

He made it sound as if it was some kind of supernatural power. Flora frowned. 'Children are just…people. Only they're usually a bit more fun.'

'You have a way with *people,* then.'

It was a nice compliment, especially since it was accompanied by his smile. Something was bugging him, but she wasn't the right person to speak to about it. She had too much baggage…

Baggage or experience? Experience was something that she could use to help her get things right this time. She'd been an impressionable teenager when she'd loved Tom, but she knew better now. There was no cosmic rule that said she had to fall for Aksel, and she could handle the regrets over never being able to trust a man enough to build a relationship. If that meant that she'd never be able to sit on the floor and play dominoes with her own child, she could deal with that, too.

Flora turned, opening the rear door of her car and dumping her bags in the footwell. Then she faced him. If all he had to throw at her were longing and regret, she'd already made her peace with them, a long time ago.

'You've said "Thank you" already, there's no need for us to stand in the cold here while you say it again. What's bugging you?'

That was obviously confronting. But the slight twitch at the corners of his mouth told Flora that challenge was one of the things that he thrived on.

He took a breath, as if preparing himself. 'My relationship with Mette's mother was over before Mette was born and we never lived together as a family.'

What was he trying to say? That he'd been an absent father who hardly knew his own child? His obvious commitment to his daughter made that difficult to believe.

'And now?'

'I can't bring her mother back, or her sight. But I'd give anything to make her happy and…' He shrugged. 'It's not working. When I saw you with her this afternoon, I saw how much it wasn't working.'

Flora thought quickly. Aksel needed the kind of professional help that didn't fall within her area of expertise.

'Maybe you should talk to Lyle Sinclair. The clinic has a family counsellor who deals with just these kinds of issues, and Lyle could organise a session for you both.'

He shook his head abruptly. 'Mette's just fine the way she is. I won't put her into counselling just because *I* need to change.'

'Maybe it's not about change, but just getting to know each other better. Kathy uses storytelling a lot in her sessions, to make things fun. I'm sure you have plenty of stories about the places you've been—'

'No.' That sounded like a hard limit. 'That part of my life is over. Mette needs to know that I'll be there for her, always. That I'm not about to leave, and go to places that she can't.'

His heart was in the right place, but his head was way

off course, and lost without a map or compass. This was something she *could* help with; Flora had grown up with a brother who hadn't always been able to do the things that she had. When Alec had been ill, she'd learned how to go out into the world, and to bring something back to share with her brother when she got home.

'Who says that you can't go together?' Flora gave an imperious twitch of her finger, indicating that he should follow her, and started to walk.

Flora seemed impatient with him, as if he was stubbornly refusing to see a simple fact that was obvious to her. On one level, Aksel just wanted to see her smile again. But on another, much more urgent level, he reckoned that Flora could be just as annoyed as she liked, if only it meant that she'd tell him what he was doing wrong. The first lesson he needed to learn was how to follow, rather than lead, and he walked beside her silently.

They reached the gravel driveway outside the clinic, and Flora stopped. 'You think that Mette doesn't know what it's like to be an explorer?'

The warmth in her eyes had been replaced by fire. Aksel swallowed down the thought that he liked that fire, and concentrated on the point that Flora seemed about to make.

'You're going to tell me different, aren't you?'

'Just think about it. She can feel the gravel under her feet, and she can hear it scrunch. If she bends down, she can probably see it. She can feel the snow…' Flora broke off, turning her face up towards the flakes that had started to drift down, and one landed on her cheek. Aksel resisted the temptation to brush it away with his finger, and it melted almost immediately.

'But she can't see any of this.' He turned towards the

mountains in the distance. He'd give his own sight if Mette could just appreciate the beauty of the world around her.

'Exactly. That's where you come in. She needs someone to explore with her, and tell her about the things she can't see for herself.'

'And if it's upsetting for her?'

'Then you respond to what she's feeling and stop. Just as long as it's Mette who's upset by it, and not you.'

She had a point, and this was a challenge he couldn't resist. Aksel's head was beginning to buzz with ideas. 'Maybe I could take a photograph of them. She might be able to hold that up close and see it.'

'*Now* you're thinking... Speak to Lyle and find out whether he thinks that might work for Mette.' Flora seemed to know that she'd lit a fuse and she wasn't taking cover. She wanted more from him.

'Maybe she'd like to go this way.' He started to walk towards the small, sheltered garden at the side of the property and found that Flora was no longer with him. She was standing still, her hands in her pockets, and one eyebrow raised slightly.

If that was the way she wanted to play it. Aksel returned to her side, holding out his arm. 'I'm going to have to guide her there, of course.'

She nodded, slipping her hand into the crook of his elbow. A frisson of excitement accompanied the feel of her falling into step beside him, and Aksel turned his mind to describing the things around them. The darkening bulk of the stone built castle. The sky, still red from the setting sun, and the clouds off to the east, which promised more snow for tonight.

She slipped so easily into a child-like wonder at the things around her. Aksel was considering asking Flora if she might accompany him and Mette when they set out on their own voyage of exploration, but he guessed what her answer might be.

No. You have to do it yourself.

'Careful…!' He'd seen her reach for a rose bush to one side of the path, and Aksel automatically caught her hand, pulling it away. 'It has thorns.'

Something that had been simmering deep beneath the surface began to swell, almost engulfing him. The thought of rose petals, wet with summer rain and vainly attempting to rival the softness of Flora's cheeks, made him shiver.

'All roses do.' She turned her gaze onto him, and Aksel saw a sudden sadness, quickly hidden. 'Will you let Mette miss the rose because of its thorns?'

That was a hard thought to contemplate. Aksel guided her hand, so that her fingers could brush the leaves. 'You must be gentle. In the summer, the rose is the softest of blooms, but the thorns will still hurt you.'

He let her fingers explore the leaves and then the stem, touching the thorns carefully. It seemed to him that the thorns of this world had done Flora some damage, but that she still chose to see roses. She had room in her heart for both Mette and for Dougal, and yet she lived alone. He wanted to ask why, but he didn't dare.

Flora looked up at him suddenly. 'What's next for us to explore, then?'

A whole spectrum of senses and experiences, none of which involved asking personal questions. Aksel took her to the trunk of an old tree, which twisted against the castle wall, and she followed the rough curves of its bark with her fingers. He explained the eerie wail of a fox, drifting towards them from somewhere beyond his own range of vision. The temptation to draw her closer, and let his body shelter her against the wind, hammered against him.

'I can hear water…' Flora seemed intent on playing this game out.

'Over here.' A small stream trickled past the flower beds, curving its way out into the surrounding countryside. Flora's excitement seemed real, and he wondered whether she was play-acting or not.

'I don't think I can get across…' Mette wouldn't be able to jump to the other side, so neither could Flora.

The temptation was just too great. He could justify it by saying that this was what he would have done with Mette, or he could just give in to it and enjoy. Right now, the urge to just enjoy was thundering in his veins.

'I could carry you.' He called her bluff, wondering who'd be the first to blink.

'You're sure you won't drop me?'

He was about to tell her that he'd carried heavier weights, over much more difficult terrain, and then he re-alised that Flora was looking him up and down. This was a challenge that he couldn't back off from.

'Let's find out.' He wound his arm around her back, waiting for her to respond, and Flora linked her hands be-hind his neck. Then he picked her up in his arms.

Stepping across the narrow stream was nothing. Having her close was everything, a dizzying, heady sensation that made Aksel forget about anything else. Her scent in-vaded his senses and all he wanted to do was hold Flora for as long as she'd allow it.

He wondered if she could feel the resonance of his heart pounding against his ribs. Feeling her arms tighten around him, he looked into her face and suddenly he was lost. Her gaze met his, seeming to understand everything, all of his hope and fears and his many, many uncertainties. He might be struggling to keep his head above water, but she was the rock that he clung to.

None of that mattered. Her eyes were dark in the twilight, her lips slightly parted. The only thing that Aksel could think about was how her kiss might taste.

He resisted. It seemed that Flora was too. This was all wrong, but he couldn't make a move to stop it.

'Are you going to put me down now?' She murmured the words, still holding him tight in the spell of her gaze. Aksel moved automatically, setting her back on her feet, and for a moment he saw disappointment in her eyes. Then she smiled.

'Where shall we go next?'

Their voyage of exploration wasn't over. And Aksel had discovered one, basic truth. That he must navigate carefully between the dangerous waters of Flora's eyes, and the absolute need to do his best for Mette.

'Over there.' Light was pooling around a glazed door, which led back into the castle. He needed that light, in order to forget the way that shadows had caressed Flora's face, in a way that he never could.

CHAPTER THREE

FLORA OPENED HER EYES. Sunday morning. A time to relax and think about nothing.

Nothing wasn't going to work. That was when Aksel invaded her thoughts. The night-time dreams of a perfect family, which were usually brushed off so easily when she woke, had been fleshed out with faces. Aksel had been there, and her children had their father's ice-blue eyes. The image had made her heart ache.

And she'd come so close yesterday. Almost done it…

Almost didn't matter. She hadn't kissed him and she wasn't going to. She'd flirted a bit—Flora could admit to that. They'd shared a moment, it was impossible to deny that either. But they'd drawn back from it, like grown-up, thinking people. It took trust to make a relationship, and that was the one thing that Flora couldn't feel any more.

She got out of bed, wrapping her warm dressing gown around her and opening the curtains. Not picturing Aksel at all. Actually, she didn't need to imagine he was there, because he was the first thing she saw when she looked out over the land that bordered the village. Kari was racing to fetch a ball that he'd just flung into the air, and he turned, as if aware of her gaze on him. Seeing her at the window, he waved.

Great. Not only was he intruding into her dreams, he

seemed to have taken over her waking moments now. Flora waved back, turning from the window.

Somehow, Aksel managed to follow her into the shower. Wet-haired, with rivulets of water trickling over his chest. Then downstairs, as butter melted on her toast, he was standing by the stove, making coffee in that little copper kettle of his.

'If he's going to stalk me, then perhaps he should do the washing-up…' Dougal was busy demolishing the contents of his bowl, and gave Flora's comment the disregard that it deserved. Aksel wasn't stalking her. She was doing this all by herself.

The doorbell rang and Dougal rushed out into the hallway, knocking over his water bowl in the process. He was pawing at the front door, barking excitedly, and Flora bent down to pick him up. Then she saw Aksel's dark shadow on the other side of the obscured glass. She jumped back, yelping in surprise, and the shadow suddenly seemed to back away too.

She opened the door, trying to compose herself. At least the real Aksel bothered to wait on the doorstep and didn't just waltz in as if he owned the place.

'Is this too early…?' Today he was clean-shaven, with just the top half of his hair caught back, leaving the rest to flow around his shoulders. How on earth did he get such gorgeous hair to look so masculine? Flora dismissed the question for later, and concentrated on the one he'd asked.

'No. Not at all.' A cold wind was whipping through into the house, and Flora stood back from the door. 'Come in.'

She led the way through to the kitchen, and both he and Kari stepped neatly around the puddle of spilt water from Dougal's bowl. He insisted that he didn't want coffee, and that she should sit down and have her breakfast while he cleared up the mess. Flora sat, taking a gulp from her mug while he fetched a cloth and wiped up the water, washing the bowl in the sink before refilling it for Dougal.

'I assume you didn't just pop in to wipe my kitchen floor for me?' Who knew that a man could look sexy doing housework? If she wasn't very careful, she would find herself fantasising about that, too.

'No. I came to ask you a favour.'

'Fire away.' Flora waved him to a seat, and picked up her toast.

'I did some reorganisation this morning, to prepare for when Mette comes back to the cottage to stay with me.' He frowned, clearly not very pleased with the results. 'I wondered if you might take a look, and tell me what you think? I won't keep you long.'

This was where the fantasy stopped. Mette was a patient at the clinic, and Aksel was a father in need of some help. It was safer, more comfortable ground, even if it was less thrilling. Flora got to her feet.

'Okay. Let's have a look.'

Aksel picked Dougal up in his arms, and all four of them squeezed through the hole in the hedge, Flora shivering as the wind tugged at her sweater. Dougal followed Kari into the sitting room, and He led the way up the stairs. Flora was surprised when he opened the door to the left because this cottage was the mirror image of hers, with the smaller bedroom and a bathroom to the right. She followed him inside.

Aksel had obviously made an effort. There was a toy box with a row of cuddly animals lined up on the top. A single bed stood at the other end of the room with the wardrobe and chest of drawers.

'This is nice. I can see you've covered all the health and safety aspects.' The room was immaculately tidy, which would help Mette find what she wanted. He'd obviously been thinking about trip hazards and sharp edges, and all of the wall sockets had protectors fitted.

'That's easy enough.' Aksel was looking around the room with a dissatisfied gaze. 'It's not very pretty, though, is it?'

It was a bit stark. But that could be fixed easily. 'Why did you choose this room for Mette?'

'It's the biggest.'

'Big isn't always best. In a very large room like this, Mette might find it difficult to orientate herself.'

Aksel thought for a moment, and then nodded, striding across the hallway and opening the door of the other bedroom. Inside, Flora could see a large double bed, which must have come from the main bedroom. This room too was scrupulously tidy, as if Aksel had decided to camp here for the night and would be moving on soon.

He looked around, assessing her suggestion. 'I think you're right. I'll move everything back the way it was.'

'Would you like a hand?' The heavy bedframe must have been a bit of a struggle.

'Thanks, but I'll manage. What else?'

'Well… I'm no expert…'

'Give me your next-door-neighbour opinion.' His smile sliced through all of Flora's resolutions not to interfere too much and she puffed out a breath, looking around.

'You're not here for long so you don't want to make any permanent changes. But it would be great to be able to change the tone and brightness of the light in here to suit her needs. Maybe get some lamps with programmable bulbs that you can take with you when you go?'

He nodded. 'That's a great idea. What else?'

'Taking her toy box downstairs and just having a few cuddly toys up here for bedtime might get her used to the idea that upstairs is for sleeping. If you use bright colours that she can see, it'll help guide her around the room. And what about some textures, a comforter or a bedspread…?'

He walked across to the nightstand next to his bed, picking up a notebook and flipping it open. 'Lights…' He scribbled a note. 'Colours… Textures… Bedspread.'

Flora nodded. 'If you got her a nice bedspread, then perhaps she could use it here and on her bed at the clinic. Then, if she wakes up in the night, she'll have something that feels familiar right there.'

Aksel nodded, scribbling another entry in the notebook. 'Good idea. Anything else?'

'What does Mette like?'

That seemed the hardest question of all to answer. 'Um… Sparkly things, mostly. And she likes it when I read to her. She always wants the same stories over and over again.'

'The ones her mother read to her?'

'Yes. I think they help her to feel more secure.'

'Then use them as a guide. Maybe choose some things that feature in her favourite stories.'

'That's a great idea, thank you.' He made another note in his notebook before putting it into the back pocket of his jeans and striding back to the main bedroom. 'I'll take the toy box downstairs now. If you could suggest a place for it…'

He was trying so hard. Maybe that was the problem, he wanted to make everything perfect for Mette and couldn't be satisfied with anything less. Flora watched as he cleared the cuddly animals from the top of the toy box, trying not to notice how small they looked in his large, gentle hands.

'Oh…wait, I'll give you a hand…' Aksel had lifted

the large wooden box alone, hardly seeming to notice its weight.

'That's all right. If you'll just stand aside.'

She could do that. Flora jumped out of his way, noticing the flex of muscle beneath his shirt as he manoeuvred the box through the doorway. She followed him as he carried it downstairs, swallowing down the lump in her throat. Aksel's strong frame was impressive when he was at rest, but in action it was stunning.

'Over there, maybe…?' He was standing in the centre of the sitting room, looking around with a perplexed look on his face. Flora shifted one of the chairs that stood around the fireside, and he finally put the box down, one hand rubbing his shoulder as he straightened up.

'Is your shoulder all right?' He raised an eyebrow, and Flora felt herself redden. Okay, so she'd been looking at his shoulders. 'Professional interest. I'm a physiotherapist, remember?'

'It's fine. It was just a little stiff this morning.'

His tone told Flora to leave it, so she did. 'Maybe we could move one of the lights so that when Mette opens the box she can see inside better.'

Suddenly Aksel grinned. 'Kari…'

The dog raised her head, moving from relaxed fireside mode to work mode immediately. In response to a command in Norwegian, she trotted over to the box and inserted her paw into a semi-circular hole cut into the side, under the lid. Flora heard a click and the lid swung open smoothly, its motion clearly controlled by a counterbalance mechanism.

The ease of opening was just the beginning. As the box opened, light flooded the inside of the box, and Flora could see that there were small LEDs around the edge, shaded at the top so that they would shine downwards and not dazzle Mette. The contents were carefully arranged in plastic baskets, so that she would be able to find whatever she wanted.

'That's fantastic! Wherever did you get this?'

'I made it. There was nothing on the market that quite suited Mette's needs.' Aksel was clearly pleased with Flora's approval.

She knelt down beside the box, inspecting it carefully. The lid opened easily enough for a child…or a dog…to lift it and the counterbalance mechanism meant that once open there was no danger of it slamming shut on small fingers. The lights came on when the lid opened and flicked off again as it closed, and they illuminated the contents of the box in a soft, clear light.

And the box itself was a masterpiece, made of wooden panels that were smooth and warm to the touch. It was quite plain but that was part of its beauty. The timber had obviously been carefully chosen and its swirling grain made this piece one of a kind.

'Mette must love it.' It was a gift that only a loving and thoughtful father could have made. And someone who was a skilled craftsman as well.

He nodded, looking around the room restlessly as if searching for the next thing that needed to be done. Aksel's response to any problem was to act on it, and he was obviously struggling with the things he could do nothing about. No wonder he was carrying some tension in his shoulders.

'We could go and do some shopping, if you wanted. It won't take long to pick out a few things to brighten Mette's bedroom up.'

'Would you mind…?' He was halfway towards the door, obviously ready to turn thought into action as soon as possible, and then stopped himself. 'Perhaps another time. Whenever it's convenient for you.'

Flora allowed herself a smile. 'Now's fine. I'll go and get my coat.'

Aksel had been struggling to get the fantasy out of his head ever since he'd opened his eyes this morning. Rumpled sheets and Flora's cheeks, flushed with sleep.

Yesterday had shown him how easy it would be to slip into loving intimacy with Flora, but her reaction had told him that she didn't want that any more than he did. The word *impossible* usually made his blood fire in his veins at the thought of proving that nothing was impossible, and it had taken Flora's look of quiet certainty to convince him that there was something in this world that truly was impossible.

He could deal with that. If he just concentrated on having her as a friend, and forgot all about wanting her as a lover, then it would be easy. When she returned, wearing a dark green coat with a red scarf, and holding Dougal's dog coat and lead, he ignored the way that the cottage seemed suddenly full of light and warmth again.

'Why don't you leave him here? They'll be fine together.' The puppy was curled up in front of the fire with Kari, and didn't seem disposed to move.

'You think so?' Flora tickled Dougal's head and he squirmed sleepily, snuggling against Kari. 'Yes. I guess they will.'

She drove in much the same way as she held a conversation. Quick and decisive, her eyes fixed firmly on where she was going. Aksel guessed that Flora wasn't much used to watching the world go by, she wanted always to be moving, and he wondered whether she ever took some time out to just sit and feel the world turn beneath her. He guessed not.

For a woman that he'd just decided *not* to be too involved with, he was noticing a great deal about her. Flora wasn't content with the just-crawled-out-of-bed look for a Sunday morning. She'd brushed her hair until it shone and wore a little make-up. More probably than was apparent, it was skilfully applied to make the most of her natural beauty. She wore high-heeled boots with her skinny jeans, and when she moved Aksel caught the scent of something he couldn't place. Clean, with a hint of flowers and slightly musky, it curled around him, beckoning his body to respond.

'So… Mette's never lived with you before?' She asked the question when they'd got out of the winding country lanes and onto the main road.

'No.' Aksel couldn't think of anything to say to describe a situation that was complicated, to say the least.

'Sorry…' She flipped her gaze to him for a moment, and Aksel almost shivered in its warmth. 'I didn't mean to pry.'

'It's all right. It's no secret. Just a little difficult to explain.'

'Ah. I'll leave it there, then.'

Flora lapsed into silence. 'Difficult to explain' didn't appear to daunt her, she seemed the kind of person who could accept almost anything. He imagined that her patients must find it very easy to confide in her. All their hopes and their most secret despair. Suddenly, he wanted to talk.

'I didn't know that I had a daughter until after Mette's mother died.'

Nothing registered in Flora's face, but he saw her fingers grip the steering wheel a little tighter. Maybe she was wondering what kind of man hadn't known about his own daughter. He wouldn't blame her—he frequently tormented himself with that thought.

'That must be…challenging.'

Her answer was just the thing a medical professional would say. Non-judgemental, allowing for the possibility of pain and yet assuming nothing. Aksel wanted more than that, he wanted Flora to judge him. If she found him wanting then it would be nothing he hadn't already accused himself of. And if she found a way to declare him innocent it would mean a great deal to him.

'What do you think?' He asked the question as if it didn't mean much, but felt a quiver deep in the pit of his stomach.

No reaction. But as she changed gear, the car jolted a little, as if it was reflecting her mood.

'I'd find it very difficult.'

Aksel nodded. Clearly Flora wasn't going to be persuaded to give an opinion on the matter and maybe that was wise. Maybe he should let it drop.

'In…lots of ways.' She murmured the words, as if they might blow up in her face. Flora wanted to know more but she wasn't going to ask.

'Lisle and I split up before either of us knew she was pregnant. I was due to go away for a while, I was leading an expedition into the Andes.' Suddenly his courage failed him. 'It's a fascinating place…'

'I'm sure.' Her slight frown told Aksel that she wasn't really interested in one of the largest mountain ranges in the world, its volcanic peaks, the highest navigable lake on the planet or the incredible biodiversity. To her, the wonders of the world were nothing in comparison to the mysteries of the human heart, and she was the kind of woman who trod boldly in that unknown territory.

He took a breath, staring at the road ahead. 'When I got

back, I heard that Lisle had gone to Oslo for a new job. I think that the job might have been an excuse...'

Flora gave a little nod. 'It does sound that way.'

There was compassion in her voice. Most people questioned why Lisle should have gone to such lengths to keep her pregnancy a secret from him, but Flora didn't seem disposed to make any judgements yet.

'I never saw her again. The first I knew of Mette's existence was when her parents called me, telling me about the accident.'

'That must have been a shock.'

It had changed his world. Tipped it upside down and focussed every last piece of his attention on the child he'd never known he had. '*Shock* is an understatement.'

She flipped a glance at him, then turned her gaze back onto the road ahead. But in that moment Aksel saw warmth in her eyes and it spurred him on, as if it was the glimmer of an evening campfire at the end of a long road.

'Olaf and Agnetha are good people. They never really agreed with Lisle's decision not to tell me about Mette, although they respected it while she was alive. When she died, they decided that Mette needed to know more than just what Lisle had told her. That she had a father but that he was an adventurer, away exploring the world.'

Flora nodded, her lips forming into a tight line. 'And so you finally got to meet her.'

'Not straight away. Mette was in hospital for a while. She had no other serious injuries, she was still in her car seat when the rescue services arrived, but one of the front headrests had come loose and hit her in the face. The blow damaged her optic nerves...'

The memory of having to stand outside Mette's room, watching through the glass partition as Agnetha sat with her granddaughter, was still as sharp as a knife. He'd understood the importance of taking things slowly, but reaching out to touch the cool, hard surface of the glass that had separated them had been agony. Aksel gripped his hands together hard to stop them from shaking.

'Olaf and Agnetha were naturally anxious to take things at whatever pace was best for Mette and I was in complete agreement with that. I dropped everything and went to Oslo, but it was two weeks before they made the decision to introduce me to her. They were the longest two weeks of my life.'

'I imagine so. It must have been very hard for them, too.'

'Yes, it was. They knew me from when I'd been seeing Lisle, but they wanted to make sure that I wouldn't hurt Mette any more than she'd already been hurt. Letting me get to know her was a risk.'

'But they took it. Good for them.'

'Not until I'd convinced them that I wouldn't walk in, shower Mette with presents and then leave again. That was why Lisle didn't tell me about her pregnancy. Because I was always leaving…'

Aksel could hear the bitterness in his own voice. The helpless anger that Lisle hadn't known that a child would make all the difference to him. She'd only seen the man who'd wanted to go out and meet the world, and she'd done what she'd felt she had to do in response to that.

'She must have cared a lot about you.'

That was a new idea. Aksel had been more comfortable with the thought that the only emotion he'd engendered in Lisle's heart was dislike. 'What makes you say that?'

'If the thought of you leaving was such an issue to her, then it must have hurt.'

Guilt was never very far from the surface these days,

but now it felt as if it was eating him up. 'I didn't think of it that way.'

'You're angry with her? For not telling you about Mette?'

Yes, he was angry. Rage had consumed him, but he'd hidden it for Olaf and Agnetha's sake. And now he hid it for Mette's sake.

'Mette loves her mother. I have to respect that.'

He was caught off balance suddenly as Flora swerved left into the service road that led to a large car park. That was the story of his life at the moment, letting other people take the driving seat and finding himself struggling to cope with the twists and turns in the road. She caught sight of a parking spot, accelerating to get to it before anyone else did, and turned into it. Aksel waited for her to reverse and straighten up, and then realised that the car was already perfectly straight and within the white lines.

'I'd want to scream. I mean, I'd go out and find a place where no one could hear me, and *really* scream. Until I was hoarse.'

So she knew something of the healing nature of the wilderness. Aksel hadn't told anyone why he'd taken the train out of Oslo towards Bergen, or that he'd set out alone in the darkness to trek to the edge of one of the magnificent fjords, roaring his anger and pain out across the water.

'I didn't scream, I yelled. But apart from that, you have it right.'

She gave a soft chuckle, regarding him silently for a moment. 'And then you went back home and read all the manuals? Did your best to be a good father, without any of the training and experience that most men get along the way?'

That was exactly how Aksel felt at times. He'd loved Mette from the first moment he'd seen her. But sometimes he found it hard to communicate with her.

'I've made a career out of dealing with the unexpected.'

Flora smiled and the warmth in the car turned suddenly to sticky heat. If he didn't move now, he was going to fall prey to the insistent urge to reach forward and touch her. Aksel got out of the car, feeling the wind's sharp caress on his face.

Flora grabbed her handbag from the back seat, getting out of the driver's seat, and Aksel took his notebook from his pocket, skimming through the list he'd made. 'I should get some Christmas-tree decorations as well while we're here.'

She turned to him, a look of mock horror on her face. 'You don't have any?'

Aksel shrugged. 'I'm used to moving around a lot. Whenever I'm home for Christmas, I go to my sister's.'

'Perfect. I love buying tree decorations, and if I buy any more I won't be able to fit them on the tree.' She scanned the row of shops that skirted the car park, obviously keen to get on with the task in hand. 'It's a good thing we came today, all the best ones will be gone soon.'

CHAPTER FOUR

IT WAS UNLIKELY that *anything* would be gone from the shops for a while yet. The stores that lined the shopping precinct were full of merchandise for Christmas, and rapidly filling up with people. Flora ignored that self-evident fact. It was never too early for Christmas.

Unlikely as it might be, Aksel seemed slightly lost. As someone who could find his way to both the North and South poles, a few shops should be child's play. But he was looking around as if a deep crevasse had opened up between him and where he wanted to be and he wasn't sure how to navigate it. Flora made for the entrance to the nearest store.

'What sort of decorations did you have in mind?' The in-store Christmas shop shone with lights and glitter, and was already full of shoppers.

'Um… Can I leave myself in your hands?'

Nice thought. Flora would have to make sure it stayed just a thought. She smiled brightly at him and made for some glass baubles, finding herself pushed up against Aksel in the crush of people.

'These are nice…'

'We'll take them. What about these?' He picked up a packet of twisted glass icicles.

'They're lovely.' Flora dropped a packet for herself into

the basket, despite having decided that she already had too many tree decorations.

As they left the shop, Aksel gazed longingly at the entrance to the DIY store, but Flora walked determinedly past it, and he fell into step beside her.

An hour later they'd filled the shopping bags that Flora had brought with her, and Aksel was laden down with them.

He peered over her shoulder as Flora consulted the list he'd torn from his notebook, ticking off what they already had and putting a star next to the more specialised home-support items that the clinic could supply him with. That left the bedspread.

'I saw a shop in the village that sells quilts. They looked nice.' He ventured a suggestion.

'Mary Monroe's quilts are gorgeous. But they're handmade so they're expensive. You can get a nice bedspread for much less at one of the big stores here…'

Aksel shook his head. 'I liked the look of the place in the village.'

'Right. We'll try that first, then.'

Aksel was shaping up to be the perfect shopping companion, patient and decisive. He didn't need to sit down for coffee every twenty minutes, and he was able to carry any number of bags. Maybe if she thought of him that way, the nagging thump of her heart would subside a little. It was a known fact that women had lovers and shopping companions, and that the two territories never overlapped.

It wasn't easy to hold the line, though. When he loaded the bags into the boot of the car, Flora couldn't help noticing those shoulders. Again. And the fifteen-minute drive back to the village gave her plenty of time to feel the scent of fresh air and pine cones do its work. By the time they drew up outside Village Quilts she felt almost dizzy with desire.

A little more shopping would sort that out. Shopping beat sex every time. And this was the kind of shop where you had to bring all your concentration to bear on the matter in hand. Mary Monroe prided herself on making sure that she was on first-name terms with all her customers, and if they could be persuaded to sit on one of the rickety chairs while she sorted through her entire stock to come up with the perfect quilt, then all the better.

But Aksel wasn't going to be confined to a chair. The introductions were made and he sat down but then sprang to his feet again. 'Let me help you with that, Mary.'

Mary was over a foot shorter than him, slight and grey-haired. But she was agile enough on the ladder that she needed to reach the top shelves, and never accepted help.

'Thank you.' Mary capitulated suddenly. Maybe she'd decided that sixty was a good age to slow down a bit, but she'd never shown any sign of doing so. And when Flora rose from her chair to assist, Mary gave her a stern glare that implied no further help was needed.

Aksel lifted the pile of heavy quilts down from the top shelf and Mary stood back. Maybe she was admiring his shoulders, too.

'Your little girl is partially blind…' Mary surveyed the pile thoughtfully.

'Yes. Something that's textured might be good for her.' Flora decided that this didn't really fall into the category of help, it was just volunteering some information.

'What about a raw-edged quilt?' Mary pulled a couple from the pile, unfolding them. 'You see the raw edges of each piece of fabric are left on the top, and form a pattern.'

The quilts were rich and thick, and each square was surrounded by frayed edges of fabric and padding. Aksel ran his fingers across the surface of one and smiled. 'This will do her very nicely. Do you have something a bit more colourful? Mette can see strong colours better.'

'That pile, up there.' Mary didn't even move, and Aksel lifted the quilts down from the shelf. Flora rose, unfolding some of the quilts.

'This one's beautiful, Mary!' The quilt had twelve square sections, each one appliquéd with flowers. Mary beamed.

'I made that one myself. It's a calendar quilt...'

Flora could see now that the flowers in each square corresponded to a month in the year. December was a group of Christmas trees on snowy white ground, the dark blue sky scattered with stars.

'Not really what you're looking for.' Mary tugged at a raw-edged quilt that was made from fabrics in a variety of reds and greens. 'How about this one?'

Aksel nodded, turning to Flora. 'What do you think.'

'Do you like it?'

'Very much.' He ran his fingers over the quilt, smiling. 'I'll take this one.'

'I have more to show you.' Mary liked her customers to see her full stock before making any decisions, but Aksel's smile and the quick shake of his head convinced her that, in this instance, they didn't need to go through that process.

'I like this one, too.' He turned his attention back to the calendar quilt, examining the different squares. 'These are all Scottish plants and flowers?'

'Yes, that's right. I design my quilts to reflect what I see around me. But this one doesn't have the texture that your daughter might like.'

'It would be something to remind us of our trip to Scotland. Perhaps I could hang it on the wall in her room. May I take this one too?'

'No, you may not.' Mary put her hands on her hips. 'My quilts are made with love, and that's why they'll keep you warm. They are *not* supposed to be hung on the wall.'

'If I were to promise to keep it in my sitting room? Something to wrap Mette in on cold winter nights and remind us both of the warm welcome we've had here. The raw-edged one will stay on her bed.' Aksel gave Mary an imploring look and she capitulated suddenly.

'That would be quite fine. You're sure you want both?'

Aksel nodded. If Mary could be an unstoppable force at times, she at least knew when she'd come into contact with an immovable object. Something had to give, and she did so cheerfully.

'You'll give this one to your daughter as a present?' She started to fold the raw-edged quilt.

'Yes.'

'I've got some pretty paper in the back that'll do very nicely. I'll just slip it into the bag and you can do the wrapping yourself.' Mary bustled through a door behind the counter, leaving them alone.

'You're sure?' Flora ran her hand over the quilts. They were both lovely, but this was a big expense, and she was feeling a little guilty for suggesting it.

'I'm sure. I'll have a whole house to furnish back in Norway, and these will help make it a home for Mette.'

'You don't have a place there already?'

'I've never been in one place long enough to consider buying a house. Mette and I have been staying with Olaf and Agnetha—their house is familiar to her and they have more than enough room. I've bought a house close by so that we can visit often.'

Flora wanted to hug him. He'd been through a lot, and he was trying so hard to make a success of the new role he'd taken on in life. She watched as Mary reappeared, bearing a large carrier bag for Aksel and taking the card that he produced from his wallet.

They stepped outside into the pale sunshine and started to walk back towards Flora's car.

'I'll give the quilt to Mette tomorrow when you're at the clinic. Will you come and help me?'

'No! It's *your* present. Aren't you going to see her this afternoon?' Flora would have loved to see Mette's face when she opened the quilt, but this was Aksel's moment.

'Yes. I just thought…' He shrugged. 'Maybe it would be more special to her if you were there.'

'It's your present. And you're her father. She can show it to me when I come and visit.' Flora frowned. 'You really haven't had that much time alone with her, have you?'

Aksel cleared his throat awkwardly. 'Almost none. I relied a lot more heavily on Olaf and Agnetha to help me than I realised.'

'And how is Mette ever going to feel safe and secure with you if you can't even give her a present on your own? You've got to get over this feeling that you're not enough for her, Aksel.' Maybe that was a little too direct. But Aksel always seemed to appreciate her candour.

'Point taken. In that case, I don't suppose you have a roll of sticky tape you could lend me?'

'Yes, I have several. You can never have too much sticky tape this close to Christmas.'

He chuckled quietly. 'You'd be happy to celebrate Christmas once a month, wouldn't you?'

Flora thought for a moment. The idea was tempting. 'Christmas is special, and once a year is just fine. It gives me loads of time to look forward to it.'

'There's that. I'm looking forward to my first Christmas with Mette.'

'You're not panicking yet?'

'I'm panicking. I just disguise it well.'

Flora grinned up at him. 'It'll be fine. Better than fine, it'll be brilliant. Christmas at the castle is always lovely.'

'Just your kind of place, then.'

Yes, it was. Cluchlochry was home, and her work at the clinic was stimulating and rewarding. Flora had almost managed to convince herself that she had everything that she wanted. Until Aksel had come along...

She felt in her pocket for her car keys, watching as Aksel stowed the quilts in the back seat with the rest of their shopping. She'd found peace here. An out-of-the-way shelter from the harsh truths of life, where she could ignore the fact that she sometimes felt she was only half living. And Aksel was threatening to destroy that peace and plunge her into a maelstrom of what-ifs and maybes. She wouldn't let him.

Aksel had spent a restless night just a few metres away from her. Even the thick stone wall between Flora's bedroom and his couldn't dull the feeling that anytime now she might burst through, bringing light and laughter. He imagined her in red pyjamas with red lips. And, despite himself, he imagined her out of those red pyjamas as well.

He set out before dawn with Kari, walking to the canine therapy centre, which was situated in the grounds of the Heatherglen Castle Estate. As they trekked past the clinic, Aksel imagined Mette, stirring sleepily under her quilt. She'd loved it, flinging her arms around his neck and kissing him. Each kiss from his little girl was still special, and every time he thought about it, his fingers moved involuntarily to his cheek, feeling the tingle of pleasure.

Esme Ross-Wylde was already in her office, and took him to meet his new charges, dogs of all kinds that were being trained as PAT dogs. For the next few weeks Aksel would be helping Esme out with some of the veterinary duties, and he busied himself reading up on the notes for each dog.

A commotion of barking and voices just before nine o'clock heralded Flora's arrival with Dougal, and Aksel resisted the temptation to walk out of the surgery and say hello. There was a moment of relative peace and then Esme appeared, holding Dougal's lead tightly.

'Flora tells me that Kari's made friends with this wee whirlwind.' She nodded down at Dougal, raising her eyebrows when, on Aksel's command, Kari rose from her corner and trotted over to Dougal. The little dog calmed immediately.

'Yes. He just needs plenty of attention at the moment.'

'I don't suppose you could take him for a while, could you? Give everyone else a bit of peace? He's a great asset when it comes to teaching the dogs to ignore other dogs, but he's getting in the way a bit at the moment.'

Aksel nodded and Esme smiled. 'Thanks. You know that Flora works at the clinic…?' The question seemed to carry with it an ulterior motive.

'Yes, she came to introduce herself on Saturday, and she's been helping me settle in. We went shopping for Mette yesterday.'

Esme chuckled. 'Shopping's one of Flora's greatest talents. Along with physiotherapy, of course.'

'We found everything that we needed.' The idea that yesterday hadn't been particularly special or much out of the ordinary for Flora was suddenly disappointing. It had been special to him, and the look on Mette's face when he'd helped her unwrap her new quilt had been more precious than anything.

'I've no need to make any introductions, then. I've been talking to the manager of a sheltered housing complex near here—her name's Eileen Ross. We're looking at setting up a dog visiting scheme there and I thought that might be something I could hand over to you. Flora visits every week for a physiotherapy clinic, maybe you could go along with her tomorrow and see how the place operates.'

'I'd be very happy to take that on. I've seen a number of these schemes before, and I know that the elderly benefit a great deal from contact with animals.' The tingle of excitement that ran down his spine wasn't solely at the thought of the medical benefits of the visit.

'So I can put this on the ever-growing list of things that you'll take responsibility for while you're here?'

Aksel nodded. He wasn't aware of such a list and wondered whether it was all in Esme's head. She ran a tight ship here at the centre, and he'd already realised that she was committed to exploring new possibilities whenever she could.

'Leave it with me. I'll have a report for you next week.'

'Marvellous. I'll give Flora a call and let her know that's what we're planning. Is an eight-thirty start all right for you?'

'That's fine. Is the sheltered housing complex within walking distance from Cluchlochry?'

Esme chuckled. 'It depends what you call walking distance. I doubt Flora would think so. You don't have a car?'

'No.'

'We have an old SUV that you can use while you're here. It's a bit bashed around and it needs a good clean, but it'll get you from A to B.'

'Thank you, that's very kind. I'll pick it up in the morning if that's okay.'

'Yes, that's fine. I'll leave the keys at Reception for you.'

CHAPTER FIVE

FLORA HAD ALLOWED herself to believe that going to Mette's room at lunchtime, when she knew Aksel would be there, was just a matter of confirming their visit to the sheltered housing complex tomorrow morning. But when she found him carefully threading Mette's fingers into a pair of red and white woollen gloves, the matter slipped her mind. The two of them were obviously planning on going somewhere as Mette was bundled up in a red coat and a hat that matched her gloves, and Aksel had on a weatherproof jacket.

'Hi, Mette.' Flora concentrated on the little girl, giving Aksel a brief smile, before she bent down towards Mette, close enough that she could see her. 'You look nice and warm. Are you going somewhere?'

Mette replied in Norwegian. Her English was good enough to communicate with all the staff here, but sometimes she forgot when she needed to use it.

'English, Mette.' Aksel gave his daughter a fond smile. If there had ever been any doubt about his commitment to the little girl, it was all there in his eyes. 'We're going on an expedition.'

'Papa says there's a river, and we have to jump across it.' Mette volunteered the information, and Flora felt a tingle run down her spine at the thought of the trickle of water, and how she'd crossed it in Aksel's arms.

Aksel flashed her a grin. 'Dr Sinclair thought that your idea was a good one.'

Okay. Flora wondered whether Aksel had shared her other ideas, and hoped that Lyle wouldn't think she'd been interfering. She'd just been trying to help…

'Don't look so alarmed. I told him that I'd asked you for some ideas and that you'd been very kind.' He smiled.

Fair enough. It was disconcerting that he'd been able to gauge her thoughts so easily from her reaction, and she wished that he'd do as everyone else did, and wait for her to voice them. But Aksel was nothing if not honest, and it was probably beyond him not to say what was on his mind.

Before she could think of a suitable answer, Lyle Sinclair appeared in the doorway, holding a flask and a large box of sandwiches. The kitchen staff never missed an opportunity to feed anyone up, and it appeared that Aksel was already on their culinary radar.

'Hello, Mette. You're off to explore with your dad, are you?' He put the sandwiches down and bent towards the little girl, who looked up at him and nodded. Lyle looked around, as if wholly satisfied with the arrangement.

'Are you going too, Flora?'

'Um… No. Probably best to leave them to it.' This was something that Aksel and Mette needed to do alone. And any reminder of the almost-kissing-him incident was to be avoided.

'Yes, of course.' Lyle beamed at her. His quiet, gentle manner was more ebullient than usual, and Flora suspected that had a great deal to do with Cass Bellow's return from the States.

'How is Cass? I haven't seen her yet.'

'She's fine.' Lyle seemed to light up at the mention of

her name. 'A little achy still, she was hoping you might have some time to see her in the next couple of days.'

'How about tomorrow afternoon? Would you like me to give her a call?'

'No, that's fine, I'll let her know and get her to call you and arrange a time. In the meantime, I won't keep you. I'll see you later, Mette.' Lyle touched Mette's hand in farewell and swept back out of the room.

'What's going on there?' Aksel had been watching quietly.

'Just a little romance. Actually, quite a lot of it, from what I've heard.' Flora liked Cass a lot, and she was happy for Lyle.

'That's nice.' Aksel's face showed no emotion as he turned his attention back to Mette's gloves, picking up the one she'd discarded on the floor. Clearly he was about as impressed with the idea of romance as Flora was, and that made things a great deal easier between them.

'You're really not going to come with us?' He didn't look up, concentrating on winding Mette's scarf around her neck.

'I'll come and wave you off.' Flora grinned at Mette. 'You've got to have someone wave you goodbye if you're going on an expedition.'

Aksel put the sandwiches into a daypack and made a show of going through its contents with Mette, explaining that the most important part of any expedition was to make sure it was properly provisioned. This particular journey required three glitter pens, a packet of sweets and Mette's rag doll.

Downstairs, Mette solemnly let the receptionist know where they were going and when they'd be back, and that they'd be documenting their journey thoroughly with photographs. Flora accompanied them outside, wrapping her arms around herself against the cold.

'I want to ride, Papa.'

'All right.' Aksel bent down, lifting Mette up and settling her securely on his shoulders, and she squealed with glee. He said something in Norwegian, clearly instructing Mette to hold on tight, and she flung her arms around his head.

He was standing completely still, blinded suddenly. Flora laughed, moving quickly to remove Mette's arms from over his eyes. 'Not like that, sweetheart. Papa can't see.'

'Thanks.' Aksel shot her a slow smile, and it happened again. That gorgeous, slightly dizzy feeling, as if they were the only two people on the planet, and they understood each other completely.

Flora wrenched her gaze away from his, reaching up to pull Mette's hat down firmly over her ears. The little girl chuckled, tapping the top of her father's head in an obvious signal to start walking.

Flora waved them goodbye, calling after them, and Aksel turned so that Mette could wave one last time. She watched them until they disappeared around the corner of the building, two explorers off to test the limits of Mette's world. Maybe Aksel's too.

Aksel had wondered whether Flora might come to say goodnight to Mette when she finished work. His disappointment when she didn't wasn't altogether on behalf of his daughter, however much he tried to convince himself that it was.

They had a connection. It was one of those things that just happened, forged out of nothing between two people who hardly knew each other. He could do nothing about it, but that didn't mean he had to act on it either. The days when he'd had only himself to consider were gone.

The evening ritual of reading Mette a story and then carrying her over to her bed calmed him a little. As he settled her down, cosy and warm under the quilt, he heard a quiet tap on the door and it opened a fraction.

'What are you still doing here?' Flora's working day had finished hours ago, but he couldn't help the little quiver of joy that gripped his heart.

'I've been working late. I just wondered how your expedition went.'

'We went across a big river! And back again.' Mette was suddenly wide awake again. 'Will you come with us next time, Tante Flora?'

Flora blushed, telling Mette that she would. Aksel wondered whether it gave her as much pleasure to hear the little girl call her *Tante* as it did when she called him Papa. He'd decided with Olaf and Agnetha that they wouldn't push her, and that Mette should call him whatever she felt comfortable with, but the first time she'd used Papa, Aksel hadn't been able to hide his tears.

'It means aunt. Don't be embarrassed, she calls a lot of people *tante* or *onkel*.' Flora's reluctance to be seen to be too close to the little girl in front of Dr Sinclair had been obvious.

'And I was hoping it was just me...' Flora smiled as if it was a joke, but Aksel saw a flash of longing in her eyes, which was hidden as quickly as it had appeared.

'Not usually so quickly.' Aksel tried to take the thought back, turning to his daughter and arranging the bedcovers over her again. 'Are you ready to say goodnight, Mette?'

'I want Tante Flora to say it with me...' Mette reached for the cabinet by the side of her bed, carefully running her fingers across its edge. Aksel bit back the instinct to help her, waiting patiently for her to find what she wanted by touch. The clinic staff had told him that he should let her do as much as she could by herself, but each time he had to pause and watch her struggling to do something that came so naturally to other children, he felt consumed with the sadness of all that Mette had lost.

'It's okay…' Flora whispered the words. They were for him, not Mette, and when he looked at her, he saw understanding. She could see how much this hurt, and was enforcing the message that it was what he must do, to allow Mette to learn how to explore her world.

Not easy. He mouthed the words, and Flora nodded.

'I know. You're doing great.'

Mette had found what she wanted, and she clutched the small electric light in her hand as she snuggled back under the covers. When she tipped it to one side, light glimmered inside the glass, as if a candle had been lit.

She hadn't done that for a few days, and Aksel hadn't pushed the issue, leaving Mette to do as she wanted. Maybe it was Flora's presence, her warmth, that had made Mette think of her mother tonight.

'Say goodnight to Mama.' Mette directed the words at Flora and she glanced questioningly at Aksel.

'Her grandmother gave her this. Mette switches it on when she wants to talk to Lisle and then we pretend to blow out the candle.'

'That's a lovely thing to do.' Flora's smile showed that she understood that this was an honour that Mette usually didn't share with people outside the family.

They each said their goodnights, Mette including Tante Flora in hers. Flora leaned forward, kissing Mette, and then turned, leaving Aksel to kiss his daughter goodnight alone.

She was waiting outside the door, though. The connection, which grew stronger each time he saw her, had told Aksel that she'd be there and it hadn't let him down yet.

'Would you like a lift home?'

Aksel shook his head. 'No. Thanks, but I want to go and have a word with Dr Sinclair. He said he'd still be here.'

'I can wait.'

'I'd prefer to walk. It clears my head.' It also didn't carry with it the temptation to ask Flora into his cottage for a nightcap. By the time he got home, he would have persuaded himself that the light that burned in her porch in the evenings was something that he could resist.

'I think I prefer a head full of clutter to walking in the cold and dark.' She gave him a wry smile and started to walk slowly towards the main staircase.

There was no one around, and they were dawdling companionably along the corridor. He could ask her now...

A sixth sense warned Aksel that he couldn't. Someone like Flora must have men lining up to ask her out, but she obviously had no partner. No children either. He wanted to ask about the welcome gifts she gave to all the kids at the clinic, and the quickly veiled sadness he'd seen in her eyes. But he didn't have the words, and something told him that even if he did, Flora would shut his enquiries down.

A couple of nurses walked past them, and Flora acknowledged them with a smile. The moment was gone.

'So... You're still okay for eight thirty tomorrow? To visit the housing complex?'

Flora nodded. 'I'll be ready.'

'Esme's offered me the use of one of the therapy centre's vehicles, so I'll drop in there to get the keys first thing and then pick you up.'

'Oh, great. I'll see you then.' She gave him a little wave, making for the main staircase, and Aksel watched her go.

Flora was an enigma. Beautiful and clever, she seemed

to live inside a sparkling cocoon of warmth. When she was busy, which seemed to be most of the time, it was entirely believable to suppose that she had everything she wanted.

But he'd seen her with Mette, and he'd seen the mask slip. Beneath it all was loneliness, and a hint of sadness that he couldn't comprehend. Maybe he saw it because he too was searching for a way forward in life. Or perhaps the connection between them, which he'd given up trying to deny, allowed him to see her more clearly.

But this chance to work together would set his head straight. Aksel had made up his mind that it would banish the thought that Flora could be anything else to him, other than a friend and colleague. And when he made up his mind to do something, he usually succeeded.

CHAPTER SIX

FLORA SAW THE battered SUV draw up outside at ten to eight the following morning. Aksel was early, and she gulped down her coffee, hurrying into the hall to fetch Dougal's lead. But the expected knock on her door didn't come.

When she looked again, she saw Aksel had opened the bonnet of the SUV and was peering at the engine. He made a few adjustments and then started the engine again. It sounded a bit less throaty than it had before.

That was a relief. The therapy centre's SUV had done more miles than anyone cared to count, and although it was reliable it could probably do with a service. Aksel looked at the engine again, wiping something down with a rag from his back pocket and then seemed satisfied, closing the bonnet and switching off the engine. Then he walked up the front path of his cottage, disappearing inside.

Fair enough. He'd said half past eight, and that would give her time to make herself some toast. She put Dougal's lead back in the hall and he gave her a dejected look.

'We'll be going soon, Dougal.' The little dog tipped his head up towards her at the mention of his name and Flora bent to stroke his head.

When she wandered back into the sitting room, still eating the last of her toast, she saw that Aksel was outside again, in the car and that it was rocking slightly as he moved around inside it. Flora put her coat on and Dougal once again sprang to the alert, realising that this time they really were going to go.

'What are you doing?' Flora rapped on the vehicle's window, and Aksel straightened up.

'Just…tidying up a bit. I didn't realise this car was such a mess when I offered you a lift.'

He tucked a cloth and a bottle of spray cleaner under the driver's seat and opened the car door. The scent of kitchen cleaner wafted out, and something about Aksel's manner suggested that he'd really rather not have been caught doing this.

'It sounds as if it's running a lot better.' Flora wondered if she should volunteer her car for the journey, but it seemed ungrateful after he'd spent time on the SUV.

'I made a few adjustments. The spark plugs really need to be replaced, I'll stop and get some if we pass somewhere that sells car parts. They'll be okay for the distance we have to do.'

'I'm sure they will. It's not exactly a trip into the wilderness. And if the SUV breaks down, we can always call the garage.'

He grinned suddenly, as if she'd understood exactly what he was thinking. 'Force of habit. When you're miles away from anywhere, you need a well-maintained vehicle. I'll just go and fetch Kari.'

The dogs were installed on the cushioned area behind the boot divider, amidst a clamour of excited barking from Dougal. Aksel stowed Flora's bag of medical supplies on the back seat, and then gave the passenger door a sharp tug to open it. Flora climbed in, noticing that both the seat and the mat in the footwell were spotlessly clean.

'You didn't need to do all this…'

'You don't want to get your coat dirty.' Aksel looked a

little awkward at the suggestion he'd done anything. He closed the passenger door and rounded the front of the vehicle.

All the same, it would have been a nice gesture on anyone's part, and on Aksel's it was all the sweeter. He clearly hadn't given the same attention to his own seat, and Flora leaned over to brush some of the mud off it before he got in.

'Anything I should know about the sheltered housing?' He settled himself into the driver's seat, ignoring the remains of the mud, and twisted the ignition key. The engine started the first time.

'It's a group of thirty double and single units, designed to give elderly people as much independence as possible. Residents have their own front doors, and each unit has a bedroom, a sitting room and a kitchenette. There's a common lounge, and a dining room for those who don't want to cook, and care staff are on hand at all times to give help when needed.'

'And what's your part in all of this?'

'I'm the Tuesday exercise lady. Mondays is chiropody, Wednesdays hairdressing. The mobile library comes on a Thursday, and Friday is shopping list day.'

'And everyone gets a rest at the weekend?'

'Kind of. Saturday is film night, and that can get a bit rowdy.'

He chuckled. 'So you just hold an exercise class?'

'No, I hold one-to-one consultations as well. I have a lady with a frozen shoulder and one who's recovering from a fractured wrist at the moment. And I also hold sessions for family members during the evenings and at weekends to show them how to assist their elderly relatives and help keep them as active as possible. Just a little of the right exercise makes a huge difference.'

'It sounds like a good place.' He manoeuvred into the

drive-through entrance of the canine therapy centre and retrieved Dougal's lead from the back seat. 'I'm almost tempted to book myself in for a couple of weeks.'

'You don't strike me as the kind of person who likes a quiet life.'

Aksel shot her a sideways glance, the corners of his mouth quirking down for a moment. 'I'm leaving what I used to be behind. Remember?'

He got out of the car, opening the tailgate and lifting Dougal out, leading him towards the glass sided entrance. Dougal bounded up to the young man at the reception desk, and Aksel gave him a smiling wave. Flora wondered exactly who he was trying to fool. Everything about Aksel suggested movement, the irresistible urge to go from A to B.

'So you're not convinced that Mette will benefit from sharing your experiences?' By the time he'd returned to the car, Flora had phrased the question in her head already so that it didn't sound too confronting.

He chuckled. 'Spare me the tact, Flora. Say what's on your mind.'

'All right. I think you're selling yourself short. And Mette.'

He started the car again. 'It's one thing to take her on pretend expeditions. But I have to change, I can't leave her behind and travel for months at a time.'

'No, of course you can't. But that doesn't mean that have to give up who you are. You can be an explorer who stays home...'

'That's a lot harder than it sounds.'

She could hear the anger in his voice. The loss.

'Is losing yourself really going to help Mette?'

'I don't know. All I know is that who I used to be kept

me apart from her for five years. I can't forgive myself for that, and I don't want to be that person any more.'

His lips were set in a hard line and his tone reeked of finality. There was no point in arguing, and maybe she shouldn't be getting so involved with his feelings. She sat back in her seat, watching the reflection of the castle disappear behind them in the rear-view mirror.

It wasn't fair, but Aksel couldn't help being angry. Flora had no right to constantly question his decisions, Mette wasn't her child. If she'd been faced with the same choice that he had, she'd understand.

But he couldn't hold onto his anger for very long, because he suspected that Flora *did* understand. She'd seen his guilt and feeling of inadequacy when faced with the task of bringing up a child. She saw that he loved Mette, too, and that he would do whatever it took to make her happy. And she saw that even though he was ashamed to admit it, he still sometimes regretted the loss of his old life.

In that old life, the one he'd firmly turned his back on, he would have loved the way that she understood him so well. He would have nurtured the connection, and if it led to something more he would have welcomed it. But now, even the thought of that made him feel as if he was betraying Mette. The anger that he directed at Flora should really be directed at himself.

By the time they drew up outside the modern two-storey building, nestling amongst landscaped gardens, he'd found the ability to smile again. It wasn't difficult when he looked at Flora. She got out of the car, shouldering her heavy bag before he had a chance to take it from her.

'The exercise does me good.' She grinned at him.

'All that weight on one shoulder?' He gave her a look

of mock reproach. 'If I were a physiotherapist, I'm sure that I'd have something to say about that.'

She tossed her head. 'Just as well you're not, then. Leave the musculoskeletal issues to me, and I won't give Kari any commands.'

'She won't listen to you anyway, she understands Norwegian.'

'If you're going to be like that…' Flora wrinkled her nose in Aksel's direction, and then directed her attention to Kari. 'Kari, *gi labb*.'

Her pronunciation left a bit to be desired, but Kari got the message. She held out her paw and Flora took it, grimacing a little at the weight of the bag as she bent over. As she patted Kari's head, Aksel caught the strap of the bag, taking it from her.

'If you're going to speak Norwegian to my dog, then all bets are off.' He slung the bag over his shoulder, feeling a stab of pain as he did so. He ignored it, hoping that Flora hadn't noticed.

Inside the building, a woman at a large reception desk greeted Flora, and they signed the visitors' book.

'Here's your list for today. Mr King says that he has a crawling pain in his leg.'

'Okay. I'll take a look at that, then.' Flora seemed undeterred by the description. 'I'll go and see Mrs Crawford first.'

'I think you'll find she's a great deal better. She said that she'd been able to raise her arm enough to brush her hair the other day.' The smiling receptionist was clearly one of those key people in any establishment who knew exactly what was going on with everyone.

'Great. Thanks. My colleague's here for a meeting with Eileen. Is she around?'

'Yes, she's in her office.' The receptionist stood, leaning over the desk. 'Is that your dog? She's gorgeous. May I stroke her?'

'Of course. Her name's Kari.'

'I'll leave you to it...' Flora shot him a smile, and grabbed the strap of her bag from his shoulder. Aksel watched as she walked away from him. Bad sign. If she turned back and he found himself smiling, that would be an even worse sign.

Flora had gone on her way, warmed by the smile that Aksel had given her, but stopped at the lift and looked back. It was impossible not to look back at him, he was so darned easy on the eye. And the way he seemed to be struggling with himself only made him even more intriguing.

Fortunately, Mrs Crawford was waiting to see her, and Flora could turn her thoughts to the improvement in her frozen shoulder. Aksel was still lurking in the part of her brain where he seemed to have taken up permanent residence, but he was quiet for the moment.

'Your shoulder seems much better, Helen, you have a lot more movement in it now. Are you still having to take painkillers to get to sleep?'

Helen leaned forward in her chair, giving her a confiding smile. 'Last night I didn't feel I needed them so I put them in the drawer beside my bed.'

'Right. You do know that you can just tell the carer you don't need them and she'll take them away again?' Flora made a mental note to retrieve the tablets before she left and have them disposed of.

'She'd come all the way up here. And I might need them at some other time. It's *my* medication, but they act as if it's all up to them whether I take it.'

Flora had heard the complaint before. Drugs were carefully overseen and dispensed when needed, and it was one of the things that Helen had been used to making her own decisions about.

'They have to do that, they'll get in all kinds of trouble if they don't store medicines safely and keep a record. Some people here forget whether or not they've taken their medication and take too much or too little.' *Some people* was vague enough to imply that Flora didn't include Helen in that.

'I suppose so. It's very annoying, though.'

'I know. Give the carers a break, they have to keep to the rules or they'll get into trouble.' Flora appealed to Helen's better nature.

Helen nodded. 'I wouldn't want them to get into trouble over me. They have enough to do and they're very kind.'

'Right, then. I'll write in your notes that the carer is to offer you the painkillers and ask whether you want them or not. Is that okay?' Flora moved round so that Helen could see over her shoulder. She liked to know what was being written about her.

'All right, dear.' Helen tapped the paper with one finger. 'Put that it's up to me whether I take them or not.'

Flora added the note, and Helen nodded in approval. She'd raised four children, and worked in the village pharmacy for thirty years to supplement the family income, and even though her three sons and daughter were determined that she should be well looked after now, she resisted any perceived loss of independence.

'Who's the young man you arrived with? He's very tall.' Helen's living-room window overlooked the drive, and she liked to keep an eye on arrivals and departures.

'That's Aksel Olsen. He's from the canine therapy centre at the castle. They're talking about setting up a dog visiting scheme.'

'To help train the dogs? I could help with that, but I'm not sure that many of the others could.'

'Well, those who can't help might benefit from having the companionship of an animal. Don't you think?'

Helen thought for a moment and nodded. 'Yes, I think they will. Where's he from? His name isn't Scottish.'

'He's Norwegian. The dog understands Norwegian, too. He's trained Kari as an assistance dog for his daughter.'

'He has a daughter? Then he has a wife, too?' Helen was clearly trying to make the question sound innocent.

'No. No wife.'

'Really?' Helen beamed. 'Well, he might be looking for one. And it's about time you found yourself someone nice and had some bairns of your own.'

'I'm happy as I am, Helen. I have everything I want.' The assertion sounded old and tired, as if she was trying to convince herself of something. Flora wondered how many times she'd have to tell herself that before she really believed that Aksel was no exception to the rule she lived by. That there was no exception to the rule. Fear of rejection made the practicalities of falling in love and having a family impossible.

Helen brushed her words aside. 'He's very good looking. And tall. And such a mane of hair, it makes him look rather dashing. I dare say that he'd be able to sweep *someone* off to lots of exciting places.'

'He's actually better looking close up. Blue eyes.' Flora gave in to the weight of the inevitable, and Helen clapped her hands together gleefully.

'I like blue eyes. Mountain blue or ocean blue?'

Flora considered the question. 'I'd say mountain blue. Like ice.'

'Oh, very nice. And is he kind?'

* * *

Flora had worked through her list of patients, and when she arrived back in the communal sitting room, she found that Helen had decided to take part in the exercise class today. It was a first, and Flora wondered whether it was an attempt to get a closer look at Aksel's blue eyes and broad shoulders, and make a better assessment of both his kindness and his capacity to sweep a girl off her feet.

'Right, ladies and gentlemen.' Everyone was here and seated in a semi-circle around her, ready for the gentle mobility exercises. 'I brought along a new CD, ballads from the sixties.'

A rumble of approval went round, and Flora slipped the CD into the player. Carefully chosen songs that reflected the right rhythm for the exercises.

'We'll start with our arms. Everyone, apart from Helen, raise your arms. Reach up as high as you can...' Flora demonstrated by raising her own arms in time to the music.

The response was polite rather than enthusiastic, but the music and a little encouragement would warm things up. 'That's lovely, Ella, try the other arm now. Helen, you're sitting this one out... Now gently lower your arms. And up again...'

This time there was a murmur of laughter and the response was a lot more energetic. '*Very* good. Once more.'

A sudden movement from Helen caught her eye, and Flora turned, following the direction of her pointing finger. Everyone was laughing now.

Aksel was leaning in the wide doorway, smiling, looking far more delicious than he had any right to. And in front of him Kari had obligingly raised one paw, lowering it again and raising the other.

Flora put her hands on her hips and walked over to

him. Behind her she could hear chatter over the strains of the music.

'You know what this means, don't you?'

Aksel shook his head, flashing her an innocent look.

'There's a spare chair right there, next to Helen.' She may as well give Helen the chance to look him over in greater detail. 'Go and sit in it.'

'Yes, ma'am.' His eyes flashed with the ice-blue warmth that she'd told Helen about, and Aksel went to sit down. Kari trotted to her side, obviously having decided that she was the star of the show.

'Right. Let's do one more arm raise.' Flora raised her arms again and Kari followed suit, raising one paw. There was more laughter, and everyone reached for the sky.

'Well done, everyone. Aksel, I think you can do a bit better than that next time…'

Flora always kept a careful eye on everyone during her exercise classes to gauge how well they were moving and that no one was overdoing things. And this time Aksel was included in that. His left arm was fully mobile but he wasn't extending his right arm fully upwards, and she guessed that it was still hurting him. His neck seemed a little stiff as well.

Kari was loving all the attention, and when the exercise session was finished she trotted forward, eager to get to know everyone. Flora started to pack up her things, leaving Aksel to lead Kari around the semi-circle and introduce her.

She'd expected that Eileen would be keeping her eye on things, and saw her standing quietly at the doorway.

'What do you think?' Suddenly it mattered to her that the dog visiting scheme was a success. That Aksel should feel useful and accepted here, rather than dwelling on all the things that he felt he'd done wrong.

Eileen nodded. 'The written plan for the scheme was very thorough and I liked the thought behind it. This is the acid test.'

Flora looked around. Kari was in off-duty mode, which meant that she was free to respond to someone other than her handler. She was greeting everyone with an out-stretched paw, and receiving smiles and pats in return.

'It looks good to me. Kari certainly made everyone a bit more enthusiastic about the exercises.' Aksel had done his part in that, too. He'd joined in without a murmur, smiling and joking with everyone. His charm had contributed almost as much as Kari's accomplishments.

'It looks *very* good.' Eileen seemed to have already made her decision. 'It might be a while before he's allowed to leave.'

It was a while, and by the time Aksel had torn himself away, promising everyone that he'd return, Flora was looking at her watch. She needed to be back at the clinic for her afternoon sessions.

As soon as he was out of the sitting room, Aksel called Kari to heel, picking up her bag and making purposefully for the reception area. He signalled a hurried goodbye to the receptionist, telling Eileen that he'd be in touch, and managed to insinuate himself between Flora and the front door so that she had no choice but to allow him to open it for her.

'How was your morning?' He gave her a broad smile. 'Did you manage to get to the bottom of Mr King's crawling leg?'

'Uh? Oh…yes, the carers keep telling him that the elastic on his favourite socks is too tight, but he won't listen. I changed them and gave his leg a rub and that fixed the crawling. You seem to have enjoyed yourself.'

'Yes, I did.'

'I see that your shoulder's still bothering you.'

'It's fine. It doesn't hurt.'

Pull the other one. There was a clear imbalance between the way that he was using his right and left arms, and Aksel seemed determined to ignore it. Just as he was determined to ignore everything else he wanted or needed. But she shouldn't push it. The clinic was full of therapists and movement specialists, and if he wanted help he could easily ask for it.

'We'll get straight back...' He dumped her bag on the back seat and started the engine. 'I saw you looking at your watch.'

'Yes, I've got afternoon sessions that I need to get back for. And if we hurry we should be back in time for you to have lunch with Mette.'

He nodded, the sharp crunch of gravel coming from beneath the tyres of the SUV as he accelerated out of the driveway.

CHAPTER SEVEN

FLORA KNEW THAT Aksel was at the clinic that afternoon, but she didn't drop into Mette's room during her break. It was bad enough that her thoughts seemed to be stalking him, without her body following suit.

Cass had come for her physiotherapy session, glowing with a happiness that matched Lyle's exactly. She'd come to the clinic as a patient, after sustaining injuries to her arm and leg during a search-and-rescue assignment. Then she'd met Lyle Sinclair. Sparks had flown, and the two had fallen head over heels in love. Lyle had been inconsolable when Cass had returned home to America, but now she was back in Cluchlochry for good. She'd spent most of the forty-minute physiotherapy session telling Flora about their plans for the future.

'The movement in your leg is a great deal better. I'm really pleased with your improvement.'

Cass sat up, grinning. 'I hardly even think about it now, only when it begins to ache. Lyle says I should still be careful…'

'Well, you don't need me to tell you that he's right, you should be taking care. But being happy helps you to heal, too.'

'Then I'll be better in no time.' Cass slid off the treatment couch, planting her feet on the floor. 'Especially as I have you to help me…'

It had been an easy session. Flora stood at the door to the treatment room, watching Cass's gait as she walked away, and Aksel intruded into her thoughts once again. Cass was so happy, and looking forward to the future, and it showed in the way she moved. Aksel was like a coiled spring, dreading the future. No wonder he had aches and pains. Tension was quite literally tearing him apart.

He might be able to ignore it, but Flora couldn't any more. His shoulder could probably be fixed quite easily at this stage, but if he did nothing it would only get more painful and more difficult to treat. This was what she did best, and if she really wanted to help him, it was the most obvious place to start.

Aksel drew up outside his cottage, trying not to notice that Flora's porch light was on. He'd decided that he wouldn't seek her out at the clinic this afternoon, and it felt almost saintly to deprive himself of that pleasure.

As he got out of the SUV, opening the tailgate to let Kari out, he saw her door open and Flora marched down the path towards him, her arms wrapped around her body in a futile attempt to shelter herself from the wind. She looked determined and utterly beautiful as she faced him, her cheeks beginning to redden from the cold and small flakes of snow sticking to her hair. Aksel decided that sainthood was overrated.

'The car sounds better than it did this morning.' That was clearly just an opening gambit, and not what she'd come outside to say.

'Yes, I changed the spark plugs.' The SUV's rusty growl had turned into a healthier-sounding purr now. Aksel closed the tailgate and reached into the passenger footwell for his shopping bags, trying not to wince as his shoulder pulled painfully.

'And have you done anything about your shoulder? I'm not taking any excuses this time.'

'In that case…no, I haven't.'

'Come inside.' She motioned towards her cottage with a no-nonsense gesture that no amount of arguing was going to overcome. He hesitated and she frowned.

'If you don't come inside now, I'm going to turn into an icicle. You don't want to have to chip me off the pavement and thaw me out, do you?'

It was obviously meant as a threat, but the idea had a certain appeal. Particularly the thawing-out part. Aksel dismissed the thought, nudging the car door shut, and Kari followed him to Flora's doorstep. When she opened the door, Dougal came hurtling out of the sitting room to greet them.

He watched as she stood in front of the hall mirror, brushing half-melted snowflakes from her shoulders and hair. 'I appreciate the concern, but there's really no need. These things tend to rectify themselves.'

She turned on him suddenly. 'What's the problem, Aksel? You have a stiff shoulder, and I'm a qualified physiotherapist. Or are you not allowed to have anything wrong with you?'

She was just a little bit too close to the truth and it stung. He wanted to be the one that Mette could rely on completely. Strong and unbreakable. But there was no point in denying any more that his shoulder felt neither of those things at the moment.

'Okay, I…appreciate the offer and… Actually, I would like you to take a look at it if you wouldn't mind. It has been a little painful over the last few days.' He put his shopping bags down, taking a bottle of wine from one. 'Don't suppose you'd like some of this first?'

She rolled her eyes. 'No, I don't suppose I would. I'm not in the habit of drinking while I'm working.'

That put him in his place. But when he walked into the sitting room, he saw that a backless chair was placed in front of the fire. She'd been concerned about him and waiting for him to come home. The thought hit him hard, spreading its warmth through his veins as he sat down.

Suddenly all he wanted was her touch.

'Take your sweater off and let me have a look.' Flora congratulated herself on how professional her tone sounded. It was exactly how this was going to be.

She stood behind him, gingerly laying her fingers on his shoulder. 'You're very tense…'

Flora was feeling a little tense herself suddenly. The lines of his shoulder felt as strong as they looked, and there was only the thin material of his T-shirt between her fingers and his skin.

'It's been a long day.'

'What happened?'

He turned suddenly and Flora snatched her fingers away, stepping back involuntarily. She couldn't touch him when the smouldering blue ice of his gaze was on her.

'I didn't come here to tell you my troubles.'

'I know. Turn around and tell me anyway.'

He turned back and she continued her examination. There was a moment of silence and she concentrated on visualising the structure and musculature of his shoulder. Suddenly Aksel spoke.

'Dr Sinclair took me through the results of Mette's latest MRI scan today. It's clear now that there isn't going to be any more improvement in her sight.'

'There was hope that there might be?' Flora pulled the neck of his T-shirt to one side, reaching to run her fingers along his clavicle.

'No, not really. The doctors in Norway told me that her condition was stable now, and there was very little chance of any change. It was unreasonable of me to hold out any hope.'

'But you did anyway, because you're her dad.'

'Yes. I wasn't expecting to come here and cry on your shoulder about it, though.'

'You can't expect muscles to heal when you're this tense, Aksel.'

Flora felt him take a breath, and he seemed to relax a little. As she pressed her thumb on the back of his shoulder he winced. 'It's a little sore there.'

She imagined it was *very* sore. The shoulder must be a lot more painful than he was letting on. 'You have a few small lumps on your collarbone. That's usually a sign that it's been broken recently.'

'Nearly a year ago.'

'And what happened? Did you get some medical treatment when you did it, or were you miles away from the nearest doctor?'

He chuckled. 'No. Actually, I'd gone skiing for the New Year. There was a doctor on hand and he treated it immediately.'

'Good. That seems to have healed well, but the muscles in your shoulders are very tight. I can give you some exercises that will help ease them out.'

'Thanks.' He reached for his sweater.

'I can work the muscles out a bit for you if you'd like. It'll reduce the discomfort.' It was also going to take every ounce of her resolve to stay professional, but she could do that.

'That would be great. Thank you.'

She was just debating whether it would be wise to ask him to remove his T-shirt so that she could see what she was doing a little better when he pulled it over his head. Flora watched spellbound as he took an elastic band from his pocket, twisting his hair up off his shoulders.

His skin was golden, a shade lighter than his hair. Slim hips and a broad, strong chest came as no surprise, but Aksel had to be seen to be believed. He was beautiful, and yet completely unselfconscious.

'Okay. Just relax…' The advice was for herself as well as Aksel. This was just a simple medical massage, which might make him feel a little sore in the morning but would promote healing. And she wanted very badly to heal him.

He could feel the warmth of the fire on his skin. Aksel closed his eyes, trying not to think about her touch. Warm, caressing and… He caught his breath as she concentrated her attention on the spot that hurt most.

'Sorry. I can feel how sore it must be there…'

'It's okay.' He didn't want her to stop. Flora seemed to know all of his sore points, the things that tore at his heart and battered his soul. He wondered whether all of her patients felt the connection that seemed to be flowing through her fingers and spreading out across his skin.

He felt almost as if he was floating. Disengaged from his body and the cares of the day. Just her touch, firm and assured.

'My brother has cystic fibrosis.' She'd been silent for a while, working out the muscles in his shoulder, and the observation came out of nowhere.

'That's why you became a physiotherapist?'

'It was what made me first think of the idea. Alec's

physiotherapist taught him techniques to clear the mucus from his airways, and he benefited a great deal from it.'

'It's a difficult condition to live with, though.' Aksel sensed that Flora had something more to say.

He heard her take a breath. 'I know how badly you want to help Mette, and how helpless you feel. I've been through all that with Alec. You're tying yourself in knots and that shows, here in your shoulder.'

'It's… I can't change how I feel, Flora.'

'I know. I'm not asking you to. Mette's lost a great deal, more than any child should have to. All she has left is you, and you owe it to her to take care of yourself.'

Aksel thought for a moment, trying to get his head around the idea. 'It sounds…as if you have a point to make.'

He heard her laugh quietly, and a shiver ran down his spine. 'My point is that you feel so guilty that your life-style kept you from her all those years that you just want to throw it all away. I can understand that, I've felt guilty about going out and doing things when Alec was ill in bed. But my mum used to tell me that if I didn't go, then I couldn't come home again and tell Alec all about it. You can share the things you've done with Mette, too. Don't be afraid to give her the real you.'

'And that'll make my shoulder better?' Flora might just be right.

'Maybe. I think the massage and exercise might help as well.'

She gripped his arm, rotating it carefully, seeming sat-isfied with the result. Then she handed him his T-shirt and Aksel pulled it over his head. The movement felt easier than it had for days.

'That feels better, thank you. Can we have that glass of wine now?'

She hesitated. 'It's not something I'd usually advise after a physiotherapy session. Water's better in terms of reducing inflammation.'

'Noted. Since I'm going to ignore your advice and have a glass anyway, you can either send me back to my cottage to drink alone, or join me.'

'In that case, I'd say it's my duty to keep an eye on you. I might need to save you from yourself.'

Aksel chuckled, getting to his feet.

The Advent candle burned on the mantelpiece. Another nineteen days to go. Aksel was sitting next to her on the sofa, and although they'd left as much space between them as possible, it still felt as if they might touch. Christmas was coming, and at the moment all that called to mind was mistletoe.

'Tell me about your family.' He sipped his wine, his tone lazy and relaxed now. He'd obviously forgiven her for forcing him to face the facts that he'd been so assiduously ignoring.

'There isn't much to tell. There's the four of us, and we travelled so much when I was a kid that we didn't see much of the rest of the family. Just at holiday time.'

'Where are your parents now?'

'They're in Italy. Dad's going to be retiring in a couple of years, so I'm not sure what will happen then. He always said he wanted to come back to Scotland. But my brother's married and lives in England, and they're trying for a child. I can't see my mum wanting to be too far away from a new grandchild.'

'What does your brother do?'

'He's a university lecturer. He fell in love with English literature when he went to Durham University, and then fell in love with his wife. The cystic fibrosis has slowed him down at times, but it's never stopped him from doing what he wants to do.'

'That's a nice way of putting it. It's what I want for Mette.'

'She can do more than you think. One day maybe she'll be leading you off on a trip around the world.'

The yearning in his face made Flora want to reach out and touch him. 'I'd like that very much.'

'My brother's never compromised...' Flora shrugged. 'It's caused its share of heartache, but we've faced it as a family.'

He nodded. There was never a need to over-explain with Aksel. He understood her and she understood him. That didn't mean they necessarily had to like what the other was saying, but the connection between them meant that neither could disregard it.

'So... You already know what frightens me. What are you afraid of?'

It was such a natural question, but one that was hard to answer. 'I'm afraid that the in vitro fertilisation for my brother and his wife will fail. They can't get pregnant on their own because of the cystic fibrosis. They'll deal with it, if it happens...'

'So that's a fear that you can face.' He was dissatisfied with her reply. 'What about the ones you can't face?'

'I have everything I want.' That must sound as much like an excuse to Aksel as it did to her. She had everything that she dared reach out for, and that was going to have to be enough.

'Having everything you want sounds nice.'

'I have a fireside, and a glass of wine. It'll be Christmas soon...' And Aksel was here. But however much she wanted to add him to the list, she couldn't.

'And...?' He reached out, allowing the tips of his fingers to touch hers. Her gaze met his and in an exquisite moment of clarity she knew exactly what he was asking.

She wanted to but she couldn't. Flora couldn't bring herself to trust any man enough to give herself to him. And the froth and excitement of a no-strings affair... It seemed great from the outside. But inside, when all the longing turned into disappointment and frustration, it hurt so much more than if it had never happened.

She moved her hand away from his, and he nodded. 'I'm sorry. I forgot all about my patient ethics for a moment.'

Flora couldn't help smiling. 'I thought *I* was the one who was supposed to be professional.'

'Oh, and I can't have ethics? I'm sure there's something in the patients' handbook about respecting your medical professional and not making a pass at them.' He grinned, his eyes dancing with blue fire.

He acknowledged the things that she didn't dare to. And he made it sound as if it was okay to feel something, as long as they both understood that actions didn't automatically follow.

'Fair point. Would it compromise your patient ethics to top up my glass?'

He chuckled. 'I don't think so. I'll do it anyway.'

This was nice. Sitting in front of the fire, drinking wine. Able to voice their thoughts and allow them to slip away. It was the best kind of friendship, and one that she didn't want to lose. Taking things any further would only mess it up.

CHAPTER EIGHT

FLORA HAD UNDERSTOOD his unspoken question, and Aksel had understood her answer. Maybe she'd also understood that in the electric warmth of her touch, he'd got a little carried away.

She wanted to stay friends. That was fine. It was probably the wisest course of action, and it was just as well that one of them had kept their head. Making love with her might well have turned into the kind of explosive need that had no part in his life since he'd found Mette.

Friends was good. It meant that he could seek her out at the clinic the next day and ask her about the trucks that had been arriving on the estate, wondering aloud if she was interested in accompanying him and Mette on another voyage of discovery.

'The Christmas carnival is a bit of a fixture here. They set it up every year. There's usually an ice skating rink.' They were walking across the grass, with Mette between them, each holding one of his daughter's hands so that she didn't fall on the uneven ground.

'I want to skate!' Mette piped up, and Aksel swallowed down the impulse to say no. The clinic was proving as much of a learning experience for him as it was for Mette, and he was beginning to understand that, *Yes, let's make that happen* was the default position.

'That sounds fun.' Flora's answer wasn't unexpected. 'Perhaps you can skate with your papa.'

Okay. He could handle that. Keeping a tight hold on his daughter and guiding her around the edge of the rink. He doubted whether Kari would be all that happy on the ice.

It wasn't hard to orientate themselves as the carnival site was a blaze of light and activity. Most of the attractions were set up, apart from a few finishing touches, and Aksel recognised a few of the clinic staff using their lunch hour to try out the skating rink. The booth for skate hire wasn't open yet, and Mette was mollified with a promise that he would take her skating as soon as it was.

'We could take a look at the maze.' Flora gestured towards a tall hedge, decked with fairy lights, which lay on one side of the carnival booths.

'There's a maze?'

'Yes, it was re-planted a few years ago, using the plans of the original one that stood in the grounds. They decided to put it here so it could be part of the Christmas carnival.'

It looked impressive. Aksel bent down, explaining in Norwegian what a maze was, and Mette started to jump up and down.

'I want to go. I want to go…'

'Let's ask, shall we?' Flora approached a man standing at the entrance, who Aksel recognised by sight as having come from the village. He turned towards Aksel and Mette, waving them towards the entrance.

It was entirely unsurprising that Aksel forged ahead of them into the maze. The paths were slightly narrower than last year, the hedges having grown since then, and they were tall enough that even he couldn't see over the top now. They were all walking blind.

'Where do we go, Papa?'

He stopped, looking around. There was a dead end in front of them, and paths leading to the right and the left.

'I'm...not sure.'

'Why don't you lead the way, then, Mette? We have to try and see if we can find our way to the centre.'

Aksel shot her a questioning look, and then understanding showed in his face. 'Yes, good idea. Why don't you tell us which way to go?'

He stepped back behind Mette, who stretched out her hand, finding the branches to one side of her. Kari watched over her, walking by her side, as she carefully walked ahead, following the line of the hedge right up to the dead end, and then turning back and to her right.

'I think she's got the right idea.' Flora fell into step beside Aksel, whispering the words to him.

'Will this work? Following the wall to your right...?' he whispered back,

Flora shot him an outraged look. 'Of course it will. We'll get there if we just stay with Mette.'

'Papa...?' Mette hesitated, suddenly unsure of herself.

'It's okay, Mette. Just keep going, we're right behind you.' He reached forward, touching his daughter's shoulder to let her know that he was there, and she nodded, confident again.

Mette led them unerringly to the centre of the maze, where a small six-sided structure built in stone was decked with fairy lights. Kari guided her towards it, and she walked around it until she found the arched doorway.

'We can go inside, Mette.' Aksel was right behind her, patiently waiting for Mette to find her own way, and he'd seen the notice pinned to one side of the arch. 'We can climb to the top of the tower if you want to.'

The tower at the centre of the maze had a curving stone staircase inside, and from the viewing platform at the top it was possible to see the whole maze, the walkways picked out by sparkling fairy lights. Mette might not be able to see them, but she could still climb, and still feel that she was the queen of this particular castle.

Aksel guided her ahead of him, ducking under the arch and letting Mette find the handrail and climb the steps. Flora followed, Kari loping up the steps at her side. The four of them could just squeeze onto the small viewing platform at the top, bounded by crenellated stonework.

'Papa! I found the way!' Mette squealed with excitement, and Aksel lifted her up in his arms.

'*Ja elskling...*' He was hugging the little girl tightly, and he seemed to have tears in his eyes. 'I'm so proud of you, Mette.'

'I'm an explorer too, Papa.'

Aksel seemed to be lost for words. Flora wanted so badly to put her arms around them both, but this was their moment. Mette had used some of the techniques that the clinic was teaching her, and they'd worked for all of them in the maze. And Aksel had found that for all his height and strength, and even though he could see, he'd not known which way to go any more than Mette had.

Flora waited while they savoured their triumph. Then she reached out, touching Mette's hand to catch her attention.

'Are you going to lead us back out again now?'

'She'd better. I don't know the way.' Aksel's voice was thick with emotion still.

Mette regarded him solemnly. 'What if I get lost, Papa?'

'You won't.' He set Mette back down on her feet, turning to guide her carefully down the staircase.

By the time they'd navigated their way out of the maze, the stallholders had almost finished setting up for the opening later on that afternoon, and the proprietor of the village tea shop was pleased to sell them sausage rolls, warm from the small oven on his stall, and made with homemade beef sausagemeat.

They wandered between the lines of stalls, and when Mette had finished eating, Aksel lifted her up onto his shoulders. Then he caught sight of it, stopping suddenly and staring at the open-sided tent.

'What's that?' He couldn't take his eyes off the large blocks of ice under the awning.

'You want to go and have a look? I'll stay here with Mette.' Flora had a feeling that this was something that Aksel would like to explore on his own.

'I...' He turned, but seemed unable to find enough momentum to walk away. Looking back, he nodded. 'Yes. If you don't mind.'

'Of course not. We can go and get some doughnuts to take back with us.'

'I'll be back in a minute.' He lifted Mette down from his shoulders and Flora took her hand, watching as Aksel strode across to the tent. She'd be very surprised if he was back in a minute.

They chose and purchased their doughnuts, and Flora looked back towards the tent to see Aksel deep in conversation with Ted Mackie, the estate manager. Ted was eyeing him up, clearly deciding whether it would be okay to let Aksel loose with a chainsaw. Flora resisted the temptation to run up to Ted, take him by the lapels of his coat, and tell him that if Aksel could be trusted to get to both Poles and back, he could be trusted with power tools. And that he really needed to do something like this.

'What's Papa doing?' Mette was unable to see her father.

'He's right over there, at one of the other stalls. Shall we go and see?' Aksel had taken the pair of work gloves that Ted had proffered, and was passing them from one hand to the other as he talked. He was tempted. Flora could see that he was *very* tempted.

She walked slowly over to the tent, wondering whether that would give Aksel time to give in to the temptation. She could see him checking out the chainsaw and running his hand over one of the large blocks of ice. Ted was nodding in agreement to something he'd said.

'Hi. We've got doughnuts.' Aksel jumped when Flora spoke, too immersed in his conversation to have noticed them approaching. Flora tried hard not to smirk.

'Oh… I suppose…' He handed the gloves back to Ted ruefully. 'I'd really like to give this a go but…'

Ted flashed Flora a glance. 'Shame. It would be good to have something to show people. It would give us a start.'

'I'd like to but…' Aksel turned, masking the regret in his face with a smile. 'We need to get you back to the clinic, Mette. You've got a play date this afternoon.'

One of the well-organised play sessions, which would help Mette to make the most of her limited sight. They were very well supervised, and Mette was already making friends at the clinic. Aksel really wasn't needed.

'If you'd like to stay here, I can take Mette back.'

'We bought you a doughnut, Papa. So you don't get hungry.'

'Thank you.' He grinned down at Mette, taking the paper bag that she was holding out towards him. 'I should come back with you, though.'

Ted had bent down to Mette and took her hand, leading her over to the blocks of ice so that she could run her hand over them to feel the icy coldness beneath her fingertips. Aksel looked about to follow, and Flora caught his sleeve.

'She can do that by herself, Aksel. Ted's looking after her.'

'I know, but…' His forehead creased into a frown. 'I'm crowding her, aren't I?'

'You're spending time with her, so that you can make a relationship. That's great.' Aksel shot her an unconvinced look. 'And, yes, you are crowding her a bit. She's learning how to explore her world.'

'And this is what the therapists at the clinic are teaching her.' He looked over at Mette thoughtfully.

'That's our job, all of us. We may have specific roles, but we all have the same aim.' Everyone who worked here on the estate was a part of that. Ted took the children on nature walks during the summer, and Mrs Renwick, the cook at the castle, held regular cookery classes for both adults and children.

'All the same, Mette's far more important than this…'

'Yes, she is. She's important to all of us, and she's just starting to feel at home at the clinic. She has a play date this afternoon, and she's going to have a great time. You can either interfere with that, or you can stay here and make her something nice.'

He narrowed his eyes. 'Are you just saying that because you know I want to stay?'

'I'm saying this because staying's okay. Mette has other things to do this afternoon.'

Aksel was frowning, now. 'I was rather hoping that she'd learn to need me.'

Flora puffed out an exasperated breath. 'She *does* need you, Aksel. She needs you to be her father, which means you're always there for her. It doesn't mean that you have to follow her around all the time. The whole point of her being here is to learn to be independent.'

Most people would have hummed and hawed about it a bit. But Aksel had the information he needed, and it was typical of him to make his decision and act on it.

'You're killing me. You know that.' He turned on his heel, walking over to Mette.

'Ted says that I can make an ice sculpture. Would you like me to make one for you this afternoon, while Tante Flora takes you back to the castle to play?'

'Yes, Papa!' Mette obviously thought that was a good idea, too.

'Okay. What would you like me to make, then?'

Flora winced. Maybe it would have been better to give Mette some suggestions, rather than allow a child's imagination to run rampant.

'A reindeer. Mama took me to see the reindeer.'

'A reindeer?' Ted chuckled, removing his flat cap to scratch his head. 'That'll be interesting. What do you think, Aksel?'

Aksel shrugged. 'If she wants a reindeer, then... I can do a reindeer.'

'Would you like me to bring Mette back here after I've finished work?' Flora reckoned that Aksel might need a bit of extra time to work out how to sculpt four legs and a pair of antlers.

'Um... Yes. That would be great, thank you.'

'Right.' Flora took Mette's hand. 'Shall we stay and watch Papa get started on your reindeer, Mette, and then we'll go back to the castle.'

Mette nodded, following Flora to a safe distance, while Ted gave Aksel the gloves and a pair of safety glasses. Running him through a few safety rules was probably unnecessary, but Ted was nothing if not thorough, and Aksel listened carefully. Then he turned towards the block of ice that Ted had indicated, standing back for a moment to contemplate his first move, before starting up the chainsaw.

Mette tugged her hat down over her ears in response to the noise. 'What's Papa doing?'

'He's cutting some ice off the top. To make the reindeer's back.'

Aksel had clearly decided to start with the easy part, and was making an incision on one side of the block of ice that ran half way along its length. Then he made a similar incision from the top, freeing a large piece of ice, which he lifted down onto the ground. He switched off the chainsaw, engaging the safety mechanism, and beckoned to Flora and Mette.

'See this big block he's sawn off. It's almost as big as you are.' She kept hold of Mette's hand, letting her feel the size of the block. 'I can't wait to see what it'll be like when we get back.'

'Neither can I,' Ted interjected. He was clearly wondering how Aksel was going to sculpt a pair of antlers too.

'You're *all* killing me...' Aksel muttered the words under his breath, but he was grinning broadly. He was clearly in his element.

He bent down, kissing Mette goodbye and telling her to enjoy her afternoon. Flora took her hand and walked away, knowing that Aksel was watching them go. It wasn't until she'd turned into one of the walkways between the stalls that she heard the chainsaw start up again.

Mette had told everyone about how her papa was using a chainsaw to make her a reindeer out of ice. When Flora arrived back at the children's unit to pick her up, the nursery nurses and some of the children already had their hats and coats on.

'Are we ready, then?' Lyle was wearing a thick windcheater and was clearly intending to join the party. Flora hoped that they wouldn't be disappointed.

'Should we phone Ted first? To see if it's finished?'

And possibly to make sure that the reindeer hadn't collapsed and they'd be greeted by an amorphous pile of ice.

Lyle chuckled. 'Aksel called me earlier for some orthopaedic advice.'

'He's hurt himself?' Flora hoped that Aksel hadn't overdone things and damaged his shoulder.

'No, it was more a matter of how thick the reindeer's legs needed to be to support the weight of the body. Interesting equation. I called Ted just now, and he says that it's all going rather well.'

Lyle looked round as Cass entered the room, displaying the sixth sense of a lover who always knew when his partner was nearby.

'I can't wait to see it.' Cass's green eyes flashed with mischief. 'There's something very sexy about a man using power tools...'

Yes, there was. And there was something almost overwhelmingly sexy about Aksel using power tools. Combine that with large blocks of ice, and it was enough to melt the most frozen heart.

'You think so? I might have to have a go, then.' Lyle raised an eyebrow and Cass laughed.

They all trooped out of the main entrance to the clinic, Mette holding her hand. It was dark now and the lights of the carnival shone brightly ahead of them, people straggling along the path that led down from the castle.

The first evening of the carnival was, as always, well attended. Charles Ross-Wylde was there, fulfilling his duties as Laird and host by greeting everyone and then melting quietly away to leave them to their fun. His sister Esme had brought a couple of the dogs from the canine therapy centre, and was clearly taking the opportunity to make sure that they weren't distracted by the lights and sounds around them.

Mette tugged at Flora's hand, remembering which way they needed to walk to get to the ice sculpture. As they approached, Flora could see Ted adjusting the lights that were placed at the bottom of the sculpture to show it off to its best effect. And Aksel's tall, unmistakeable silhouette standing back a little.

He turned, seeming to sense that they were there, and walked towards them. Shooting Flora a smile, he addressed Mette.

'Would you like to come and see your reindeer?'

'Yes, Papa!'

Flora watched as he led his daughter over to the reindeer, letting her stand close so that she could see the lights reflected in the ice. It was beautiful, standing tall and proud, a full set of antlers on its head. The lights glistened through the ice, making it seem almost alive.

Over the noise of the carnival, Flora could hear Mette's excited chatter. Lyle came to inspect the reindeer and Mette took his hand, pulling him closer to take a look. Aksel stood back, leaving his daughter with Lyle and Cass, and walked over to Flora.

'That is downright amazing.' Flora grinned up at him.

'I had a bit of help. One of the antlers snapped off, and Ted and I had to re-attach it. And Dr Sinclair's anatomical knowledge was invaluable.'

'Yes, I heard about that. I'm a little more interested in *your* anatomy.' Flora frowned. She could have phrased that a little better. Somehow, a perfectly innocent enquiry about his shoulder seemed to have turned into a barely disguised chat-up line.

'My shoulder's fine. If that's what you mean.' The slight quirk of his lips showed that Aksel was quite prepared to call her bluff, and Flora decided to ignore the invitation.

'I'm glad you haven't undone the work I did on it.'

'It might be a bit stiff in the morning…'

Flora returned his smile. 'If it is, I'll be officially reporting you to Lyle for some more orthopaedic advice.' A repetition of last night was probably to be avoided.

'You make that sound like a threat.'

'Don't worry. It is.'

CHAPTER NINE

AKSEL WOKE UP the following morning feeling more re-freshed from sleep than he had in a long time. It was a bright, clear day, and although his shoulder was a little sore, it was nothing that a hot shower and some stretching exercises wouldn't banish. He was ready for the day, and the day seemed that much better for the possibility that it might bring another chance to see Flora.

He wasn't disappointed. When he arrived at the clinic, after a morning's work at the therapy centre, he found that Mette was absorbed in a learning game with one of the children's therapy assistants. He kissed his daughter and told her that he wouldn't interrupt, and then wandered aimlessly down to one of the patient sitting rooms.

He saw Flora sitting in one of the wing-backed chairs by the great fireplace, which had been made bright and wel-coming with an arrangement of Christmas greenery. He recognised the sandy-haired man in the chair opposite. One of the children's play leaders had told him that this was Andy Wallace and that he didn't much like to be touched, in a broad hint that Aksel should steer Mette clear of him.

Flora was leaning towards Andy, and the two seemed to be deep in conversation. Aksel turned to walk away, but then Flora looked up and beckoned him over.

Andy didn't offer to shake hands when Flora introduced the two men but nodded quietly in Aksel's direction, clearly taking his time to sum him up.

'We're just having tea. Would you like to join us?' Flora smiled at him.

There was no *just* about it. Flora had been talking quietly to Andy, no doubt discussing the next step of what looked like a long road back to full health. Andy's leg was supported by a surgical brace and his eyes seemed haunted. But if Flora thought that it was okay for him to join them, then he trusted her.

'Thank you. Can I get you a refill?' He gestured to the two empty cups on the small table between them.

'Not for me, thanks. Andy?'

Andy proffered his cup, and Aksel carried it over to the side table where coffee and tea were laid out. He put a fresh herbal teabag into Andy's cup and reached for a coffee capsule for himself. Flora leaned forward, saying a few words to Andy, and he nodded. All the same, when Aksel operated the coffee machine, Andy jumped slightly at the noise.

'Where's Mette?' Flora turned to him as he sat down.

'She's…got something going with the play assistants. Apparently I'm surplus to requirements at the moment.' Aksel made a joke of it, but it stung more than he cared to admit.

Flora nodded, smiling at Andy. 'Aksel's not used to that.'

Andy let out a short, barked laugh. 'I can identify with *surplus to requirements*.' He nodded down at his leg, clearly frustrated by his own lack of mobility.

'It's nothing…' The comparison was embarrassing; Andy clearly had life-changing injuries.

'Don't let Flora hear you say that. She has a keen nose

for *nothing*.' Andy gave a wry smile, and Flora grinned back at him.

'Nothing's a code word around here. Meaning something.' Flora's observation sounded like a quiet joke, and Aksel wondered if it was aimed at him or Andy. Probably both of them.

'In that case, it's something. And I'm handling it.' Aksel's smiling retort made both Andy and Flora laugh. He was beginning to like Andy, and Aksel pulled out his phone, flipping to the picture he'd taken yesterday and handing the phone to Andy.

'Oh, she's a bonny wee lass. What's that she's standing next to?'

Flora smiled. 'Ted Mackie has an ice-sculpting stall at the carnival. With chainsaws. Aksel made the mistake of telling Mette that he'd sculpt whatever she wanted for her, and he ended up having to do a reindeer.'

Andy chuckled. 'You made a decent job of it. Why is your daughter here?'

'She was in a car accident, and she's lost most of her sight. Anything that's more than a few feet away from her is just a blur.'

'You've done the best thing for her, bringing her to the clinic. They'll help her make the most of what she has.' Andy's reaction was like a breath of fresh air. Someone who knew the nature of suffering but didn't dwell on it, and who preferred to look at what could be done for Mette, and not express horror at what couldn't be changed.

'Thanks. That's good to hear.'

Flora had leaned back in her chair, seemingly in no hurry to go anywhere. The talk drifted into quiet, getting-to-know-you mode. Andy had been in the army and had travelled a lot, and the two men swapped stories about places they'd both visited. Andy's story about patching up a broken-down SUV from the only materials to hand struck a chord with Aksel, and the two men laughed over it. And Aksel's story about the mystery of the missing coffee supplies made Andy chuckle.

Finally, Flora looked at her watch. 'I hate to break this up, but it's time for your physio now, Andy.' She was clearly pleased with the way things had gone. And Aksel had enjoyed their talk. Andy had a well-developed sense of humour, and he'd led an interesting life.

Andy rolled his eyes. 'Another chance for you to torment me?' He clearly thought a lot of Flora.

'Yes, that's right. I don't get paid if I can't find something to torment my patients with.' Flora gave Andy a bright smile, helping him to his feet and pulling in front of him the walking frame that stood by the side of his chair.

'I'd like to see the pictures of your expedition to the Andes.' Andy turned to Aksel.

'Sure. I'll bring them in tomorrow. Is it okay for me to bring Mette with me?' Aksel wondered if a child might be too much for Andy but he smiled.

'I'd like that. As long as she doesn't find me boring.' Andy glanced down at his leg. Aksel shook his head, sure that if anyone could see past Andy's injuries then his daughter could.

Flora broke in briskly. 'If you send me the pictures, I can print them out for you. Perhaps Mette will be able to see them better that way?'

'Thanks. I think she will.'

The two men nodded goodbye, and Flora followed as Andy walked slowly towards the doorway. She turned, giving Aksel a grin.

'If you're at a loose end, you can always go and sculpt something else. I'm very partial to unicorns, and now you have this down to a fine art it should be child's play…'

'Don't listen to her, man.' Andy called out the words. 'She's far too bossy.'

Bossy and beautiful. Soft and sweet and yet surprisingly strong. Intelligent, warm... The list just went on. Aksel had given up trying to complete it, because there was always more to say about Flora.

He called out an acknowledgement to Andy, wondering if Flora had lip-read the words that had formed silently on his lips. Or maybe she'd tapped into the connection between them and she just knew, because she shot him a look of amused surprise.

You want a unicorn...? If that was what Flora wanted, then that's what she'd get.

The ice unicorn stood next to the reindeer, and Ted Mackie had told Aksel that it had attracted both attention and admiration. He hadn't told Flora about it, even though she was the one person that it was intended to please. She was sure enough to hear about it, and he hoped she'd know it was *her* unicorn.

He'd arranged a schedule with Lyle for when he should bring Mette home. Both of them agreed that Mette was settling in well, and Aksel was anxious that she wouldn't miss any of the activities that the clinic ran for its patients.

'Are you sure you're happy with this? It's a little less than we originally envisaged.' Lyle gave him a searching look, and Aksel realised that his own attitude had changed since they'd last spoken about this. The question was less of a tug of war and more a meeting of minds now.

'I'm very happy with it. My relationship with Mette has been much better since she's been here. I have you to thank for that. She's gained a lot of confidence.' Aksel had wondered if he should say that Flora had given *him* the confidence to see that.

Lyle had nodded, smiling. 'I'm glad you feel that way. I think that your daily visits are very important for Mette, she knows that you're always there for her.'

He'd gone to the children's unit to see Mette and she'd greeted him with a hug and a kiss. When he'd asked her if she'd like to spend the day with him tomorrow, she'd tugged at the play assistant's arm excitedly, telling her that she was going to explore a new place with her papa.

Then he'd texted Flora, asking her if she was free. There had been no mention of unicorns, which had been a little disappointing, but her 'Yes' had made up for that.

Aksel arrived at the clinic just as the children were finishing their breakfast. He packed some things into his day-pack, although in truth nothing was needed. But Mette liked the idea of packing for a journey.

His shoulder had improved a great deal. The massage had done wonders and he suspected that Flora's wake-up call had something to do with it as well. He lifted Mette up onto his shoulders, perched on top of his day-pack, and felt his stride lengthen as they started the two-mile walk home, the rhythm of his steps quieting his heart. Aksel began to tell Mette the story of his trip up to a remote village in the Andes.

'Were there crocodiles, Papa?'

Not that he'd noticed. But, then, Mette's idea of a crocodile was her smiling stuffed toy. 'Yes, there were crocodiles. We gave them some chocolate so they wouldn't eat us.'

'And penguins?'

'Yes. We had to go fishing and catch them some tea, so they'd tell us the right way to the village.' If he was going to enter into the realms of fantasy, then he may as well just go for it.

'Did your feet hurt?'

'A little bit. I had a big blister on my toe.' He'd made a rookie mistake on the way back down, allowing water to get inside one of his boots, and frostbite had taken hold.

'Did it get better, Papa?'

'Yes, it got better. And when we reached the village, at the top of the high snowy mountain, the people there welcomed us and gave us food and comfortable beds, with warm quilts like yours.'

Mette whooped with joy, and the achievement seemed greater than the walk up to the isolated village, in terrible weather conditions, had been.

They had warm drinks together when they arrived back at the cottage, and Mette insisted on keeping her hat on, since she was an explorer. Then there was a knock at the door, and Flora burst into the cottage, bringing the same sunlight with her that she took everywhere.

'I like the new look.' She grinned up at him and Aksel's hand shot awkwardly to the small plait that ran from his right temple and was caught into the elastic band that held the rest of his hair back.

'Mette's rag doll has plaits…' He shrugged as if it was nothing. When Mette had demanded that she be allowed to plait his hair this morning, it had felt like another step towards intimacy with his daughter, and he hadn't had the heart to unravel the uneven braid.

'I'm glad you kept it. She has excellent taste.' Flora obviously approved wholeheartedly. 'I hear that Ted Mackie's acquired an ice unicorn…'

Aksel wondered if she really hadn't been to see it, or she was just teasing. 'Has he?' He decided to play things cool.

'It's beautiful. I have about a million pictures of it.' She stood on her toes, kissing his cheek so briefly that he only realised she'd done it after the fact. 'Thank you.'

His cheek tingled from the touch of her lips as he followed Flora into the sitting room, where Mette was playing with Kari. Aksel decided that the hours spent sculpting the unicorn had been well worth it, and that he'd be tempted to create a whole menagerie of fantastic creatures in exchange for one more fleeting kiss.

It was agreed that they would walk down to the marketplace to see the village Christmas tree and the Christmas market. Aksel called Kari, putting on the yellow vest that denoted that she was at work now.

'Mette's already using Kari as her assistance dog?'

'No, but Esme suggested that it might be a good idea to let her see her at work a bit, just to get her used to the idea. Where's Dougal?'

'I took him up to the therapy centre, they're minding him. I didn't want him to get under Mette's feet.' Flora took a green and red striped bobble hat from the pocket of her red coat, pulling it down over her ears, and Aksel chuckled. She looked delightful.

'What are you? One of Santa's elves?'

'Right in one.' She shot him an innocent look, tugging at the hat. 'What gave me away?'

CHAPTER TEN

CLUCHLOCHRY'S MARKET SQUARE was paved with cobble-stones, and boasted an old market cross, worn and battered by many winters. The market was already in full swing, with fairy lights hung around the canvas-topped stalls, and the village Christmas tree standing proudly in one corner, smothered in lights. As this was a Saturday morning, carol singers and a band had turned out to give the market a festive air.

The band struck up a melody that Mette recognised, and she started to sing along in Norwegian. Aksel lifted her up out of the crush of people, and heard Flora singing too, in English. At the end of the carol she joined in with the round of applause for the band, and Mette flung her arms up, wriggling with delight.

'Shall we go over to the village hall first?' Flora indicated a stone building next to the church. 'There are lots of stalls in there as well.'

Aksel nodded his agreement, and Flora led the way, while he followed with Mette. Kari trotted by her side, and every now and then the little girl held out her hand, putting it on Kari's back. It was a start. Soon, hopefully, Mette would be learning to rely on Kari to guide her.

Inside, it looked as if there had been some kind of competition between the stallholders to see who could get the most Christmas decorations into their allotted space. Aksel saw a large reindeer twinkling above one of them, and decided not to point it out to Mette, in case she wanted to take it home with her.

'Oh, look.' Flora had caught sight of yet another stall that she wanted to visit. 'I heard that Aileen was here, we should go and see her knitwear. She might have something that Mette would like.'

Aksel nodded his agreement, and Flora led him over to the stall, introducing him to Aileen Sinclair, an older woman with greying hair, confiding the information that Aileen was Lyle's mother and that she did a *lot* of knitting. That was self-evident from the racks of hats and scarves, and the sweaters laid out on two tables. Aileen smiled at him, sizing him up with an experienced eye.

'I don't know whether I can find anything to fit you, hen.' Aileen seemed willing to try all the same, sorting through a small pile of chunky cableknit sweaters. 'No, there isn't much call for extra-large, and Mrs Bell bought the last one for her son. If there's something you like, we can always make it up for you.'

'Thank you.' Aksel began to dutifully look through the sweaters. 'Actually, we were looking for something for my daughter.'

Flora lifted Mette up so that she could run her hand across the fine, lace knitted children's jumpers. Aileen greeted Mette with another of her beaming smiles, producing a tape measure from her pocket, and began to measure Mette's arms.

'What colour do you like, Mette?' Flora always asked Mette what she liked rather than suggesting things to her.

'Red.' Mette had caught sight of Aileen's bright red sweater, under her coat.

'Very good choice. Maybe a lacy one?' Aileen glanced at Flora and she nodded.

Piles of sweaters were looked through, knocked over and then re-stacked, in what looked like a completely arbitrary search. Finally three pretty sweaters, which looked to be around Mette's size, were laid out on top of the others.

'What do you think, Aksel?' Flora turned to him questioningly.

'They're all very nice.' Aksel wasn't prepared to commit himself any further than that and Flora frowned at him.

'You're no help.'

'Everyone should stick to what they're good at.' And Flora was very good at shopping. She always seemed to pick out the nicest things, buying the best she could afford and yet not over-spending. That was why she always looked immaculate.

He watched as Flora encouraged Mette to run her hand across each of the sweaters to feel their softness and warmth. She picked one, and Flora unzipped her coat so that Aileen could hold it up against her and make sure it fitted properly. The general consensus of opinion seemed to be that this was the perfect sweater, and Aksel reached into his pocket for his wallet.

He was too slow. As Aileen wrapped the sweater carefully in pretty paper, sticky-taping the ends down, Flora had whipped a note from her purse and handed it over.

'Thank you. I'll get your change.' Aileen plumped the package into a paper carrier bag and gave it to Mette.

'Don't worry about the change, Aileen. You don't charge enough for these already, I still have the one I bought from you three years ago. You'd make a lot more money if you didn't make them to last.'

Aileen flushed with pleasure. The sweaters were clearly more a labour of love than a money-making exercise.

Mette whirled around, eager to show Aksel her carrier bag, and Flora caught her before she lost her balance. He examined the bag, declared it wonderful, and Aileen bade them a cheery goodbye.

Then it was on to the other stalls. Flora was endlessly patient, letting Mette sniff each one of the home-made soaps on offer and choose the one she liked the best. The avuncular man at the fudge stall offered them some samples to taste, and Aksel was allowed to make the choice of which to buy. The indoor market was a whirl of colours, tastes, textures and smells, and Aksel found himself enjoying it as much as Mette obviously was.

'Are you hungry yet?' Flora clearly was or she wouldn't have asked the question. 'There's a pub on the other side of the green that serves family lunches whenever the market's open.'

A family lunch. That sounded good, and not just because Aksel was hungry too. He could really get used to this feeling of belonging, with both Mette *and* Flora.

'Good idea. They won't mind us taking Kari in?' Despite her yellow service coat, Kari wasn't working as Mette's assistance dog just yet.

'No, of course not. They're used to people coming in with dogs from the canine therapy centre, and they welcome them.'

Flora managed to find a table close to one of the roaring fires, and while she stripped off Mette's coat, Aksel went to the bar, ordering thick vegetable soup with crusty bread, and two glasses of Christmas punch. When he returned with the tray, Mette and Flora were investigating their purchases together. This seemed to be an integral part of the shopping experience, and Mette was copying Flora, inserting her finger into the corner of each package so that they could catch a glimpse of what was inside.

'Why don't you open them?' Aksel began to clear a space on the table between them, and Flora shot him a horrified look.

'Hush! We can't open them until we get home.'

'Ah. All right.' Aksel found that the thought of Flora and Mette spreading out their purchases for a second and more thorough inspection was just as enticing as this was. This complex ritual was more than just going out and shopping for something that met your needs. It was about bonding and sharing, and the excitement of finding a sweater that was the right colour and design, and fitted perfectly.

He was learning that there were many things he *could* share with Mette, and wondered if this would ever be one of them. At the moment, it seemed an impossible set of rules and conventions, which were as complicated as any he'd seen on his travels. It occurred to him that Mette really needed a mother, and the thought wasn't as difficult to come to terms with as it had been. He could be a good father, without having to do everything himself.

Flora and Mette were whispering together, and he couldn't hear what they were saying over the swell of conversation around them. Then Flora turned to him, her eyes shining.

'We're giving you ten out of ten. Possibly ten and a half.'

That sounded great, but he wasn't sure what he'd done to deserve it. 'What for?'

'For being our ideal shopping companion.' Flora didn't seem disposed to break the score down, but Mette had no such reservations.

'Because you carry the bags, Papa. And you don't rush, and you buy soup. And fudge.'

Aksel hadn't realised that this could cause him so much pride. And pleasure. 'Thank you. I'm…honoured.'

Mette gave him a nod, which said that he was quite

right to feel that way, having been given such an accolade. Flora smiled, and suddenly his whole world became warm and full of sparkle.

'The Christmas tableau will be open by the time we've finished. And then I'd like to pop over to Mary's stall if you don't mind. I heard she has some nice little things for Christmas gifts.'

'That sounds great. I'd like that.' He wasn't quite sure what a Christmas tableau was, but he'd go with the flow. Aksel leaned back in his seat, stretching his legs out towards the fire. Making sense of the proceedings didn't much matter, he'd been voted ten out of ten as a shopping companion, and that was a great deal more than good enough.

The Christmas tableau turned out to be housed in a three-sided wooden structure outside the church. Inside were Mary and Joseph, an assortment of shepherds and three kings, along with one of the dogs from the therapy centre. Aksel wasn't quite sure how it had ended up there, but he assumed its presence had something to do with Esme, and that she'd probably had a hand in choosing its festive, red and white dog coat.

'Mette!' As they opened the gate to the churchyard, the shortest and broadest of the three kings started to wave, handing a jewelled box to one of the other kings and ducking past the crowd that was forming around the tableau.

Mette turned her head, recognising the voice, and tugged at Aksel's hand. 'It's Carrie. Where is she?'

It was the first time that Aksel had heard Mette say anything like that. Usually she ignored the things she couldn't see, and she'd been known to throw a temper tantrum when she couldn't find something she wanted.

'She's coming over to you now, sweetheart.' Flora volunteered the information, and Mette nodded. Now that the king was a little closer, he realised it *was* Carrie, one of the children's nurses from the clinic, and almost unrecognisable under a false beard and a large jewelled hat. Her small frame was completely disguised by what looked like several layers of bulky clothes under her costume.

'Hi, Carrie. Keeping warm?' Flora grinned at her.

'I'm a bit hot, actually.' Carrie pushed her beard up, propping it incongruously on the rim of her hat, and bent down to greet Mette. 'The costume was a bit big so I've got two coats on underneath this. Along with a thick sweater *and* thermal underwear.'

'Sounds reasonable to me. You've got a couple of hours out here. The shepherds are already looking a bit chilly.'

'Don't worry about them. The vicar's brought a couple of Thermos flasks along, and we've got an outdoor heater behind the manger, that's why everyone's crowding around it. You'd be surprised how warm it gets after a while.' Carrie volunteered the information and Flora laughed.

'That's good to know. I'll make sure I'm standing next to the heater when it's my turn.'

It was impossible that Flora wouldn't take a turn, she was so much a part of the life of the village. Aksel wondered what she'd be dressing up as and decided to wait and see.

'Would you like to come and see the stable, Mette?' Carrie bent down towards her. 'We've got a rabbit…'

'Yes, please.' Mette took her hand, waving to Aksel as Carrie led her away.

'A rabbit?' Aksel murmured the words as he watched her go.

'The vicar's not afraid to improvise, and I don't think there were any sheep available.' Flora chuckled. 'And anyway, don't you think it's the best stable you've ever seen?'

It was. The costumes were great, and there was a sturdy manger and lots of straw. A couple of other children, besides Mette, had been led up to the tableau by their parents, and had been welcomed inside by the shepherds and kings. Carrie was carefully showing Mette around, talking to her and allowing her to touch everything. The place shone with sparkling lights to re-create stars, and the warmth and love of a small community.

'Yes. The very best.'

CHAPTER ELEVEN

AKSEL WAS RELAXED and smiling as they watched Mette explore the stable with Carrie. So different from the man Flora had first met. The clinic tended to do that to patients and their families. Flora had seen so many people arrive looking tense and afraid, and had watched the secure and welcoming environment soothe their fears and allow them to begin to move forward. It was always good to see, but she'd never been so happy about it as she was now.

It was hard not to wonder what things might have been like if she and Aksel had met before they'd both been changed by the world. Whether they might have been able to make a family for more than just the space of a day. But for all the hope that the clinic brought to people's hearts, there was also the understanding that some things couldn't be changed, and it was necessary to make the best of them. She should enjoy today for what it was, and let it go.

Carrie delivered Mette back to her father, and she chattered brightly about having seen the rabbit and stroked it, as they walked towards Mary's stall. It was a riot of colour. Along with a few small quilts, there were fabric bags, with appliquéd flowers, patchwork lavender bags tied with ribbon, and quilted hats with earflaps. Mary was, unusually, not in the thick of things but sitting on a rickety stool and leaving her husband and Jackie, the young mum who helped out in the shop on Saturdays, to deal with the customers.

Flora greeted her with a smile. 'Hello, Mary. It's cold enough out here…'

Mary was sitting with her hands in her pockets, and her woollen hat pulled down over her ears and brow. Most of the stallholders prided themselves on being out in all weather, however cold, but maybe Mary should consider going into the pub for a while to get warm.

Mary nodded, her expression one of deep thought.

'These look wonderful.' Flora indicated the lavender bags and Aksel hoisted Mette up so she could smell them. 'How much are they?'

Mary smiled suddenly. 'Thruppence.'

Okay…. Flora had never heard of thruppenny lavender bags being a thing, but there were three in each bundle. They'd be tagged with a price anyway. Mary went back to staring in her husband's direction and Flora wondered if maybe they'd had an argument about something.

Hats were tried on, lavender sniffed, and the fabric bags admired. They found a hat for Mette, its bright reds and greens matching her coat, and Aksel encouraged Flora to treat herself to one of the fabric bags. It would be perfect for carrying some of the smaller items that she used most regularly in the course of her job, and it would be nice to visit the residents at the sheltered living complex carrying a bag that didn't scream that it was *medical*.

Mary smiled at her, and Flora put the bag and the hat down in front of her. 'I'd like to take these, Mary.'

'Ah, yes.' Mary sprang to her feet. 'The hat's for…the little girl.'

It was unlike Mary to forget a name. 'Yes, it's for Mette.'

'Of course. Red.' Mary stared at the hat and then seemed to come to her senses. 'That's two pounds for the hat, plus three and fourpence for the bag. Fourteen and six altogether, dear.'

Mary held out her hand to receive the money. Something was very wrong. Flora leaned across, studying her face in the reflection of the fairy lights above their heads.

'Are you all right, Mary?'

'I just have a bit of a headache, dear. How much did I say it was?'

Mary *wasn't* all right. Flora glanced at Aksel and saw concern on his face too. Even if he didn't follow the vagaries of pounds, shillings and pence, it was obvious that Mary was confused and calculating the bill in coins that had been obsolete for almost fifty years.

Flora squeezed around the edge of the stall, taking Mary's hand. It felt ice-cold in hers. 'Mary, can you sit down for me, please?'

'No, dear.'

'What's the matter?' Mary's husband, John, had left the customer he was serving and come over to see what was happening.

'I don't know. Mary doesn't seem well, has she hit her head or anything recently?'

John Monroe had been a county court judge before he'd retired, and his avuncular manner covered an ability to sum up a situation quickly and take action.

'Sit down, hen.' He guided Mary to the stool, keeping his arm around her when she sank down onto it, and turning to Flora. 'She bumped her head when we were setting up the stall. She said it was nothing, and she seemed fine…'

'Okay, where?' Flora gently peeled off Mary's hat and realised she hadn't needed to ask. A large bump was forming on the side of her head.

'We need to get her into the warm, John.' Flora looked

around at the crowded market. 'Go and fetch the vicar. I think that the church is the best place.'

John hesitated, not wanting to leave Mary, and Flora caught his arm. 'Go now, please.'

Aksel had dropped their shopping bags and Jackie stowed them away under the stall. Mette seemed to understand that something was wrong, and she stood quietly, her arms around Kari's neck. Jackie took her hand and Aksel bent down next to Mary, supporting her on the stool. Flora pulled out her phone.

'I'm going to call Charles.' She hoped that she wasn't overreacting but in her heart she knew that she wasn't. And she knew that Charles Ross-Wylde would rather she called, if she thought someone needed his help.

Charles answered on the second ring, and Flora quickly told him what had happened, answering his questions and breathing a sigh of relief when he told her he'd be there as soon as he could. She ended the call, and Aksel glanced up at her.

'Charles is on his way, and he's going to call an ambulance.' Flora murmured the words quietly, so that Mary didn't hear. 'This may be a bad concussion or a brain bleed, so we must be very careful with her and take her somewhere warm and quiet.'

'Fourteen and six... Fourteen...and...seven...' Mary seemed to be in a world of her own, and Aksel nodded, concern flashing in his eyes.

The vicar arrived, along with Carrie, who was red-faced and breathless from running, her beard hanging from one ear. She took Mette's hand and Aksel turned to her.

'Will you take her, please, Carrie?'

'Of course. You see to Mary, and I'll look after Mette and Kari.'

'I'll go and open up the church lounge.' The vicar was

fumbling under his shepherd's costume for his keys. 'It's nice and warm in there.'

Now all they had to do was to persuade Mary to go with them. Flora knelt down beside her. 'Mary, we're going to the church.'

'Are we?' Mary gazed dreamily around her, as if she wasn't quite sure what direction that was. 'All right.'

Mary went to stand up, swaying suddenly as she lost her balance. Aksel caught her, lifting her up, and she lay still and compliant in his arms.

People were gathering around the stall, some offering help. The only help they could give was to stand back, and Flora cleared a path for Aksel. As everyone began to re-alise what was happening, the crowd melted away in front of them, leaving them a clear route to the church.

They walked around the side of the ancient building to a more modern annexe. The vicar was waiting for them, holding the swing doors open, and he ushered Aksel through to the quiet, comfortable lounge. There was a long, upholstered bench seat at one side of the room, and Aksel carefully laid Mary down, while Flora fetched a cushion for her head.

'Mary, love....' John knelt down beside her and took her hand, but Mary snatched it away. Aksel laid his hand on John's shoulder.

'She's confused, John. We just need to keep her calm at the moment.'

'Is there any tea?' Mary tried to sit up, and Aksel gently guided her back down again.

'The vicar's just making some. He'll be along in a min-ute.' His answer seemed to satisfy Mary, and she lay back. Aksel kept talking to her, reassuring her and keeping her quiet.

Flora's phone rang and she pulled it from her pocket.

Charles sounded as if he was in the car, and she quickly told him where to find them.

'That's great. I'll be there soon, and an ambulance is on its way too…' The call fizzled and cut out, and Flora put her phone back into her pocket. Maybe Charles had just driven into a black spot, or maybe he'd said all he wanted to say.

'What's the matter with her, Flora?' John was standing beside her, waiting for her to end the call.

'I'm not sure, but it seems to be a result of the bump on her head.' Flora didn't want to distress John even further by listing the things it could be. 'We need to keep her quiet. Charles is on his way and the ambulance will be here soon.'

'What have I done…?' Tears misted John's eyes. 'She said it was nothing. She seemed a bit subdued, but I thought she was just cold. I was going to take her to the pub for lunch as soon as I'd finished with the customer I was serving.'

'It's okay. In these situations people often try to deny there's anything wrong with them and they'll hide their symptoms. And they'll push away the people they love most. We'll get her to the hospital and they'll help her.' There was nothing more that Flora could say. If this was what she thought it was, then Mary was gravely ill.

John nodded. 'Is there *anything* I can do?'

'Has Mary taken any medication? Did she take some-thing for the headache?'

'She didn't say she had one. And, no, she tries to avoid taking painkillers if she can.'

That could be a blessing in this particular situation. 'No aspirin, or anything like that? Please try to be sure.'

'No. Nothing. I've been with her all day, she hasn't taken anything.' John shook his head.

'Okay, that's good.' Flora smiled encouragingly at

him. 'Now, I want you to sit down and write down exactly when Mary bumped her head, and how she's seemed since. Please include everything, whether you think it's important or not.'

'Right you are.'

Maybe John knew that Flora was giving him something to do but he tore a blank sheet from one of the stack of parish magazines that lay on top of the piano and hurried over to a chair, taking a pen from his jacket pocket. Maybe the details would come in useful…

Flora knelt down beside Aksel. 'You should go and get Mette now. I can manage.'

Flora didn't want him to leave. Her own medical knowledge was enough to care for Mary until Charles arrived, but he was so calm. So reassuringly capable. But however much Mary might need him, however much Flora *did* need him, she knew that he couldn't leave Mette.

'One minute…' He got to his feet, striding towards the door. A brief, quiet conversation with someone outside, and he returned.

'You're sure you want to stay?' Aksel had obviously made a decision and from the look on his face it troubled him a little. But he'd come back.

'Carrie's going to take Mette and Kari back to the clinic and I'll meet her there later. She's in very good hands.'

'Yes, she is. Thank you.'

He gave a little nod, and knelt back down beside Mary, taking her hand. Flora had to think now. She had to remember all the advanced first-aid courses she'd been on, and the physiology and pathology elements of her degree course. She took a deep breath.

Leaning forward, she looked for any blood or fluid discharge from Mary's ears and nose. Checked that she was conscious and alert, and noticed that her pupils were of an unequal size and that a bruise was forming behind her ear. Then she picked up Mary's hand.

'Can you squeeze my hand, Mary?'

The pressure from Mary's fingers was barely noticeable. 'As tight as you can.'

'I think I must have hurt it.' Mary looked up at her, unthinking, blank trust written on her face. It tore at Flora's heart, and she knew that she must do everything she could to help Mary.

'Let me massage it for you.' It wouldn't do her head injury any good, but it would keep Mary calm, and that was important.

'Thank you. I feel a bit sick.'

Aksel carefully moved Mary, sitting her up, and Flora grabbed the rubbish bin, emptying it out on the floor. Mary retched weakly, and then relaxed.

'That's better. I'm sorry…'

'It's okay. You're okay now.' Flora made sure that Mary's mouth was clear, and Aksel gently laid her down in the recovery position. Flora was aware that John was watching them, and couldn't imagine his agony, but she had to concentrate on Mary.

She talked to Mary, soothing her, watching her every reaction. It seemed a very long time before the door opened and the vicar ushered Charles into the room.

John shot to his feet, watching and listening. Flora carefully relayed all the information she had to Charles, and he nodded, bending down towards Mary to examine her. Mary began to fret again, and by the time he'd finished she was trying to push him away. Charles beckoned to Flora.

'Can you keep her quiet?'

'Yes.' Flora knelt down, taking Mary's hand, and she seemed to settle. She heard Charles talking softly to John behind her, and then the arrival of the ambulance crew.

Then she had to move back as the paramedics lifted Mary carefully onto a stretcher.

'I couldn't have done better myself, Flora. Well done.' Charles didn't wait for her answer, turning to usher John out of the room.

The lights from the ambulance outshone the fairy lights on the stalls in the marketplace. The noise and bustle seemed to have quietened down, and many of the stall-holders watched as Mary was lifted into the ambulance and Charles and John followed.

Suddenly she felt Aksel's arm around her shoulders. As the ambulance negotiated the narrow street around the perimeter of the market square, people began to crowd around her, wanting to know what had happened to Mary.

'I'm sorry, we can't say exactly what's happened, that's for the doctors at the hospital to decide. Mary's in good hands.' Aksel gave the answer that Flora was shaking too much to give. Then he hurried her over to Mary's stall.

'Jackie, will you be okay to pack up the stall?'

Jackie nodded. 'Yes, I've called my husband and he's on his way down with his mates. They'll be here in a minute. How's Mary?'

'I'm afraid we don't know, but Charles Ross-Wylde is with her and she's in very good hands.' Aksel repeated the very limited reassurance that he'd given to everyone else.

'Okay. I'll wait for news. Carrie came and took your shopping bags, she's taken them back to the clinic with Mette.'

'Thanks, Jackie. Are you sure you'll be all right on your own?'

'Yes, of course. Look, there's my husband now.'

Jackie waved, and Aksel nodded. He turned away, his arm tightly around Flora.

'Do you want to go the long way home? Or take the more direct route?'

'What's the long way? Via Istanbul?'

Aksel chuckled. 'No, via the clinic. I'm going to go home and pick up the SUV, then go to see Mette. I'll either walk you home or you can come with me.'

'I'll come with you.' Being at home alone didn't much appeal at the moment. 'Thanks for staying with me, Aksel. I know you didn't want to leave Mette.'

'No, I didn't. But Mette was all right and I reckoned I might be needed here.'

'Yes, you were.' Flora was going through all of the things she'd done in her head, trying to think of something that she'd missed. Something she might have done better.

'Mary's going to be all right. Largely because of you...'

'You're just saying that. I'm not a doctor.'

'No, but you used your medical knowledge to do as much as any doctor on the scene could have. You kept her quiet, you made sure she didn't choke. You acted professionally and decisively.'

'But if something happens to her...' Flora didn't want to think about it. If there was something that she'd missed, and Mary didn't survive this... She couldn't bear to think about it.

He stopped walking, turning to face her. His eyes seemed dark, and his shadow all-encompassing.

'Listen. Mary was surrounded by people, and no one realised there was something wrong. If you hadn't noticed and done something about it, this wouldn't have ended as well as it has. You were the one who gave her a chance, Flora.'

His trust in her reached the dark corners of her heart. 'You were pretty cool-headed yourself.'

'Well, I've been in a few situations before.'

Flora would bet he had. 'I don't know what I would have done without you.'

He chuckled. 'I do. You would have done exactly the same—taken care of Mary, checked all her symptoms, and acted quickly. I might not cross the line from animal medicine into human medicine, but those things are essential in any kind of emergency.'

'You make me feel so much better.' He'd lifted a heavy weight from her shoulders. Whatever happened now, she'd know that she'd done all she could.

'Mary was lucky that you were there, Flora. Never think otherwise.'

They'd reached the SUV, parked outside his cottage, and Aksel felt in his pocket for the keys and opened the door for Flora. He was clearly keen to see Mette. *She* wanted to see Mette. Both of them had found a place in her heart, and now she didn't want to let them go.

The process of winding down had taken a while, but helping Mette to unpack the bags that lay in the corner of the room had helped. Aksel had been persuaded to tell a story about his travels, and she found herself joining in with Mette's excitement at the twists and turns of his narrative.

As they were leaving her phone rang. She pulled it out of her pocket, seeing Charles's number on the display, and when she answered, she heard John's voice on the line.

She listened carefully to what he had to say, feeling the tension ebb out of her. 'That's really good news, John…'

'Words can't express my gratitude, for what you did this afternoon Flora…' John's voice was breaking with emotion.

'I'm glad I could help. Make sure you get some rest tonight, you'll be able to see her in the morning. I'll come as soon as she's allowed visitors.' Flora ended the call, aware suddenly that Aksel was staring at her, waiting to hear John's news.

'This isn't bad news, is it?'

Flora shook her head. 'No, it's very good news. We were right about it being a brain haemorrhage and Mary was taken into surgery straight away. The operation was a success, and they're hopeful that, in time, Mary will make a full recovery.'

'That's wonderful. How's John, does he need a lift from the hospital? I can go there now and take him home.'

'No, he's okay. Charles is still there and he got some-one from the estate to fetch his car from the village and bring it to the hospital. Benefits of being the Laird.' A great weight seemed to have been lifted from Flora's chest, and she felt that she could really breathe again. 'John said… he was glad that I'd been there.'

'Yes. I was glad you were there, too. Let's go home, shall we?'

It seemed so natural to just nod and take his arm. As if the home that they were going to was *their* home and not two separate cottages. As they walked out of the clinic to-gether, towards the battered SUV, it didn't seem to mat-ter that she was leaning on his arm. Just for tonight, until she reached her own front door, she could rely on Aksel's strength and support.

CHAPTER TWELVE

FLORA HAD BEEN wondering whether to ask Aksel over for Sunday lunch, but she'd seen him set out towards the clinic with Kari by his side at eleven o'clock. She opened the refrigerator, staring at its contents. Suddenly she didn't feel like going to the trouble of cooking.

She made herself a sandwich, rounding it off with apple pie and ice cream as she watched a film on TV. Then she picked up a book, curling up on the sofa with Dougal and working her way through a couple of chapters.

The doorbell rang, and she opened her front door to find Aksel standing in the front porch. 'Shouldn't you be at the clinic?' The question slipped out before she'd had time to think.

'I went in a little early today and had lunch with Mette. I left her making paper angels with the other children.'

There was always something going on at the clinic, and Mette had obviously been drawn into the Sunday afternoon activities. 'That's good. The world always needs more paper angels.'

He nodded. 'Would you like to come for a walk?'

'A walk? I was planning to sit by the fire and make a few welcome gifts for the kids.'

'Sounds nice. A lot less chilly.' Something in his eyes beckoned her.

'The forecast's for snow later on this evening.'

He nodded, looking up at the sky. 'That looks about right. Are you coming?'

It was a challenge. Aksel was asking her to trust him, and in Flora's experience trusting a man didn't usually end well.

But Aksel was different. And what could happen on a windy, snowy hillside? Certainly nothing that involved exposing even a square inch of flesh.

'Why not? Come in, I'll get my coat.'

'You'll need a pair of sturdy shoes.' He glanced at the shoe rack in the hall.

'Even *I* wouldn't tackle the countryside in high heels. I have walking boots.' They were right at the back of the wardrobe, and Flora made for the stairs.

When she came back downstairs, his gaze flipped from her boots to the thick waterproof coat she wore and he gave a little nod of approval. As he strode across the road and towards the woods ahead of them, Flora struggled to keep up and he slowed a little.

'Where are we going?'

'I thought up to the old keep.' He pointed to the hilltop that overlooked the village, where piles of stones and a few remnants of wall were all that was left of the original castle seat of the Ross-Wylde family. 'Is that too far?'

It looked a long way. The most direct route from the village was up a steep incline, and Aksel was clearly heading for the gentler slope at the other side, which meant they had to go through the woods first.

'I can make it.' She wasn't going to admit to any doubts. 'Looks like a nice route for a Sunday afternoon.'

He kept his face impressively straight. If Aksel had any doubts about her stamina, he'd obviously decided to set them aside in response to her bravado. Perhaps he reckoned that he could always carry her for part of the way.

'I think so.' His stride lengthened again, as if he'd calculated the exact speed they'd need to go to get back by teatime. Flora fell into step with him, finding that the faster pace wasn't as punishing as it seemed, and they walked together along the path that led into the trees.

The light slowly began to fail. Flora hoped they'd be home soon, although Aksel didn't seem averse to stumbling around in the countryside after dark. She felt her heel begin to rub inside her boot and wondered if she hadn't bitten off more than she could chew.

Only their footsteps sounded in the path through the trees. It was oddly calming to walk beside him in silence, both travelling in the same direction without any need for words. Their heads both turned together as the screaming bark of a fox came from off to their left, and in the gathering gloom beneath the trees Flora began to hear the rustle of small creatures, which she generally didn't stop to notice.

He stopped at the far end of the wood, and Flora was grateful for the chance to catch her breath. Aksel was staring ahead of him at a red-gold sunset flaming across the horizon. It was nothing new, she'd seen sunsets before. But stumbling upon this one seemed different.

'You're limping. Sit down.' He indicated a tree trunk.

Flora had thought she was making a pretty good job of *not* limping. 'I'm okay.'

'First rule of walking. Look after your feet. Sit.' He was brooking no argument and Flora plumped herself down on the makeshift seat. Aksel knelt in front of her, picking up her foot, and testing the boot to see if it would shift.

'Ow! Of course it's going to hurt if you do that…'

she protested, and he ignored her, unlacing the boot. He stripped off her thin sock, the cold air making her toes curl.

'You're getting a blister.' He balanced her foot on his knee, reaching into his pocket and pulling out a blister plaster. It occurred to Flora that maybe he'd come prepared for her as she couldn't imagine that he ever suffered from blisters.

All the same, it was welcome. He stuck the plaster around her heel, and then pulled a pair of thick walking socks from his pocket.

'Your feet are moving around in your boots. These should help.'

'I thought walking boots were meant to be roomy.' She stared at the socks. They had *definitely* been brought along for her benefit.

'They're meant to fit. When your foot slips around in them, that's going to cause blisters.' He slid her boot back on and relaced it. 'How does that feel?'

She had to admit it. 'Better. Thanks.'

He nodded, unlacing her other boot. Running his fingers around her heel to satisfy himself that there were no blisters, he held the other sock out and she slid her foot into it. She reached for her boot, and he gave her a sudden smile.

'Let me do it. You need to lace them a bit tighter.'

Flora gave in to the inevitable. 'Rookie mistake?'

'Yes.' His habitual honesty wasn't making her feel any better.

'You might mention that it can happen to anyone. With new boots.' The boots weren't exactly new, but they hadn't been used much.

'It *can* happen to anyone. I let water get into one of my boots once, and lost the tips of two toes to frostbite.'

'Hmm. Careless.'

He looked up at her, smiling suddenly. 'Yes, it was. Looking at the way your teammates are walking comes as second nature because your feet are the only things you have to carry you home.'

They weren't exactly in the middle of nowhere. One of the roads through the estate was over to their right, and Flora had her phone in her pocket, so she could always call a taxi. But as Aksel got to his feet, holding out his hand to help her up, that seemed about as impossible as if they'd been at the South Pole.

She took a couple of steps. 'That's much more comfortable.'

'Good. Let me know if they start to hurt again, I have more plasters.'

Of course he did. If there was a next time, she'd make him hand over the plasters and lace her boots herself. She'd show him that she could walk just as far as he could. Or at least to the top of the hill and back down again.

As the ground began to rise, Flora's determination was tested again. She put her head down, concentrating on just taking one step after another. The incline on the far side of the hill hadn't looked that punishing, but it was a different matter when you were walking up it.

Aksel stopped a few times, holding out his hand towards her, and she ignored him. She could do this herself. It was beginning to get really dark now, and snow started to sting her face. This was *not* a pleasant Sunday afternoon stroll.

Finally they made it to the top and Aksel stopped, looking around at the looming shapes of the stones. Flora would have let out a cheer if she'd had the breath to do it.

'Perhaps we should take a rest now. Before we go back down.'

Yes! It was cold up here, but there must be some place where the stones would shelter them. Flora's legs were shaking and she suddenly felt that she couldn't take another step. She followed him over to where a tree had grown up amongst the stones, its trunk almost a part of them, and sat down on a rock, worn smooth and flat from its exposed location. Heaven. Only heaven wasn't quite so cold.

'I won't be a minute. Stay there.'

She nodded. Wild horses couldn't get her to move now. Aksel strode away, the beam of his torch moving to and fro among the stones. He seemed to be looking for something. Flora bent over, putting her hands up to her ears to warm them.

When he returned he was carrying an armful of dry sticks and moss. Putting them down in front of her, he started to arrange them carefully in two piles.

'What are you going to do now? Rub two sticks together to make a fire?' Actually, a fire seemed like a very good idea. It was sheltered enough here from the snow, which was blowing almost horizontally now.

'I could do, if you want. But this is easier.' He produced a battered tin from his pocket, opening it and taking out a flint and steel. Expertly striking the flint along the length of the steel, a spark flashed, lighting the pile of tinder that he'd made. He carefully transferred the embers to the nest of branches, and flames sprang up.

This was *definitely* a good idea. Flora held her hands out towards the fire, feeling it begin to warm her face as Aksel fuelled it with some of the branches he'd set to one side. She felt herself beginning to smile, despite all he'd put her through.

'This is nice.' When he sat down next to her she gave him a smile.

'Better than your fire at home?' His tone suggested that he thought she'd probably say no.

'Yes. In a strange kind of way.' Flora was beginning

to see how this appealed to Aksel. They'd only travelled a short way, but even though she could still see the lights of the village below her, she felt as if she was looking down from an entirely different planet. The effort of getting here had stripped everything away, and she felt unencumbered. Free, even.

CHAPTER THIRTEEN

AKSEL HAD PUSHED her hard, setting a pace that would stretch even an experienced walker. He'd wanted her exhausted, unable to sustain the smiles and the kindnesses that she hid behind and defended herself with. But Flora was a lot tougher than he'd calculated. She'd brushed away all his attempts to help her, and kept going until they'd got to the top of the hill.

But her smile *was* different now. As she warmed herself in front of the fire, Aksel could see her fatigue, and the quiet triumph in meeting the challenge and getting here. He'd found the real Flora, and he wasn't going to let her go if he could help it.

The blaze seemed to chase away the darkness that stood beyond it, illuminating the faces of the rocks piled around them as if this small shelter was the only place in the world. Right now, he wished it could be, because Flora was there with him.

'Now that we're here…' she flashed him a knowing smile '…what is it you want me to say?'

She knew exactly what he'd done. And it seemed that she didn't see the need for tact any more.

'Say whatever you want to say. What's said around a camp fire generally stays there.'

She thought for a moment. 'All right, then, since you

probably have a lot more experience of camp-fire truth or dare games, you can start. What's the thing you most want?'

Tricky question. Aksel wanted a lot of things, but he concentrated on the one that he could wish for with a good conscience.

'Keeping Mette from harm.'

'That's a good one. You'll be needing to get some practice in before she hits her teens.'

'What's that supposed to mean?' Aksel explored the idea for a moment and then held up his hand to silence Flora. 'On second thoughts, I don't think I want to know.'

'That's just as well, really. Nothing prepares any of us for our teens.'

She was smiling, but there was quiet sadness in her tone. Aksel decided that if he didn't call her bluff now, he was never going to. This wasn't about Mette any more, it was all about Flora.

'All right. I'm going to turn the question on its head. What would you avoid if you could go back in time?'

'How long have you got?'

'There's plenty of fuel for the fire here. I'll listen for as long as I can convince you to stay.'

She stared into the fire, giving a little sigh. 'Okay. Number one is don't fret over spots. Number two is don't fall in love.'

'The spots I can do something about. I'm not sure that I'm the one to advise anyone about how not to fall in love.' Aksel was rapidly losing control of his own feelings for Flora.

'All you can do is be there for her when she finds herself with a broken heart.'

The thought was terrifying. But he wouldn't have to contend with Mette's teenage years just yet, and the question of Flora's heart was a more pressing one at the moment. He would never forgive himself if he lost this chance to ask.

'Who broke yours?'

'Mine?' Her voice broke a little over the word.

'Yes. What was his name?'

'Thomas Grant. I was nineteen. What was the name of the first girl who dumped you?'

Aksel thought hard. 'I don't remember. I went away on a summer camping trip with my friends, and by the time I got back she was with someone else. I don't think I broke her heart, and she didn't break mine.'

'If you can't remember her name, she probably didn't.' Flora was trying to keep this light, but these memories were obviously sad ones.'

'So… Thomas Grant. What did he do?'

'He…' Flora shrugged, as if it didn't matter. Aksel could tell that it did. He waited, hoping against agonised hope that if she looked into her own heart, and maybe his, she'd find some reason to go on.

'I went to university in Edinburgh to study physiotherapy. He was in the year above me, studying history…' She let out a sigh. 'I fell in love with him. I didn't tell my parents for a while, they were in Italy and I thought I'd introduce him to them first. I think my mum probably worked it out, though, and so Dad would have known as well.'

'An open secret, then.' It didn't sound so bad, but this had clearly hurt Flora. Aksel supposed that most really bad love affairs started well. The only real way to avoid hurt, was never to fall in love.

'Yes. We decided to tell our parents over the summer. We'd been talking about living together during our second year and…he seemed very serious. He even spoke about getting engaged. So I asked him to come to Italy with me for a fortnight. Mum and Dad really liked him and we had a great holiday. Alec wasn't too well that summer...'

Something prickled at the back of Aksel's neck. He knew that the end of this story wasn't a good one, and wondered what it could have to do with Flora's brother. His hand shook as he picked up a stick, poking the fire.

'You know, don't you, that cystic fibrosis is an inherited condition?' She turned to look at him suddenly.

'Yes.' Aksel searched his brain, locating the correct answer. 'It's a recessive gene, which means that both parents have to carry the gene before there's any possibility of a child developing cystic fibrosis.'

'Yes, that's right. Tom knew that my brother had cystic fibrosis, I never made any secret of it and I'd explained that since both my parents have the gene there was a good chance that I'd inherited it from one of them. Not from both, as my brother did, because I don't have the condition.'

'There's also a chance you haven't.'

She nodded. 'There's a twenty five percent chance of inheriting the gene from both parents. Fifty percent of inheriting it from one parent, and a twenty five percent chance of inheriting it from neither parent. The odds are against me.'

She didn't know. The realisation thundered through his head, like stampeding horses. Aksel hadn't really thought about it, but taking the test to find out whether she'd inherited the faulty gene seemed the logical thing to do, and he wondered why Flora hadn't. He opened his mouth and then closed it again, not sure how to phrase the question.

'When we came home to Scotland, we went to stay with his parents for a week. I told them about myself, and talked about my family. Tom told me later that I shouldn't have said anything. His parents didn't want their grandchildren to run the risk of inheriting my genes.'

'But that's not something you have to keep a secret…' Aksel had tried to just let her tell the story, without intervening, but this was too much. Anger and outrage pulsed in his veins.

'No. I don't think so either.'

'But… Forgive me if this is the wrong thing to say, I'm sure your whole family would rather that your brother didn't have cystic fibrosis. That doesn't mean it would be better if your parents had never married, or your brother hadn't been born.'

Tears suddenly began to roll down her cheeks. Maybe he *had* said the wrong thing. 'Thank you. That's exactly how I feel.'

'So they were wrong.' Surely *someone* must have told her that. 'What did your parents say?'

'Nothing. I didn't tell them, or Alec. It would have really hurt them, and I couldn't tell my own brother that someone thought he wasn't good enough. He's a fine man, and he's found someone who loves him and wants to raise a family with him.'

The defiance in her voice almost tore his heart out. Flora had stayed silent in order to keep her brother from hurt. She'd borne it all by herself, and her tears told him that with no way to talk about it and work it through, the wound she'd been dealt had festered.

'Did he listen? To his parents?'

'Yes, he listened. It probably had a lot to do with the fact that they were funding his grant, and they threatened to withdraw their support if he didn't give me up.'

'Don't make excuses for him, Flora. Don't tell me that it's okay to even contemplate the thought that my daughter, or your brother, are worth less than anyone else.'

She laid her hand on his arm, and Aksel realised that he was shaking with rage. Maybe that was what she needed to see. Maybe this had hurt her for so long because she'd never talked about it, and never had the comfort of anyone else's reaction.

'No one's ever going to tell Mette that she's anything other than perfect. I'm not going to tell Alec that either.'

She'd missed herself out. Flora was perfect too, whether or not she carried the gene. But, still, she hadn't found out...

'You don't know whether you carry the gene or not, do you?'

She shook her head miserably.

'Flora, it's no betrayal of your brother to want to know.'

'I know that. In my head.' She placed her hand over her heart. 'Not here...'

Suddenly it was all very clear to him. 'You just want someone to trust you, don't you?'

Surprise showed in her face. 'I never thought of it that way. But, yes, if I take the test I want someone who'll stick by me whatever the result. If it turns out that I don't carry the gene, then I'll never know what would have happened if I did, will I? I suppose that's just foolishness on my part.'

It was the foolishness of a woman who'd been badly hurt. One that Aksel could respect, and in that moment he found he could love it too, because it was Flora's.

'Anyone who really knew you would trust you, Flora. *I* trust you.'

She gave a little laugh. 'Are you making me an offer?'

Yes. He'd offer himself to her in a split second, no thought needed. But he couldn't gauge her mood, and the possibility that she might not be entirely serious made him cautious.

'I just meant that you can't allow this to stop you from taking what you want from life. You deserve a lot more than this.'

* * *

The sudden anger wasn't something that Flora usually felt. There was dull regret and the occasional throb of pain, but this was bright and alive. And it hurt, cutting into her like a newly sharpened blade.

'And that's why you brought me up here, is it? To take me apart, piece by piece?' On this hilltop, with the village laid out below them like a child's toy, it felt as if she could sense the world spinning. And it was spinning a great deal faster at the thought that Aksel wanted to know what made her tick.

'I brought you here because…it's possible to walk away from the everyday. To see things more clearly than you might otherwise. And because I wanted to know why someone as beautiful and accomplished as you are seems so sad.'

No. She couldn't hear this. Aksel needed to take the rose-coloured spectacles off and understand who she really was.

'I'm *not* sad. I just see things the way they are.'

'That no one's ever going to accept you for who you are? That's just not true, Flora.'

'Well that's not my experience. And for your information, I didn't give up on men completely, I just…approach with caution.'

He shook his head, giving a sudden snort of laughter. 'I've never thought that sex was much like stopping at a busy road junction.'

Trust Aksel. But his bluntness was always refreshing. She'd been skirting around the word and now that he'd said it… They were talking about sex. And unless Flora was very much mistaken, this wasn't a conversation about sex generally, it was about the two of them having sex. Despite all the reasons why it shouldn't, the thought warmed her.

'I'm not going to have sex with you, Aksel. I can't…'

Flora didn't have the words to tell him why and she buried her face in her hands in frustration.'

'You don't have to give me any reasons. *No* is enough.'

Not many men took rejection the way that Aksel did. He'd pushed her on so many other things but this was where he drew the line. His smile let slip a trace of regret, but he accepted what she said as her final answer.

It wasn't final, though. Everything they were to each other, all the things they'd shared came crashing in on Flora. She couldn't let him believe that she didn't want him. The problem was hers, and she had to own it.

'It's not you. It's me.'

'It's a good decision, Flora. We've both been hurt. I'm leaving in five weeks, and you'll be staying here.'

And despite all that she wanted him. Maybe *because* of it. A relationship that had to end in five weeks didn't seem quite so challenging as something that might end because her genetic make-up, something she couldn't change, wasn't deemed good enough.

'But I *want* to explain…'

His face softened suddenly. 'There's no better place to do that than at a camp fire.'

'After Tom left me I had a few no-strings affairs, with men I knew. I thought it would help me get over him, but… they just didn't turn out right.' Flora couldn't bring herself to be more specific than that. She was broken, and even Aksel couldn't mend her.

'They ended badly?' Aksel came to the wrong conclusion, which was hardly surprising. She was going to have to explain.

'No, they ended well, it was all very civilised. But things didn't work physically. For me, I mean…'

He was looking at her steadily. She could almost see

his brain working, trying to fit each piece of the puzzle together, and when he did, she saw that too.

'I think that when two people have sex, an orgasm is something that you create together.'

Sex and *orgasm*. All in the same sentence and without a trace of embarrassment or hesitation. That made life a lot easier.

'I don't want to fake it with you, Aksel. And that's all I know how to do now.'

Tears began to roll down her cheeks. She wanted to be with him, and all that she'd lost hurt, in a way it never had before. Flora heard the scrape of Aksel's all-weather jacket as he reached for her, and she shied away.

'The way I see it is that we have a connection. I don't know why or how, but I do know that I want to be close to you, in whatever way seems right. Do you feel that?' The tenderness in his face made her want to cry even more.

'I feel it. But it's too late…' Flora made one last attempt to fight the growing warmth that wanted so much more than she was able to give.

'Maybe I just ask you to my place for a glass of wine. We put our feet up in front of the fire…'

Frustration made her open her mouth before she'd put her brain in gear. 'You don't get it, Aksel. I want wild and wonderful sex with you, and frankly a glass of wine doesn't even come close…' Flora clapped her hand over her mouth before she blurted anything else out.

The trace of a smile hovered around his lips. 'You're killing me, Flora. You know that, don't you?'

'I know. I'm sorry.'

'That's okay. You're worth every moment of it.' Aksel leaned forward, murmuring in her ear, 'Close your eyes. I won't touch you, just imagine…'

Here, alone with him on a windy hilltop, warmed by the crackling flames of a fire, Flora could do that. She could leave her anger behind, along with everything that stood between them, and visualise his kiss and the feel of his fingers tracing her skin. She shivered with pleasure, opening her eyes again.

'You're smiling.' He was smiling too. The knowledge that he'd been watching her face, knowing that she was thinking of him, sent tingles of sensuality down her spine.

'That was a great kiss. One of the best.'

He raised his eyebrows. 'So we kissed? I'm glad you liked it. Any chance I might get to participate in the next one?'

He was closer now, and Flora closed her eyes again. This time she didn't have to imagine the feel of his lips on hers. They were tender at first, like the brush of a feather, and when she responded to him the kiss deepened. She grabbed the front of his jacket, pulling him close, and felt his arms wrap around her.

Arousal hit her hard. The kind of physical yearning that she'd searched for so many times and which had eluded her. It was impossible to be cold with Aksel.

'That was much better. There are some things I can't imagine all on my own.'

He grinned suddenly. 'I liked it much better, too.'

'Would you like…to continue this? Somewhere more comfortable?'

'Will you promise me one thing?' He hesitated.

'What's that?'

'Don't fake it with me, Flora. However this turns out is okay, but I need you to be honest with me.'

She stretched up, kissing his cheek. 'No secrets, no lies. It's what I want, too.'

* * *

The thought that Flora had trusted him enough to feel that this time might be different was both a pleasure and a challenge. Aksel kicked earth onto the smouldering remains of the fire and shouldered his backpack, holding her hand to guide her down the steepest part of the hill, which led most directly to her cottage.

Flora unlocked her front door, stepping inside and turning to meet his gaze when he didn't follow her.

'Have you changed your mind?'

'No. But it's okay for you to change yours. At any time.'

She replied by pulling him inside and kicking the door shut behind them, then stretching up to kiss him. It was impossible that she didn't feel the electricity that buzzed between them and when she gave a little gasp of pleasure, unzipping his jacket so that they could nuzzle closer, it felt dizzyingly arousing. He wanted her so badly, and she seemed to want him. The thought that he might not be able to please her as he wanted to clawed suddenly at his heart.

Maybe he shouldn't take that too personally. Flora had been quick enough to tell him that he wasn't in charge of everything that happened around him. He would be a kind and considerate lover, and if things didn't work out the way they wanted, he'd try not to be paralysed by guilt.

'I'll love you the best that I can…' The urgent promise tore from his lips.

'I know you will. That's all I want.' She took his hand and led him up the stairs.

CHAPTER FOURTEEN

HE WAS LETTING her dictate the pace. Caught between urgent passion and nagging fear, Flora had no idea what she wanted that pace to be. Aksel pulled back the patchwork quilt that covered her bed and sat down, waiting for her to come to him.

She opened the wooden box that stood on top of the chest of drawers, rummaging amongst the collection of single earrings and pieces of paper that she shouldn't lose. Right at the bottom, she found the packet of condoms.

'I have these. I hope they're not out of date…' Her laugh sounded shrill and nervous.

'Let's see.' He held out his hand, and she dropped the packet into it. Aksel examined it carefully and then shot her a grin. 'They're okay for another six months.'

'Good. Maybe we'll save one for later.' The joke didn't sound as funny as she'd hoped. In fact, it sounded stupid and needy, but his slow smile never wavered.

Aksel caught her hand, pressing it to his lips. She sank down onto his knee and he embraced her, kissing her again, and suddenly there was only him. Undressing her slowly. Allowing him to patiently explore all the things that pleased her was going to be a long journey, full of many delights.

'Stop…' She'd let out a sigh of approval when he got

to the fourth button of her shirt, and he paused, laying his finger across her lips. 'Be still. Be quiet, for as long as you can.'

'How will you know the difference?' In Flora's rather limited experience, most men wanted as much affirmation as they could get.

He gave a small shrug. 'If I don't know the difference when I hear it, then I really shouldn't be here.'

Flora put her arms possessively around his neck. This guy was *not* going anywhere. And if he wanted her to fight the rising passion until there was no choice but to give in to it, then that was what she would do.

She kept silent, even though her limbs were shaking as he undressed her. The touch of his skin against hers almost made her cry out, but she swallowed the sound. Flora had never had a man attend to her pleasure so assiduously before, and while the physical effect of that was evident in the growing hunger she felt, the emotional effect was far more potent.

He moved back onto the bed, sitting up against the pillows, and lifting her astride him. Face to face, both able to see and touch wherever they pleased. She reached round to the nape of his neck, undoing the band that was tied around his hair, and letting it fall forward.

'Is that what you want?' He smiled suddenly.

'Yes.' She kissed him again. 'I want that too.'

Aksel laughed softly. 'What else?'

It was an impossible question. 'It's too long a list. I don't think I know where to start...'

'How about here, then?'

She felt his arm coil around her back, pulling her against his chest. His other hand covered her breast, and she felt the brush of his hair against her shoulder as he kissed her neck. Flora closed her eyes, trying to contain her excitement.

She couldn't help it. Her own ragged cry took her by surprise. Wordless, unmodulated, it was as if Mother Nature had climbed in through a window and stripped away everything but instinct and pleasure. She felt Aksel harden, as if this was what he'd been waiting for. If she'd known that it would feel so good, she'd have been waiting for it too.

'I want you so much, Flora…'

But he was going to wait until she was ready. Flora reached for the condoms, her hands shaking. When she touched him, to roll one on, she saw his eyes darken suddenly, an involuntary reaction that told her that he too was fighting to keep the last vestiges of control.

When she lifted her body up and took him inside, Aksel groaned, his head snapping back. And his large gentle hands spread across her back.

This time things were going to be different. No faking it, and… No thought either. She was thinking too much. Flora felt herself tremble in his arms, returning his kisses as the tension built. A soft, rolling tide that must surely grow.

He sensed it too. The fragile, tingling feeling rose and then dissipated, leaving her shaken but still unsatisfied. All the same, it was something. More than she'd experienced for a long time.

Aksel didn't question her, but as he held her against his chest she could hear his heartbeat. He wanted to know.

'It was nice… Something.'

'Not everything, though?' His chest heaved, with the same disappointment that Flora felt. Nagging frustration turned once more to hunger.

'Can we try again?' He was still inside her. Flora knew that he must feel that hunger too.

'Maybe we should stop. I don't want to hurt you.'

'You won't. I want to try again, and this time I…don't want you to be so gentle.'

He hesitated. Flora knew that she was asking a lot of him. *Just take me. Make me come.* Maybe that was too much weight of expectation to put on any man.

But she knew that he wanted to. She wriggled out of his arms, moving away from him. Bound now only by gaze.

'Don't you want me?'

'Are you crazy, Flora? You're everything any man could want, and far more than I have a right to take…'

'But I'm asking you to do it anyway.'

For one moment, she thought he'd turn away from her. And then he moved, so quickly that he'd caught her up and pinned her down on the bed before she knew quite what was happening. His eyes were dark, tender and fierce all at the same time.

'Take my hand.' His elbows were planted on either side of her, and she reached up, feeling his fingers curl around hers in what seemed a lot like a promise. Whatever happened next, he'd be right there with her.

They'd faced passion together, and then faced disappointment. The kind of disappointment that a man—Aksel, anyway—found difficult to forget. If Flora hadn't already given him a good talking to about the nature of guilt, he'd be feeling far too responsible, and much too guilty to do this.

But when he'd tipped her onto her back, she'd gasped with delight, smiling up at him and putting her hand in his when he asked her. Trapped in her gaze, entering her for the second time was even better than the first. Better than anything he'd ever done, and it felt liable to overshadow anything he ever *would* do again.

She wrapped her legs around his back, and he felt her skin against his, warm and welcoming. He began to move, and her eyes darkened as her pupils dilated. Her body responded to his, a thin sheen of perspiration forming on her brow.

Aksel watched her carefully, revelling in all the little signs of her arousal. Suddenly she gasped, her whole body quivering for a moment in anticipation and her hand gripping his tightly. And then that sweet, sweet feeling as Flora clung to him, choking out his name.

It broke him. His own orgasm tore through him, leaving him breathless, his heart hammering in his chest. When he was able to focus his eyes again, the one thing he'd most wanted was right in front of him.

'You're smiling.'

Flora reached up, her fingertips caressing the side of his face. 'So are you.'

'Yes.' Aksel had the feeling that it was one of those big, stupid after-sex smiles. One that nothing in this world could wipe from his face. 'I'm not even going to ask. I know you weren't faking that.'

The thought seemed to please her. As if she'd wanted him to feel the force of her orgasm, without having to be told.

'I loved it. Every moment.'

'I loved it too.'

Her hand was still in his, and he raised it to his lips, kissing her fingers. Easing away from her for a moment, he arranged the pillows and she snuggled against him, laying her head on his chest, so soft and warm in his arms. Aksel let out a sigh of absolute contentment.

* * *

Flora had slept soundly, and she woke before dawn. The clock on the bedside table glowed the numbers six and twelve in the darkness. Twelve minutes past six was more Aksel's wake-up call than it was hers.

But he was still asleep. And she felt wide awake and more ready to meet the day than she usually did at this time in the morning.

She moved, stretching her limbs, and his eyelids fluttered open. Those blue eyes, the ones that had taken her to a place she'd been afraid to go last night.

Afraid... The clarity of early morning thoughts wondered whether it might just be the case that she'd been afraid all these years. Afraid to give herself to a man who didn't trust her enough for her to trust him back.

But she'd given herself to Aksel. In one overwhelming burst of passion that really should have been accompanied by booming cannons, waving flags, and perhaps a small earthquake. And she couldn't help smiling every time she thought about it.

He stretched, and she felt the smooth ripple of muscle. Then he reached for her hand, the way he had last night. He was still here, with her. Still protecting her from the doubts and fears.

'God morgen.' He leaned over, kissing her brow.

He'd lapsed into Norwegian a few times last night as they'd lain curled together in the darkness. It was as if his thoughts didn't wait to be translated before they reached his tongue, and although Flora didn't know what he'd said, the way he'd said it had left her in no doubt. They had been words of love, whispered in the quiet warmth of an embrace, and meant to be felt rather than heard.

'Are you...?' Did he feel as good as she did? Did he want this moment to last before the day began to edge it out? Flora couldn't think of a way of saying that in any language.

He chuckled, flexing his limbs again. 'I am. Are you?'

'Yes. I am too.'

All she needed was to lie here with him, holding his hand. But the sound of paws scrabbling at the kitchen door broke the silence.

'That's Dougal. He won't stop until I let him out…' Flora reluctantly tried to disentangle herself from Aksel's embrace, but he held on to her.

'I'll go. If you'd like to stay here, then I'll make you some breakfast.'

That would be nice, but even the time it took to make a couple of pieces of toast would be too long an absence. Flora let go of his hand and sat up. Even that was too much distance and she bent to kiss him again.

'I'll go. Are you hungry?'

He shook his head. 'Coffee or juice would be nice.'

She could let Dougal out, give him some food and water, and make coffee in two minutes flat if she hurried. 'Will you still be naked when I get back?'

Aksel grinned. 'You can count on it.'

She took the road into the estate as fast as the freezing morning would allow, and dropped Aksel off at the therapy centre at ten to nine, leaving him to take Dougal inside. If anyone noticed, then giving a next-door neighbour a lift into work couldn't excite any comment. She made it up to her office at one minute to nine, tearing off her coat and sitting down at her desk. Her first session of the morning wasn't until half past nine, and she could at least look as if she was at work, even though her mind was elsewhere.

Her whole body felt different, as if it was still bathed in Aksel's smile. Science told her that it was probably the effect of feel-good neuro-transmitters and hormones, but rational thought had its limitations. Aksel seemed to have no limitations at all.

When she closed her eyes, she could still feel him. He'd brushed off her suggestion that surely there wasn't anything more he might explore, and had taken her on a sensory journey that had proved her wrong. Aksel made foreplay into an exquisite art, and he obviously enjoyed it just as much as she did.

'Flora, we've a new patient....' Her eyes snapped open again to see Charles Ross-Wylde staring at her from the doorway. 'Are you all right?'

'Oh. Yes, I'm fine. Just concentrating.' Flora wondered if it looked as if she'd just spent two hours having stupendous sex. In the three years she'd been here, she'd never seen Charles show any interest in anything other than work, and he might not understand.

'Yes. Of course. As long as you're not feeling unwell.'

'No!' She could have sounded a little less emphatic about that as Charles was beginning to look puzzled. Best get down to business. 'You've a new patient for me to see...?'

The day wasn't without its victories. Andy Wallace had mentioned that Aksel had popped in, bringing Mette with him, and that they'd talked about ice carving and the long road that led across the Andes. The friendship seemed to have given Andy the final push to take his first step unaided.

Flora had tried to conceal her blushes when Andy had talked about Aksel, but he was in the habit of watching everyone closely. When they'd finished their session together, Andy had asked her to give Aksel his best when she saw him, smiling quietly when Flora had said she would.

Dougal seemed a little calmer when she picked him up from the centre, and didn't make his usual frenetic dash around the cottage. He lay down in front of the fire, growling quietly.

'What's the matter, Dougal?' Flora bent down to stroke him, and he gave her his usual response, his tail thumping against the hearth. She walked into the kitchen, wondering if he'd follow, and he bounded past her, pawing at the cupboard where she kept his food. Whatever it was, it didn't seem to have affected his appetite.

She knew that Aksel would come. He'd be late, staying at the clinic until Mette was ready to go to bed, but he'd come. She heard the sound of the battered SUV outside, and smiled. He usually walked back from the castle, but tonight he was in a hurry.

The doorbell rang and she opened the door. Aksel was leaning against the opening of the porch, grinning.

'Are you coming in?'

'Are you going to ask me in?' There didn't seem to be any doubt in his mind that she would.

'Since you're holding a bottle of wine, then yes.'

He stepped inside, and Flora took the bottle from his hand, putting it down on the hall table. Without giving him the chance to take off his coat, she kissed him.

'I thought you wanted the wine,' he teased her, kissing her again hungrily.

'Isn't that just an excuse? To call round?'

'Yes, it's an excuse. Although if you'd prefer to just sit around the fire and drink it…' Aksel seemed determined to give her the choice, even though their kisses had already shown that neither of them wanted to spend the rest of evening anywhere else than in bed.

'No. I want you stone-cold sober. Upstairs.'

Aksel chuckled. 'I'll have you stone-cold sober, too. And calling out my name, the way you did last night.'

The thought was almost too much, but there was still something she had to do. Dougal was lying in front of the fire, still making those odd growling sounds.

'Will you take a look at Dougal first?'

'Of course. What's the matter with him?' Aksel walked into the sitting room, bending down to greet Dougal.

'I'm not sure. He's eating fine, and he doesn't seem to be in any pain. But he's making these odd noises.'

Aksel nodded, trying to stop Dougal from licking him as he examined him. Then he nodded in satisfaction. 'There's absolutely nothing wrong with him. He's trying to purr.'

'What?' That didn't sound like much of a diagnosis. 'Like a cat?'

'Yes.' Aksel tickled Dougal behind his ears and he rolled on his back, squirming in delight and growling. 'When I arrived at work this morning, I went to the office to finish up my report for Esme on the dog visiting scheme. I took Dougal with me to keep him out of the way as everyone was busy.'

'And you have a cat in the office at the canine therapy centre? Isn't that a bit of an explosive mix?'

Aksel shrugged, getting to his feet. 'Cats and dogs aren't necessarily natural enemies. A dog's instinct is to chase smaller animals, and a cat's instinct is to sense that as an attack, and flee. It's all a big misunderstanding, really.'

'Okay, so there was a cat at the centre...'

'Yes, someone brought it in, thinking that they might take it. Esme wasn't about to turn it away because... Esme doesn't know *how* to turn an animal in need away. And Dougal's natural instinct seems to be to make friends with everything that moves, and so by the end of the morning the two of them were curled up together. The cat was purring away and Dougal… I guess he was just trying to make friends.'

'So now we've got a dog that thinks he's a cat on our hands.' Flora looked down at Dougal, and he trotted up to her, rubbing his head against her leg.

'Maybe he'll grow out of it.'

Maybe. It made the little dog even more loveable, if that was at all possible. And talking of loveable…

'So… Mette and Kari are at the castle, and they're both fast asleep by now. Dougal's okay, apart from a few minor identity issues.' She approached Aksel, reaching up to wrap her arms around his neck. 'That just leaves you and me.'

'And more than twelve hours before it's time to go back to work.' Aksel grinned, and picked her up in his arms.

CHAPTER FIFTEEN

THEY LAY ON the bed together, naked. Aksel had made love to her, and each time he did, it was more mind-blowing than the last. Things were going to have to plateau at some point, or Flora's nerve endings were going to fry.

'You know, don't you? When someone you're with has an orgasm.' Flora wondered whether the other guys she'd been with had known too. Maybe they had, and just hadn't cared.

'I do with you.' He grinned lazily. 'I suppose you want to know how.'

Yes, she did. Very much, because it seemed to please him so much. 'Tell me.'

'Your pupils dilate. You start to burn up, and you cry out for me. Then your muscles start to contract…'

'You like that?' Flora traced her fingertips across the ripple of muscles in his chest.

'You know I do. And you can't fake any of that.'

'Strictly speaking… I think you could try.'

'No, you wouldn't fool me.' Aksel curled his arm around her, pulling her a little closer. 'What we have is honesty, and I'd know if that ever changed.'

It was a good answer. They *were* honest with each other. It had been something that had just happened from day one. Perhaps it was that which had guided them past all the traps and obstacles, and led them here.

'Well, honestly…' Flora propped herself up on one arm so that she could look into his eyes '…you are the most perfect, beautiful man I've ever seen.'

He didn't believe that. Aksel thought that his body was a workhorse that got him from one place to another, along with anything he carried with him. Vanity didn't occur to him.

'I'd urge you to make an appointment with your optician if you think I'm perfect.'

'You have a great body. *Very* nice arms.'

'Uneven toes…' He wiggled the toes on his left foot, two of which had been amputated above the distal phalangeal joint.

'Not very uneven. You only lost the tips of your toes, and they tell a story.'

'One that I won't forget in a hurry. Frostbite's painful.'

'And the mark on your arm?'

'That's where I was bitten by a snake. In South America.'

'And this one?' Flora ran her finger across a scar on his side.

'I was in a truck that tipped over while fording a river. The current turned out to be a bit stronger than we anticipated.'

'And you have a couple of small lumps along your clavicle where you broke it. The muscles in your shoulders are a little tight because you worry. A little tension in your back because Mette loves it when you carry her on your shoulders. Most people's bodies reflect who they are, and how they've lived, and yours is perfect.'

'And you… You really *are* perfect, Flora. You're made

of warmth and love, and that makes you flawlessly beautiful.' He chuckled. 'Apart from that little scar on your knee.'

'It's not as good a story as yours are. I fell off my bike when I was a kid.'

Aksel reached up, pulling her down for a kiss. 'It's a great story. The scar's charming, along with the rest of you.'

Flora ran her fingers through his hair. Thick and blond, most women would kill for hair like that.

'Okay…so what's with the hair, then?' He knew that she liked it spread over his shoulders, instead of tied back, especially when they made love.

'It makes you look free, like a wild creature. Is that why you grew it so long?'

He shrugged. 'I don't know. Maybe I just never got around to cutting it. I like the sound of that, though.'

She kissed him again. 'Don't get around to cutting it, Aksel. That's perfect too.'

Aksel was happy. He felt free when he made love to Flora. And even when they weren't making love, the contentment that he felt whenever he was in her company was making him feel that maybe there was a little life left in his battered, careworn heart.

Tonight he'd be sleeping apart from Flora, though. He'd arranged to bring Mette home for the afternoon, and she'd stay the night with him at the cottage, before returning to the clinic the next morning. It had gone without saying that this was something that he needed to do alone.

He'd decided on some games, and had bought all of Mette's favourite foods. When he arrived home with her, he spread the colourful quilt on her bed, walking her around the cottage to remind her of the layout.

Everything just clicked into place, as if he'd been there

all of Mette's life. She enjoyed her afternoon, and dozed in his arms as he told her the story about how crocodiles and penguins had helped him to reach the top of a high mountain in safety.

'I want to say goodnight to Mama.'

Aksel realised suddenly that in his determination to get everything right, he'd forgotten all about Mette's electric candle and had left it by her bed at the clinic. But it was important that his daughter felt she could speak to her mother whenever she wanted to. He reached for one of the Christmas candles that Flora had arranged on his mantelpiece, putting it into the grate.

'We'll use Tante Flora's candle, shall we? Just for tonight.'

Mette nodded, and Aksel fetched matches from the kitchen and lit the candle. They sat together on the hearthrug, saying their goodnights, and Mette leaned forward and blew out the candle. Aksel carried her upstairs, settled her into her bed and kissed her goodnight.

At a loose end now, and not wanting to go downstairs just yet in case Mette stirred, he went to his own bedroom and lay down on the bed, staring at the ceiling. This was the first night that he'd been completely alone with her, and it was a responsibility that brought both happiness and a measure of terror.

Aksel woke up to the feeling of something tugging at his arm. Opening his eyes, he realised that Kari had hold of his sweater in her jaws and was pulling as hard as she could to make him wake up and get off the bed. A moment later the smoke alarm started to screech a warning that made his blood run cold.

'Mette…' He catapulted himself off the bed and into her room. The bedclothes were drawn to one side and Mette was nowhere to be seen. Remembering that children had a habit of hiding when they sensed danger, he wrenched open the wardrobe doors, but she wasn't there either.

As he ran downstairs, he could smell smoke, but he couldn't see where it was coming from. Mette was curled up at the bottom of the stairs, crying, and he picked her up, quickly wrapped her in his coat, then opened the front door and ran with her to the end of the path.

'Papa. Kari made me go away from the fire.'

Cold remorse froze his heart suddenly. He could see a flicker of flame through the sitting-room window. Kari must have herded Mette out of danger, shutting the door behind them as she'd been taught. He held his daughter close, feeling tears run down his face.

'It's all right, Mette. Everything's all right. You're safe…'

The sound of an alarm beeping somewhere woke Flora up. It wasn't coming from inside the cottage, and she rolled drowsily out of bed, sliding her feet into her slippers and peering out of the window. She saw Aksel outside with Mette in his arms, Kari sitting obediently at his feet.

Running downstairs, she grabbed her coat, not stopping to put it on. As soon as she was outside, the faint smell of smoke hit her and she hurried over to Aksel.

'Are you both all right?'

He raised his face towards her, and Flora saw tears. Mette realised that she was there, although she must be practically blind in the darkness, and reached out from the warm cradle of his arms.

'Papa says we're safe.' Aksel seemed too overwhelmed to speak, and Mette volunteered the information.

'That's right. You're safe now.'

She looked up at Aksel questioningly, and he brushed his hand across his face. 'There's a fire, I think it's pretty much contained to the sitting room. Will you take Mette while I go and have a look.'

'No, Aksel. Wait for the fire brigade. Have you called them?'

'My phone's inside. Please, take her.'

It seemed that Aksel was more comfortable with dealing with the situation than he was with taking care of his daughter right now. Flora wondered how the fire had started. She took Mette, holding the little girl tight in her arms.

'Papa's just looking to see how big the fire is.' As Aksel walked back up the path, peering through the front windows, Mette craned round to keep him in view.

'It's all right, he's quite safe. He isn't getting too close, so the fire won't burn him.'

Mette seemed more confident of that than Flora felt. 'My papa fights crocodiles.'

'There you are, then. If he can fight crocodiles then a little fire will be easy…'

She watched, holding her breath as Aksel walked back towards them, his face set in a look of grim determination.

'It's just the hearth rug at the moment. Will you look after Mette while I go and put it out?'

'You should leave it, until the fire brigade gets here. We'll go inside and call them now…'

'I can put it out, there's a fire extinguisher in the kitchen. And if we leave it, then it may spread to the chimney. I don't know how long it's been since it's been swept, and I want to avoid that.'

A chimney fire could easily spread to her cottage. Flora dismissed the thought. What mattered was that they were all safe. 'No, Aksel…'

He was going anyway. She may as well accept it, and work with what was inevitable. Flora transferred Mette into his arms for a moment while she wriggled out of her own coat, wrapping it around the little girl so that his was no longer needed.

'If you must go, put your coat on, it'll protect your arms. And put a pair of boots on as well.'

He looked down at his feet, seeming to realise for the first time that he was only wearing a pair of socks. 'Okay. You're right. You'll take Mette inside?'

She was shivering, her pyjamas giving no protection against the wind. But she wasn't moving until she saw that Aksel was safe. 'If you must go, go now. Before the fire gets any worse. And no heroics, Aksel. Back off if it looks to be getting worse.'

He nodded. Giving Kari a curt command, he strode back up the path, opening the door to his cottage.

Kari was on the alert now, sniffing the air and looking around. Aksel had clearly ordered the dog to protect them, and she was taking her task seriously. Flora hugged Mette close, pulling her coat down around the child's feet.

'Papa's just going to put out the fire. He won't be a minute.' She said the words as if it was nothing. Maybe it *was* nothing to Aksel, but right now it seemed a great deal to her.

She watched as Aksel's dark figure approached the fire. A plume of shadows emitted from the fire extinguisher and the flames died almost immediately. He disappeared for a moment and then reappeared with a bucket, tipping its contents over the ashes to make sure that the fire was well and truly out.

Okay. Everything was okay, and now all she wanted to do was to get warm. By the time Aksel reappeared her teeth were chattering.

'Everything all right?'

'No.' He took his coat off and wrapped it around her. 'You're freezing.'

'The fire's out, though...' He was hurrying her towards her own front door, his arm around her shoulders.

'Yes. I made sure of it.' Aksel pushed the door open and glorious warmth surrounded her suddenly. 'Come and sit down.'

He was gentle and attentive, but his eyes were dead. Whatever he felt was locked behind an impervious barrier.

'Stay with Mette and I'll make a hot drink.' Flora was trying to stop shivering.

'No, I'll do that. You sit and get warm.' He picked up the woollen blanket that was folded across the back of the sofa and waited until Flora had sat down, then tucked it around her and Mette. Then he disappeared into the kitchen.

He came back with two cups of tea, and Flora drank hers while he went upstairs to the bathroom to wash his hands and face. When he came back and sat down, Mette crawled across the sofa, snuggling against him and yawning. Flora waited for the little girl to fall asleep before she asked the inevitable question.

'What happened?'

'I was asleep upstairs. Kari and Mette were downstairs, and Kari herded Mette out into the hallway and shut the door. Then she came to wake me up.' He held out his hand, and Kari ambled over to him. He fondled the dog's ears and she laid her head in his lap.

'You taught her to do that?'

He nodded. 'I didn't even know that Mette was out of bed.'

'What was she doing downstairs?'

'From the looks of it, she'd gone downstairs and lit a candle in the grate. It must have fallen over onto the hearth rug...' His voice cracked and broke with emotion.

'Where did she get the matches from?' Aksel had clearly already tried and convicted himself, without even listening to the case for the defence.

'They were in one of the high cupboards in the kitchen. I didn't think she could get to them, but when I went back inside I saw that she'd dragged a chair across the room. She must have climbed up on it, then got up onto the counter top and into the cupboard.'

It was quite an achievement for a six-year-old with poor sight. 'What made her so determined to light a candle in the middle of the night?' Flora's hand flew to her mouth. She knew the answer.

'When I packed her things, I forgot her electric candle. So I lit a real one for her. It's all my...' He fell silent as Flora flapped her hand urgently at him.

'Don't. You're not to say it. It's *not* your fault.'

'That's not borne out by the facts.' His face was blank, as if he'd accepted his guilt without any question.

Flora took a breath. Whatever she said now had to be convincing. 'Look, Aksel, I talk to a lot of parents in the course of my work. The one thing that everyone agrees on is that you can't watch your children twenty-four hours a day. It isn't possible. But you've come up with a good second-best, and you trained Kari to watch over her.'

He narrowed his eyes. 'You're just making excuses for me.'

'No, I'm not. You let her say goodnight to her mother, Aksel, she needs to do that. And you put the matches away, somewhere that should have been out of her reach.'

'She *did* reach them, though.'

'Well, you might be able to take part of the blame for that one. She takes after her father in being resourceful. I imagine she has all kinds of challenges up her sleeve...'

'All right. You're making me panic now.'

If he didn't like that, then he *really* wasn't going to like the next part. 'You need to let her know, Aksel, that she mustn't play with matches.'

He sighed. 'Yes. I know. Her grandmother always told her off when she was naughty…'

'Yeah, right. You can't rely on her to be the bad guy now.'

Right on cue, Mette shifted fitfully in his arms, opening her eyes. 'Papa, the fire's out?'

'Yes.'

'Did you save all the crocodiles, and the penguins?' Mette was awake again now, and probably ready to play. Aksel's face took on an agonised look, knowing that the time had come for him to be the bad guy.

'Yes, the crocodiles and penguins are all fine. Mette, there's something I have to say to you.'

Mette's gaze slid guiltily towards Flora and she struggled not to react. Aksel had to do this by himself.

'I love you very much, Mette, and you know that you can talk to Mama any time you want.' He started with the positive. 'But you mustn't touch matches or light candles when I'm not there. And you mustn't climb up onto cupboards either. You could hurt yourself very badly.'

A large tear rolled down Mette's cheek. Flora could almost see Aksel's heart breaking.

'Is the fire my fault, Papa?'

'No. It's my fault. I didn't tell you not to do those things, and I should have. But I want you to promise not to do them again.' He waited a moment for Mette to respond. 'You have to say it, please, Mette. "I promise…"'

Mette turned the corners of her mouth down in a look of abject dismay. Even Flora wanted to forgive her immediately, and she wondered whether getting to the North Pole had presented quite as much of a challenge to Aksel as this.

'I promise, Papa.' Another tear rolled down her cheek and Aksel nodded.

'Thank you.' Finally he broke, cuddling Mette to his chest. 'I love you very much.'

'I love you too, Papa.'

'What was it you wanted to say to Mama?' He kissed the top of his daughter's head.

'I forgot to tell her all about our house. And that I like my room…'

'All right. We'll go back to the clinic and find your candle. And you can tell Mama all about it.'

'When?'

'Right now, Mette.'

Mette nodded, satisfied with his answer, and curled up in his arms, her eyelids drooping again drowsily. Flora handed him the woollen blanket and he wrapped his daughter in it, leaving her to sleep. Finally his gaze found Flora's.

'Forget wrestling crocodiles. That was the most difficult thing…'

'*Have* you wrestled a crocodile?'

'Actually, no. Mette thinks I have, but that's not as dangerous as it sounds because she thinks that her cuddly crocodile is a true-to-life representation. I tell her a story about crocodiles and penguins that I met when I was in the Andes.'

'Right. Even I could wrestle a cuddly toy. I didn't know there were crocodiles in the Andes.'

'There aren't. She added a few things in as we went along. The penguins act as tour guides and show you the right way to go.'

'Penguins are always the good guys.'

He nodded, finally allowing himself a smile. 'I'm going to take her back to the clinic, now.'

'What? It's three in the morning, Aksel. Why don't you just stay here?'

'I said that we'd go now so that she can talk to Lisle. And I want her to wake up somewhere that's familiar to her.'

'But…' Flora saw the logic of it but this felt wrong. 'She's asleep. It seems a shame to take her out into the cold now when you can let her sleep and take her back first thing in the morning.'

'You heard me promise her, Flora. I'll stay the night so that I'll be there whenever she wakes up. You can't help me with this.'

There was more to this than just practicality. More than a promise. She could feel Aksel slipping away from her, torn by his guilt and the feeling that he'd let his daughter down.

Flora had to let him go. He'd feel differently about this in the morning and realise that he could be a father to Mette and a lover to her as well.

'Okay. You'll be back in the morning?'

'Yes.' He reached for her, and Flora slid towards him on the sofa. His kiss was tender, but it held none of the fire of their nights together.

'You're tired. You'll sleep in?'

If she could sleep at all. Dread began to pulse through her. What if he decided that this was where their relationship had to end? She pushed the thought away. She *had* to trust Aksel. There was no other choice.

'I'll phone in and take a couple of hours off work, I don't have any patients to see in the morning. I'll be here when you get back.'

He nodded. 'I'll come as soon as I can.'

CHAPTER SIXTEEN

FLORA WAS UP early and let herself into Aksel's cottage with the spare key that he'd left with her. The place stank of smoke, and there were deposits of soot all around the sitting room, but apart from that the damage was relatively minor. She tidied the kitchen, putting away the evidence of Mette having climbed up to reach the matches, and tipped the remains of the hearth rug into a rubbish bag. Then she brewed a cup of strong coffee to jolt her tired and aching limbs into action and started to clean.

Ten minutes after she'd returned to her own cottage for more coffee and some breakfast, Flora heard the throaty roar of the SUV outside in the lane. Running out to embrace him seemed as if it would only make the awful what-ifs of last night a reality again, and she forced herself to sit down at the kitchen table and wait for him to come to her.

When he did, he looked as tired as she felt. But the first thing he did, when she let him into the cottage, was hug her. His body seemed stiff and unresponsive, but it was still a hug. Things were going to be all right.

'I appreciate the clean-up, but I was hoping to find you'd slept in this morning.' He sat down at the kitchen table while she made him coffee.

'Your early mornings are starting to rub off on me.' It wouldn't do to tell him she'd been awake most of the night, worrying. Normal was good at the moment, even if she was going to have to fake it.

She put his coffee down in front of him and sat down. 'So how's Mette?'

'Fine. She told me that a fire's a very second-league adventure. Fighting crocodiles is much more exciting.' He smiled suddenly, and Flora laughed.

'Shame. If we could have tempted a few out of the loch then you could have done that too.'

He laughed, but there was no humour in his eyes. They were going through the motions of believing in life again, without any of the certainty.

'Aksel, I… What happened last night was a terrible accident. Mette's all right and so are you.'

'Yes. I know.' He might know it, but he didn't seem to believe it.

'You're a good father. You can keep her safe. We'll do it together, we'll go through the whole cottage and check everything… We can learn from this and make sure that it doesn't happen again.'

He looked at her blankly. 'We?'

'Yes, *we*. You're not alone with this, we'll do it together.'

'*I* need to do it, Flora. When I go back to Oslo…' They both knew what happened then. When he went back to Oslo, she would stay here in Cluchlochry, and it would be an end to their relationship. Aksel couldn't bring himself to rely on her.

She'd thought about this. It was far too early to say anything, but maybe it needed to be said now. Maybe they both needed to know that their relationship didn't have to be set in stone, and that it did have a future.

'When you go back to Oslo, there's nothing to stop me from visiting, is there?' Flora decided to start slowly with this.

He looked up at her. The look in his eyes told Flora that maybe she hadn't started slowly enough.

'I just… It seems so very arbitrary, to put an end date on this. What we have.'

'We'll always have it, Flora. There's no end date on that.'

It was a nice thought. A romantic thought, which didn't bear examination. Over time, the things they'd shared would be tarnished and forgotten.

'That's not what I meant. I was thinking in a more… literal sense.' Flora's heart began to beat fast. This wasn't going quite the way she'd hoped, and she was beginning to dread what Aksel might say.

'You're thinking of coming to Norway?'

'Well… I'm a free agent. I can come and see you, can't I?'

This wasn't about Mette any more. It was about Aksel's determination to do things on his own. About hers to find someone who trusted her. It was a bright winter morning, warm and cosy inside with snow falling outside the window, but Flora could feel the chill now, instead of the heat.

He was still and silent for a moment. When he looked at her, Flora could only see the mountain man, doggedly trudging forward, whatever the cost. Whatever he left behind.

'Do you seriously think that if you came to Norway, I'd ever let you go?'

Flora swallowed hard. That sounded like a *no*.

'Okay.' She shrugged, as if it didn't matter to her. 'That's okay, I won't come, then.'

'Flora…' He reached across the table, laying his hand on her arm. The sudden warmth in his eyes only made her angry and she pulled away from him.

'I heard what you said, Aksel.' He didn't want her. Actually, not wanting her would have been relatively okay. Flora knew that he wanted her but that he was fighting it.

'I didn't mean…' He let out a breath, frustration showing in his face. Clearly he didn't know quite what he meant. Or maybe he did, and he wasn't going to say it. In a moment of horrible clarity Flora knew exactly what he meant.

Aksel wouldn't take the risk of things becoming permanent between them. She'd trusted him, and he was pushing her away now. They'd tried to be happy—and surely they both deserved it. But Aksel was going to turn his back on that and let her down.

'Don't worry about it. I know what you're saying to me. That you're in control of this, and it comes to an end when you go. Well, I'm taking control of it and it ends now. I'm going to work.'

'Flora…' he called after her, but Flora had already walked out of the kitchen. Pulling on her coat, she picked up Dougal's lead, which was all she needed to do to prompt him to scrabble at the front door.

He'd made her feel him. He'd been inside her, in more ways than just physically, and she'd dared to enjoy it. Dared to want more. When he caught her up in the hallway, and she turned to look at him, she still loved him. It would always be this way with Aksel, and she had to make the break now, for her own sanity's sake.

'Can't we talk about this?'

'I think we've said all we need to say, haven't we? If you see me again, just look the other way, Aksel. I don't want to speak to you, ever again.'

She pulled open the front door, slamming it in his face. Aksel would be gone by the time she got home from work this evening, and hopefully he'd take what she'd said seriously. If they saw each other in the village, or at the clinic, she'd be looking the other way, and so should he.

* * *

He'd messed up. Big time. Aksel had been in some very tight spots, but he couldn't remember one as terrifying and hopeless as this.

He'd spent most of the night sitting in the chair next to Mette's bed, staring into the darkness and wondering how he could make things right. How he could be a father to Mette, and love Flora as well. He'd come to no conclusion.

Last night's fire wasn't the issue. But it had shaken him and dredged up feelings that he'd struggled to bury. Lisle's lies. His guilt over not having been there for Mette. And when Flora had spoken of coming to Norway to visit…

He knew what she'd been doing. She'd been trying to patch things up and convince them both that nothing was the matter. Flora always tried to mend what was broken, and he loved her for it. But she deserved someone better than him. Now that he was responsible for Mette, could he ever be the man that Flora could trust?

The question hammered at him, almost driving him to his knees. He'd travelled a long way, and it had seemed that he'd finally found the thing that he hadn't even known he'd been looking for. Did he really have to turn his back on Flora? Aksel couldn't bear it, but if it had to be done, then it was better for it to be done now.

He took a gulp of his coffee, tipping the rest into the sink and clearing up the kitchen. Then he signalled to Kari to follow him out into the cold, crisp morning air. As Aksel shut Flora's front door behind him, he knew only two things for sure. That this hurt far more than anything he'd experienced before. And that now he had to go on the most important journey of his life. One that he'd told himself he'd never make, and which might just change everything.

* * *

Anger had propelled Flora through the morning. But anger was hard to sustain, particularly where Aksel was concerned. When she couldn't help thinking about his touch, the honesty in his clear blue eyes, and the way he gave himself to her...

But now he'd taken it all away. As the day wore on, each minute heavy on her hands, the sharp cutting edge of her fury gave way to a dull ache of pain. She hurried home after work, trying not to notice that his cottage was quiet and dark, no lights showing from the windows.

Flora spent a sleepless night, thinking what might have been, and wondering if a miracle might happen to somehow bring it all back again. The feeble light of morning brought her answer. It had been good between them, and Aksel was the man she'd always wanted. But he couldn't handle the guilt of feeling himself torn in two directions, and Flora couldn't handle trusting him and then having him push her away.

She'd decided that she must go and see Mette, because it wouldn't be fair to just desert the little girl. Making sure that Aksel wasn't at the clinic that morning, she spent an hour with Mette, putting on a happy face even though she was dying inside, and then went back to her treatment room, locking the door so that she could cry bitter tears.

It seemed that Aksel had got the message. He knew that she didn't want to see him, and he was avoiding her too. He was perceptive enough to know that things weren't going to work out between them, and it was better to break things off now. He might even be happy about that. Flora was a claim on his time and attention that he didn't need right now.

The second time she passed his cottage, on the way to her own front door, was no easier than the first. It looked as empty as it had last night, and Flora wondered whether he'd found somewhere else to stay.

But then she'd gone to the window to close the curtains and seen the light flickering at the top of the hill, partly obscured by the ruins of the old keep. Flora knew exactly where Aksel was now. This was his signal fire, and it was meant for her.

He might have just phoned... If Aksel had called her then she could have dismissed the call, and that would have been an end to it. But the fire at the top of the hill burned on, seeming to imprint itself on her retinas even when she wasn't staring out of the window at it.

She needed something to take her mind off it. Her Christmas card list was always a good bet, and she fetched it, along with the boxes of cards that she'd bought, sitting down purposefully in front of the fire with a pen and a cup of tea. But her hand shook as she wrote. Wishing friends and family a happy Christmas always made her smile but, knowing that this year she'd be spending hers without Aksel, the Christmas greetings only emphasised her own hollow loneliness.

She gathered the cards up, deciding to leave them for another day. Drawing the curtains apart, she saw the light of the fire still twinkling out in the gloom...

Aksel had built the fire knowing that Flora would see it. And knowing that he'd stay here all night if he had to, and then the following night, and each night until she came. However long it took, he'd be here when Flora finally decided to climb the hill.

Maybe it wouldn't be tonight. It was getting late, and the lights of her cottage had been flicking on and off, tracing what seemed to be an irregular and undecided progress from room to room. Soon the on and off of the lights upstairs would signal that Flora had gone to bed, which left little chance that she'd come to him tonight.

All the same, he'd be here. Wrapped in his sleeping bag, until the first rays of dawn told him that he had to move now, work the cold stiffness from his limbs, and get on with another day.

His fire was burning low, and he went to fetch more fuel from the pile of branches that he'd stacked up nearby. The blaze began to climb through the dry twigs, brightening as it went, and he missed the one thing he had been waiting and watching for. When he looked down toward the village again, Flora's porch light was on.

He cursed his own inattentiveness, reaching for his backpack. His trembling fingers fumbled with the small binoculars, and he almost dropped them on the ground. Focussing them down towards Flora's cottage, he saw her standing in her porch, wearing her walking boots and thick, waterproof jacket, and looking up in his direction. Aksel almost recoiled, even though he knew that she couldn't see him. And then she went back inside the cottage again.

He bit back his disappointment. It had been too much to expect from this first night. But then she reappeared, pulling a hat onto her head, and as she started to walk away from the cottage a small thread of light issued from her hand. He smiled, glad that she'd remembered to bring a torch with her.

Aksel tried to calm himself by wondering which route she'd take. The most direct was the steepest, and it would be an easier walk to circle around the bottom of the hill before climbing it. She crossed the bridge that led from the village to the estate and disappeared for a moment behind a clump of bushes. And then he saw her again, climbing the steep, stony ground and making straight for him.

He waited, his eyes fixed on the small form labouring up the hill. When she fell, and the torch rolled skittishly back a few feet down the slope, he sprang to his feet, cursing himself for bringing her out here in the dark. But before he could run towards her, she was on her feet again, retrieving the torch.

Aksel forced himself to sit back down on the stony bench he'd made beside the fire. He *had* to wait, even though it was agony to watch Flora struggle like this. He had to trust that she'd come to him, and she had to know that she would too, however hard the journey.

His heart beat like a battering ram, and he suddenly found it difficult to breathe. The fire crackled and spat, flames flaring up into the night. The moment he'd longed for so desperately would be here soon, and despite working through every possible thing she might say to him, and what he might say in reply, he was completely unprepared.

When she finally made it to the top of the hill, she seemed rather too out of breath to say anything. Flora switched off her torch, putting her hands on her hips in a stance that indicated she wasn't going to take any nonsense from him.

'It's warmer by the fire...' He ventured the words and she frowned.

'This had better be good, Aksel. If you think I came up here in the middle of the night to hear something you might have said anywhere...'

'When might I have said it? You told me you never wanted to speak to me again.'

The logic had seemed perfect to him, but it only seemed to make her more angry. 'You could have slipped a note under my front door. It's not so far for either of us to walk.'

'I trusted you to come to me.'

She stared at him. 'I really wish you hadn't said that.'

Because it was the one thing he could have said to stop her from walking away from him? A sharp barb of hope bit into his heart.

'Sit down. Please.'

Flora pressed her lips together, hesitating for agonising moments. Then she marched over to the stone slab that he was sitting on, plumping herself down on the far end so that their shoulders didn't touch.

She was angry still, but at least she was sitting down. Aksel wasn't sure where to start, but before he could organise his thoughts, Flora did it for him.

'Where have you been, Aksel? You haven't been at the cottage and Mette told me that you weren't coming in to see her today.'

'You went to see Mette?' Of course she had. Flora wouldn't let a little thing like a broken heart get in the way of making sure that a child wasn't hurt by her absence. And from the way that she seemed to hate him so much, Aksel was in no doubt that her heart was just as wounded as his.

'Yes. I made sure that you weren't there already.'

Good. Hate was a lot more akin to love than indifference was. 'I was in Oslo.'

'Oslo? For two days?'

'Just a day. I went to see Mette yesterday afternoon and left straight from there. I got back a couple of hours ago. The flight only takes an hour from Glasgow.'

She turned the edges of her mouth down. 'And it was such a long way when I was thinking of making the trip.'

He deserved that. 'I meant it when I said that I wouldn't be able to let you go, and that this is your home. I went to Oslo to talk with Olaf and Agnetha. About making this *my* home and Mette's.'

'You need their permission?' He could hear the fight beginning to go out of Flora's tone. She was starting to crumble, and if she wasn't in his arms yet, then maybe she would be if he gave it time.

'No, I don't. I'm Mette's father, and I make decisions about what's best for her, you taught me that. I wanted their blessing, and to reassure them that moving here didn't mean that they wouldn't get to see her.'

Flora stared at him. 'And…?'

'They told me that they expected me to get a house with a nice guest room, because they'll be visiting.'

A tear ran down her cheek. 'Aksel, please. What exactly are you saying?'

Now was the time. He had to be bold, because Flora couldn't be. He had to trust her, and show her that she could trust him. Aksel hung onto her hand for dear life.

'There's so much I want to say to you. But it all boils down to one thing.'

Flora had stumbled up a hill in the pitch darkness, and probably skinned her knees. If, in the process, she'd come to realise that nothing could keep her away from Aksel, she wanted to hear what he had to say for himself first.

The flickering flames bathed his face in warmth, throwing the lines of worry across his forehead into sharp relief. The taut lines of his body showed that he was just as agitated as she was.

'What's the one thing?'

'I love you.'

That was good. It was very good because, despite herself, she loved him.

'Seriously?' Maybe he could be persuaded to say it again…

'Yes, seriously. I love you, Flora.' He was smiling at her in the firelight.

'I…love you too.'

He didn't argue. Putting his arms around her, he enveloped her in a hug.

'I was so horrible to you. I'm sorry, Aksel.' The things she'd said made Flora shiver now.

'You were afraid. I was afraid too, and our fear was all that we could see. But I'd be the bravest guy in the world if you'd just forgive me.'

'You mean I'm more scary than wrestling crocodiles?'

'Much more. But the thing that scares me most is losing you.'

Flora kissed him. So much nicer than words. But even the wild pleasure of feeling him close, embraced in his fire on a cold, dark night, couldn't entirely wipe away the feeling that there were some things they really did need to talk about.

'Aksel… What if…?'

'What-ifs don't matter.' He kissed her again, and Flora broke away from him with an effort.

'They *do* matter, Aksel. I need to know. I want you to say it, because I can't keep wondering what might happen if we make a go of this, and decide to have children some day.'

'I'd like children very much. A boy, maybe. Or a girl. One or more of each would be more than acceptable…' He was grinning broadly now.

'Stop it! Don't even say that if you can't also say that there's a risk that one or more of our children might have cystic fibrosis.'

He took her hands between his. 'I know that there *may* be a risk, but only if I carry the gene as well. I love you and I trust you. It's not that I don't care about these possibilities, I just have no doubts that we can face it and do the right thing. And there are other things we need to do first.'

He trusted her. He'd take her as she was, with all the doubts that raised, and he'd make them into certainties. 'What other things do we need to do first?'

'First, I need to tell you that I intend to marry you. I'll work very hard towards making you so happy that you won't be able to resist asking…'

'What? I have to ask you?'

Aksel nodded. 'You have to ask me, because you already know what my answer will be. I'll wait.'

'You're very sure of yourself.'

'I'm very sure of *you*. And I'll be doing my best to wear you down…' He took her into his arms and kissed her. He'd answered none of her questions, but they were all irrelevant now. The only thing that mattered was that they loved each other.

'And how are you going to do that?'

He gave her a gorgeous grin. 'Close your eyes and imagine…'

Aksel wasn't sure whether he had a right to be this happy. But he'd take it. He'd stamped the fire out hastily, lucky not to singe his boots in the process, and he and Flora had hurried back down the hill. The only question that was left to ask was whether they'd spend the night in his bed or hers.

He reckoned that last night had to count towards the *wearing down* process. And then this morning, when they'd made love again, before rushing to work.

If Lyle noticed the coincidence of Aksel wanting to take Mette out after lunch and Flora asking for the afternoon off, he'd said nothing. The old SUV was now running smoothly and even though the outside left a little to be desired, it was now thoroughly clean inside and had a child seat in the back.

'Where are we going?' Flora felt as excited as Mette was.

'Wait and see.' Aksel took the road leading to the other side of the estate, through snow-covered grasslands, and then they bumped a little way across country to the half-acre plantation of Christmas trees. The larger ones, for the castle and the village marketplace had already been felled, but there were plenty of smaller ones that would fit nicely in Flora's cottage. He left Flora to help Mette out of the car seat, and opened the boot to retrieve the chainsaw he'd borrowed from Ted Mackie.

'No!' Flora clapped her hand over her mouth in horror when she saw him eyeing the plantation. 'We can't do that…isn't tree rustling some kind of crime?'

'I got permission from Charles. He says I can take whichever tree I want. Anyway, trees can't run away, so I'm sure it wouldn't technically be rustling.'

'Is it Christmas Eve tomorrow?' Mette started to jiggle up and down in excitement.

'In Scotland we can put up our tree as soon as we like, we don't have to wait until the day before Christmas Eve.'

Mette's eyes grew rounder. 'I *like* Scotland, Papa. Do we have *two* Christmases?'

'No, but there's Hogmanay.' Aksel grinned as Mette looked perplexed. 'You'll have to wait and see what that is.'

Mette nodded, and Aksel leaned towards Flora, her soft scent curling around him. 'I like Scotland, too.'

They took their time choosing, wandering through the plantation hand in hand, while Mette relied on Kari to guide her through the snow. Mette declared that she wanted a tree tall enough for her to climb up to the sky, and Aksel explained that they couldn't get one like that into the cottage. In the end, Flora settled the argument by choosing one they all liked.

'Stand back…' He started up the chainsaw, grinning at Flora, and then cut a 'V' shape in the trunk. Flora hung tightly onto Mette's hand as she screamed excitedly. The tree fell exactly where Aksel had indicated it would.

He'd brought some netting, and Aksel wrapped the tree up in it, bending the larger branches upwards. Then he lifted the tree onto one shoulder to take it to the car. The raw power in his body never failed to thrill Flora. But there was more now. They were becoming a family.

'How long do I have to hold out for? Before I ask you to marry me?' Mette was busy scooping snow up to make a snowman, and Flora watched as Aksel loaded the tree into the car.

'Be strong.' He grinned at her. 'I'm finding that persuading you is much nicer than I'd thought. I have a few more things in mind.'

'What are they?'

'Breakfast in bed on Christmas morning. A Hogmanay kiss. Taking you back to Norway to meet my family after the New Year.'

Flora had always thought that the most romantic proposal must be a surprise. But planning it like this was even better than she'd dreamed. 'That sounds wonderful. Don't think that I won't be thinking of some things to persuade you.'

'So how long before we give in?' He leaned forward, growling the words into her ear as if they were a challenge.

'I think that decorating the tree's going to be the first big test of our resolve. Christmas Eve might prove very tempting…'

'Yes. That'll be difficult.' He took her hand, pulling off her glove and pressing her fingers to his lips.

'You'll be ready with your answer?' Flora smiled up at him.

'Oh, yes.' He wrapped his arms around her, kissing her. 'I'll be ready.'

EPILOGUE

Oslo, one year later

IT WAS THE night before Christmas Eve, and the family had gathered for Christmas. The big tree at Olaf and Agnetha's house was the centrepiece of the celebrations, and both Aksel's and Flora's parents were spending Christmas here this year. Everyone had admired the appliquéd Christmas stockings, a present from Mary Monroe, who had made a complete recovery and was back working at her beloved quilt shop three days a week.

Mette had fallen asleep as soon as her head had touched the pillow, and Aksel and Flora had tiptoed next door to their own room.

'Mum was telling me how welcome your parents have made her and Dad. They've been showing them around Oslo.' Flora slid onto the bed, propping herself up on the pillows next to Aksel, and he put his arm around her.

'I'm glad they get on so well. And with Olaf and Agnetha too.'

Flora nodded. 'I'm really going to miss this year. We did so much.'

They'd arranged a wedding and bought a house, one of the large stone-built properties just outside the village. Mette understood that her new family would always be there for her, and was gaining in confidence and exploring her world a little more each day. Aksel had been working at the canine therapy centre, after the previous vet had decided not to return from her maternity leave, and helping Ted Mackie organise adventure trips on the estate for the clinic's residents.

'I've got something to get us started on next year. I had an email from Charles this morning. He's signed the papers for the land, and it's now officially ours. We can start to build in the New Year.'

This had been Aksel's dream project, and Flora had fallen in love with it too. The small parcel of barren land, right on the edge of the estate, was no good for anything other than being ideally situated to build. Charles had sold it for a nominal amount, after Aksel had approached him with his plans for an adventure centre for people with disabilities.

'So it's a reality. That's fantastic!' Flora hugged him tight.

'Charles is as excited about it as I am. He offered to make a contribution towards the building costs, but I told him that if he wanted to do something, he could turn up and help dig out the foundations. He liked that idea much better.'

'I'm glad you decided that you weren't going to entirely give up on exploring. Even if these trips will be a little different.'

'They'll be even more challenging.' Aksel took her hand, pressing her fingers to his lips. 'And I'll never be away from my family for too long.'

'Well, maybe your family will just pack their bags every once in a while and come with you.'

He grinned. 'You know I'd love that.'

'I have something for you as well.' Flora reached under the pillow, giving him the small, carefully wrapped package.

'Am I supposed to open this now?' He grinned at her.

'Yes.' She watched as he tore the paper, then turned the little fabric crocodile with sharp embroidered teeth over in his hands.

'All right. You've given me a crocodile to wrestle…?' He'd got the message and he was smiling at the thought of whatever challenge she was going to present him with now. 'Whatever it is you have in mind, the answer's yes.'

Flora nudged him in the ribs. 'You don't know what the question is yet.'

'It'll be Christmas Eve soon. And I trust you…'

It was his trust that had brought Flora to this point. They'd talked about this, and he'd told her that she'd know when the time was right. And she *did* know.

'You said that when we decided to start a family, we'd both take the test for the cystic fibrosis gene. Together…'

A broad grin spread across his face. He knew now exactly what she wanted.

'Yes. I did.'

'Are you ready, Aksel?'

He nodded. 'I've been ready for a long time. You?'

'I'm ready. If it turns out that we both carry the gene we have lots of options. Would it be irresponsible of me to say that we don't need to decide anything now? We'll know what to do if and when we find ourselves in that situation?'

'Nope. Life's one big exploration. You can't know what's ahead of you, but if you're travelling with someone you trust, you can be sure that you'll face it together.'

This felt like the first step in a journey that Flora

couldn't wait to make. She kissed him, nestling into the warmth of his arms.

'So I'm going to be a dad again.' Aksel hugged her tight. 'I'm not going to miss a moment of it this time. I'll find someone else to lead the trips…'

'Whatever happens, it won't be for a little while. And when it does, you can have both, Aksel, you don't have to choose.' Sometimes she still had to remind him of that.

'How do you do it, Flora? Every time I think that I'm about as happy as it's possible to be, you manage to make me happier.'

'Trust me Aksel. There's a lot more to come, for both of us.'

He laughed, pure joy spilling out of him. 'Oh, I trust you. Always.'

* * * * *

CHRISTMAS WITH THE SINGLE DAD

LOUISA HEATON

For Mrs Duff, my first English teacher, for telling me I had a wonderful imagination and that I was never to stop writing.

CHAPTER ONE

SYDNEY HARPER CONFIRMED her appointment details on the surgery's check-in touchscreen and headed into the waiting room.

It was full. Much too full. Eleven of the twelve available chairs were filled with faces she recognised. People she saw every day in the village. One or two of her own clients from the veterinary practice she ran. Were they *all* before her? Would she be sitting in this waiting room all morning to see Dr Preston? She had patients of her own waiting—it was a busy time of year. Close to Christmas. No doubt everyone was trying to see their doctor before the festive season.

With a sigh at the thought of the inevitable wait she strode in, looking for the book she always kept in her bag for situations such as this.

At the empty seat she sat down and opened the book, slipping her bookmark into her fingers. She tried to focus on the words upon the page, but her eyes were tired and she kept reading the same sentence over and over again. The words were refusing to go in and make sense.

It was happening again. Every year when it started to get close to *that date* her body rebelled and she couldn't sleep. The date would be hanging heavy in the near future, along with the dread of having to get through

Christmas again, reliving what had happened before, every moment as clear as if it had just occurred. The shock. The fear. The *guilt*.

The difficulty getting to sleep. Then the difficulty *staying* asleep. She'd keep waking, staring at the clock, staring at those bright red digits, watching them tick over, minute to minute, hour to hour. Feeling *alone*. So alone in the dark! With no one to talk to. No one to go to, to reassure herself that everyone was fine.

That first year—the first anniversary of when it had happened—she'd got up and stood in the doorway of Olivia's old room, staring at her daughter's empty bed. She'd stood there almost all night. Trying to remember what it had looked like when it had been filled with life and laughter and joy.

The second year after it had happened she'd got up again and, determined not to stand in the doorway for another night, gawking at nothing, she'd decided to make herself useful. She'd cleaned. Scrubbing the oven in the middle of the night until it shone like a new pin was perfect therapy as far as she was concerned. She could get angry with the burnt-on bits. Curse at them. Moan about the ache in her back from all the bending over. But it felt better to be focused on a real physical pain than a mental one.

Last year, when the anniversary of Olivia's death had come around, she'd decided to visit Dr Preston and he'd given her a prescription for some sleeping pills and told her to come and see him if it happened again.

This year, though her oven could no doubt do with another clean, the idea of being up all night again—alone again—just wasn't an option. She hated losing all this sleep. And it wasn't just the one night any more. She was losing sleep earlier and earlier, up to a month or more before the anniversary.

So here she was.

All she needed was a quick prescription. She could be in and out in seconds. Get back to her own patients— Fletcher the Great Dane, who needed his paw checked after a grass seed had become embedded under his pad, a health check on two new ferrets and the first set of jabs for Sara's new kitten. There were others, she knew, but they were her first three and they would be waiting. Even now. Patiently watching the clock in *her* waiting room.

The screen on the wall in front of her gave a beep and she looked up to see if she was being called in. It wasn't, but the person next to her got up out of her chair and left. Sydney was glad for the space, but it didn't last long, Mrs Courtauld, owner of a retired greyhound, settled into the newly vacant seat.

'Hello, Sydney. How nice to see you. How are you doing?'

'Mrs C! I'm fine. How are you?'

'Oh, you know. The usual aches and pains. That's why I'm here. My knees are giving me a bit of gyp. They have been ever since Prince knocked me over in the park and broke my wrist.'

'You did get quite a knock, didn't you?'

'I did! But at my age you expect a bit of wear and tear in the old joints. I'm no spring chicken now, you know. I get out and about each day if I can. It's good to keep mobile.'

Sydney nodded, smiling. 'But you're still looking great, Mrs C.'

'You're too kind, young Sydney. I do have mirrors in the house—I know how old I look. The skin on my neck is that red and saggy I'm amazed a farmer hasn't shot me, thinking I'm an escaped turkey.'

Sydney laughed. 'Ridiculous! I'd be happy to look like you if I ever make it to pensionable age.'

Mrs Courtauld snorted. 'Of course you'll make it to my age! What are you now? Thirty-three? Thirty-four?'

'Thirty-five.'

'You see? Loads of years left in you.' She thought for a moment, her eyes darkening, and she looked hard at Sydney in concern. 'Unless, of course, you're here because there's something wrong? Oh, Sydney, you're not dreadfully ill, are you?'

Mrs Courtauld's face filled with motherly concern and she laid a liver-spotted wrinkly hand on Sydney's arm.

'Just not sleeping very well.'

Mrs Courtauld nodded, looking serious. 'No. 'Course not. The anniversary is coming up again, isn't it? Little Olivia?'

Sydney swallowed hard, touched that Mrs Courtauld had realised the date was near. How many in the village had forgotten? *Don't cry.*

'Yes. It is,' she answered, her voice low. She wasn't keen on anyone else in the waiting room listening in.

Mrs Courtauld gripped Sydney's hand and squeezed it. 'Of course. Understandable. I'm the same each year when it comes round to my Alfred's birthday. Ten years since I lost him.' She paused as she looked off, as if into the distance. But then she perked up again. 'I laid some flowers at Alfred's grave the other day and I thought of you. Your little Olivia's plot is so close. I hope you don't mind, but I put an amaryllis against her headstone.'

Oh.

Sydney wasn't sure how to respond. That was sweet. It was nice to think that Olivia had a bright, beautiful flower to brighten up her plot. Nice for her to be remembered in that way.

She hadn't been to the graveyard for a while. It was just so impossibly bleak and devastating to stand there and look down at the headstone, knowing her daughter was…

She swallowed hard.

Don't even think it.

It hurt too much. Going to the grave just kept proving that she was dead, making Sydney feel helpless and lost—a feeling she couldn't bear. She'd found that by staying away, by existing in her dreams and her memories, she could still see her daughter alive and well and she never had to stare at that cold, hard, depressing ground any more.

Blinking back the tears, she was about to thank Mrs Courtauld when the computer screen that announced patient's names beeped into life and there was her name. Ms Sydney Harper. Dr Jones's room.

She got up quickly, then did a double-take, looking at the screen again. Dr *Jones?*

But she'd booked in with Dr Preston. *He* was her doctor, not this Jones person! And who was it? A locum? A new partner? If it was, and she'd been passed on to someone else…

She shoved her book back into her bag, wondering briefly if she ought to go and check with Reception and see what had happened, but the doctor was probably waiting. If she faffed around at Reception she might lose her appointment altogether—and she needed those tablets!

Clearing her throat, she pushed through the door and headed down the corridor. To the left, Dr Preston's room. To the right, Dr Jones's.

Sydney hesitated outside the door, her hand gripping the handle, afraid to go in. What if this new doctor wanted to *ask questions?* She wasn't sure she was ready to tell the story *again*. Not to a stranger. Dr Preston knew everything. There was no need to explain, no need for her to sit in front of him and embarrass herself by bursting into tears, because he *knew*. Knew what she'd gone through and was *still* going through. He often saw her in the village and would call out with a cheery wave, ask her how she was doing. She appreciated that.

A newcomer might not understand. A locum might be loath to hand out a prescription as easily.

Please don't ask me any probing questions!

She sucked in a breath and opened the door, not knowing what or who to expect. Was Dr Jones a woman? A man? Young? Old?

She strode in, her jaw set, determined to be as brief as possible so she could get her prescription and get out again but she stopped as her gaze fell upon the extremely handsome man seated behind the doctor's desk.

Her breath caught in her throat and somehow paralysed it. He was a complete shock to her system. Totally unexpected. It was like walking into a room expecting to see a normal person—some old guy in a boring shirt and tie…maybe someone bald, with old-fashioned glasses and drab brown trousers—but instead laying eyes upon a movie star in all his airbrushed glory.

The man was dressed in a well-fitting dark suit, with the brightest, bluest eyes she'd ever seen. There was a gorgeous smile of greeting upon his face. The type that stopped your heart. That stopped you breathing for a moment.

Oh, my!

Sydney had not noticed a good-looking man since Alastair had left. There was no point. Men were not on her radar. She wasn't looking for another relationship. What was the use? She'd only end up getting blamed for everything.

She was sure those men were out there. Somewhere. Even though Silverdale Village wasn't exactly overrun with hot guys. The type who ought to star in Hollywood movies or get their kits off for a charity calendar. She'd just never noticed. Living too much in her own head.

But *this* guy? Dr Jones?

I'm staring at him! Like a goldfish with my mouth hanging open! Speak, Sydney. Say something. Anything! So he knows he's not dealing with a mute.

She turned away from him to close the door, shutting her eyes to compose herself and take in a steadying breath. Hoping her cheeks had stopped flushing, hoping he hadn't noticed the effect he'd had on her.

He's just a guy.

Just.

A.

Guy.

She blew her breath out slowly before she turned around, telling herself to try and sound haughty and distant, whilst simultaneously feeling her cheeks flame hot enough to sizzle bacon. 'I…um… I don't mean to be rude, but I made an appointment to see Dr Preston…?'

An angel had walked into his consulting room.

An angel with long, luscious waves of chocolate-coloured hair and sad grey eyes. Big, sad eyes, tinged with red, in the fresh face of an English rose.

Startled, he dropped his pen, fumbling for it when it fell from his fingers and smiling in apology. What the hell had just happened? Why was he reacting like this? She was just a patient!

He'd not expected to feel suddenly...*nervous*. As if he'd never treated a patient before. Tongue-tied. Blind-sided by his physical response to this woman. He could feel his normal greeting—*Morning, take a seat, how can I help?*—stifled in his throat and he had to turn to his computer, glancing at the screen briefly to gather his thoughts before he could speak.

Sydney Harper.

Beautiful. Enchanting.

A patient!

Reel your thoughts back in and show that you know what you're doing.

He cleared his throat. 'Er...yes, you did... But he...er...got overbooked.' He paused briefly, noticing the way she hovered uncertainly at the door. The way her long cardigan covered her almost to mid-thigh, the shapeless garment hiding any figure she might have. The way her heavy tartan skirt covered her legs down to her boots. The way her fingers twisted around each other.

Curious... Why is she so frightened? Why do I get the feeling that she tries her best not to be noticed?

He could see her gaze darting about the room, as if she were looking for means of escape, and suddenly curiosity about this woman overrode any previous nervousness.

'Is that okay?'

'I'd prefer to see Dr Preston. He knows me. I'm *his* patient.'

Nathan glanced back at the computer, so that he wouldn't stare at her and make her feel even more un-comfortable. Did Dr Preston *really* know her? The last time she'd been into the surgery had been—he checked the screen—a year ago. A lot could change in a year.

He should know.

Forget that. Concentrate on your work.

He was itching to know what ailed her. What he could help her with. How to keep her in the room and not have her bolt like a skittish horse.

Purely on a professional basis, of course. I'm not interested in her in that *way.*

What had brought her to the surgery today? She looked anxious. A bit stressed. Not entirely comfortable with this change.

He gave her his best friendly smile. 'Why don't you take a seat? You never know, I might be able to help. Doctors do that.' He tried to reassure her, but she approached the chair opposite him as if she were a gazelle trying to sidle past a ravenous lion.

He waited for her to sit and then he looked her over. A little pale, though her cheeks were flushed. Her pulse was probably elevated. Her blood pressure rising. What had made her so anxious? He was intrigued. But he'd learnt a valuable trick as a doctor. Silence was a wonderful tool. People would feel compelled to fill it. They'd start talking. Eventually.

So he waited, noting how white her knuckles were as they clutched the bag upon her lap.

And he waited.

She was looking at anything *but* him. Checking out the room as if it were new to her before she finally allowed herself to glance at his face. Her cheeks reddened in the most delightful way, and she was biting her bottom lip as she finally made eye contact.

'I need some sleeping pills. Dr Preston told me to come again if I needed a repeat.'

Ah. There we go!

'You're not sleeping well?'

Her cheeks reddened some more, and again she averted her eyes. 'Not really. Look, I'm needed back at work, so if you could just write me a prescription? I don't want to keep my clients waiting.'

Nathan Jones sat back in his swivel chair and appraised her. He was curious as to why she needed them. 'Sleeping pills are really a last resort. I'll need a few details from you first of all.'

The flash of alarm in her eyes was startling to observe. And if she twisted the strap of her handbag any more it would soon snap.

Sydney shook her head. 'I don't have long.'

'Neither do I. So let's crack on, shall we? Eight minutes per patient can go by in the blink of an eye.' He was trying to keep it loose. Casual. Non-threatening. This woman was as taut as a whip.

She let out an impatient breath. 'What do you need to know?'

'Tell me about your sleep routine.'

Does your husband snore? Does he toss and turn all night, keeping you awake? Wait... What the...?

Why was he worrying about whether she had a husband or not? He wasn't looking to go *out* with this woman. She was a patient! At least for now. He had no doubt that the second she bolted from his consulting room she would make sure she never had to see him again!

'What about it?'

'Is it regular?'

'I work long days at the veterinary surgery across the road from here. I'm the only vet there, so I'm on call most nights, and since the new homes got built I've been busier than ever.'

'So you get called out a lot?'

'I do.'

He nodded and scribbled a note. 'And are you finding it difficult to drop off to sleep?'

'Yes.'

'Worried about your beeper going off? Or is it something else?'

She looked at him directly now. 'Look, Dr Preston has given me the pills before. I'm sure he won't mind if you give me some more.'

She didn't like him prying. He glanced at her records, his eyes scanning the previous note. Yes, she was correct. She'd been given sleeping pills by Dr Preston this time last year...

'...due to the sudden death of the patient's daughter three years ago, patient requested tranquillisers...'

He felt a lump of cold dread settle in his stomach as he read the notes fully.

She'd lost her *child*. Sydney Harper had lost her daughter and she couldn't sleep when the anniversary of her death got close. It happened every year. *Oh, heavens.*

He closed his eyes and gritted his teeth, mentally apologising.

'I...er...yes. I can see that in your notes.'

How terrible. The most awful thing that could ever happen to a parent. And it had happened to her and he was trying to poke around in her despair when it was clear in her notes why she needed the pills. But would he be being a good doctor just to give them to her? Or would he be a *better* doctor if he tried to stop her needing them? They could be addictive...

'I'm sure he won't mind if you give me some more tablets.'

Nathan had a daughter. Anna. She was six years old and she was all he had in this world. He couldn't imagine losing her. She was everything to him right now. What this poor woman had been through...! No wonder she looked the way she did.

'I can write you a prescription, but...' He paused. 'Have you ever been offered counselling?'

She looked directly at him, her demeanour suggesting she was about to explain something to a child. 'I was. And I did go to start with. But it didn't help me so I stopped going.'

'Perhaps you weren't ready for it then. Would you be interested in trying it again now? It might help you with this sleeping issue. I could arrange it for you.'

The computer whirred out the prescription and he grabbed it from the printer and passed it over to her.

'Counselling is not for me. I don't...talk...about what happened.'

'Maybe that's the problem?' The words were out before he could censor them. He bit his lip with annoyance. Too late to take the words back. He needed to cover their crassness. And quickly. 'Have you tried a different night-time routine? Warm milk? A bath? That kind of thing?'

But she'd stood up, was staring down at him, barely controlling the anger he could see brewing behind her eyes. 'Are you a father, Dr Jones?'

He nodded solemnly, picturing his daughter's happy, smiling face. 'I am.'

'Have you ever experienced the loss of a child?'

He could see where she was going with this, and felt horrible inside. He looked away. 'No. Thankfully.'

'Then don't tell me that *warm milk—*' she almost spat the words '—will make me better.' She spun on her heel and when she got to the door, her hand on the handle, she paused, her head low, then glanced over her shoulder, her teeth gritted. 'Thank you for my prescription.'

Then she left.

He felt as if a hurricane had blown through the room. He felt winded. Stunned. He had to get up and pace, sucking in a lungful of air, running both hands through his hair before he stood and stared out of the window at the sparrows and starlings trying to take food from the frozen feeders hanging outside. The smaller birds were carefully picking at the peanuts, whereas the starlings were tossing white breadcrumbs everywhere, making a mess.

No, he had *not* experienced the same pain that Sydney had gone through. He would never want to. But he *did* know what it felt like to realise that your life had changed for evermore.

People dealt with tragedies in different ways. Some found comfort in food. Some in drink or drugs. Some kept it all inside. Others found it easy to talk out their feelings and frustrations. A few would blindly choose to ignore it and pretend it had never happened.

He felt deflated now that she'd left his room. Sydney Harper was intense—yes—and hurting—definitely—but there was something about her. He couldn't quite put a finger on it.

It bothered him all day. Through seeing all his patients. The chest infection, the sprained ankle, a case of chicken pox, talking someone through using his asthma medication. His thoughts kept returning to his first patient at his new job.

Sydney Harper.

Beautiful. Elegant.

Fragile.

And then it came to him. The reason why he couldn't forget her. The reason he kept going over and over their interaction that morning.

I'm attracted to her.

The thought stopped him in his tracks. No. He

couldn't—*wouldn't*—be. He had nothing to offer her. Besides, he had a child to take care of. Clearly!

No. That way danger lay.

He doubted he would ever see her again. Not as his *patient*. She had clearly wanted to see Dr Preston, and the way she'd stormed from the room had left him feeling a little bit stunned. He'd *never* had a patient walk out on him like that.

A fiancée, yes.

The mother of his child, yes.

But never a patient.

Sydney strode from the room feeling mightily irritated with Dr Jones, but not knowing why. Because she had the prescription she needed. She'd obtained what she'd wanted when she'd made the appointment. But now that she was out from under Dr Jones's interested, *unsettling* gaze she felt restless and antsy. Almost angry. As if she needed to go running for a few miles to get all of that uncomfortable adrenaline out of her system. As if she needed to burn off some of the inner turmoil she was feeling. As if she needed to let out a giant enraged scream.

Averting her gaze from the people in the waiting room, she went straight back to Reception and leant over the counter towards Beattie the recetptionist—the owner of a moggy called Snuggles.

'Beattie, I've just been seen by Dr Jones. Could you make a note on my records that when I make an appointment to see Dr Preston—my *actual* doctor—that I should, indeed, *see* Dr Preston?'

Beattie looked up at her in surprise. 'You didn't *like* Dr Jones?'

Her jaw almost hit the floor.

'*Like* him? Liking him has nothing to do with it. Dr

Preston is my GP and that is who I want to see when I phone to make an appointment!'

Beattie gave an apologetic smile. 'Sorry, Syd. Dr Jones offered to see you as Dr Preston was overrun and he knew you were in a rush to get back to work.'

Oh. Right. She hadn't thought of that. 'Well, that was very kind of him, but...'

It *had* been very kind of him, hadn't it? And what was she doing out here complaining? Even though she'd got what she needed.

Deflating slightly, she relaxed her tensed shoulders. 'Next time just book me in with Richard.'

'Will do. Anything else I can help you with?'

Not really. Though a niggling thought had entered her head... 'This Dr Jones that I saw today... Just a locum, is he? Just here for the day?'

She tried to make it sound casual. But it would be nice to know that she wouldn't be bumping into him in the village unless she had to. Not after she'd stormed out like that. That wasn't her normal behaviour. But something about the man had irritated her, and then he'd made that crass suggestion about warm milk...

'No, no. He's permanent.' Beattie's face filled with a huge grin. 'He moved to the village a week ago with his daughter. Into one of the homes on the new estate.'

'Oh. Right. Thank you.'

Permanent. Dr Jones would be living here. In Silverdale.

'Please don't tell me he's got an aging pet dog or anything?'

'I don't think so. But you'll run into him at the committee meetings for the Christmas market and the village nativity.'

What? She'd only just decided to return to those meetings. Had been looking forward to them!

'Why?'

Beattie looked at her oddly. 'Dr Preston is cutting down on his commitments now that he's nearly retired. He's asked Nathan to take over. You didn't like him? We all think he's gorgeous! Have you seen him smile? I tell you, that man's a heartbreaker!'

A heartbreaker? Not if *she* had anything to do with it.

Sydney grimaced, but thanked Beattie once again and left the surgery, pausing to wait for traffic to rush by so she could cross the road over to her own practice.

The new doctor was going to be on the Christmas committee. And she'd just agreed to go back. To help. She'd told them she would *be there*. Her heart sank at the thought of it as she neared her place of work.

Silverdale Veterinary Surgery was a relatively small building, comprised of two old cottages that had been knocked through inside and transformed from homes into a business.

Sydney loved it. It was clinical and businesslike, but still retained its old-world charm with white walls and large exposed oak beams and, outside, a thatched roof. There were even window boxes, which she'd learnt to tend. They overflowed with primulas and pansies in the spring, but right now were hung with dark green ivy and indigo lobelia. And *no* fairy lights. Even if everyone else seemed to think it was okay to start decorating for Christmas in *November!*

She'd never been a green-fingered person. Not before she'd got married. But when Olivia came along the little girl had loved being in the garden and growing pretty things. Although Sydney had managed to kill the first few plants they'd got, they'd eventually learned together and their flowers had begun to thrive. There'd been nothing she'd liked better than to watch Olivia use her pink tin watering can to water them each evening, when it was cool. And Syd's talent with flowers had not gone unnoticed around the village either. She'd often been in charge of the flower stalls at the Christmas market each year.

When she'd been involved, anyway.

She pushed through the door and saw that her waiting room was pleasingly busy. There was Mr Shepherd, as expected, with his Great Dane, Sara with her new kitten, and no doubt in the box by Janet's feet were her two ferrets, Apollo and Zeus.

'Morning, everyone! Sorry to keep you waiting.'

Her anxiety was gone here. This was her home turf. Her safe haven. The place that *she* controlled. Was in charge of. Where there were no surprises. Well, nothing life-changing, anyway. Not to her. Here she could cure illnesses. Make things better. As much as she could.

Her clients waved and smiled and said good morning, too. They weren't too bothered about waiting for her. And she appreciated them for that.

In the staff room, she put on her green veterinary top and prepared to start work.

This was better.

This she could do.

This she was in control of.

Nathan stood in the playground, surrounded mostly by mothers waiting for their children to come out of infant school. As always, he felt like a complete fish out of water here. All the mothers stood in little groups, chatting and laughing. They all *knew* each other. And him…? He was the lone male, feeling awkward. Sure that he was standing out like a sore thumb.

He could feel their eyes on him. Judging him. Assessing him. Were they talking about him? Could they see his awkward gait? His limp? Could they see what was wrong with him? *It feels like they can.* He almost felt as if he was carrying a huge sign naming his condition around his neck.

Silverdale Infants had seemed the perfect place for Anna when he'd first come to the village for his job interview. He'd scouted the place out and asked the head-teacher to give him a tour. He'd walked through the school with her, looking in the classrooms, seeing the happy children and their paintings, listening to them singing in assembly and watching as they'd sat for story-time in their impossibly small chairs. He'd genuinely felt his daughter would be happy there. It had a good vibe. The head was a nice woman and Miss Howarth, Anna's teacher-to-be, seemed really lovely and welcoming.

Nathan had just had his first day in his new job and this had been Anna's first day at her new school. He could only hope that it had gone as well as his own day, and that she would come running out with a big smile on her face. Then, perhaps, the lump of anxiety in his stomach would disappear and they'd be able to go home and he'd cook dinner.

Nathan hated being away from Anna. Giving her into the care of someone else. But he had to work and she had to learn—and weren't schools considered *in loco parentis?*

He was grateful for the flexible hours his new job afforded him. Since Gwyneth had left them he'd had to become both father *and* mother to Anna. And he didn't think he was doing too badly. Anna seemed happy enough, only occasionally asking why she didn't have a mummy, like other children. Those days were hard.

When he could see the hurt in his daughter's eyes. And when it happened he would curse Gwyneth inwardly, whilst outwardly he would throw everything he had at making his daughter happy.

He just couldn't give her the mother that she wanted. He wasn't ready to be with someone new. To open himself up to possible hurt and betrayal. To being left again. And why put Anna through the hope of getting to know someone when they might walk away and break her heart, too?

He didn't bad-mouth Gwyneth to Anna. It wasn't up to him to tell Anna how to feel about her mother. Anna might want to find her one day and see her. Talk to her. Ask her things. Did he want Anna to grow up resentful and hating her mother? No. Even if it was hard for him. Because Gwyneth had abandoned them both. And that hurt. Not so much now, but it still caused pain whenever he thought about his and Anna's future.

He sighed as he thought about his mistake in getting involved with Gwyneth. She'd been so much fun to begin with, but—as was sometimes the way with relationships—they'd both realised something was missing. And then they'd discovered she was pregnant...

Life was short. And he would not have Anna spending hers moping about for a mother who had no interest in her whatsoever. He was only sorry that he hadn't noticed Gwyneth's shallowness earlier on. Before he'd got in too deep.

The school bell rang and he braced himself. Now he'd know. Had it gone well?

Crossing his fingers in his jacket pockets, trying not to shiver in the late November cold, he looked for her familiar face amongst the mass of children pouring out through the door, all of them almost identical in their little green jumpers and grey skirts or trousers.

Then he saw her and his heart lifted.

'Daddy!'

She was *smiling*. Beaming at him as she ran to his open arms, clutching a painting that was still slightly wet. Nathan scooped her up, hefting her onto his hip, trying not to grimace at the pain in his shoulder.

'What do we have here?' He glanced at the painting. There were daubs of brown and green that he guessed was a tree, and to one side was a large black blob with ears. 'Is that Lottie?'

Anna nodded, grinning, showing the gap where her two front teeth were missing. 'Yes!'

Lottie was their pet rabbit and his one concession to Anna's demands to fill their house with pets of all shapes and sizes. Anna *adored* animals, and ever since she'd started at nursery had plagued him with requests for cats or dogs or parrots or anything that had fur, feathers or a cute face.

Knowing that they would both be out all day—him at work, she at school—he'd not thought a dog or a cat was appropriate, but he'd given in and allowed her a rabbit. It had the added bonus of living outdoors and its presence had stopped Anna from 'rescuing' injured insects and bringing them in to be 'nursed'.

'It looks just like her.' He squinted as he saw a small daub of bright orange. 'Is that a carrot?'

'No, Daddy. Silly! That's a worm.'

'Oh, right.' He gently placed his daughter back on the ground, being careful not to grimace or wrench himself further. 'So how did it go? Was it good? Did you make friends?'

She nodded. 'Lots and lots.'

She proceeded to list them as they walked back to the car. There seemed an *awful* lot, and to his ears it sounded as if she'd just memorised the register, but he nodded and smiled at her as she told him about Hattie with the bright pink glasses, and George who had held her hand as they'd walked to assembly.

They were soon home. Nathan still had half their life packed away in boxes after the move, but he knew they'd get there eventually. All the important stuff was unpacked. And Anna's room had everything. He'd done that first. Everything else could wait for when he had the time. He just had to decide where he wanted it all to go.

The house was brand-new, so had none of that old-world character the rest of the cottages in the village had. He had tiles on his roof, not thatch. A modern fake fireplace rather than an old rustic one with real flames. Flat, smooth walls rather than whitewashed ones with crooked oak beams.

Still, the place would get its character eventually.

'I'm going to see if Lottie missed me.' Anna ran through the house towards the back door, so she could go into the garden.

'Not yet, young lady,' he called after her. 'Go upstairs and get out of your uniform first.'

'Daddy, please!'

'It was raining this morning, Anna. I'm not having you getting your uniform covered in mud and straw. Please go and get changed.'

She pouted, but only briefly, and then she ran back past him, clambering up the stairs as he took their bags through to the kitchen, pinned her painting to the fridge with a magnet that was shaped like a banana. He'd picked up some vegetables from a farm shop, so he popped those in the fridge, then switched on the kettle for a drink.

Upstairs, he heard a small *thunk* as Anna kicked off her shoes and soon enough she was trotting back down the stairs, wearing a weird combination of purple corduroy skirt, green tee shirt and a rather loud orange and yellow cardigan.

'Nice… I'm liking your style.' He was keen to encourage her to wear what she wanted and to pick her own clothes. He'd learned that it was important—it helped Anna to develop her independence and allowed her to express herself. And he needed Anna to be a strong character. He wanted to encourage her at all times to feel happy about herself and her own decisions. To feel valued and beautiful. Because she *was* beautiful. With her mother's good looks but thankfully none of her character.

'Will you do me a juice, Daddy?'

'Sure thing, poppet.' He watched her twist the back door key and trot out into the garden. It wasn't huge out there, and as theirs was one of the original show houses it was just plain grass, with one side border of bushes. Nothing too impressive. Nothing that needed that much work. Something he figured he'd get to later. Maybe in the New Year.

But it had the rabbit hutch. The main reason for Anna to go and play outside. He was hoping to get her a trampoline, or a bike, or something. Maybe for Christmas.

He was just diluting orange juice with some water when he heard his daughter let out a blood-curdling scream.

'Daddy!'

'Anna?' His body froze, his heart stopped beating just for a millisecond, and then he was dropping the glass into the sink and bolting for the back door. What on earth had happened? Why had she screamed? Was she hurt?

Oh, please don't let her be hurt!

'Daddy!'

She ran into his arms, crying, and he held her, puzzled. What was it? Had she fallen over? What?

'Let me look at you.' He held her out at arm's length to check her over, but she looked fine. No scuffed knees, no grazes, no cuts. Just a face flooded with tears. What the…?

'Lottie's *bleeding*!' She pointed at the hutch before burying her face in his shirt.

He looked over the top of her head and could now see that the hutch had a broken latch and poor Lottie the rabbit sat hunched within, breathing heavily and audibly, with blood all over her and in the straw around her, as if she'd been involved in some sort of weird rabbit horror movie.

'Oh…' He stood up and led Anna away and back into the kitchen, sitting her down on one of the chairs by the table. 'Stay here.'

'She's bleeding, Daddy.'

'I know, honey. We'll need to take her to the vet.'

He didn't know if the poor thing might have to be put to sleep. There was a lot of blood, and Lottie looked like she might be in shock. He dashed for the cupboard under the stairs, where they'd put Lottie's carrier and got it out. Then he grabbed some latex gloves from under the sink and headed for the garden.

'I'll get Lottie. Can you get your shoes on for me? And your coat?'

'Where are we going?'

'The vet. The animal doctor. She'll need to check her over.'

'What if she dies, Daddy?' Anna sobbed, almost hiccupping her words.

He hadn't imagined this. He'd agreed to have Lottie knowing that rabbits lived for around ten years, hoping that they wouldn't have to face this day until Anna was in her teens. But not this early. Not *now*. He wasn't sure how she'd handle a pet's death at this age.

'Let's cross that bridge when we come to it. Get your shoes on. We need to get her there quickly.'

Nathan headed into the garden, slipped on the gloves and picked up the poor, shocked rabbit and placed her in the box. Normally she fought going in the carrier. But there was no fight today. His heart sank at the thought of having to tell his daughter her rabbit might die. Had Anna not been through enough?

He pulled off the bloodied gloves and quickly discarded them in the bin.

He could only hope that the veterinary surgery was still open.

CHAPTER TWO

IT HAD BEEN a long, tiring day. After her doctor's appointment Sydney had come back to the surgery and seen her first ten patients, and then she'd got round to her surgeries—a dental clean, two spays on cats, a dog to be neutered. Lunch had been quick, and then there had been more appointments: kitten visits, puppy checks, suture removals, an elderly dog that had had to be euthanised. Then she'd returned phone calls, given owners blood test results and now she was finishing off her paperwork. Filling in records. There were three animals being kept in overnight, but Lucy, her veterinary nurse, was giving them their final check before they left for the evening.

'I'll be ready to put my feet up tonight. Have you seen my ankles?' said Lucy.

Sydney smiled sympathetically. Lucy did seem to be suffering lately.

Almost all the lights were off, except for in her office and at the surgery entrance, and Sydney was just debating whether to have a cup of tea here or go home and have it there when she heard a loud banging on the surgery's front door.

A last-minute emergency?

She hurried through, switching on the lights as she

went, and stopped when she saw who was on the other side of the door.

Dr Jones.

Oh.

Her pause was barely noticeable. At least she hoped so. Then she was rushing to the door, her cheeks flaming at having to let in the dishy doc. Though, judging by the look of worry on his face, he wasn't here to continue his conversation about warm milk.

She opened the door and Dr Jones came in, carrying a pet carrier. Behind him, a little uncertainly, followed a little girl with chestnut-brown hair in two ponytails held by pink bobbles, her face tearstained, pale and stunned. Seeing the little girl, so like Olivia—*no, so like her father*—startled her and her stomach twisted painfully. As if she'd been punched in the gut.

She dragged her gaze away from the little girl and looked over at the doctor. 'Dr Jones? Can I help?'

Am I stammering? I feel like I'm stammering.

'My daughter's rabbit. I think it's been attacked.'

He lifted up the carrier, so she could see through the barred door, but it was impossible to gauge the extent of the animal's injuries.

Sydney glanced quickly at the little girl. She looked around Olivia's age. Maybe a bit older. She wasn't sure. But she was young, and she didn't need to see Sydney examining the rabbit if it was in a bad way. There were a lot of foxes out here in Silverdale Village. It was a very rural area, surrounded by farms and woodlands. Occasionally they even saw deer. The likelihood that there were animal predators around was very high.

All business now, she took the carrier from the doctor. 'Maybe your daughter should sit in the waiting room whilst I take a look?'

The little girl slipped her tiny hand into her father's. 'Don't leave me, Daddy.'

Dr Jones looked torn, but then he nodded. 'I'll sit with you.' He looked up at Sydney. 'Is that okay? If I sit out here with Anna?'

Anna. A lovely name.

'Of course. I'll just take a quick look.'

She hurried the rabbit through to the surgery, closing the door behind her and leaning back against it for a moment whilst she gathered herself.

That's Anna. Anna! Not Olivia.

The table where she usually examined pets had already been cleaned down, so she laid the carrier upon it and opened it up.

Inside was a very scared, very shocked black rabbit. From what she could see at this stage it had injuries to the top of its head, its left eye looked damaged, and there were other fine puncture marks across its back and legs. Sydney held it gently whilst she checked it over. The ears looked okay, as did its throat, and it seemed to be breathing fine, if a little loudly. She listened to its chest through her stethoscope and tried to get a better look at the eye, but she couldn't tell if it was ruptured or not.

Poor thing.

She suspected it might die of shock. She felt for its pulse. It was slow and faint, but that was typical for an animal like this in such a situation. Its gums were pale, too and its ears cool.

There wasn't much she could do at this point. Technically, she couldn't see any *fatal* injuries. The shock itself might be the killer here. All she could do at the moment was give the rabbit a painkilling injection and some antibiotics. But she'd need to check with Dr Jones first, in case they requested euthanasia.

Sydney put the rabbit back into the carrier and secured it, then headed to the waiting room, her own heart thumping rapidly at the thought of returning to speak to him.

'Dr Jones?'

He looked up when she called his name and then patted his daughter's hand and told her to stay in her seat before he came over to her and whispered in a low voice, 'How is she?'

Sydney also kept her voice low, not wanting to upset Anna. 'She's in a great deal of shock. Can you tell me what happened?'

He shrugged. 'We're not sure. I'd been at work all day and then went to pick Anna up from school. She found Lottie like that when we got back.'

She nodded. 'She has sustained a great deal of damage to her left eye, but it's hard to see at the moment whether the eyeball itself has been ruptured. If it has, we might have to remove it, but at this stage I think we need to see if she'll survive the night.'

Dr Jones let out a heavy sigh and glanced at his daughter. 'Do you think Lottie might die?'

'It's fifty-fifty. I can give her a painkiller and some antibiotics if you wish. The bite marks are quite small and thin, possibly caused by a cat or a fox. Their mouths are filled with bacteria, so the chance of infection is high. There aren't any fatal injuries, but shock can kill an animal like this. It's up to you what measures you'd like me to take.'

She left the implication hanging. Did he want to see if the rabbit survived? Or did he want her to put the rabbit to sleep?

Dr Jones thought for a moment. 'Lottie is Anna's world. She loves animals. If there aren't any fatal injuries I think I owe it to her to see if Lottie makes it through the night. She won't be in any pain?'

'There'll be some discomfort, but the painkillers should help her an awful lot. I'll give her the injections, but if you can take her home, keep her somewhere warm and safe where she won't be disturbed. Do you have an indoor cage?'

He shook his head. 'I don't.'

'A bathroom, then. It's the safest place—somewhere there aren't any cables or wires to chew.'

'Will she want to eat?'

'You must get her to try. When a rabbit goes into shock it sometimes stops eating, and it will just lead to further complications if her digestive system shuts down. Offer her all her favourites and try to get her to drink, too. I'll need to see her first thing in the morning. Can you bring her in then?'

'Before surgery, yes. About eight?'

She nodded. 'I'll be here.'

Sydney slipped back inside her room and administered the injections. She really hoped on their behalf that Lottie would survive, but the poor thing had been through a terrible ordeal.

Back in the waiting room, she handed the carrier to Dr Jones and then, hesitantly, after thinking twice about doing so, she knelt in front of Anna. She tried not to notice the way the little girl's eyes looked into hers with so much hope. The way tears had welled in her eyes.

'Stay nice and quiet for her. No loud noises. Lottie needs to rest. Can you help her do that?'

Anna nodded. 'Yes.'

'Good.' She stood up again, frighteningly taken in by the little girl's big blue eyes. So similar to Olivia's it was unsettling. How was it possible that this little girl should remind her so strongly of her own?

Backing away, she held open the door for them, eager for them to go. So she could breathe again.

'What do I owe you?' Dr Jones glanced over at the till.

'We'll sort it in the morning. Don't worry. And good luck.'

She watched them go and backed away from the door. They were a nice family, little Anna and her father. Was there a wife at home, waiting for news? It hadn't sounded like it. *He'd* been at work, *he'd* picked his daughter up from school. No mention of anyone else.

It doesn't matter. You're not interested in him anyway. Dr Jones is off limits!

So why was she thinking about him? Just because he was handsome? No. She wasn't that shallow. It must be because of the way she'd walked out on him that morning after her consultation. She'd been rude and had not apologised for it, either. She'd been defensive. Abrupt. Even though he had suggested the most ridiculous thing. And now she'd helped with their rabbit; that was all. They'd all had a shock and she knew how that felt. She wanted it to be easier for them.

Poor rabbit.

She hoped it was still alive in the morning.

Nathan had a sleepless night. It wasn't just because of the rabbit. Though he *was* worrying about getting up in the morning and finding her dead on the floor of the bathroom. If that happened then he wanted to deal with everything before Anna saw any of it. She shouldn't have to see that.

But, no. It was his own body that had kept him from sleeping.

Yesterday he'd tried to give advice on getting a good

night's sleep to Sydney and he felt a bit hypocritical. Yes, there were tried and tested methods—relaxation, a milky drink, a warm bath, checking you had a comfortable bed—but they didn't work for him, either.

The spasticity he suffered from his multiple sclerosis kept *him* awake at night.

It wasn't as bad as it was for some people, and he knew he was lucky that no one just looking at him could guess his condition. He liked it that way. Fought to keep it so. But that didn't stop the damned stiffness that never seemed to go away. Sometimes he would lie there, trying to relax, and he would feel his muscles tightening so hard it almost felt like a vice. Then he would have to rub at his arm or his leg and hope that it would go away. It never did. And he knew it wouldn't. But that didn't stop him from trying.

So he'd spent the night alternately staring at the ceiling and getting up to check that the rabbit was still breathing.

At five a.m. he crawled out of bed, ready for a cup of tea, and checked on Lottie once more.

She's still alive. Thank goodness!

He gave her some dandelion leaves from the back garden and happily watched as she chewed them down, Her appetite was still good. Then he tried to pipette some water into her mouth—which she didn't like—so he decided to leave her a small bowl to drink from instead.

Anna was thrilled when she woke to find Lottie moving about in the bathroom. The rabbit's left eye still looked pretty mangled, though, and Anna was keen for the time to pass so she could go to the vet with her dad before school.

'You won't be at the vet, Anna. I'm dropping you at breakfast club, as normal.'

'But, Daddy, I want to go! Please?'

'No, Anna. I'm sorry.'

It was important that she kept to her routine. He hated changing things in Anna's life. And, though the incident with Lottie was out of the ordinary, it didn't mean that Anna's life had to be disturbed. It had changed enough already. Her mother had walked out on them both, not to mention that he had his diagnosis to deal with. Life for Anna would change dramatically at some point, if his condition worsened. Best to keep things as normal as he could, for however long he could. He would not have her upset unnecessarily.

Anna pouted for a bit, but got in the car happily and whispered good things to Lottie through the carrier door as he drove. 'You'll be okay, Lottie. The vet will take good care of you.'

With his daughter at breakfast club, Nathan drove to work, parked, and then walked across the road to the veterinary surgery with Lottie in her carrier once more. He was kind of proud of his daughter's little rabbit. Getting through a severe trauma and surviving. It was like finding a kindred spirit, and after getting up all night to check on her he felt he was bonding with her. And though last night he'd almost expected to have to tell Sydney to put Lottie to sleep, the fact that she'd lived... Well, he was kind of rooting for her now.

He was looking forward to seeing Sydney's reaction. She was an intriguing woman, and he was keen for her to see that the rabbit was still alive and find out her plan of action. But picturing the look of surprise on her face, or even trying to imagine what her smile might be like, was doing surprising and disturbing things to his insides. Things he didn't want to examine too closely for fear of what they might mean.

The bell above the door rang as he walked through,

clutching the carrier, and he headed over to the reception desk, where a veterinary nurse sat.

'Lottie Jones to see Sydney, please.'

'Ah, yes. Please take a seat—you'll be called through in a moment.'

He sat and waited, his nerves strangely on edge. For the rabbit? For himself? For seeing Sydney again? Last night when he'd lain awake he'd thought about her a great deal. She was very beautiful, and totally out of his league, but…she intrigued him. For all that she'd been through— the loss of her daughter—she seemed surprisingly together. A little terse, maybe, but professional and she clearly cared for her animal charges.

What made her tick? What kept her going? Her bravery in the face of immense tragedy was a very positive force, and he liked to surround himself with positive people. He needed that; he tried to stay positive himself. Perhaps just by knowing her a little bit better he might learn her secret? If she ever forgave him for what he'd said. She was a strong woman. Determined. He could see that. The complete antithesis of Gwyneth.

He shook his head as he thought of his thoughtless advice to her. *Warm milk?*

So busy was he, feeling embarrassed for what he'd said, that he wasn't ready when she opened her surgery door and called his name. 'Dr Jones?'

He looked up, startled. Today, her long brown hair was taken up into a messy ponytail. There were little wavy bits hanging free around her face, and even without make-up she looked amazing. He quickly cursed himself for noticing.

He got up, loudly cleared his throat and took the carrier through to her consulting room, determined to be distant and professional.

'She's still with us. Lottie survived the night.'

He placed the carrier onto her examination table and stood quite far back, as if the physical distance would somehow stop him stealing glances at her.

Her eyebrows rose in surprise. 'Okay. Let's have a look at her.'

He watched as Sydney's very fine hands opened the carrier and she gave Lottie a thorough assessment, listening to her chest and abdomen with her stethoscope, taking the rabbit's temperature, checking the bites and scratches and finally examining the wounded eye.

He tried not to take notice of the small beauty mark on Sydney's bared neck, her delicate cheekbones, or the way she bit her bottom lip as she concentrated. She had a very fine mouth. With full, soft-looking lips.

Dragging his eyes away from her mouth, he stared hard at Lottie. *Focus on the rabbit!*

'It's impossible for me to see if the eyeball itself has ruptured. The damage is too extensive. But until the swelling goes down I don't think we should assume that it has. I'm going to prescribe antibiotic drops for her eye, more painkillers, and a drug to keep her digestive system working which is an oral medicine. Rabbits don't like receiving oral meds, so if you can put the medicine in a food that you know she will eat you can get it into her that way.'

He nodded, keeping his gaze fixed firmly on Lottie's thick black fur so that he didn't accidentally start staring into Sydney's soft grey eyes. 'Okay. How often does she need the meds?'

'The eye drops three times a day, the oral meds four times a day. Will you be able to do that?'

He thought about his work schedule. It would be tough.

But manageable. Perhaps if he kept Lottie in her carrier at work? In an unused room?

'I'll find a way.'

'I'll need to see her in about four days' time. The swelling should have gone down by then, we'll know if the antibiotics have worked, and I'll be able to see if the eye needs to be removed.'

He risked a glance at her wide almond-shaped eyes. 'She'd cope with that?'

'Not all rabbits do well with surgery, and if we do have to remove the eye then she could be susceptible to further infection. Keep it clean. Bathe it with cooled boiled water when you can—three or four times a day.'

'Like a proper patient.' He smiled and closed the door on the carrier once again. 'Thank you, Sydney, for seeing us last night. I appreciate that you were probably closed and your staff were ready to go home.'

She glanced away, her cheeks glowing slightly, before she began typing notes into her computer. 'It was no problem.'

He watched her where she stood by the computer. It was better with her further away and not looking at him. He could think more clearly. And he wanted to make things right between them. He hated it that she'd left his consulting room feeling stressed and angry. Hated it that he'd insulted her daughter's memory with a crass piece of advice.

'I'd like to thank you properly, if I may? We got off to a bad start the other day and... Well, we both live in this village. It'd be nice to know I've not upset the first person I got to properly meet. Would you join me for a coffee some time? I'd really appreciate the chance to apologise.'

What on *earth are you doing?*

The invitation had just come out. He cursed himself

silently, knowing she would refuse him, but, hell, he kind
of wanted her to say *yes*. He couldn't just see her about
rabbits and sleeping tablets. Part of him wanted to know
more about her. About that strong side of her that kept
her going in the cruel world that had taken her daughter.
That inner strength of hers…

But he also got the feeling that if they were given the
chance the two of them might become friends. It had been
a long time since he'd sat down and just chatted with a
woman who wasn't a patient, or some cashier in a shop,
someone with whom he could pass the time of day.

'Oh, I don't know. I—' She tucked a stray strand of
hair behind her ear and continued typing, her fingers
tripping over one another on the keyboard, so that he
could see she had to tap 'delete' a few times and go back,
cursing silently.

He focused on her stumbling fingers. Tried not to
imagine himself reaching for her hands and stilling them.
'Just coffee. I don't have an evil plan to try and seduce
you, or anything.'

Shut up, you idiot. You're making it worse!

Now she looked at him, her hands frozen over the
keys. Her cheeks red. Her pause was an agonising silence
before her fingers leapt into life once more, finishing her
notes before she turned to him and spoke.

'That's kind of you, but—'

'Just a chat. Anna and I don't really know anyone
here, and—well, I'd really like to know you.' He smiled.
'As a friend.'

It could never be anything else. Despite the fact that
she was the most beautiful creature he had ever seen.
Despite the fact that he could see her pulse hammering
away in her throat. That her skin looked so creamy and

soft. That he wanted to lift that stray strand of hair from her face and...

'I—'

'No pressure. Not a date. Just...coffee.'

He realised he was rambling, but he was confused. *She* confused him. Made him feel like he was tripping over his own words even though he wasn't. Made him surprised at what came out of his own mouth.

He'd not reached out to a woman like this since Gwyneth had left. He'd tried to become accustomed to the fact that he would spend the rest of his life alone. That he would not parade a stream of women past Anna. That he would not endanger his heart once again because on the one occasion he had given it to a woman she had ripped it apart.

The only female who would have his undying love was his daughter.

Which was as it should be.

Anna didn't need the huge change that a woman in their lives would bring. He was lucky that Gwyneth had left before Anna knew who she was or formed a bond.

But he missed being able just to sit with a woman and chat about everyday things. He missed asking about another person's day. He missed having adult company that didn't involve talks about unusual rashes, or a cough that wouldn't go away, or *could you just take a look at my boil?* And he imagined that Sydney would be interesting. Would have intelligent things to say and be the complete opposite of his ex-fiancée.

That was all he wanted.

All he *told* himself he wanted.

He waited for her to answer. Knowing she would turn him down, knowing it would hurt for some reason, but knowing that he'd had to ask because... Well, because he'd said something stupid to her the other day and he needed to apologise in the only way he knew how.

He waited.

Just a coffee?

Was there really such a thing as 'just a coffee' when a guy asked you out?

Because that was what he was doing. Asking her out. Like on a date. Right? And though he said there was no pressure, there was *always* pressure. Wasn't there?

Besides, why would she want to meet him for a drink? For a chat? This was the man who had got her so riled up yesterday, what with his probing questions and his damned twinkling eyes.

Did he not know how attractive he was? Because he seemed oblivious to it. Either that or he was a great actor. With great hair, and an irresistible charm about him, and the way he was looking at her right now... It was doing unbelievable things to her insides. Churning her up, making her stomach seem all giddy, causing her heart to thump and her mouth to go dry. She hadn't felt this way since her schoolgirl crush had asked her to the local disco. And her hands were trembling. *Trembling!*

Why had he asked her out? Why did he want to go for coffee? She had nothing to talk to him about. She didn't know this guy. Except that he was a hot doctor with effortlessly cool hair and eyes that melted her insides every time he smiled at her. Oh, and that he had a daughter. A beautiful little girl who seemed very lovely indeed, but who made her feel uncomfortable because she reminded her too much of Olivia.

If he wanted to apologise to her then why didn't he just do it? It wouldn't take a moment. No need for them to go to a coffee shop. He could say it here. Now. Then she could thank him, and then he could go, and it would all be over.

Why would she get any kind of involved with this man? He was dangerous in so many ways. Intelligent, good-looking, attractive. Not to mention his adorable daughter... She pushed the thought away. *No.*

She wanted to say, *We have nothing to talk about.* She wanted to say, *But there's no point.* She wanted to yell, *You're so perfect you look airbrushed. And I can't have coffee with you because you make me feel things that I don't want to feel and think of things I sure as hell don't want to think about!*

But she said none of those things. Instead she found herself mumbling, 'That'd be great.' Her voice almost gave out on that last word. Squeaking out of her closed throat so tightly she wondered if only dogs would have been able to hear it.

Oh, no, did I just agree to meet him?

The goofy smile he gave her in return made her temperature rise by a significant amount of degrees, and when he said goodbye and left the room she had to stand for a minute and fan her face with a piece of paper. She berated herself inwardly for having accepted. She would have to turn him down. Maybe call the surgery and leave a message for him.

This was a mistake.

A big mistake.

Nathan waited for his computer system to load up, and whilst he did he sat in his chair, staring into space and wondering just what the hell he had done.

Sydney Harper had said yes to his coffee invitation. *Yes!*

It was unbelievable. There must have been some

spike, some surge in the impulse centre of his brain that had caused his mind to short circuit or something. His leg muscles would sometimes spasm and kick out suddenly—the same must have happened with his head. And his mouth.

He had no doubt that they would get on okay. She would show up—a little late, maybe—pretend that she couldn't stay for long, have some excuse to leave sooner than she'd expected. Maybe even get a friend to call her away on an invented emergency. But...they'd get on okay. He'd apologise right away for what he'd said. Be polite as could be.

Surely it was a good thing to try and make friends when you moved to a new area? That was all he was doing.

And how many guys have you invited for coffee?

The only people he really knew in Silverdale were Dr Preston, some of the staff at the medical centre and his daughter's teacher at school, and they were more colleagues than actual friends. He'd left all his old friends behind when he'd moved from the city to this remote village. They kept in touch online. With the odd phone call and promises to meet up.

Sydney could be a *new* friend. A female friend. That was possible. How could it *not* be in today's modern age? And once he got past her prickly demeanour, made her realise he was sorry and showed her that he was no threat to her romantically, then they could both relax and they would get on like a house on fire.

He had no doubt of that.

So why, when he thought of spending time with Sydney, did he picture them kissing? Think of himself reaching for her hand across the table and lifting it to his lips while he stared deeply into her eyes. Inhaling the scent of her perfume upon her wrist…

And why did that vision remind him of Gwyneth's twisted face and her harsh words?

'I can't be with you! Why would anyone *want to be with you? You're broken. Faulty. The only thing you can offer is a lifetime of pain and despair and I didn't sign up for that!'*

Determined not to be haunted by his ex-fiancée's words, he angrily punched the keys on his keyboard, brought up his files and called in his first patient of the day.

Sam Carter was a thirty-two-year-old man who had just received a diagnosis of Huntington's Disease. His own father had died from it quite young, in his fifties, and the diagnosis had been a terrible shock to the whole family after Sam had decided to have genetic testing. Now he sat in front of Nathan, looking pale and washed out.

'What can I do for you, Sam?'

His patient let out a heavy sigh. 'I dunno. I just… need to talk to someone, I guess. Things are bad. At home. Suddenly everything in my life is about my diagnosis, and Jenny, my wife… Well…we'd been thinking about starting a family and now we don't know what to do and…'

Nathan could see Sam's eyes reddening as he fought back tears. Could hear the tremor in his patient's voice. He understood. Receiving a diagnosis for something such as Huntington's was very stressful. It changed everything. The present. The future. His own diagnosis of multiple sclerosis had changed *his* life. And Anna's. It had been the final axe to fall on his farce of a relationship.

'What did your consultant say?'

Sam sniffed. 'I can't remember. Once he said the

words—that I had Huntington's—I didn't really hear the rest. I was in shock… He gave us leaflets to take home and read. Gave us some websites and telephone numbers of people who could help, but…' He looked up at Nathan and met his eyes. 'We wanted to start a *family!* We wanted babies! And now… Now we don't know if we should. Huntington's is a terrible disease, and I'm not sure I want to pass that on to my children.'

Nathan nodded. It was a difficult thing to advise upon as a general practitioner. He didn't have a Huntington's specialty. He didn't want to give Sam the wrong advice.

'I hear what you're saying, Sam. It's a difficult situation and one that you and your wife must come to an agreement about together. I'm sure your consultant could discuss giving you two genetic counselling. A counsellor would be able to advise you better about the possibility of passing Huntington's to your children and what your options might be in terms of family planning. Have you got another appointment scheduled with your consultant soon?'

'In a month.'

'Good. Maybe use the time in between then and now to think of what questions you want to ask him. Just because you have Huntington's, and your father did too, it does not mean that any children you and Jenny have, will develop it. It's a fifty per cent chance.'

'They could be carriers, though.'

'That's a possibility, yes. Your consultant will be much better placed to talk this over with you, but if I'm right CVS—chorionic villus sampling—can be used to gain some foetal genetic material and test for the disease. And I believe there's also a blood test that can be performed on Jenny to check the cell-free foetal DNA, and that would carry no risk of miscarriage. How are you coping on a day-to-day level?'

'Fine, I guess. I have a chorea in my hand sometimes.' A chorea was a hand spasm. 'But that's all, so far.'

Nathan nodded. 'Okay. What about sleeping? Are you doing all right?'

'Not bad. I've lost some sleep, but I guess that's down to stress. My mind won't rest when I go to bed.'

'That's understandable. If it gets difficult then come and see me again and we'll look at what we can do.'

'How long do you think I've got, Dr Jones? My dad died young from this; I need to know.'

Nathan wanted to reassure him. Wanted to tell him that he would live a long life and that it would all be fine. But he couldn't know that. He had no idea how Sam's Huntington's would affect him. It affected each sufferer differently. Just like multiple sclerosis did.

'It's impossible to say. You've just got to take each day as it comes and live it the best you can. Then, whenever the end does arrive, you'll know you lived your life to the fullest.'

Sam smiled. 'Is that *your* plan, Doc?'

Nathan smiled back. It certainly was. Living his life and trying to be happy was his number one aim. And he wanted the people around him to be happy too. The fact that he'd upset Sydney the way he had... Perhaps that was why he had asked her to coffee.

'It is.'

Sydney stared at her reflection in the mirror. 'What on earth am I doing?' she asked herself.

Her make-up was done to perfection. Her eyeliner gave a perfect sweep to the gentle curve of her eyelid. The blusher on her cheeks highlighted her cheekbones and her lipstick added a splash of colour, emphasising the fullness of her lips. Her eyelashes looked thicker and darker with a coating of mascara, making her grey eyes lighter and clearer. Her normally wavy hair had been tamed with the help of some styling spray, and the earrings in her ears dangled with the blue gems that had once belonged to her grandmother.

She looked completely different. Done up. Like a girl getting ready for a date. Like a girl who was hoping that something might happen with a special guy.

It's just coffee! Why have you put in this much effort? Is it for him?

Grabbing her facial wipes, she rubbed her face clean, angry at herself, until her skin was bare and slightly reddened by the force she'd used upon it. She stared back at her new reflection. Her normal reflection. The one she saw every day. The one bare of pretence, bare of cosmetics. Mask-free.

This is me.

She was *not* getting ready for a date! This was coffee. Just coffee. No strings attached. They were just two people meeting. Associates. She did *not* have to get all dressed up for a drink at The Tea-Total Café.

So she pulled the dress off over her head and put on her old jeans—the ones with the ripped knees—slipped on a white tee and then an oversized black fisherman's jumper and scooped her hair up into a scruffy bun, deliberately pulling bits out to give a casual effect. Then she grabbed her bag, thick coat and scarf and headed out, figuring that she'd walk there. It wasn't far. The wind might blow her hair around a bit more. She would *not* make any effort for Dr Jones.

Striding through the village, she hoped she looked confident, because she wasn't feeling it. She had more nerves in her stomach now than she'd had taking her driving test or her final exams. Her legs were weak and her nerves felt as taut as piano strings.

It was all Dr Jones's fault—that charming smile, those glinting blue eyes, that dark chestnut hair, perfectly tousled, just messy enough to make it look as if he hadn't touched it since rolling out of bed.

She swallowed hard, trying *not* to think of Dr Jones in bed. But Sydney could picture him perfectly…a white sheet just covering his modesty, his naked body, toned and virile as he gazed at her with a daring smile…beckoning her back beneath the sheets…

Stop. It.

She checked her mobile phone. Had the surgery been in touch? A last-minute patient? An emergency surgery, maybe? Something that would force her to attend work so she didn't have to go? But, no. Her phone was annoyingly clear of any recent messages or texts. She was almost tempted to call the surgery and just check that things were okay—make sure no cows on the nearby farms were about to calve. Right now she'd be much happier standing in a swamp of mud or manure with her arm in a cow's insides. Instead she was *here*.

She stood for a moment before she entered, psyching herself up.

The bell above the door rang as she went inside and she was met by a wall of heat and the aroma of freshly brewed coffee and pastries. Praying he wouldn't be there, she glanced around, ready to flash a smile of apology to the staff behind the counter before she ducked straight out again—but there he was. Dashing and handsome and tieless, dressed in a smart grey suit, the whiteness of his shirt showing the gentle tan of his skin.

He stood up, smiling, and raised a hand in greeting. 'Sydney. You made it.'

Nervous, she smiled back.

Dr Jones pulled a chair out for her and waited for her to sit before he spoke again. 'I wasn't sure what you'd like. What can I get you?'

He seemed nervous.

'Er…just tea will be fine.'

'Milk and sugar?'

She nodded, and watched as he made his way over to the counter to place her order. He looked good standing there. Tall, broad-shouldered. Sydney noticed the other women in the café checking him out. Checking *her* out and wondering why she might be with him.

You can have him, ladies, don't worry. There's nothing going on here.

He came back moments later with a tray that held their drinks and a plate of millionaire's shortbread.

She was surprised. 'Oh. They're one of my favourites.'

He looked pleased. 'Mine too. Help yourself.'

She focused on making her tea for a moment. Stirring the pot. Pouring the tea. Adding sugar. Adding milk. Stirring for a while longer. Stopping her hand from shaking. Then she took a sip, not sure what she was supposed to be talking about. She'd been quite rude to this man. Angry with him. Abrupt. Although, to be fair, she felt she'd had reason to be that way.

'So, how long have you lived in Silverdale?' he asked.

I can answer that.

'All my life. I grew up here. Went to the local schools. I left to go to university, but came back after I was qualified.'

She kept her answer short. Brief. To the point. She

wasn't going to expand this. She just wanted to hear what he had to say and then she would be gone.

'And you now run your own business? Did you start it from scratch?'

'It was my father's business. He was a vet, too.'

'Does he still live locally?'

'No. My parents moved away to be closer to the coast. They always wanted to live by the sea when they retired.'

She paused to take another sip of tea, then realised it would be even more rude of her if she didn't ask *him* a question.

'What made you come to live in Silverdale?'

'I grew up in a village. Loved it. Like you, I left for university, to do my medical training, and then after Anna was born I decided to look for a country posting, so that Anna could have the same sort of childhood I had.'

She nodded, but knew he was glossing over a lot. Where was Anna's mother? What had happened? Anna wasn't a baby any more. She was five years old, maybe six. Was this his first country posting?

Who am I kidding? I don't need to know.

Sydney gave him a polite smile and nibbled at one of the shortbreads.

'My name's Nathan, by the way.'

Nathan. A good name. Kind. She looked him up and down, from his tousled hair to his dark clean shoes. 'It suits you.'

'Thanks. I like *your* name, too.'

The compliment coupled with the eye contact was suddenly very intense and she looked away, feeling heat in her cheeks. Was it embarrassment? Was it the heat from the café's ovens and the hot tea? She wasn't sure. Her heart was beginning to pound, and she had a desperate desire to start running, but she couldn't do that.

Nor could she pretend that she was relaxed. She didn't want to be here. She'd said yes because he'd put her on the spot. Because she hadn't been able to say no. Best just to let him know and then she could go.

She leaned forward, planting her elbows on the desk and crossing her arms in a defensive posture.

'You know…this isn't right. *This*. Meeting in a coffee shop. With you. I've been through a lot and you…' she laughed nervously '…you make me *extremely* uncomfortable. When I met you yesterday, in your surgery, I was already on edge. You might have noticed that. What with your doctor's degree and your—' she looked up '—your incredible blue eyes which, quite frankly, are ridiculously much too twinkly and charming.'

She stood, grabbing her bag and slinging it over her shoulder.

'I'm happy to help you with your daughter's rabbit, and I'll be the consummate professional where that poor animal is concerned, but *this*?' She shook her head. 'This I cannot do!'

She searched in her bag to find her purse. To lay some money on the table to pay for her tea and biscuit. Then she could get out of this place and back to work. To where she felt comfortable and in control. But before she could find her purse she became aware that Nathan had stood up next to her and leaned in, enveloping her in his gorgeous scent.

'I'm sorry.'

Standing this close, with his face so near to hers, his understanding tone, his non-threatening manner, his apology… There was nothing else she could do but look into his eyes, which were a breathtaking blue up close, flecked with tones of green.

She took a step back from his gorgeous proximity. 'For what?'

'For what I said to you. In our consultation. My remark was not intended to insult you, or the memory of your daughter, by suggesting that you could get over it with the help of...' he swallowed '...warm milk. But you were my first patient, and I knew you were in a rush, and I got flustered and...' His voice trailed off as he stared into her eyes.

Sydney quickly looked away, aware that the other customers in the café might be watching them, sensing the tension, wondering what was going on.

'Sydney?'

She bit her lip, her cheeks flushing, before she turned back to meet his gaze. 'Yes?'

'I promised this was just coffee. We've had tea and shortbread which may have changed things slightly, but not greatly. So please don't go. We're just drinking tea and chomping on shortbread. Please relax. I'm not going to jump your bones.'

'Right.' She stared at him uncertainly, imagining him *actually* jumping her bones, but that was too intense an image so, giving in, she sank back into her seat and broke off a piece of shortbread and ate it.

Her cheeks were on fire. This was embarrassing. She'd reacted oddly when all he'd expected was a drink with a normal, sane adult.

She glanced up. He was smiling at her. She hadn't blown it with her crazy moment. By releasing the steam from the pressure cooker that had been her brain. He was still okay with her. It was all still okay. He wasn't about to commit her to an asylum.

'I'm out of practice with this,' she added, trying to explain her odd behaviour. 'Could you please pretend that you're having tea with a woman who behaves normally?'

He picked up his drink and smiled, his eyes twinkling with amusement. 'I'll try.'

She stared back, uncertain, and then she smiled too. She hadn't scared him off with her mini-rant—although she supposed that was because he was a doctor, and doctors knew how to listen when people ranted, or nervously skirted around the main issue they wanted to talk about. Nathan seemed like a good guy. One who deserved a good friend. And good friends admitted when they were wrong.

'I'm sorry for walking out on you like that yesterday.'

'It's not a problem.'

'It is. I was rude to you because I was unsettled. I thought you were going to ask questions that I wasn't ready to answer and I just wanted to get out of there.'

'Why?'

'Because you made me nervous.'

'Doctors make a lot of people nervous. It's called White Coat Syndrome.'

She managed a weak smile. 'It wasn't your white coat. You didn't have one.'

'No.'

'It was you. *You* made me nervous.'

He simply looked at her and smiled. He was understanding. Sympathetic. Kind. All the qualities she'd look for in a friend.

But he was also drop-dead gorgeous.

And she wasn't sure she could handle *that*.

CHAPTER THREE

HE WAS SITTING there trying to listen to Sydney, hearing her telling stories of veterinary school and some of the cases she'd worked on, but all he could think about as he sat opposite her was that she was so very beautiful and seemed completely unaware of it.

It was there even in the way she sat. The way she held her teacup—not using the handle but wrapping her hands around the whole cup, as if it was keeping her warm. The way her whole face lit up when she laughed, which he was beginning to understand was rare. He'd wondered what she would look like when she smiled and now he knew. It was so worth waiting for. Her whole face became animated, unburdened by her past. It was lighter. Purer. Joyous. And infectious. Dangerously so.

And those eyes of hers! The softest of greys, like ash.

He was unnerved. He really had just wanted to meet her for this drink and clear the air after yesterday's abrupt meeting in his surgery. And to thank her for helping Lottie after her attack. But something else was happening. He was being sucked in. Hypnotised by her. Listening to her stories, listening to her talk. He liked the sound of her voice. Her gentle tone.

He was trying—*so hard*—to keep reminding himself that this woman was just going to be a friend.

Sydney worked hard. Very hard. All her tales were of work. Of animals. Of surgeries. She'd not mentioned her daughter once and he knew *he* couldn't. Not unless she brought up the subject first. If she wanted to share that with him then it had to be *her* choice.

He understood that right now Sydney needed to keep the conversation light. This was a new thing for her. This blossoming friendship. She was like a tiny bird that was trying its hardest not to be frightened off by the large tom cat sitting watching it.

'Sounds as if you work very hard.'

She smiled, and once again his blood stirred. 'Thank you. I do. But I enjoy it. Animals give you so much. Without agenda. Unconditionally.'

'Do you have pets yourself? It must be hard not to take home all the cases that pull at your heart strings.'

'I have a cat. Just one. She's ten now. But she's very independent—like me. Magic does her own thing, and when we both get home after a long day she either curls up on my lap or in my bed.'

Her face lit up as she spoke of Magic, but she blushed as she realised she'd referenced her bed to him.

A vision crossed his mind. That long dark hair of hers spread out over a pillow. Those almond-shaped smoky eyes looking at him, relaxed and inviting, as she lay tangled in a pure white sheet...

But he pushed the thought away. As lovely as Sydney was, he couldn't go there. This was friendship. Nothing else. He had Anna to think about. And his health.

He had no idea for how long he would stay relatively unscathed by his condition. His MS had been classified as 'relapsing remitting multiple sclerosis'. Which meant that he would have clear attacks of his symptoms, which would slowly get better and go away completely—until the next attack. But he knew that as the disease progressed his symptoms might not go away at all. They would linger. Stay. Get worse with each new attack, possibly leaving him disabled. But he was holding on to the thought that it wouldn't happen soon. That he would stay in relative good health for a long time.

But he could not, in any good conscience, put anyone else through that. Who deserved that?

And he had a child to think about. A child who had already lost her mother because of him. Who did not know what it was like to have that kind of female influence in her life. Bringing someone home would be a shock to Anna. It might upset her. It might bring up all those questions about having a mother again.

Sydney Harper was just going to be his *friend*.

That was all.

He smiled as she talked, trying not to focus all of his attention on her mouth, and pushed thoughts of what it would be like to kiss her completely out of his head.

Later, he offered to walk her back to work.

'Oh, that's not necessary. You don't have to do that,' she protested.

'I might as well. I'm heading that way to pick up my pager as I'm on call tonight.'

She nodded her reluctant acceptance and swung her bag over her shoulder. Together they exited into the street.

It was a cold November day. With blue skies, just a few wispy white clouds and a chill in the air when they moved into the shade and lost the sun.

They walked along together, respectfully a few inches apart. But she was *so* aware of him and trying her hardest not to be.

Nathan Jones was delicious. Of course she was physically attracted to him. Who wouldn't be? Aside from his good looks, this man was intelligent. A good listener. Not at all judgemental. He'd seemed really interested in her. He'd asked questions without being too probing and really paid attention to her answers.

She was very much aware that although they had just spent an hour in each other's company she still didn't know much about him. They'd both edged around serious subjects. They'd both avoided talk of past traumas and upsets. And they'd both kept everything light. Unthreatening. No mention of the baggage that each of them had to be carrying.

She liked that about him. It was as if he knew what she needed.

She frowned, spotting someone from the local council up a ladder, arranging the Christmas lights. 'It gets earlier and earlier each year.'

Nathan nodded. 'I love Christmas.'

She certainly didn't want to talk to him about *that*!

She changed the subject. 'Do you know your way around Silverdale yet?' she asked him, aware that the village had many tiny roads, closes and cul-de-sacs. And now, with the new build of over two hundred new homes on the edge of Silverdale, a lot of new roads had popped up that even *she* was unfamiliar with.

'Not really. But the GPS system in the car helps.'

'If you ever need help finding your way I could help you out. I know most places. Just pop in and ask at the desk.'

He looked at her. 'Thanks. If I ever get a call-out to the middle of nowhere I'll be sure to call in and pick you up first.'

Sydney glanced at him quickly, then looked away. That

was a joke, surely? She'd meant that he could call in to her *work* and ask whoever was on Reception.

She felt his gaze upon her then, and she flushed with heat as they came to a stop outside her veterinary practice.

'Well, thank you for the tea. And the shortbread.'

'It was my pleasure.'

'I'll see you at the end of the week? When you bring in Lottie again?' she added.

The rabbit was due another check-up, so she could look at its eye and see if it needed removing or not.

'Hopefully I'll see you before that.'

Her heart pounded in her chest. What did he mean? 'Why?'

'Because we're friends now, and friends see each other any time—not just at preordained appointments.' He smiled and held out his hand.

She blushed. 'Of course.'

She took his hand in hers and tried to give him a firm handshake, but she couldn't. All she could think of was that he was touching her. And she him! And that his hand felt warm and strong. Protective. It felt good, and she briefly imagined what it might feel like if he pulled her into his arms and pressed her against his chest.

He let go, and when he did she felt an odd sense of disappointment.

Now, why am I feeling that?

She stared back at him, unsure of how to say goodbye to this new friend. Should she give a small wave and go inside? Should they just say goodbye and walk away? Or should there be some sort of kiss on the cheek?

But if I kissed him and liked it...

'Well...maybe I'll see you later, then?'

He nodded. 'Yes.'

'Right. Bye.'

'Goodbye, Sydney.'

And then, with some hesitation, he leaned in and kissed the side of her face.

She sucked in a breath. His lips had only brushed her cheek, and were gone again before she could truly appreciate it, but for the millisecond he'd made contact her body had almost imploded. Her heart had threatened to jump out of her chest. Her face must have looked as red as a stop sign.

She watched him turn and walk across the road to his place of work and she stood there, breathing heavily, her fingers pressed to her face where his lips had been, and wondered what the hell she was doing.

With this *friendship* with Dr Nathan Jones.

Technically, they hadn't done *anything*. Just shared a pot of tea. A plate of shortbread. A quick chat and a walk to work.

But all she could think of was how he'd looked when he'd smiled at her. His beautiful blue eyes. The way he'd listened, the way he'd filled the space of the cafeteria chair, all relaxed and male and virile. How attracted she was to him physically. How his lips had felt...and how frightened that made her feel.

Sydney turned and went into her own place of work.

She needed to cool down.

In more ways than one.

And she needed to stay away from Dr Nathan Jones. He was going to be trouble.

The kiss had been an impulse. To fill an awkward pause. It was just what he did when he left female friends or relatives. He kissed them goodbye.

It didn't *mean* anything. The fact that he'd breathed in

her scent as he'd leaned in…the fact that his lips had felt scorched the second they'd touched her soft cheek…the fact that he'd got a shot of adrenaline powerful enough to launch an armada meant nothing.

Did it?

It was just that it was something new. A new friendship. The fact that she was the most stunningly beautiful woman he'd met in a long time had nothing to do with it. He felt for her. She'd been through a trauma. The loss of a daughter was something he simply couldn't imagine. The fact that she was still standing, smiling and talking to people was a miracle, quite frankly. He couldn't picture going through that and having the power or strength to carry on afterwards. And she was so nice! Easy to talk to. Friendly once you got past that prickly exterior she'd erected. But he could understand why that was there.

What he felt for her was protective. That was all. And didn't friends look out for one another?

Crossing the road, he called in to the surgery and picked up his pager for the evening, along with a list of house calls that needed to be completed before he had to pick up Anna at three-thirty. He had a good few hours' worth of work ahead of him, but he was distracted.

A simple coffee had been something else.

And he was afraid to admit to himself just what it had been.

Sydney sat hunched up on her couch, clutching a mug of cold tea and worrying at a loose bit of skin on her lip. Behind her head lay Magic the cat, asleep on the back of the couch, her long black tail twitching with dreams. The house was silent except for the ticking of the clock in the hallway, and Sydney's gaze was upon the picture of her daughter in the centre of the mantelpiece.

In the picture Olivia was laughing, smiling, her little hands reaching up to catch all the bubbles that her mum was blowing through a bubble wand.

She could remember that day perfectly. It had been during the summer holiday before Olivia was due to start school and it had been a Sunday. Alastair—Sydney's husband and Olivia's father—had gone to the supermarket to do a food-shop and Sydney and Olivia had been playing in the back garden. Her daughter had been so happy. Chasing bubbles, giggling. Gasping when Sydney made a particularly large one that had floated up higher and higher until it had popped, spraying them with wetness. She'd been chasing down and splatting the smaller ones that she could reach.

'Mummy, look!' she'd said when she'd found a bubble or two resting on her clothes.

Sydney remembered the awe and excitement in her daughter's eyes. They'd been happy times. When they'd all believed that life for them was perfect. That nothing could spoil it. Olivia had been about to start infant school; Sydney had been going back to work full-time. It had been their last summer together. The last summer they'd enjoyed.

Before it had all changed. Before it had all gone dreadfully wrong.

Why did I not listen when she told me she had a headache?

She tried to keep on remembering that summer day. The sound of her daughter's deep-throated chuckles, the smile on her face. But she couldn't.

Every time she allowed herself to think of Olivia her thoughts kept dragging her back to that morning when she'd found her unconscious in her bed. To the deadly silence of the room except for her daughter's soft, yet ragged breaths. To the dread and the sickness in her stomach as she'd realised that something was desperately, deeply wrong. That her daughter wouldn't wake up no matter how much Sydney called her name. To the moment when she'd unzipped her onesie to see *that rash*.

If Olivia had lived—if meningitis had not got its sneaky grasp on her beautiful, precious child—then she would have been nine years old now. In junior school. There'd be school pictures on the mantel. Pictures that showed progress. Life. But her pictures had been frozen in time. There would be no more pictures of Olivia appearing on the walls. No more videos on her phone. No paintings on her fridge.

And I could have prevented it all if only I'd paid more attention. Alastair was right. It was all my fault.

Sydney put down her mug and hugged her knees. The anniversary of Olivia's death was getting closer. It was a day she dreaded, that relentlessly came round every year, torturing her with thoughts of what she might have done differently. Tonight she would not be able to sleep. At all.

I can't just sit here and go through that insomnia again!

She got up off the couch and looked about her for something to do. Maybe declutter a cupboard or something? Deep-clean the kitchen? Go through her books and choose some for the bookstall at the Christmas market? Something… Anything but sit there and dwell on *what ifs*!

The doorbell rang, interrupting her agonising.

She froze, then felt a rush of relief.

Thank goodness! I don't care who you are, but I'm going to talk to you. Anything to get my mind off where it's going!

She opened the door.

Nathan!

'Oh. Hi.' She'd never expected him to turn up at her door. How did he know where she lived?

Nathan looked a little uncomfortable. Uncertain. 'I… er…apologise for just turning up at your house like this.'

'Is it Lottie?'

He shook his head and scratched at his chin, looking up and down the road. 'No. I've…er…got a call-out. Nothing urgent, but…'

She'd thought that what he'd said previously about calling in on her had been a joke. Had he actually meant it?

Spending more time with the delicious Nathan since that kiss on her cheek had seemed a bad idea. She'd made a firm decision to avoid him. And now here he was!

As if in answer to her unspoken question he looked sheepish as he said, 'I looked up your home address at work. Sorry. It's just… I tried to use my GPS, but it hasn't been updated for a while and it led me to a field, so… I need your help.'

He needed to find an address! She *had* offered to help him with that, and though she'd told herself—harshly—not to spend time alone with Nathan Jones again, she was now reconsidering it. After hours of feeling herself being pulled down a dark tunnel towards all those thoughts that tortured her on a nightly basis—well, right now she welcomed his interruption. What else would she be doing anyway?

Not sleeping. That was what. The damn pills he'd given her just didn't seem to be having the desired effect. Were they different from last year's? She couldn't remember.

Nathan though was the king of light and fluffy, and that was what she needed. Plus it would be interesting to see what he did at work. And she would be helping by telling him the way to go. Anything was better than sitting in this house for another night, staring at the walls, waiting for sleep to claim her.

'Sure. I'll just get my keys.'

She tried not to be amused by the look of shock on his face when she agreed. Instead she just grabbed her coat, locked up and headed out to his car—a beat-up four-wheel drive that, quite frankly, looked as if it deserved to be in a wrecker's yard. There were dents, one panel of the car was a completely different colour from the rest of it, and where it wasn't covered in rust it was covered in mud. Even the number-plate was half hanging off, looking as if it wanted to escape.

She looked at the vehicle uncertainly. 'Does that actually work?'

He smiled fondly at it. 'She's old, but she always starts. I promise it's clean on the inside.' He rubbed the back of his neck.

Sydney almost laughed. 'Don't worry. I've got a matching one over there.' She pointed at her own vehicle and saw him notice the dried sprays of mud—not just up the bodywork, but over the back windows too.

He smiled, relaxing a little. 'That makes me feel much better.'

Sydney smiled and got into his car. 'Where are we going?'

'Long Wood Road?'

She nodded. 'I know it. It's a couple of miles from here. Take this road out of the village and when you get to the junction at the end turn right.'

'Thanks.' He gunned the engine and began to drive.

Strangely, she felt lighter. More in control. And it felt great not to be sitting in her cottage, staring at those pictures.

'Who are you going to see?'

'Eleanor Briggs?'

'I know her. She has a Russian Blue cat called Misty.'

'I'm not seeing her about Misty. I'm afraid I can't say why. Patient confidentiality prohibits me sharing that with you.'

'That's okay.' She smiled as he began heading to the outskirts of Silverdale.

It felt good next to him. Comfortable. Was that because this was business? And because he was working?

The focus isn't on me. Or us. This is just one professional helping out another.

She'd never been comfortable with being the focus of people's attention. Even as a child she'd tried to hide when she was in the school choir, or a school play. Trying her hardest not to be given a main role, trying not to be noticed. At university, when she'd had to give a solo presentation on the dangers of diabetes in dogs, she'd almost passed out from having to stand at the front of the lecture hall and present to her lecturers and tutor. The *pressure!*

But here they were, stuck in a car together, music on the radio, and she was much more relaxed. This was much better than being stuck at home, staring at old pictures that broke her heart.

Glancing at him driving, she noticed he'd rolled up his sleeves and that his forearms were lightly tanned, and filled with muscle as he changed gear. A chunky sports watch enveloped his wrist. He had good arms. *Attractive* arms. She glanced away.

A song came on that she knew and quietly she began singing and bobbing her head to the music.

Nathan looked over at her. 'You like this?'

Sydney nodded and he turned up the sound. She began to sing louder as it got to the chorus, laughing suddenly as Nathan joined in. Out of tune and clearly tone deaf.

They began to drive down a country road.

Silverdale was Sydney's whole life. A small pocket of English countryside that she felt was all hers. The place where she'd hoped to raise her daughter. In its community atmosphere where everyone looked out for one another.

Pushing the thought to one side, she turned back to Nathan. He was concentrating on the road now that the song was over and the DJ was babbling, his brow slightly furrowed, both hands gripping the wheel.

'You need to take the next left. Long Woods Road.'

Nathan indicated, following the twists and turns of her directions, and soon she was pointing out Eleanor's small cottage. They turned into the driveway and parked in front of the house. Killing the engine, he turned to her. 'Thank you. I wouldn't have got here without you.'

'And I wouldn't have had my eardrums assaulted.'

He raised an eyebrow.

'Your singing.'

'I have a lovely voice. I'll have you know that when I was in my school choir I was the only child not selected to sing a solo.'

She smirked. 'You should be proud.'

'I am.'

Then he grinned and reached for his bag, which was down by her feet. She moved slightly, out of his way, as he lifted it up and past her.

He was smiling still. Looking at her. She watched as his gaze dropped to her mouth and instantly the atmosphere changed.

Sydney looked away, pretending that something out of the window had caught her eye.

'Will you be okay for a while? I can leave the radio on.'

She didn't look at him, but dug her phone from her

pocket. 'I've got my phone. I'm playing a word game against my veterinary nurse.'

Nathan said nothing, but got out of the car. Once he was gone, she suddenly felt *alone*. His presence had filled the car, and now that he was gone it seemed so empty. The only reminder a very faint aroma of cologne. She would never have thought that spending time with Nathan would be so easy, after their coffee together. But he'd been just what she needed tonight. Bad singing included.

In the sky above stars were beginning to filter through the dark, twinkling and shining. She looked for the biggest and brightest. Olivia's star. The one she had once pointed out to her daughter as her very own special light. Just remembering that night with her daughter made her eyes sting with unshed tears, but she blinked them away.

I can't keep crying. I've got to be stronger than this!

She switched on her phone and stared at the game she no longer wanted to play.

It was pitch-black along the country roads as they followed behind another four-wheel drive that was towing a horsebox. In the back, Sydney could see a large black horse, easily fifteen hands high. Was it the Daltons? They had a horse like that. Though she guessed it could be the Webbers' horse. They had one like it too. Or maybe it wasn't anyone she knew. She didn't get called out to *all* the horses in the Silverdale area. There was a specialised equine veterinary service in Norton Town. Sometimes she worked alongside it.

As they drove back along Long Wood Road, Sydney realised she was feeling more relaxed and happy than she had for a few weeks. It was strange. Perhaps it was a good thing not to be wallowing in her memories tonight.

Perhaps getting out and about and doing something was the right thing to do.

I need a hobby. An evening class. Something. Maybe it'll be better when we start those meetings for the Christmas market and fête.

What she knew for sure was that she had felt better when she'd seen Nathan returning to the car. Seen his smile. Felt his warmth. Knowing that he wasn't the type to pry into her past. He made her feel weirdly comfortable, despite the physical response she felt. It was something she hadn't felt for a long time, and she was really glad she'd agreed to come out with him and spend some more time with him.

She was just about to say something about it—thank him for earlier—when she spotted something, off to Nathan's right, illuminated by the lights of the vehicles. It was a small herd of deer, running across the field at full pelt.

'Nathan, look!' She pointed.

There had to be seven or eight. Mostly fully grown and running hard. The lead deer had full antlers, like tree branches.

And they were heading straight for the road.

'I think I'm going to slow down.'

But as Nathan slowed their vehicle it became clear that the vehicle in front, with the horse trailer, had continued on at a normal speed.

Sydney leaned forward. 'Have they not seen them? What can we do?'

Nathan hit his horn, hoping it would make the driver ahead pay attention, or at least startle the deer into heading in another direction, but neither happened.

The biggest deer burst through the undergrowth, leaping over the ditch and straight out onto the road—right in front of the other vehicle.

Sydney watched, horrified, and brake lights lit up her face as the car in front tried to swerve at the last minute, but failed. The horsebox at the back wobbled, bouncing from left to right with the weight of the horse inside, before it tipped over and pulled the car straight into the ditch. The rest of the deer leapt by, over the road and into the next field.

Nathan hit the brakes, stopping the car. 'Call for help.'

Her heart was pounding madly in her chest. 'What are you going to do?'

'I'm going to check for casualties. After you've contacted emergency services go into the boot of the car and find the reflective triangle and put it in the road. We're on a bend here, and we need to warn other traffic. We're sitting ducks.'

Then he grabbed his bag and was gone.

She watched him run over to the car through the light of the headlamps as she dialled 999 with shaking fingers. As she watched Nathan trying to talk to someone she saw the driver fall from the driver's side. Then her gaze fell upon the horse in the horsebox. It was moving. Alive.

I have to get out there!

But she had no equipment. No bag. No medicines. She felt helpless. Useless! She'd felt this way just once before.

I'll be damned if I feel that way again!

'Which service do you require?' A voice spoke down the phone.

'*All of them*. We need them all.'

CHAPTER FOUR

SYDNEY DASHED TO the boot of Nathan's car and panicked as she struggled to open it. At first she couldn't see the reflective triangle he'd mentioned—his boot was full of *stuff.* But she rummaged through, tossing things to one side, until she found it. Then she dashed to the bend in the road and placed it down, hoping that it would be enough of a warning to stop any other vehicles that came that way from running into them.

She ran over to the ditched car and horsebox, glancing quickly at the horse in the back. It was neighing and huffing, making an awful lot of noise, stamping its hooves, struggling to find a way to stand in a box that was on its side. She couldn't see if it had any injuries. She hoped not. But there wasn't much she could do for the horse anyhow. She needed to help Nathan and the people in the car.

She'd already seen the driver was out of the vehicle. He was sitting in the road, groaning and clutching at his head. He had a bleeding laceration across his brow, causing blood to dribble down his face and eyes.

Nathan was in the ditched vehicle, assessing whoever was in the front seat.

Sydney knelt down, saw the head wound was quite deep and pulled the scarf from around her neck and tied it around the guy's scalp. 'You need to come with me. Off the road. Come and sit over here.'

She pointed at the grass verge.

'I didn't see... I didn't notice... We were arguing...' the man mumbled.

He was in shock. Sydney grabbed the man under his armpits and hauled him to his feet. Normally she wouldn't move anyone after a car accident. She knew that much. But this man had already hauled himself out of the vehicle and dropped onto the road before Nathan got there. If he'd done any damage to himself, then it was already done. The least she could do was get him out of the middle of the road and to a safer zone.

The man was heavy and dazed, but he got to his feet and staggered with her to the roadside, where she lowered him down and told him to stay. 'Don't move. Try and stay still until the ambulance gets here. I've called for help—they're on their way.'

The man looked up at her. 'My wife...*my son!*'

He tried to get up again, but Sydney held him firmly in place. 'I'll go and help them, but you *must* stay here!'

The man looked helpless and nodded, trembling as he realised there was blood all over his hands.

Sydney ran back over to the ditched car, heard a child crying and noticed that Nathan was now in the back seat. He called to her over his shoulder.

'There's a baby. In a car seat. He looks okay, but I need to get him out of the vehicle so I can sit in the back and maintain C-spine for the mother.'

Sydney nodded and glanced at the woman in the front seat. She was unconscious, and her air bag had deployed and lay crumpled and used before her. There was no bleeding that she could see, but that didn't mean a serious injury had not occurred. If a casualty was unconscious, that usually meant shock or a head injury. She hoped it was just the former.

'I'm unclipping the seatbelt.'

Sydney heard a clunk, then Nathan was backing out, holding a car seat with an indignant, crying infant inside it, bawling away.

The baby couldn't be more than nine months old, and had beautiful fluffy blond hair. But his face was red with rage and tears, and his little feet in his sleep suit were kicking in time with his crying.

'Shh… It's okay. It's okay… I've got you.' Sydney took the heavy seat with care, cooing calming words as she walked back across the road to take him to his father.

In the distance she heard the faint, reassuring sound of sirens.

'Here. Your little boy. What's his name?' she asked the man, who smiled with great relief that his son seemed physically okay.

'Brandon.'

That was good. The man's bump to the head hadn't caused amnesia or anything like that. 'And your name…?'

'Paul.'

'Okay, Paul. You're safe. And Brandon's safe—he doesn't look injured—and that man helping your wife is a doctor. She's in good hands. He knows what he's doing.'

'Is she hurt? Is Helen hurt?'

Sydney debated about how much she should reveal—should she say that Helen was unconscious? Or stay optimistic and just tell him she was doing okay? The truth won out.

'I don't know. She's unconscious, but Nathan—that's Dr Jones—is with her in the car and he's looking after her. Do you hear those sirens? More help will be with us soon.'

The sirens were much louder now, and Sydney knew she was breathing faster. Hearing them get closer and closer just reminded her of that morning when she'd had to call an ambulance for Olivia. Wishing they'd get to her faster. Feeling that they were taking for ever. Praying that they would help her daughter. She could see the same look in Paul's eyes now. The distress. The *fear*.

But this was an occasion where she actually had her wits about her and could do something.

'I need to go and help Nathan.'

She ran back across the road. The car's radiator or something must have burst, because she could hear hissing and see steam rising up through the bonnet of the vehicle. She ducked into the open door.

Nathan was in the back seat, his hands clutching Helen's head, keeping it upright and still. His face was twisted, as if *he* was in pain.

'Is she breathing still?' he managed to ask her.

Is she *breathing*? Sydney wasn't sure she wanted to check—her own shock at what had happened was starting to take effect. What if Helen wasn't breathing? What if Helen's heart had stopped?

'I—'

'Watch her chest. Is there rise and fall?'

She checked. There was movement. 'Yes, there is!'

'Count how many breaths she takes in ten seconds.'

She looked back, counting. 'Two.'

'Okay. That's good.'

She saw Nathan wince. Perhaps he had cramp, or something? There was some broken glass in the car. Perhaps he'd knelt on it? She pushed the thought to the back of her mind as vehicles flashing red and blue lights appeared. An ambulance. A fire engine, and further behind them she could see a police car.

Thank you!

Sydney got out of the car and waved them down, feeling relief flood her.

A paramedic jumped out of the ambulance and came over to her, pulling on some purple gloves. 'Can you tell me what happened?'

She gave a brief rundown of the incident, and pointed out Paul and baby Brandon, then filled him in on the woman in the car.

'Okay, let's see to her first.' The paramedic called out to his partner to look after the driver and his son whilst he checked out Helen, still in the car with Nathan.

Sydney ran back over to Paul. 'Help's here! It's okay. We're okay.' She beamed, glad that the onus of responsibility was now being shouldered by lots of other people rather than just her and Nathan.

As she stood back and watched the rescue operation she realised there were tears on her face. She wiped them away with a sleeve, aware of how frightened she'd been, and waited for Nathan to join her, shivering. She wanted to be held. To feel safe. She wanted to be comforted.

The morning she'd found Olivia she'd been on her own. Alastair had already left for work. So there'd been no one to hold her and let her know it was okay. She'd needed arms around her then and she needed them now. But Alastair had never held her again.

If she asked him, Nathan would hold her for a moment. She just knew it. Sensed it. What they'd just experienced had been traumatic. But she remained silent, clutching her coat to her. She just stood and watched the emergency services get everything sorted.

And waited.

Nathan was needed by the paramedics, and then by

the police, and by the time he was free she was not. The horse needed her—needed checking over.

She told herself a hug wasn't important and focused on the practical.

Paul and Brandon had been taken to hospital in one ambulance; Helen had been extricated and taken away in another, finally conscious. The horsebox had been righted and the horse had been led out to be checked by Sydney. It had some knocks and scrapes to its legs, mostly around its fetlocks—which, in humans, was comparable to injuries to an ankle joint—but apart from that it just seemed startled more than anything.

They'd all been very lucky, and Sydney now stood, calming the horse, whilst they waited for an animal transporter to arrive.

Nathan stood watching her. 'That horse really feels safe with you.'

She smiled. 'Makes a change. Normally horses see me coming with my vet bag and start playing up. It's nice to be able to comfort one and calm it down.'

'You're doing brilliantly.'

She looked at him. He looked a little worn out. Wearied. As if attending to the patients in the crash had physically exhausted him. Perhaps he'd had a really long day. Just like being a vet, being a doctor had to be stressful at times. Seeing endless streams of people, each with their own problems. Having to break bad news. She knew how stressful it was for her to have to tell a customer that their beloved pet was dying, or had to be put to sleep. And when she *did* euthanise a beloved pet she often found herself shedding silent tears along with the owner. She couldn't help it.

Perhaps it was the same for Nathan. Did seeing people in distress upset him? Wear him out?

'*You* did brilliantly. Knowing what to do...who to treat. How to look after Helen. I wouldn't have thought to do that.' She stroked the horse's muzzle.

'It's nothing.'

'But it is. You probably saved her life, keeping her airway open like that. She could have died.'

'At least they're in safe hands now.'

She looked at him and met his gaze. 'They were *already* in safe hands.'

She needed to let him know that what he'd done today had *mattered*. Paul still had a wife. Brandon still had a mother. Because of *him*. A while ago she'd almost lost her faith in doctors. She'd depended on them to save Olivia, and when they'd told her there was nothing they could do...

At first she hadn't wanted to believe them. Had *raged* at them. Demanded they do *something*! When they hadn't she had collapsed in a heap, hating them—and everyone—with a passion she had never known was inside her. Today, Nathan had proved to her that doctors did help.

'How do you think the horse is doing?'

Sydney could feel the animal was calmer. It had stopped stamping its hooves and snorting as they'd stood there on the side of the road, watching the clean-up operation. It had stopped tossing its head. Its breathing had become steadier.

'She's doing great.'

'Paul and Helen aren't the only ones in safe hands.' He smiled and sat down on the bank beside her, letting out a breath and rolling his shoulders.

She stared at him for a moment, shocked to realise that she wanted to sit next to him, maybe to massage his shoulders or just lean her head against his shoulder. She wanted that physical contact.

Feeling that yearning to touch him surprised her and she turned away from him, focussing on the horse. She shouldn't be feeling that for him. What was the point? It was best to focus on the horse. She knew what she was doing there.

It didn't take long for the accident to be cleared. The police took pictures, measured the road, measured the skid marks and collected debris. The car was pulled from the ditch and lifted onto a lorry to be taken away, and just as Sydney was beginning to doubt that a new horse-box would ever arrive a truck came ambling around the corner and they loaded the mare onto it to take her back to her stable.

Sydney gave the truck driver her details and told her to let Paul know that she'd be happy to come out and check on the horse, and that he was to give her a call if she was needed urgently.

Eventually she and Nathan got back into his car and she noticed that it was nearly midnight. Normally she would be lying in bed at this time, staring at the ceiling and worrying over every little thought. Wide awake.

But tonight she felt tired. Ready for her bed even without a sleeping pill. It surprised her.

Nathan started the engine. 'Let's take you home. Our little trip out lasted longer than either of us expected.'

'That's okay. I'd only have been awake anyway. At least this way I was put to good use.'

'You've not been sleeping for some time?'

She shook her head and looked away from him, out of the window. 'No.'

He seemed to ruminate on this for a while, but then he

changed the subject. 'Good thing I didn't get any more house calls.'

That was true. What would he have done if he'd got a page to say that someone was having chest pains whilst he'd been helping Helen? They'd been lucky. All of them.

It was nice and warm in Nathan's car as he drove them steadily back to Silverdale. For the first time Sydney felt the silence between them was comfortable. She didn't need to fill the silence with words. Or to feel awkward. The circumstances of the emergency had thrown them together and something intangible had changed.

It felt nice to be sitting with someone like that. Even if it *was* with a man she had at first disliked immensely.

A jolt in the road startled her, and she realised she'd almost nodded off. She sucked in a breath, shocked that she'd felt comfortable enough to fall asleep.

She glanced at Nathan just as he glanced at her, and they both quickly looked away.

Sydney smiled.

It was beginning to feel more than nice.

It was beginning to feel *good*.

Nathan pulled up outside Sydney's cottage and killed the engine. He looked out at the dark, empty street, lit only by one or two streetlamps, and watched as a cat sneaked across the road and disappeared under a hedge after being startled by his engine.

Despite the accident he'd had a good time tonight. It had felt really good to spend time with Sydney, and he felt they'd cleared the air after their misunderstandings at their first meeting and the awkward coffee.

Turning up at her door to ask for help with directions had almost been a step too far for him. He'd joked about asking her for her help, but when he'd tried to find

Eleanor's cottage on his own his stupid GPS had made him turn down a very narrow farming lane and asked him to drive through a muddy field! He'd got out and checked that there wasn't a farmhouse or something near, where he might ask for help, but there'd been nothing. Just fields. And mud. Plenty of mud!

He'd argued with himself about going to her house. Almost not gone there at all. He knew her address. He'd seen it on his computer at work and for some reason it had burnt itself into his brain. She didn't live far from her place of work, so it had been easy to find her, but he hadn't known what sort of reception he'd get. She might have slammed the door in his face.

He'd felt awkward asking for help, but thankfully she'd agreed to go with him, and it had been nice to have her with him in his car, just chatting. It had been a very long time since he'd done that with anyone. The last time had been with Gwyneth. She'd always talked when they were driving—pointing things out, forming opinions on people or places that they passed. Her judgemental approach had made him realise just how insecure she'd been, and he'd done his best to try and make her feel good about herself.

Tonight, Sydney had been invaluable at the accident site—something he knew Gwyneth would never have been. She'd not been great with blood.

Sydney had been brilliant, looking after the driver and the baby, and then she'd managed to calm the horse and check it over. He wouldn't have known how to handle such a large animal. He barely coped with looking after a rabbit, never mind a terrified horse that had been thrown around in a tin box.

Now they were back to that moment again. The one where he normally kissed people goodbye. And suddenly there was that tension again. He wasn't sure whether he should lean over and just do it. Just kiss her.

'Thanks for everything tonight. I couldn't have done it without you,' he said honestly.

She'd grabbed her handbag from the footwell on her side and sat with it on her knee. 'No problem. I couldn't have done it without you either.'

Though half her face was in shadow, he could still see her smile.

'Well…goodnight, Sydney.'

'Goodnight, Nathan.'

She stared at him for a moment, and then turned away and grabbed the latch to open the door. It wouldn't budge and she struggled with it for a moment or two.

'Sorry…sometimes it catches.'

He leant over her for the handle and she flinched as he reached past her and undid the door for her. He sat back, worried that he'd made her start.

She hurried from the vehicle without saying a word, throwing the strap of her bag over her shoulder and delving into her coat pocket for her house keys.

Disappointment filled his soul. He didn't want her to walk away feeling awkward. That flinch, it had been… He wanted…

What do I want?

'Sydney?' He was out of his car before he could even think about what he was doing. He stood there, looking over the top of his car, surprising even himself. The night air had turned chill and he could feel goosebumps trembling up his spine.

She'd turned, curious. 'Yes?'

'Um…' He couldn't think of anything to say! What was he even doing, anyway? He couldn't turn this friendship with Sydney into anything more. Neither of them was ready for that. And there was Anna to think of too. He was sure Sydney would not want to take on someone with a little girl—not after losing her own. And surely she wouldn't want to take on someone who was ill?

Gwyneth had made it quite clear that he wasn't worth *her* time and affection. That he had somehow ruined her life with his presence. Did he want to put someone else through that? Someone like Sydney? Who'd already been through so much? He'd end up needing her more than she needed him, and he'd hate that imbalance. He knew the state of his health. His condition would make him a burden. And Anna had to be his top priority. And yet...

And yet something about her *pulled* at him. Her energy. Her presence. Those grey eyes that looked so studious and wise, yet at the same time contained a hurt and a loss that even he couldn't fully understand. He'd lost his fiancée, yes, but that had been through separation. It wasn't the same as losing a child. Nowhere near it. He and Gwyneth had hardly been the love story of the century.

Even though he'd only known Sydney for a couple of days, there was something in her nature that...

'Remember to take your sleeping pill.'

Remember to take your sleeping pill? Really? That's what you come up with?

Her face filled with relief. 'Oh. Yes, I will. Thank you.'

Relief. *See?* She was being polite. She was probably desperate to get inside and away from him, because he clearly had no idea how to talk to women, having spent the last few years of his life just being a father and—

Being a father is more important than your ability to chat up women!

'You get a good night's sleep yourself. You've earned it.'

He opened his mouth to utter a reply, but she'd already slipped her key into the lock. She raised her hand in a brief goodbye and then was inside, her door closing with a shocking finality, and he was left standing in the street, staring at a closed door.

Nathan watched as Sydney switched on the lights. He ducked inside his car as she came to her window and closed the curtains. He stared for a few minutes, then tore his gaze away, worried about what her neighbours might think. He started the engine, turned up the heater and slowly drove away. Berating himself for not saying something more inspiring, something witty—something that would have had her...*what?*

That wasn't who he was. Those clever, witty guys, who always had the perfect line for every occasion, lived elsewhere. He didn't have a scriptwriter to think up clever things for him to say that would charm her and make her like him more. He wasn't suave, or sophisticated, or one of those charming types who could have women at their beck and call with a click of their fingers.

And he didn't *want* to be a man like that. He was a single dad, with a gorgeous, clever daughter who anyone would be lucky to know. He led an uncomplicated life. He worked hard.

What did he want to achieve with Sydney? And why was he getting involved anyway? His own fiancée—the woman he'd been willing to pledge his entire life to—had walked away from him, and if someone who'd once said they loved him could do that, then a relative stranger like Sydney might do the same thing. She didn't strike him as someone looking to settle down again, to start a relationship in a ready-made family. Especially not with another little girl after losing her own.

Did she?

No.

So why on earth could he not get her out of his head?

* * *

Nathan was fighting fatigue. Over the last few days he'd been having a small relapse in his symptoms, and he'd been suffering with painful muscle spasms, cramps, and an overwhelming tiredness that just wouldn't go away. That accident had aggravated it. It was probably stress.

As he downed some painkillers he knew he'd have to hide his discomfort from his daughter. She mustn't see him weaken. Not yet. It was still early days. He didn't want her to suspect that there was something wrong. He had to keep going for her. Had to keep being strong. Normally he could hide it. And he needed his energy for today. Anna was still too young to understand about his condition. How did you explain multiple sclerosis to a six-year-old?

Today Lottie was due for her next check-up, and he was feeling some anticipation at seeing Sydney. At work, during breaks, he often found himself itching to cross the road on some pretext, just to see if she was there, but for the life of him he couldn't think of anything to say. His inner critic kept reminding him that seeing her was probably a bad idea. The woman practically had 'Keep Out' signs hanging around her neck, and she'd certainly not divulged anything too personal to him. She hadn't even mentioned her daughter to him.

And yet…

'Anna! Come on, it's time to go.'

'Are we taking Lottie now?'

'We are. But we're walking because…' he reached for a plausible excuse '…it's a nice day.' He smiled, reaching out for the counter as a small wave of dizziness affected his balance briefly. Of all his symptoms, dizziness and feeling off-balance were the worst. He couldn't drive like this. It would be dangerous. And at least the crisp, fresh winter air would make him feel better.

'Yay!' Anna skipped off to fetch Lottie's carrier.

He managed to stop the world spinning and stood up straight, sucking in a deep breath.

The rabbit was doing quite well, Nathan thought. She was eating and drinking as normal, had come off the medication and was settled back outside. The bite wounds had healed cleanly and Lottie's eye had escaped surgery, much to both his and Anna's delight. They were hopeful for a full recovery.

With Lottie in her box, Nathan locked up and they headed to the veterinary practice. He still wasn't feeling great—quite tired and light-headed—but he tried to keep up a level of bright chatter as they walked along the village roads.

His daughter hopped alongside him, pointing out robins and magpies and on one particular occasion a rather large snail.

The walk took a while. They lived a good couple of miles from the practice and his arms ached from carrying Lottie, who seemed to get weightier with every step, but eventually they got there, and Nathan settled into a waiting room seat with much relief.

He didn't get to enjoy it for too long, though.

Sydney had opened her door. 'Do you want to bring Lottie in?'

Sydney looked well, though there were still faint dark circles beneath her eyes. It felt good to see her again. He carried Lottie through and put her onto the examination table.

'How's she doing?'

He nodded, but that upset his balance and he had to grip the examination table to centre himself.

Had Sydney noticed?

He swallowed, suppressing his nausea. 'Er…good. Eating and drinking. The eye's clean and she seems okay.' He decided to focus on Sydney's face. When he got dizzy like this it helped to focus on something close to him. She wasn't moving that much, and he needed a steady point to remain fixed on.

'Let's take a look.'

Sydney frowned, concern etched across her normally soft features as she concentrated on the examination. She was very thorough, reminding him of her capability and passion. She checked Lottie's eye, her bite wounds, her temperature and gave her a thorough going-over.

'I agree with you. She seems to have recovered well. I think we can discharge this patient.' She stood up straight again and smiled.

'That's great.'

He realised she was looking at him questioningly.

'Are you okay?'

Nathan felt another wave of nausea sweep over him as dizziness assailed him again. 'Er…not really…'

Had the walk been too much? Was he dehydrated?

Sydney glanced at Anna uncertainly, then came around the desk and took Nathan's arm and guided him over to a small stool in the corner. 'I'll get you some water.'

He sank his head into his hands as the dizziness passed, and was just starting to feel it clear a bit when she returned with a glass. He tried not to look at Anna until he was sure he could send her a reassuring smile to say everything was okay.

He took a sip of the drink. 'Thanks.'

'Missed breakfast?'

He gratefully accepted the excuse. 'Yes. Yes, I did. Must have got a bit light-headed, that's all.'

'Daddy, you had toast with jam for breakfast.' Anna contradicted.

He smiled. 'But not enough, obviously.'

'You had three slices.'

He smiled at his daughter, who was blowing his cover story quite innocently. He was afraid to look at Sydney, but she was making sure Lottie was secure in her cage.

Then she turned to look at him, staring intently, her brow lined. 'Are you safe to get home, Dr Jones?'

He stood up. 'We walked here. And I'm fine.' He didn't want to let her see how ill he felt.

'You don't look it. You look very pale.'

'Right…' He glanced at Anna. 'Perhaps I just need some more fresh air.' He took another sip of water.

Sydney stood in front of him, arms crossed. 'You don't seem in a fit state to walk home yet. Or to take care of Anna.'

'I am!' he protested.

'You had nystagmus. I know your world is spinning.'

Nystagmus was a rapid movement of the eyes in response to the semi-circular canals being stimulated. In effect, if the balance centre told you your world was spinning, your eyes tried to play catch-up in order to focus.

'Look, let me tell my next client I'll be ten minutes and I'll drive you both back.'

'No—no, it's fine! I can't disrupt your workday, that's ridiculous. I'm okay now. Besides, that would annoy your patient. I'm fine.'

He stood up to prove it, but swayed slightly, and she had to reach for him, grabbing his waist to steady him.

'Honestly. I just need to get some air for a moment. I could go and sit down across the road at the surgery, maybe. Check my blood pressure. Have a cup of sweet tea. It'll pass—it always does.' He smiled broadly, to show her he was feeling better, even though he wasn't.

She let go of him. 'You're sure?'

No.

'Absolutely.'

He saw her face fill with doubt and hesitation. 'Maybe Anna could stay here with me. She could look after the animals in the back. Give them cuddles, or something.'

Anna gasped, her smile broad. '*Could* I, Daddy?'

He didn't want to impose on Sydney. He could see it had been tough for her to offer that, and she was working. Anna should be *his* responsibility, not someone else's.

'Er... I don't know, honey. Sydney's very busy.'

'It's no problem. Olivia used to do it all the time.' She blushed and looked away.

Her daughter.

'Are you sure?'

'I'm sure. You're clearly unwell today. She can stay with me for the day and I'll drive you both home when I finish. Around four.'

Anna was jumping up and down with joy, clapping her hands together in absolute glee at this amazing turn of events.

He really didn't want to do this, but what choice did he have? Sydney was right. And hadn't he wanted to move to a village to experience this very support?

'Fine. Thank you.' He knelt to speak to his excited daughter. 'You be good for Sydney. Do what you're told and behave—yes?'

She nodded.

Standing up, he felt a little head rush. Maybe Sydney was right. Perhaps he *did* need a break.

He was just having a difficult time letting someone

help him. It irked him, gnawing away at him like a particularly persistent rodent. How could he look after his daughter if he was going to let a little dizziness affect him? And this was just the *start* of his condition. These were mild symptoms. It would get worse. And already he was relying on other people to look after his daughter—Sydney, of all people!

'Perhaps she ought to stay with—'

Sydney grabbed his arm and started to guide him towards her exit. 'Go and lie down, Dr Jones.'

Nathan grimaced hard, then kissed the top of his daughter's head and left.

It had been a delight to have Anna with her for the day. The invitation to look after Nathan's little girl had just popped out. She'd not carefully considered exactly what it would mean to look after the little girl before she'd said it, and once she had she'd felt a small amount of alarm at her offer.

But Anna had been wonderful. She was sweet, calm with the animals, with a natural affection and understanding of them that those in her care gravitated towards, allowing her to stroke them. The cats had purred. Dogs had wagged their tails or showed their bellies to be rubbed. And Anna had asked loads of questions about them, showing a real interest. She'd even told Sydney that she wanted to be a vet when she was older! That had been sweet.

Olivia had liked being with the animals, but she'd only liked the cuddling part. The oohing and aahing over cute, furry faces. Anna was different. She wanted to know what breed they were. What they were at the vet's for. How Sydney might make them better. It had been good to share her knowledge with Nathan's daughter. Good to see the differences between the two little girls.

Once they were done for the day, and the last of the records had been completed, she smiled as Lucy complained about her sore back after cleaning cages all afternoon, but then sat down to eat not one but two chocolate bars, because she felt ravenous.

They sat together, chatting about animal care, and Anna listened quietly, not interrupting, and not getting in the way.

When she'd gathered her things, Sydney told Anna it was time to go.

'Thank you for having me, Sydney.'

She eyed the little girl holding her hand as they crossed the road to collect Nathan. 'Not a problem, Anna. It was lovely to have you. Let's hope your daddy is feeling better soon, hmm?'

'Daddy always gets sick and tired. He pretends he's not, but I know when he is.'

'Perhaps he *is* just tired? He does a very important job, looking after everyone.' But something niggled at her. The way Nathan had been, and the nonchalant way Anna had mentioned that *'Daddy always gets sick and tired...'*

Was Nathan ill? And, if so, what could it be? Just a virus? Was he generally run-down? Or could it be something else? Something serious?

They quickly crossed to the surgery and collected a rather pale-looking Nathan. He insisted he was feeling much better. Suspecting he wasn't quite being truthful, she got him into the car and started the engine, glancing at Anna on the back seat through the rearview mirror.

Anna smiled, and the sight went straight to Sydney's heart. To distract herself, she rummaged in the glovebox to see if she had any of Olivia's old CDs. She found one and slid it into the CD player, and soon they were singing along with a cartoon meerkat and a warthog.

Driving through the village, she found herself smiling, amazed that she still remembered the words, and laughing at Anna singing in the back. It felt *great* to be driving along, singing together. She and Olivia had always used to do it. It was even putting a smile on Nathan's face.

Much too soon she found herself at Nathan's house, and she walked them both up to their front door, finally handing them Lottie's carrier.

Nathan smiled broadly. 'Thanks, Sydney. I really appreciate it. I got a lot of rest and I feel much better.'

'Glad to hear it. Anna was brilliant. The animals adored her.'

'They all do. Thanks again.'

'No problem. See you around.'

She began to walk away, turning to give a half wave, feeling embarrassed at doing so. She got in her car and drove away as fast as she could—before she was tempted to linger and revel in the feeling of family once again.

It felt odd to be back in the car, alone again after that short while she'd been with Anna and Nathan. The car seemed empty. The music had been silenced and returned to the glovebox.

By the time she got home her heart physically ached.

And she sat in her daughter's old room for a very long time, just staring at the empty walls.

CHAPTER FIVE

SOMEHOW IT HAD become December, and November had passed in a moment. A moment when natural sleep had continued to elude her, but her strange, mixed feelings for the new village doctor had not.

She'd listened as her own clients had chatted with her about the new doctor, smiled when they'd joked about how gorgeous he was, how heroic he was. Had she heard that he'd saved lives already? One woman in the village, who really ought to have known better, had even joked and blushed about Dr Jones giving her the kiss of life! Sydney had smiled politely, but inside her heart had been thundering.

She'd seen him fleetingly, here and there. A couple of times he'd waved at her. Once she'd bumped into him in the sandwich shop, just as a large dollop of coleslaw had squeezed itself from her crusty cob and splatted onto her top.

'Oh!' He'd laughed, rummaging in his pockets and pulling out a fresh white handkerchief. 'Here—take this.'

She'd blushed madly, accepted his hankie, and then had stood there wiping furiously at her clothes, knowing that he was standing there, staring at her. When she'd looked up to thank him *he'd* blushed, and she'd wondered what he had been thinking about.

Then they'd both gone on their way, and she'd looked over her shoulder at him at the exact moment when he'd done the same.

She felt that strange undercurrent whenever they met, or whenever she saw him. She kept trying to ignore it. Trying to ignore *him*. But it was difficult. Her head and her heart had differing reactions. Her head told her to stay away and keep her distance. But her heart and her body sang whenever he was near, as if it was saying, *Look, there he is! Give him a wave! Go and say hello! Touch him!*

Today frost covered the ground like a smattering of icing sugar, and the village itself looked very picturesque. Sydney was desperate to get out and go for a walk around the old bridleways, maybe take a few pictures with her camera, but she couldn't. There was far too much to do and she was running late for a committee meeting.

The Silverdale Christmas market and nativity was an annual festive occasion that was always held the week before Christmas. People came from all around the county, sometimes further from afield, and it was a huge financial boost to local businesses during the typically slower winter months. Unfortunately this year it was scheduled to fall on the one day that she dreaded. The anniversary of Olivia's death.

Sydney had previously been one of the organisers, but after what had happened with Olivia she hadn't been involved much. Barely at all. This year she'd decided to get back into it. She'd always been needed, especially where the animals were concerned. She'd used to judge the Best Pet show, and maintain the welfare of all the animals that got involved in the very real nativity—donkeys, sheep, cows, goats, even chickens and geese! But she'd also been in charge of the flower stalls and the food market.

It was a huge commitment, but one she had enjoyed in the past. And this year it would keep her busy. Would stop her thinking of another Christmas without her daughter. Stop her from wallowing in the fact that, yet again, she would not be buying her child any gifts to put under a non-existent tree.

She sat at the table with the rest of the committee, waiting for the last member to arrive. Dr Jones was late. Considerably so. And the more they waited, the more restless she got.

'Perhaps we should just make a start and then fill Dr Jones in if he ever gets here?' Sydney suggested.

Everyone else was about to agree when the door burst open and in he came, cheeks red from the cold outside, apologising profusely. 'Sorry, everyone, I got called out to some stomach pains—which, surprisingly, turned out to be a bouncing baby boy.'

There were surprised gasps and cheers from the others.

'Who's had a baby?' asked Malcolm, the chairman.

Nathan tucked his coat over the back of his chair. 'Lucy Carter.'

Sydney sat forward, startled. '*My* Lucy Carter? My veterinary nurse?'

His gaze met hers and he beamed a smile at her which went straight to her heart. 'The very same.'

'B-but...she wasn't pregnant!' she spluttered with indignation.

'The baby in her arms would beg to differ!'

'But...'

She couldn't believe it! Okay, Lucy had put some weight on recently, but they'd put that down to those extra chocolate bars she'd been eating... *Pregnant? That's amazing!* She felt the need to go and see her straight away. To give her a hug and maybe get a cuddle with the newborn.

'It was a shock for everyone involved. But they're both doing well and everyone's happy. She told me to let you know.'

A baby. For Lucy. That was great news. And such a surprise!

It meant more work for Sydney for a bit, of course, but she'd cope. She could get an agency member of staff in. It would be weird, not seeing Lucy at work for a while. They'd always worked together. They knew each other's ways and foibles.

She sighed. Everyone else seemed to be moving on. Lucy and her new baby. Alastair and his new bride, with a baby on the way. Everyone was getting on with their lives. And she...? She was still here. In the village she's been born in. With no child. No husband. No family of her own except her elderly parents, who lived too far away anyway.

She looked across at Nathan as he settled into his seat and felt a sudden burst of irritation towards him. She'd been looking forward to getting involved in these meetings again, getting back out there into the community, and yet now her feelings towards him were making her feel uncomfortable. Was it because he'd brought news that meant her life was going to change again?

'Let's get started, shall we?' suggested Malcolm. 'First off, I'd like to welcome Dr Nathan Jones to the committee. He has taken over the role from its previous incumbent, Dr Richard Preston.'

The group clapped, smiled and nodded a welcome for their new member. Sydney stared at him, her face impassive. He looked ridiculously attractive today. Fresh-faced. Happy. She focused on his hands. Hands that had just recently delivered a baby. And she felt guilty for having allowed herself to succumb to that brief, petty jealousy. She looked up at his face and caught him looking at her, and she looked away, embarrassed.

'I'd also like to welcome Sydney back to the committee! Sydney, as I'm sure most of you know, took a little… sabbatical, if you will, from the organisation of this annual event, and I'm most pleased to have her back in full fighting form!'

She smiled as she felt all eyes turn to her, and nodded hellos to the group members she knew well and hadn't worked with for so long. It did feel good to be back here and doing something for the community again. The Christmas market and nativity was something she hadn't been able to find any pleasure in for some time, but now she was ready.

At least she hoped she was.

'The market is going to be held in the same place as always—the centre of the village square—and I believe we've already got lots of things in place from last year. Miriam?'

Miriam, the secretary, filled them in on all the recent developments. Lots of the same stalls that came every year had rebooked. Music was going to be covered by the same brass band, and the school was going to provide a choir as well.

Sydney listened, scribbling things down on her pad that she'd need to remember, and thought of past activities. There was a lot to take in—she'd forgotten how much organising there was!—and as her list got longer and longer she almost wished she could write with both hands.

She'd also forgotten how soothing these meetings could be sometimes. The hum of voices, the opinions of everyone on how things should be done, the ebb and flow of ideas… She truly appreciated the need for all this planning and preparation. Even though sometimes the older members of the committee enjoyed their dedication to picking over details a little too much.

Briefly, she allowed her mind to wander, and the memory that sprang to her mind was of a happier year, when Olivia had played the part of Mary in the nativity. In the weeks beforehand Sydney had taught her how to ride the donkey, shown her how to behave around the other animals. She remembered holding her daughter's hand as they walked through the market stalls, making sure she didn't eat too many sweets or pieces of cake, and listening to her singing carols in the choir.

She smiled, feeling a little sad. She had those memories on camera. Alastair had videoed Olivia riding the donkey in the nativity, with her fake pregnancy bump. Olivia had loved that belly, rubbing her hands over it like a real pregnant mother soothing away imaginary kicks.

'And that brings us back to our star players for the nativity,' Malcolm continued. 'I have been reliably informed by Miss Howarth of Silverdale Infants School that our Mary this year will be played by Anna Jones, and Joseph will be Barney Brooks…'

Sydney was pulled from her reverie. *Anna? Dr Jones's Anna? She was going to play Mary?* Visions flashed through her mind. Anna wearing Olivia's costume… Anna riding Olivia's donkey… Anna being the star of the show…?

It simply hadn't occurred to her when she came back that someone else would be playing Olivia's part. But of course. There had already been new Marys in the years that she'd stayed away. She'd just not seen them, hiding away in her house every year, longing to clap her hands over her ears to blot out the sound of all those Christmas revellers. It had been torture!

It hurt to hear it. It was as if Olivia had been replaced. Had been *forgotten*...

Her chair scraped loudly on the floor as she stood, grabbing her notepad and pen, her bag and coat, and muttering apologies before rushing from the room, feeling sick.

She thought she was on her own. She thought she would get to her own car in peace. But just as she was inserting her key into the lock of her car she heard her name being called.

'Sydney!'

She didn't want to turn around. She didn't want to be polite and make small talk with whoever it was. She just wanted to go. Surely they wouldn't mind? Surely they'd understand?

She got into her seat and was about to close the door when Nathan appeared at her side, holding the car door so she couldn't close it.

'Hey! Are you okay?'

Why was he here? Why was he even bothering to ask? Why had he come after her?

'I just want to go, Nathan.'

'Something's upset you?'

'No, honestly. I just want to get home, that's all.'

'Is it Lucy? Are you worried about work?'

'No.' She slipped on her seatbelt and stared resolutely out through the windshield rather than looking at him. Her voice softened. 'I'm thrilled for Lucy. Of course I am!'

'Is it me?'

Now she looked at him, her eyes narrowing. 'Why would it be you?'

He shrugged. 'I don't know. Things haven't exactly been...straightforward. There's a...a tension, between us. We didn't exactly get off to the best start, did we?'

'It's not you,' she lied.

'Well, that's good, because they've asked me to work closely with you, seeing as I'm new and you're an established committee member.'

What? When did I miss that bit?

'Oh.'

'That's quite good, really, because—as you heard— Anna came home from school today and told me she's been picked to play the part of Mary. Apparently that means riding a donkey, and she's never done that before, so...'

'So?'

Push the memory away. Don't think about it.

'So we'll need your help.'

He smiled at her. In that way he had. Disarming her and making her feel as if she ought to oblige him with her assistance. His charming eyes twinkling.

'Know any good donkeys? Preferably something that isn't going to buck and break her neck?'

There was someone in the village who kept donkeys. They were used every year for the nativity. And she trusted the animals implicitly.

'Do you know the Bradleys? At Wicklegate Farm?'

He pretended to search his memory. 'Erm...no.'

'Do you know where Wicklegate Farm even *is*?'

He shook his head, smiling. 'No.'

Feeling some of her inner struggle fade, she smiled back. Of course he didn't. 'I suppose I'd better help you, then. Are you free next Saturday?'

'Saturday? All day.'

She nodded and started her engine. 'I'll pick you up

at ten in the morning. I know your address. Does Anna have any riding clothes?'

'Er...'

'Anything she doesn't mind getting dirty?'

'My daughter is always happy to wallow in some mud.'

'Good. Tell her I'm going to teach her how to ride a donkey.'

'Thanks.'

He stood back at last, so she could finally close her car door. She was about to drive off, eager to get home, when Nathan rapped his knuckles on her glass.

She pressed the button to wind the window down, letting in the cold evening air. 'What?'

'Lucy's at home. And waiting for your visit.'

She nodded, imagining Lucy in her small cottage, tucked up in bed, looking as proud as Punch with a big smile on her face.

'Has she picked a name for him?'

'I believe she has.'

'What is it?'

He paused, clearly considering whether to say it or not. 'She's named him Oliver.'

Oliver. So close to...

A lump filled her throat and she blinked away tears. Had Lucy chosen that name in honour of her own daughter? If she had, then...

Sydney glanced up at Nathan. 'I'll see you on Saturday.' And she quickly drove away, before he could see her cry.

Nathan had driven round to Paul and Helen's to check up on them after the accident. They lived on the outskirts of Silverdale and were pretty easy to locate, and he pulled into their driveway feeling optimistic about what he would find. Helen had been released from hospital a while ago and he only needed to remove Paul's stitches from the head laceration.

As he drove in he saw the horse grazing in a field, a blanket wrapped around its body, and smiled. They'd all been very lucky to escape as easily as they had. The accident could have been a lot worse.

But as he pulled up to the house, he spotted another vehicle.

Sydney's.

Why was she here? To check on the horse? It had to be that. It was odd that she was here at the exact same time as him, though.

Just lately she'd been in his thoughts a lot. The universe seemed to be conspiring to throw the two of them together, and whilst he didn't mind that part—she was, after all, a beautiful woman—she did tend to remind him of all his faults and of how he could never be enough for her.

His confidence had taken a knock after Gwyneth's departure. Okay, they'd only been staying in their struggling relationship because she'd learnt she was expecting a baby and Nathan had wanted to be there for her. He'd always had his doubts, and she'd been incredibly high-maintenance, but he'd honestly believed she might change the closer she got to delivering. That they both would.

She hadn't. It had still been, *Me, me, me!*

'Look at all the weight I'm putting on!'

'This pregnancy's giving me acne!'

'I'm getting varicose veins!'

'You do realise after the birth I'm going straight back to work?'

Nathan had reassured her. Had promised her it would be amazing. But it had been *his* dream. Not hers.

It had only been when she'd left him for someone else

that he'd realised how much relief he felt. It had stung that she'd left him for someone better. Someone unencumbered by ill health. Someone rich, who could give her the lifestyle she craved. But he'd felt more sorry for his baby girl, who would grow up with a mother who only had enough love for herself.

In the weeks afterwards, when he'd spent hours walking his baby daughter up and down as he tried to get her off to sleep, he'd begun to see how one-sided their relationship had always been.

Gwyneth had always been about appearances. Worrying about whether her hair extensions were the best. Whether her nails needed redoing. How much weight she was carrying. Whether she was getting promoted above someone else. She'd been a social climber—a girl who had been given everything she'd ever wanted by her parents and had come to expect the same in adulthood.

He'd fallen for her glamorous looks and the fact that in the beginning she'd seemed really sweet. But it had all been a snare. A trap. And he'd only begun to see the real Gwyneth when he'd got his diagnosis. Multiple sclerosis had scared her. The idea that she might become nursemaid to a man who wasn't strong, the way she'd pictured him, had *terrified* her.

When Nathan had discovered his illness, and Gwyneth had learned that their perfect life was not so perfect after all, her outlook had changed and she'd said some pretty harsh things. Things he'd taken to heart. That he'd believed.

He didn't want to burden Sydney with any of that.

She'd looked after his daughter for a few hours, she'd looked after and cured their rabbit, she was kind and strong...

She's the sort of woman I would go out with if I could...

But he couldn't.

She'd lost her only daughter. And where was the child's father? From what he'd heard around the village, the father had left them just a couple of months after Olivia had passed away. Shocking them all.

It seemed the whole village had thought the Harpers were strong enough to get through anything. But of course no one could know how such a tragic death would affect them.

Hadn't Sydney been through enough? He had a positive mind-set—even if he did sometimes take the things that Gwyneth had yelled at him to heart. He tried to remain upbeat. But just sometimes his mind would play tricks with him and say, *Yeah, but what if she was right?*

Besides, he wasn't sure he could trust his own judgement about those kinds of things any more. Affairs of the heart. He'd felt so sure about Gwyneth once! In the beginning, anyway. And he'd wanted to do everything for her and the baby. Had wanted the family life that had been right there in front of him. Ready and waiting.

How wrong could he have been?

He'd been floored when she'd left. She'd been high-maintenance, but not once had he suspected that she would react that way to his diagnosis. To having a baby, even. She'd been horrified at what her life had become and had been desperate to escape the drudgery she'd foreseen.

And Nathan had *known* Gwyneth. Or thought he had.

He didn't *know* Sydney. As much as he'd like to.

And he sure as hell didn't want his heart—or Anna's—broken again.

Getting out of the car, he looked up and saw Paul, Helen and Sydney coming out of the house. Helen was standing further back, her arms crossed.

'Dr Jones! Good of you to call round! You've arrived just in time. Your wife was just about to leave.'

He instantly looked at Sydney. My *wife?*

Sydney blushed madly. 'We're not married!'

Paul looked between the two of them. 'Oh, but we thought... Partners, then?'

'No. Just...friends. Associates. We just happened to be in the car together, that's all...' he explained, feeling his voice tail off when he glanced at Sydney's hot face.

'Really? You two look perfect for each other.' Paul smiled.

Nathan was a little embarrassed, but amused at the couple's mistake. 'Hello, Sydney. We seem to keep bumping into each other.'

She shook his hand in greeting. 'We do.'

'Did you get to see Lucy?'

'I did. The baby is gorgeous.'

'He is.' He was still holding her hand. Still looking at her. Someone seemed to have pressed 'pause', because for a moment he lost himself, staring into her grey eyes. It was as if the rest of the world had gone away.

Paul and Helen looked at each other and cleared their throats and Nathan dropped Sydney's hand.

'You're leaving?'

'I just came to check on the horse. No after-effects from the accident.'

'That's good. How about you, Paul? Any headaches? Anything I should be worried about?'

'No, Doc. All well and good, considering.'

'How about you, Helen?'

'I'm fine. Physically.'

'That's good.'

Sydney pulled her car keys from her pocket. 'Well, I must dash. Good to see you all so well. Paul. Helen.' She looked over at Nathan, her gaze lingering longer than it should. 'Dr Jones.'

He watched her go. Watched as she started her engine, reversed, turned and drove out of the driveway. He even watched as her car disappeared out of sight, up the lane.

Suddenly remembering that he was there to see Paul and Helen, he turned back to them, feeling embarrassed. 'Shall we go in? Get those stitches seen to?'

Paul nodded, draping his arm around Nathan's shoulder conspiratorially. 'Just friends, huh?'

He felt his cheeks colour. They'd caught him watching her. Seen how distracted she made him.

'Just friends.'

Inside the house, Helen disappeared into the kitchen to make a cup of tea.

'So, Paul... How are you?' He noted the stitches in his scalp. He'd certainly got a nasty laceration there, but apart from that obvious injury he seemed quite well.

'I'm good, Doc, thanks.' Paul settled into the chair opposite.

They had a lovely home. It was a real country cottage, with lots of character and tons of original features. There was a nice fire crackling away in the fireplace. It looked as if they were in the process of putting some Christmas decorations up.

'So I need to remove your stitches. How many days have they been in?'

'Too long! I'm really grateful for you coming out like this. I was going to make an appointment to come and say thanks to you. For saving me and Helen. And Brandon, too, of course.'

'It wasn't a problem. We were just in the right place at the right time.'

'You were in the perfect place.' He looked down at

the floor and then got his next words out in a quiet rush, after he'd turned to check that Helen wasn't listening. 'Helen and I didn't see that deer coming across the field because we were arguing.'

'Oh?' Nathan sensed a confession coming.

'I…er…hadn't reacted very well to the fact that… well…' He looked uncomfortable. 'Helen had had a miscarriage. Two weeks earlier. The hospital said they'd send you a letter… We hadn't even known she was pregnant, but she had this bleed that wouldn't stop, and we ended up at A&E one night, and they found out it was an incomplete miscarriage. She needed a D&C.'

Nathan felt a lurch in his stomach. 'I'm very sorry to hear that.'

'Yeah, well…apparently *I* wasn't sorry enough. Helen got mad with me because I wasn't upset about losing the baby. But neither of us had even *known* about the pregnancy! How could I get upset over a baby I didn't know about?' Paul let out a heavy breath. 'She thought I didn't care. We were arguing about that. Yelling…screaming at each other—so much so that Brandon started too. We didn't notice the deer because I wasn't paying attention.' He sounded guilty. 'And now, because I didn't notice the deer running in front of us, and because I didn't notice my wife was pregnant, *I'm* the bad guy who nearly got us all killed.'

How awful for them! To lose a baby like that and then to have a serious accident on top of it. They were both very lucky to have got out alive. Brandon, too. It could all have gone so terribly wrong.

'Well, I can sort your stitches for you. And I'm not so sure I would *want* to stop Helen being mad. She's had a terrible loss, Paul. You both have. And she needs to work through it.'

'I know, but…'

'There are support groups. Ones specifically for women who have suffered miscarriage. I can give you some information if you drop by the surgery. Or maybe I could ask Helen if she wants to come in and have a chat with me? You may not have known about the pregnancy, but she still lost a baby. A D&C can be a traumatic event in itself, when you think about what it is, and it can help some women to talk about things. She's had a loss and she needs to work her way through it. And I'm sure, in time, so will you.'

Paul rubbed at his bristly jaw. 'But even *she* didn't know.'

'It doesn't matter. It was still a baby, Paul. Still a loss. A terrible one. And she knows *now*. She probably feels a lot of guilt, and the easiest person to take that out on is you.'

'Does she think *I've* not been hurt too? To not even know she was pregnant and then to see her so scared when she wouldn't stop bleeding? And then to learn the reason why?' He shook his head, tears welling in his eyes. '*Why* didn't I know?'

'You're not to blame. It's difficult in those early weeks.'

'I keep thinking there must have something else I could have done for her. Something I could have said. To see that pain in her eyes… It broke my heart.'

Nathan laid a hand on Paul's shoulder.

'It *has* hurt me. I *am* upset. And I feel guilty at trying to make her get over something when she's just not ready to. Guilty that I won't get to hold that baby in my arms…'

'Grief takes time to heal. For both of you.'

Paul glanced at his hands. 'But she won't talk to me. She doesn't talk to me about any of the deep stuff because she thinks I don't care. She never shares what she's feeling. How are you supposed to be in a relationship with someone who won't tell you what's really going on?'

With great difficulty.

He looked at Paul. 'You wait. Until she's ready. And when she is…you listen.'

Nathan was so glad he'd never had to go through something like this with Gwyneth. They'd come close, when she'd thought there might still be time for an abortion, but the thought of losing his child…? It was too terrible even to think about.

Sydney would understand.

Just thinking about her now made him realise just how strong she was to have got through her daughter's death. And on her own, too.

'So I've just got to take her anger, then?'

'Be there for her. Be ready to talk when she is. She's grieving.'

Was Sydney still grieving? Was that why she wasn't able to talk to him about what had happened? Should he even *expect* her to open up to him?

He opened his doctor's bag and pulled out a small kit to remove Paul's stitches. There were ten of them, and he used a stitch-cutter and tweezers to hold the knots each time he removed them. The wound had healed well, but Paul would be left with a significant scar for a while.

'That's you done.'

'Thanks. So I've just got to wait it out, then?'

'Or you could raise the subject if *you* feel the need. I can see that you're upset at the loss, too. Let her know she can talk to you. That you're ready to talk whenever she is.'

Paul nodded and touched the spot where his stitches

had been. 'Maybe I will. I know I've lost a baby, but I'm even more scared of losing my wife.'

Nathan just stared back at him.

Sydney felt odd. She had to call round to Nathan's house in a minute, so she could take them to Wicklegate Farm and teach Anna how to ride the donkey. But for some reason she was standing in front of her wardrobe, wondering what to wear?

It shouldn't matter!

Deliberately she grabbed at a pair of old jeans, an old rugby shirt that was slightly too big for her and thick woolly socks to wear inside her boots.

I have no reason to dress up for Dr Jones.

However, once dressed, she found herself staring at her reflection in the mirror, messing with her hair. Up? Down?

She decided to leave her hair down and then added a touch of make-up. A bit of blush. Some mascara.

Her reflection stared back at her in question.

What are you doing?

Her mirror image gave no response. Obviously. But that still didn't stop her waiting for one, hoping she would see something in the mirror that would tell her the right thing to do.

She even looked at Magic. 'Am I being stupid about this?'

Magic blinked slowly at her.

She *liked* Nathan, and that was the problem. She liked it that he was comfortable to be with. She liked it that he was great to talk to. That he was very easy on the eye.

There was some small security in the fact that his little girl would be there, so it was hardly going to be a seduction, but... But a part of her—a small part, admittedly—

wondered what it would be like if something were to happen with them spending time together. What, though? A kiss? On the cheek? *The lips?* That small part of her wanted to know what it would feel like to close her eyes and feel his lips press against hers. To inhale his scent, to feel his hands upon her. To sink into his strong caress.

Alastair, in those last few months, made me feel like I had the plague. That I was disgusting to him. It would be nice to know that a man could still find me desirable.

She missed that physical connection with someone. She missed having someone in her bed in the morning. Someone to read the papers with. To talk to over a meal. She missed the comfort of sitting in the same room as another person and not even having to talk. Of sharing a good book recommendation, of watching a movie together snuggled under an old quilt and feeding each other popcorn. Coming home and not finding the house empty.

But so what? Just because she missed it, it didn't mean she had to make it happen. No matter how much she fantasised about it. Nathan was a man. And in her experience men let you down. Especially when you needed them the most. She'd already been rejected once, when she was at her lowest, and she didn't want to go through that again.

It was too hard.

So no matter how nice Nathan was—no matter how attractive, no matter how much she missed being *held*—nothing was going to happen. Today was about Anna. About donkeys and learning how to ride.

She remembered teaching Olivia. It had taken her ages to get her balance, and she'd needed a few goes at it before she'd felt confident. She hadn't liked pulling at the reins, had been worried in case it hurt the donkey.

Thinking about the past made her think of the present. Her ex-husband, Alastair, had moved on. He'd found someone new. Was making a new family. How had he moved on so quickly? It was almost insulting. Had she meant nothing to him? Had the family they'd had meant less to him than she'd realised? Perhaps that was why he'd walked away so easily?

Everyone in the village had been shocked. *Everyone.* Well, she'd make sure that everyone knew *she* wasn't moving on. Keeping Nathan and Anna at arm's length was the right thing to do, despite what she was feeling inside.

She considered cancelling. Calling him and apologising. Telling him that an emergency had cropped up. But then she'd realised that if she did she would still have to meet him again at some point. It was best to get it over and done with straight away. Less dilly-dallying. Besides, she didn't want to let Anna down. She was a good kid.

She held her house keys in her hand for a moment longer, debating with her inner conscience, and her gaze naturally strayed to a photograph of Olivia. She was standing with her head back, looking up to the sun, her eyes closed, smiling at the feel of warmth on her face. It was one of Sydney's favourite pictures: Olivia embracing the warmth of the sun.

She always enjoyed life. Even the small things.

Sydney stepped outside and locked up the cottage. She needed to drive to Nathan's house. The new estate and the road he lived on was about two miles away.

It was interesting to drive through the new builds. The houses were very modern, in bright brick, with cool grey slate tiles on their roofs and shiny white UPVC windows. They were uniformly identical, but she could see Nathan's muddy jalopy parked on his driveway and she pulled in behind it, letting out a breath. Releasing her nerves.

I can do this!

She strode up to the front door, trying to look businesslike, hoping that no one could see how nervous she suddenly felt inside. She rang the bell and let out a huge breath, trying to calm her scattered nerves.

The door opened and Nathan stood there. Smiling. 'Sydney—hi. Come on in.' he stepped back.

Reluctant to enter his home, and therefore create feelings of intimacy, she stepped back. 'Erm…shouldn't we just be off? I told the owners we'd be there in about ten minutes.'

'I'm just waiting for Anna to finish getting ready. You know what young girls are like.'

She watched his cheeks colour as he realised what he'd said, and to let him off the hook decided to step in, but keeping herself as far away from him physically as she could.

'I do…yes. Anna?' she called up the stairs.

Sydney heard some thumps and bumps and then Anna was at the top of the stairs. 'Hi, Sydney! I can't decide what to wear. Could you help me? *Please?*'

Anna wheedled out the last word, giving the cutest face that she could.

The look was so reminiscent of Olivia that Sydney had to catch her breath.

'Erm…' she glanced at Nathan, who shrugged.

'By all means…'

'Right.'

Sydney ascended the stairs, feeling sweat break out down her spine. She turned at the top and went into Anna's room. Her breath was taken away by how *girly* it was. A palace of pink. A pink feather boa hung over the mirror on a dresser, there were fairy lights around the headboard, bubblegum-coloured beanbags, a blush-pink carpet and curtains, a hammock in the corner filled with all manner of soft, cuddly toys and a patchwork quilt upon the bed.

And in front of a large pink wardrobe that had a crenelated top, like a castle, Anna stood, one hand on one hip, the other tapping her finger against her lips.

'I've never ridden a donkey. Or a horse! I don't know what would be best.'

Sydney swallowed hard as she eyed the plethora of clothes in every colour under the sun. 'Erm…something you don't mind getting dirty. Trousers or jeans. And a tee shirt? Maybe a jumper?'

Anna pulled out a mulberry-coloured jumper that was quite a thick knit, with cabling down the front. 'Like this?'

Syd nodded. 'Perfect. Trousers?'

'I have these.' Anna pulled a pair of jeans from a pile. They had some diamanté sequins sewn around the pockets. 'And this?' She pointed at the tee shirt she was already wearing.

'Those will be great. I'll go downstairs whilst you're getting dressed.'

'Could you help me, Sydney? I can never do the buttons.'

Sydney stood awkwardly whilst Anna changed her clothes, and then knelt in front of the little girl to help her do up her clothes. It had been ages since she'd had to do this. Olivia had always struggled with buttons. These two girls might almost have been made out of the same mould. Of course there were so differences between the girls, but sometimes the similarities were disturbing. Painful.

She stood up again. 'Ready?'

Anna nodded and dashed by her to run downstairs. 'I'll get my boots on!'

She sat at the bottom of the stairs and pulled on bright green wellington boots that had comical frog eyes poking out over the toes.

Sydney stood behind her, looking awkwardly at Nathan.

'Will I need boots, too?' he asked.

She nodded. 'It's a working farm…so, yes.'

She watched as they both got ready, and it was so reminiscent of standing waiting for Olivia and Alastair to get ready so they could go out that she physically felt an ache in her chest.

They had been good together. Once. When she and Alastair had married she'd truly believed they would be in each other's arms until their last days. Shuffling along together. One of those old couples you could see in parks, still holding hands.

But then it had all gone wrong.

Alastair hadn't been able to cope with losing his little girl and he'd blamed her. For not noticing that Olivia was truly ill. For not acting sooner. The way he'd blanked her, directed his anger towards her, had hurt incredibly. The one time she'd needed her husband the most had been the one time he'd failed her completely.

When Nathan and Anna were both ready she hurried them out of the door and got them into her car.

'Can you do your seatbelt, Anna?'

'Yes!' the little girl answered, beaming. 'I can't wait to ride the donkey! Did Daddy tell you I'm going to be Mary? That's the most important part in the play. Well… except for baby Jesus…but that's just going to be a doll, so…' She trailed off.

Sydney smiled into the rearview mirror. How many times had she driven her car with Olivia babbling away in the back seat? Too many times. So often, in fact, that she would usually be thinking about all the things she had to do, tuning her daughter out, saying *hmm*...or *right*...in all the right places, whenever her daughter paused for breath.

And now...? With Anna chatting away...? She wanted to listen. Wanted to show Nathan's little girl that she heard her.

I can't believe I ignored my daughter! Even for a second!

How many times had she not truly listened? How many times had she not paid attention? Thinking that she had all the time in the world to talk to her whenever she wanted? To chat about things that hadn't meant much to her but had meant the world to her daughter?

'All eyes will be on you, Anna. I'm sure you'll do a great job.'

Nathan glanced over at her. 'I appreciate you arranging this. I don't suppose you're a dab hand with a sewing machine, are you?'

She was, actually. 'Why?'

'The costume for Mary is looking a bit old. The last incumbent seems to have dragged it through a dump before storing it away and now it looks awful. Miriam has suggested that I make another one.'

She glanced over at him. 'And you said...?'

'I said yes! But that was when I thought a bedsheet and a blue teacloth over the head was all that was needed.'

'You know... I might still have Olivia's old outfit. She played Mary one year.'

'She did?' Nathan was looking at her closely.

'I still have some of her stuff in boxes in the attic. Couldn't bear to part with it. Give me a day or two and I'll check.'

'That's very kind of you.'

She kept her eyes on the road, trying not to think too

hard about going up into the attic to open those boxes. Would the clothes still have Olivia's scent? Would seeing them, touching them, be too painful? There was a reason they were still in the attic. Unsorted.

She'd boxed everything up one day, after a therapist at one of her grief counselling sessions had told her it might be a good thing to do. That it might be cathartic, or something.

It hadn't been.

She'd felt that in boxing up her daughter's clothes and putting them somewhere they couldn't be seen she was also been getting rid of all traces of her daughter. That she was hiding Olivia's memory away. And she'd not been ready. She'd drunk an awful lot of wine that night, and had staggered up into the attic to drag all the boxes back downstairs, but Alastair had stopped her. Yelled at her that it was a *good* thing, and that if she touched those boxes one more time then he would walk out the door.

She'd sobered up and the next morning had left the boxes up there—even though she'd felt bereft and distraught. And dreadfully hungover.

Alastair had left eventually, of course. Just not then. It had taken a few more weeks. By then it had been too late to drag the boxes back down. Too scary.

'What was she like?'

'Hmm?' She was pulled back to the present by his question. 'What?'

'What was Olivia like?' he asked again.

She glanced over at him quickly. He sounded as if he really wanted to know, and no one had asked her that question for years. All this time she'd stayed away from people, not making connections or getting close because she hadn't wanted to talk about Olivia. It had been too painful. But now she *wanted* to talk about her.

Was thrilled that he'd asked, because she was *ready* to talk about her. He'd made it easy to do so.

'She was…amazing.'

'Who's Olivia?' asked Anna from the back seat.

Sydney glanced in the rearview mirror once again and smiled.

The donkey was called Bert and he had a beautiful dark brown coat. The farmer had already got him saddled before their arrival and he stood waiting patiently, nibbling at some hay, as Sydney gave Anna instructions.

'Okay, it's quite simple, Anna. You don't need Bert to go fast, so you don't need to nudge him with your feet or kick at his sides. A slow plod is what we want, and Bert here is an expert at the slow plod and the Christmas nativity.'

'Will he bite me?'

She shook her head. 'No. He's very gentle and he is used to children riding him. Shall I lift you into the saddle?'

Anna nodded.

Sydney hefted Anna up. 'Put your hands here, on the pommel. I'll lead him with the reins—the way we'll get the boy playing Joseph to do it.'

'Okay.'

'Verbal commands work best, and Bert responds to *Go on* when you want him to start walking and *Stop* when you want him to stand still. Got that?'

Anna nodded again.

'Why don't you give that a try?'

Anna smiled. 'Go on, Bert!'

Bert started moving.

'He's doing it, Sydney! He's *doing* it! Look, Daddy— I'm riding!'

'That's brilliant, sweetheart.'

Sydney led Bert down the short side of the field. She turned to check on Anna. 'That's it. Keep your back straight…don't slouch.'

They walked up and down. Up and down. Until Sydney thought Anna was ready to try and do it on her own. She'd certainly picked it up a lot more quickly than Olivia had!

'Okay, Anna. Try it on your own. Head to the end of the field and use the reins to turn him and make him come back. Talk to him. Encourage him. Okay?'

She knew Anna could do it. The little girl had connected with the donkey in a way no other had, and the animal responded brilliantly to her. Sydney really didn't think Anna would have a problem on the night of the nativity. Bert was putty in her hands.

They both stood and watched as Anna led Bert confidently away from them and down the field. Sydney almost felt proud. In fact, she *was* proud.

She became aware that Nathan was staring at her, and then suddenly, almost in a blink, she felt his fingers sliding around hers.

'Thank you, Sydney.'

She turned to him and looked into his eyes. The intensity of the moment grew. It felt as if her heart had sped up but her breathing had got really slow. Her fingers in his felt protected and safe, and he stroked the back of her hand with his thumb in slow, sweeping strokes that were doing strange, chaotic things to her insides, turning her legs to jelly.

'What for?' she managed to say.

'For helping me when it's difficult for you. I appreciate the time you're giving me and my daughter. I…'

He stopped talking as he took a step closer to her, and

as he drew near her breathing stopped completely and she looked up into his handsome blue eyes.

He's going to kiss me!

Hadn't she thought about this? Hadn't she wondered what it might be like? Hadn't she missed the physical contact that came with being in a relationship? And now here was this man—this incredibly *attractive* man—holding her hand and making her stomach do twirls and swirls as his lips neared hers, as he leaned in for a kiss...

Sydney closed her eyes, awaiting the press of his lips against hers.

Only there was no kiss.

She felt him pull his hand free from hers and heard him clearing his throat and apologising before he called out, 'You're doing brilliantly, Anna! Turn him round now—come on. We need to go home.'

Sydney blinked. What had happened? He'd been about to kiss her, hadn't he? And she'd stood there, like an idiot, waiting for him to do it.

How embarrassing!

Anna brought Bert to a halt beside them, beaming widely.

'I think that's enough for today. You've done really well, Anna.'

Anna beamed as her father helped her off the donkey, and then she ran straight to Sydney and wrapped her arms around her. 'Thanks, Sydney! You're the best!'

Sydney froze at the unexpected hug, but then she relaxed and hugged the little girl back, swallowing back her surprise and...for some reason...her tears. 'So are you.'

The farmer took Bert back to his field with the other donkeys, once he'd removed the saddle and tack, and Sydney and Anna said goodbye. Then they all got back into Sydney's car and she started to drive them home.

'Thank you for…er…what you've done for Anna today,' said Nathan.

She took a breath and bit back the retort she wanted to give. 'No problem.'

'You know…taking time out of your weekend…'

'Sydney could stay for dinner, couldn't she Daddy? We're having fajitas!' Anna invited from the back.

She would have loved nothing more than to stay. Her time spent with Anna had been wonderful, and the times when she'd looked across at Nathan and caught him looking at her had been weirdly wonderful and exciting too.

But after what had just happened—the almost-kiss… He'd been going to do it. She knew it! But something had stopped him. Had got in the way.

Was it because he'd suddenly remembered Anna was there? Had he not wanted to risk his daughter seeing them kissing? Or was it something else?

She was afraid of getting carried away and reading too much into this situation. She'd helped out. That was all. She'd felt a connection that Nathan hadn't. Getting too involved with this single dad was perhaps a step too far. Where would it end? If she spent too much time with them, where would she be?

She shivered, even though the car heater was pumping out plenty of hot air. 'I'm sorry, I can't. I've got a…a thing later.'

'Maybe another time?' Nathan suggested, looking embarrassed.

As well you might!

'Sure.'

There can't ever be another time, no.

She watched them clamber from her car when she dropped them off. Nathan lingered at the open window of the car, as if he had something else to say, but then he looked away and simply said goodbye, before following his daughter up the path.

Sydney drove off before he could turn around and say anything else.

I really like them. Both of them.

But was it what they represented that she liked? This dad. This little girl. They were a ready-made family. Being with them might give her back some of what she'd lost. They offered a chance of starting again. So was it the *situation* that she liked? Or *them* as individuals?

Nathan was great. Gorgeous, charming, someone she enjoyed being around. And Anna was cute as a button, with her sing-song voice and happy-go-lucky personality.

Was it wrong to envy them? To envy them because they still had each other?

Was it wrong to have wanted—to have *craved*—Nathan's kiss?

Feeling guilty, she drove home, and she was just about to park up when she got a text. A cat was having difficulties giving birth and she needed to get to the surgery immediately to prep for a Caesarean section.

Suddenly all business—which was easy because she knew what she was doing—she turned the car around and drove to the surgery.

Nathan sent Anna upstairs to get changed into some clean clothes that didn't smell of donkey and farm. Then he headed into the kitchen, switching on the kettle and sinking into a chair as he waited for it to boil.

What the hell had he done?

Something crazy—something not *him*—had somehow slipped through his defences and he'd found himself taking hold of Sydney's hand, staring into her sad grey eyes. And he had been about to *kiss her*!

Okay, so he'd been fighting that urge for a while, and it was hardly a strange impulse, but he *had* thought that he'd got those impulses under control.

Standing there, looking down into her face, at her smooth skin, her slightly rosy cheeks, those soft, inviting lips, he'd wanted to so badly! And she'd wanted him to do it. He'd wanted to, but…

But Anna hadn't been far away, and he'd suddenly heard that horrid voice in his head that still sounded remarkably like Gwyneth, telling him that no one, and especially not Sydney, would want him. Not with his faulty, failing body. Not with his bad genes. Not with a child who wasn't hers…

How could he ask her to take on that burden—especially with the threat of his MS always present? He knew the chances of the MS killing him were practically zero. Okay, there would be difficulties, and there would be complications—there might even be comorbidities such as thyroid disease, autoimmune conditions or a meningioma. But the MS on its own…? It was unlikely.

But it had been enough to make him hesitate. To think twice. And once he'd paused too long he'd known it was too late to kiss her so he'd stepped away. Had called out to Anna…said they needed to go.

Sydney deserved a strong man. A man who would look out for her and care for her and protect her. What if he couldn't do that?

Fear. That was what it had been. Fear of putting himself out there. Of getting involved. Of exposing himself to the hurt and pain that Gwyneth had caused once. How could he go through again? How could he expose Anna to that now that she was older? She would be aware now if she grew to love someone and then that someone decided it was all too much and wanted out.

Anna being a baby had protected her from the pain of losing her mother. And today he had saved himself from finding out if he could be enough for someone like Sydney. Gwyneth had made him doubt what he had to offer. She had probably been right in what she'd said. He didn't know what his future would be like. He couldn't be certain, despite trying his best to remain positive. But it was hard sometimes. Dealing with a chronic illness… sometimes it could get to you.

The kettle boiled and he slowly made himself a cup of tea. He heard Anna come trotting back down the stairs and she came into the kitchen.

'Can I have a biscuit, Daddy?'

'Just one.'

She reached into the biscuit barrel and took out a plain biscuit. 'I loved riding Bert. He was so cute! I love donkeys. Do *you* love donkeys, Daddy?'

He thought for a moment. 'I do. Especially Bert.'

She smiled at him, crumbs dropping onto the floor. 'And do you love Sydney?'

His gaze swung straight round to his daughter's face. 'What?'

'I think you like her.'

'What makes you say that?' he asked in a strangled voice.

'Your eyes go all funny.' She giggled. 'Joshua in my class—he looks at Gemma like that and he *loves* her. They're boyfriend and girlfriend.'

Nathan cleared his throat. 'Aren't they a little young to be boyfriend and girlfriend?'

Anna shrugged, and then skipped off into the other room. He heard the television go on.

She noticed quite a lot, did Anna.

Curious, he followed her through to the lounge and

stood and watched her for a moment as she chose a channel to watch.

'Anna?'

'Yes?'

'If I did like Sydney…how would you feel about that?'

Anna tilted her head to one side and smiled, before turning back to the television. 'Fine. Then you wouldn't be all alone.'

Nathan stared at his daughter. And smiled.

CHAPTER SIX

IT HAD BEEN a long time since Sydney had had to play 'mother', and now she had the pleasure once again. The cat she'd raced to had recovered from its surgery, but had disowned her kittens afterwards. It happened sometimes with animals, when they missed giving birth in the traditional way and there just wasn't that bond there for them.

The four kittens—three black females and a black and white male—were kicking off their December in a small cat carrier at her home and she was on round-the-clock feeding every two hours.

Sydney was quite enjoying it. It gave her purpose. It gave her a routine. But mostly it gave her something to do during the long hours of the lonely nights. Even if she *was* still torturing herself with what might have happened between her and Nathan.

I wanted him to kiss me and I made that perfectly clear!

She'd hardly fought it, had she? Standing there all still, eyes closed, awaiting his kiss like some stupid girl in a fairytale. He must have thought she was a right sap. Perhaps that was what had put him off...

Disturbed from her reverie by the sound of her doorbell, she glanced at the clock—it was nearly eight in the morning—and went to answer the door.

It didn't cross her mind that she'd been up all night, hadn't combed her hair or washed her face, or that she was still wearing yesterday's clothes and smelt slightly of antiseptic and donkey at the same time.

She opened the door to see Nathan and Anna standing there. 'Er... Hi... Sorry, had we arranged to meet?' She felt confused by their being there. And so early, too.

'We were out getting breakfast,' Nathan explained. 'Anna wanted croissants and jam. We didn't have any and...' He blinked, squirming slightly. 'I thought you might like to share some with us.'

He raised a brown paper bag that was starting to show grease spots and she suddenly realised how hungry she was.

Her mouth watered and her stomach ached for the food and nourishment. Warm, buttery croissants sounded delicious!

Even though she still felt embarrassed after yesterday, the lure of the food overpowered the feeling.

'Sure. Come on in.' She stepped back, biting her lip as they passed, wondering if she was making a huge mistake in accepting. Hadn't this man humiliated her just yesterday? Unintentionally, perhaps, but still... And today she was letting him in to her house? She had no idea where her boundaries were with them any more.

Following the scent of food to her kitchen, she washed her hands and got out some plates, then butter from the fridge.

'I don't have any jam...'

'We do!' Anna chirruped. 'Blackberry, apricot and strawberry!' She put a small bag holding the jars onto the kitchen counter.

Sydney nodded. 'Wow! You *do* come prepared, don't

you? There can't be many people wandering around with a full condiments selection.'

Nathan grinned. 'We weren't sure which one you liked, so…'

He was trying to say sorry. She could see that. The croissants, the jam, the sudden breakfast—these were all part of his white flag. His olive branch. His truce. She would be cruel to reject it. Especially as it was going to be so nice. When had she last had a breakfast like this?

'I like apricot, so thank you for getting it for me.'

She smiled and mussed Anna's hair, and then indicated they should all sit at the table. Sydney filled the kettle, and poured some juice for Anna, and then they all settled down to eat.

Her home was filled with laughter, flaky pastries and the wonderful sound of happiness. It was as if her kitchen had been waiting for this family to fill it, and suddenly it no longer seemed the cold empty room she knew, but a room full of life and purpose and identity.

For an hour she forgot her grief. She let down her barriers and her walls and allowed them in. Despite her uncertainty, they were good for her. Anna was wonderfully bright and cheerful and giggly. And those differences between her and Olivia were growing starker by the minute. Anna liked looking at flowers, but had no interest in growing them. She knew what she wanted to be when she was grown up. She liked building things and being hands-on. She was such a sweet little girl, and so endearing, and Nathan…

They just got on well together. It was easy for them all.

Sydney was licking the last of the croissant crumbs from her fingers when Nathan said, 'How come you don't have any Christmas decorations?'

His question was like a bucket of ice-cold water being

thrown over her. It was a reality check. It pulled her back to her *actual* life and not the temporarily happy one she'd been enjoying.

'I don't do Christmas.'

He held her gaze, trying to see beyond her words. Trying to learn her reasons.

Anna looked at her in shock. 'Don't you believe in Santa Claus?'

Sydney smiled at her. If only it were that simple. 'Of course I do. Santa is a very good reason to enjoy Christmas.' She thought for a moment. 'Anna, why don't you go and take a look at what's in the blue cat carrier in my lounge? Be gentle, though.'

Anna gasped and ran into the other room, and Sydney turned back to face Nathan. She sucked in a breath to speak but nothing came out. Thankfully he didn't judge or say anything. He just waited for her to speak. And suddenly she could.

'Olivia died just before Christmas. It seems wrong to celebrate it.'

He swallowed. 'Do you want to talk about it?'

She did…but after the way he'd been with her yesterday… Did she want to share the innermost pain in her heart with a man who could blow so hot and cold? What would be the point in telling him if he wasn't going to stick around? If he wasn't going to be the kind of person she needed in her life? Because she was beginning to think that maybe there *could* be someone. One day. Maybe.

Could the person be Nathan?

She didn't want to feel vulnerable again, or helpless. But sitting in her home night after night, *alone*, was making her feel more vulnerable than she'd ever realised. Yet still she wasn't sure whether to tell him everything.

He stared at her intently, focusing on her eyes, her lips, then on her eyes again. What was he trying to see? What was he trying to decide?

He soon let her know, by confiding something of his own.

'I have MS—multiple sclerosis. To be exact, I have relapsing remitting multiple sclerosis. I have attacks of symptoms that come on suddenly and then go away again.'

She leaned forward, concerned. Intrigued. Was this what had been wrong with him the other day? When he'd been all dizzy at the veterinary surgery? And that time at the accident site?

'MS…?'

'I was diagnosed the week before Anna was born. It was a huge shock—nothing compared to losing a child, but it had tremendous repercussions. Not only my life, but Anna's too. Anna's mother walked out on us both during a time in which I was already reeling. Only a couple of weeks after we'd had Anna, Gwyneth left us…but it doesn't stop us from celebrating Anna's birthday each year. She gets presents, a cake, a party, balloons. You *should* enjoy Christmas. You *should* celebrate. There aren't many times in our lives where we can really enjoy ourselves, but Christmas is one of them.'

Sydney stood up and began to clear away the breakfast things. She'd heard what he'd said, but his story hardly touched hers. 'That's completely different.'

He got up and followed her into the kitchen, grabbed her arm. 'No, it isn't.'

She yanked her arm free. 'Yes, it is! My child *died*. Your girlfriend walked out. There's a *big* difference.'

'Sydney—'

'Do you think I can *enjoy* being reminded every year

that my daughter is dead? Every time Christmas begins—and it seems to get earlier every year—everywhere I look people are putting up decorations and trees and lights, buying presents for each other, and they're all in a happy mood. All I can see is my daughter, lying in a hospital bed with tubes coming out of her, and myself being told that I need to say goodbye! Do you have *any* idea of how that feels? To know that everybody else is *happy* because it's that time of year again?'

He shook his head. 'No. I couldn't possibly know.'

'No.' She bit back her tears and slumped against the kitchen units, lost in memories of that hospital once again. Feeling the old, familiar pain and grief. 'I became the saddest I could ever be at this time of year— when everyone else is at their happiest. I can't sleep. It's hard for me. I could *never* celebrate.'

Nathan stood in front of her and took one of her hands in his, looking down at their interlocked fingers. 'Perhaps you need to stop focusing on the day that she died and instead start focusing on all the days that she lived...'

His words stunned her. A swell of anger like a giant wave washed over her and she had to reach out to steady herself. It was that powerful.

How *dared* he tell her how she ought to grieve? How she ought to remember her daughter! He had no idea of how she felt and here he was—another *doctor*—telling her what she needed to do, handing out advice.

She inhaled a deep breath through her nose, feeling her shoulders rise up and her chin jut out in defiance as she stared at him, feeling her fury seethe out from her every pore.

'*Get out.*'

'Sydney—'

He tried to reach for her arm, but seeing his hand

stretched out towards her, without her permission, made her feel even more fury and she batted him away.

'You don't get to tell me how to deal with my grief. You don't get to tell me how I should be thinking. You don't get to tell me anything!'

She stormed away from him—out of her kitchen, down the hallway, towards her front door, which she wrenched open. Then she stood there, arms folded, as tears began to break and her bottom lip began to wobble with the force of her anger and upset.

She felt as if she could tackle anything with the strength of feeling she had inside her right now. Wrestle a lion? *Bring it on.* Take down a giant? *Bring it on.* Chuck someone out of her home? *Bring. It. On!*

Nathan followed her, apology written all over his features. 'Look, Syd, I'm sorry. I—'

She held up a finger, ignoring the fact that it was shaking and trembling with her rage. 'Don't. Don't you *dare*. I don't want to hear any of it. Not from you. You with your *"drink warm milk"* advice and your *"why not try grief counselling?"* and your *"focus on the days she lived"* advice. You couldn't *possibly* understand what I am going through! You couldn't even kiss me, Dr Nathan Jones, so you don't get to tell me how to live.'

He stared back at her, his Adam's apple bobbing up and down as he swallowed hard. Then he sighed and called out for his daughter. 'Anna? We need to go.'

They both heard Anna make a protest at having to leave. She was obviously having far too much fun with the orphaned kittens.

But she showed up in the doorway and looked at both her father and Sydney. 'Are we leaving?'

''Fraid so.' Nathan nodded and gave her a rueful smile. 'We need to head back now. Sydney's got things to do.'

'Not fair, Daddy! I want to stay with the kittens. Sydney, can I stay for a little bit—*pleeeeeease*?' She added a sickly sweet smile and clutched her hands before her like she was begging for a chance of life before a judge.

Nathan steered her out through the front door. 'Another time, honey.' As he moved out of the door he turned briefly to Sydney. 'I'm sorry I've upset you. I didn't mean anything by it.'

She closed the door, and as it slammed, as she shut out the sight of Nathan and Anna walking away down her front path, she sank to the floor and put her head in her hands and sobbed. Huge, gulping sobs. Sobs that caused her to hiccup. Sobs that took ages to fade away, leaving her crouched in the hallway just breathing in a silence broken only by the ticking clock.

Finally she was able to get to her feet, and listlessly she headed back to the kitchen to clear away the breakfast things.

Sydney had felt numb for a few hours. It was a strange feeling. Having got that angry, that upset, it was as if she'd used up a year's worth of emotions all in a few minutes, and now her body and her mind had become completely exhausted, unable to feel anything.

Now she sat in her empty home, looking at the pictures of her daughter, and felt…*nothing*. No sadness. No joy. She couldn't even bring herself to try and remember the days on which they'd been taken, and when she tried to remember the sound of her daughter's chuckles she couldn't conjure it up.

It was like being frozen. Or as if she could move, breathe, live, exist, but the rest of the world was seen through a filter somehow. It was as if her memories were gone—as if her feelings had been taken away and in their place a giant nothingness remained.

She didn't like it. It made her feel even more isolated than she had been before. Lonely. She didn't even have her daughter's memories to accompany her in the silence.

She wasn't ready to forget her daughter. To lose her. She needed to remind herself again. To reconnect.

Sydney looked up. Olivia's things were in the attic. Her clothes. Her toys. Her books. Everything. She hadn't been able to go up in the loft for years because of them, but perhaps she needed to at this moment.

So, despite the tiredness and the lethargy taking over every limb, muscle and bone, she headed up the stairs and opened up the attic, sliding down the metal ladder and taking a deep breath before she headed up the steps.

There was a stillness in the attic. As if she'd entered a sacred, holy space. But instead of vaulted ceilings with regal columns and priceless holy relics gleaming in soft sunlight there was loft insulation, piles of boxes and a single bulb that was lit by pulling a hanging chain.

She let out a long, slow breath as some of her numbness began to dissipate, and in its place she felt a nervous anxiety begin to build.

Was she right to be doing this? She hadn't looked through these things for so long!

Am I strong enough? What if it's too much?

But then there was another voice in her head. A logical voice.

It's only clothes. Books. Toys. Nothing here can hurt you.

Doubt told her that something might. But she edged towards the first box, labelled *'Costumes'*, and began to unfold the top, not realising that she was biting into her bottom lip until she felt a small pain.

The contents of the box were topped with taffeta. A dress of some sort. Sydney lifted it out to look at it, to try and force a memory. And this time it came.

Olivia had wanted a 'princess dress' for a party. They'd gone shopping into Norton town centre together, her daughter holding on to her hand as she'd skipped alongside her. They'd gone from shop to shop, looking for the perfect dress, and she'd spotted this one. With a beautiful purple velvet bodice and reams upon reams of lilac taffeta billowing out from the waist.

Olivia had looked perfect in it! Twirling in front of the mirror, this way and that, swishing the skirt, making it go this way, then that way around her legs.

'Look, Mummy! It's so pretty! Can I have it?'

Sydney smiled as she pulled out outfit after outfit. A mermaid tail, another princess dress, this time in pink, a Halloween costume festooned with layers and layers of black and orange netting. Sydney hesitated as she dipped into the box and pulled out a onesie made of brown fur. It had a long tail, and ears on the hood. Sydney pressed it to her nose and inhaled, closing her eyes as tears leaked from the corners of them.

Olivia had loved this onesie. She'd used to sleep in it. She'd been wearing it when… The memory came bursting to the fore.

The morning I found you.

She smiled bravely as she inhaled the scent of the onesie once again. It had been washed, but she was convinced it still had her daughter's scent.

An image of that awful morning filled her head. The day before Olivia had said she had a headache. She hadn't wanted to go to school. But Sydney had had a long day of surgeries, and Alastair had had work, so they'd needed their daughter to go in.

At the end of the day, when Sydney had gone to pick her up, Olivia had seemed in a very low mood—not her normal self. When they'd got home she'd said she was tired and that her head still hurt, so Sydney had given her some medicine and a drink and told her she could go to bed. She'd kept checking on her, but her daughter had been sleeping, so she'd just put it down to some virus.

When Alastair had got home he'd been celebrating a success at work, and that night they'd gone to bed and made love. The next morning Alastair had left early. Sydney had called for Olivia to come down for breakfast but she hadn't answered. So she'd gone up to get her and instantly known something was wrong. The second she'd walked into her daughter's bedroom.

She'd not been able to wake her. She'd called her name, shaken her shoulders—nothing. Olivia had been hot, and Sydney had gone to unzip the onesie, and that was when she'd seen the rash and called 999.

Sydney laid the onesie down. This was the last thing that Olivia had worn. It was too sad to focus on. Too painful.

She dug further into the box and pulled out a pirate costume.

Now, this has a happier memory!

There'd been a World Book Day and all the school's children had been asked to come in as one of their favourite characters. At the time Olivia had been into pirate stories, but none of the characters had been girl pirates, so she'd decided that she would be a pirate anyway. Sydney had rolled up a pair of blue jeans to Olivia's calves, bought a red and white striped tee shirt and a tricorne hat, and used an eye patch that they'd been gifted in an old party bag.

Olivia had spent all day answering every question Sydney had asked her with, *'Arr!'* and, *'Aye, Captain!'*

Sydney laughed at the memory, her heart swelling with warmth and feeling once again. Seeing her daughter happy in her mind's eye, hearing that chuckle, seeing her smile, feeling her—

She stopped.

Oh... Could Nathan be right? That I need to focus on the days she lived?

No. No, he couldn't be right. He hadn't experienced grief like this—he didn't know what he was talking about.

But I do feel good when I remember the good times...

Perhaps holding on to the grief, on to the day she died, on to the *pain* was the thing that anchored Sydney in the past? Maybe she was holding herself back? Isolating herself so that she could wallow in her daughter's memory. Was that why Alastair had moved on? Had he been able to let go of the misery and instead chosen to remember his daughter's vibrant life, not just her death?

Stunned, she sat there for a moment, holding the pirate tee shirt and wondering. Her gaze travelled to the other boxes. Books. Toys. Clothes. Was holding on to her daughter like this the thing that was keeping her from moving on? Perhaps keeping her daughter's things in the attic had kept Olivia trapped in a place that tortured them both.

I know I have to try to move on...but by letting go of my past will I lose my daughter?

The thought that maybe she ought to donate some of Olivia's stuff to a charity shop entered her head, and she immediately stood up straight and stared down at the open box.

Give her things away?

No. Surely not. If she gave Olivia's things away, how on earth would she remember her?

You've remembered her just fine with all this stuff packed away in the attic for four years...

She let out a breath. Then another. Steadier. It calmed her racing heart. What if she didn't do it all in one go? What if she just gave away a few pieces? Bit by bit? It might be easier that way. She'd keep the stuff that mattered, though. The onesie. Olivia's favourite toys—her doll and her teddy bear Baxter. Maybe one or two of her daughter's favourite books. The last one they'd been reading, for sure.

Maybe...

She saw the look on Nathan's face as he'd left. *'I'm sorry I upset you...'*

I need to apologise.

Guilt filled her and she suddenly felt sick. Gripping her stomach, she sat down and clutched the onesie for strength. For inspiration.

She would have to apologise. Make it up to him. Explain.

If he even wants to listen.

But then she thought, *He will listen.* He was a doctor. He was good at that. And she needed to let him know that she cared.

As she thought of how she could make it up to him she saw some other boxes, further towards the back of the attic. She frowned, wondering what they were, and, crouching, she shuffled over to them, tore off the tape and opened them up.

Christmas decorations.

Perhaps she could show Nathan in more than one way that she was trying to make things right...

She'd used to love Christmas. Olivia had *adored* it.

What child didn't? It was a season of great fun and great food, rounded off with a day full of presents.

She particularly remembered the Christmas before Olivia had died. She'd asked for a bike and Sydney and Alastair had found her a sparkly pink one, with tassels on the handlebars and a basket on the front adorned with plastic flowers.

Olivia had spent all that Christmas Day peddling up and down on the pathways and around the back garden, her little knees going up and down, biting her bottom lip as she concentrated on her coordination. And then later that day, after they'd all eaten their dinner, pulled crackers, told each other bad jokes and were sitting curled up on the sofa together, Olivia had asked if next Christmas she could have a little brother or sister.

Sydney's gaze alighted on the bike, covered by an old brown blanket...

She swallowed the lump in her throat. Olivia would have loved a sibling. A little baby to play with. What would she have made of Anna? No doubt the girls would have been best friends.

Thinking of Anna made her think of Nathan. She was so very grateful for him coming over today. Offering his olive branch. He had given her a new way of thinking. And how had she reacted? Badly! She'd seen it as an attack on her rather than seeing the kind and caring motivation behind it.

She could see now what he'd been trying to say. And she had missed it completely. It was true. She had been focusing so much on her daughter's death that she had forgotten to focus on her daughter's life.

And Nathan had also told her about his MS. It had been so brave of him to share that with her, and it must have been troubling him for some time. It must have been why he'd been so ill that day she'd looked after Anna. And hadn't Anna said her daddy was always sick and tired?

Poor Nathan. But at least he knew what he was fighting. It had a name. It had a treatment plan. She would have to look it up online and see what relapsing remitting multiple sclerosis really was. Especially if—as she was starting to hope—they were going to be involved with each other. It would be good to know what to expect and how to help.

Nathan had given her a gift. A way to try and lift the burden that she'd been feeling all this time. The guilt. The grief. He'd given her something else to think about. Told her to try and remember Olivia in a different way. A less heartbreaking way.

Could she do it?

Maybe she could start by honouring the season…

Sydney lifted up a box of decorations and began to make her way back down the ladder.

CHAPTER SEVEN

Mrs Courtauld had arrived for her appointment. She was there for a blood pressure check, and though she could have made an appointment to see the practice nurse to get it done she'd deliberately made a doctor's appointment to see Nathan.

She came into his room, shuffling her feet, and settled down into a chair with a small groan.

He forced a smile. 'Mrs Courtauld...how are you?'

'Oh, I'm good, Doctor, thank you. I must say *you* look a bit glum. I've been round the block enough times to know when someone's *pretending* to be okay.'

He laughed. 'I'm sorry. I'll try to do better. Are you ready for Christmas?'

Sydney's rejection of him had hurt terribly. Although he didn't think she'd rejected him because of his health—unlike Gwyneth—the way she'd thrown him out still stung.

'Of course I am! Not that there's much preparation for me to do...not with my Alfred gone, God rest his soul. But my son is going to pick me up on Christmas Eve and I'm going to his house to spend the season.'

'Sounds great. Let someone else look after you and do all the work. Why not?'

'I've brought those things that you asked for.' She

reached down into her shopping trolley and pulled out a small packet wrapped in a brown paper bag and passed it across the table to him. 'I asked around and so many people wanted to help. I hope it's the kind of thing you were after. Surprisingly, there was quite a bit that people had.'

He peeked inside and smiled. It *was* rather a lot. More than he could have hoped for. But would it be any good now?

'Perfect. Thank you, Mrs C. I appreciate all the trouble you went to to coordinate this. Now, shall we check your blood pressure?'

She began to remove her coat. 'Anything for our Sydney.' She looked at him slyly. 'Will you be spending Christmas together, then?'

He felt his face colour, but smiled anyway, even though he suspected that the chance of his spending Christmas with Sydney had about the same odds as his MS disappearing without trace. Choosing not to answer, he wheeled his chair over to his patient.

Mrs Courtauld couldn't know that they'd had a falling out. He'd been trying to help Sydney, but maybe it had come out wrong? He'd been going over and over what he'd said, trying to remember the *way* he'd said it as well as *what* he'd said, and he'd got angry at himself.

His patient rolled up her sleeve, staring at him, assessing him. 'She deserves some happiness, young Sydney. She's had her sadness, and she's paid her dues in that respect. Enough grief to last a thousand lifetimes. It's her turn to be happy.' She looked up at him and made him meet her gaze. 'And you could do that for her, Doctor. You and that little girl of yours.'

'Thanks, Mrs C.'

'Call me Elizabeth.'

He smiled and checked her blood pressure.

* * *

A bell rang overhead as Sydney walked into the charity shop. There was only one in Silverdale, and sales from it aided the local hospice. She hadn't been in for a long time, but was reassured to see a familiar face behind the counter.

'Syd! Long time, no see! How are you?'

Sydney made her way to the counter with her two bags of clothes. It wasn't much. But it was a start. 'Oh, you know. Ambling on with life.'

'We've missed seeing you in here. We could always rely on you to come in most weekends, looking for a new book or two.'

'I'm sorry it's been a while.' She paused for a moment. She could back out if she wanted to. She didn't have to hand these items over. 'I've…er…brought in a few things. Children's clothes.'

'Children's…? Oh, wait…not *Olivia's*?'

Her cheeks flushed with heat and she nodded. 'Just one or two outfits. Thought I'd better start sorting, you know.'

Lisa nodded sadly. 'Sometimes it's what we need to do, to move forward.'

She didn't want to cry. Wasn't that what Nathan had said in a roundabout way? And look at how she had treated him for it! Perhaps everyone had been thinking the same, but she'd been the only one not to know.

'It's all been laundered and pressed. You should be able to put it straight out.' She placed the two bags on the counter and Lisa peered inside, her fingers touching the fabric of a skirt that Olivia had worn only once, because she'd been going through a growth spurt.

'That's grand, Syd. I'll have a sort through and maybe make a window display with them. Launch them with style, eh?'

Unable to speak, Sydney nodded. Then, blinking back tears, she hurriedly left the shop.

Outside in the cold air she began to breathe again, sucking in great lungsful of the crisp air and strangely feeling a part of her burden begin to lift.

It had been a difficult thing to do, but she'd done it. She'd made a start. Hopefully next time it would be easier. But doing it in little instalments was better than trying to get rid of it all in one go. She knew that wasn't the way for her. Slow and steady would win this race.

But now she had a really hard thing to do. She had to see Nathan. Apologise. There was one last committee meeting tonight and perhaps there, on neutral ground, she could let him know that she'd been in the wrong. That it would be nice if he could forgive her. But if not...

She dreaded to think of *if not*...

Those hours in the attic—those hours spent sorting her daughter's clothes for donation—had made her begin to see just how much she had begun to enjoy and even to depend upon Nathan's friendship.

She'd been a fool to react so badly.

She could only hope he would forgive her in a way Alastair had never been able to.

It was the last committee meeting before the big day. The Christmas market and nativity—and the anniversary of Olivia's death—were just two days away, and this was their last chance to make sure that everything was spick and span and organised correctly. That there were no last-minute hiccups.

There was palpable excitement in the room, and Miriam had even gone to the trouble to supply them with chocolate biscuits to help fuel their discussion.

Sydney sat nervously at one end of the table, far from

Nathan, anxious to get the opportunity to talk to him and put things right. Her mind buzzed with all the things she needed to say. Wanted to say. She'd hoped she'd have a chance to talk to him before the meeting started, but he'd come in late once again and grabbed his place at the table without looking at her.

'The marquees are all organised and will be delivered tomorrow and erected on-site. Items for the tombola are all sorted, and Mike has promised us the use of his PA and sound system this year.' Miriam beamed.

'How are we doing regarding the food stalls? Sydney?'

She perked up at the sound of her name and riffled through her notes, her hands shaking. 'The WI ladies in the village are in full cake-making mode and most will bring their cakes down in the morning for arrangement. The manageress of The Tea-Total Café has promised us a gingerbread spectacular, whatever that may be.'

'Sounds intriguing. Any entries this year for the Best Pet competition?'

She nodded. 'The usual suspects. I'm sure Jim will be hoping to win back the trophy from Gerry this year.' She smiled, hoping Nathan would look at her so she could catch his eye, but he just kept gazing down at his own notes.

She could almost feel her heart breaking. Had she hurt him so much with her words the other day that he couldn't even *look* at her now? Was she shut out of his world completely? It hurt to think so.

But then he looked up, glanced at her. 'Can I enter Lottie?'

She turned to him and smiled hopefully. 'You can.'

Though they were seated two chairs apart, she itched to reach for his hand across the table. To squeeze his fingers. Let him know that she was sorry. That she hadn't meant what she'd said. That she'd had a knee-jerk reaction because she was frightened of letting go.

But then he looked away again as he scribbled something into his notes.

Her heart sank.

Malcolm filled them in on what was happening with the beer tent, the businesses that had applied to have a stall and sell their wares, who'd be covering first aid and said that licences for closing the road to the council had been approved.

'All that's left that's out of our hands is the nativity. Dr Jones, I believe your daughter is going to be the star attraction this year? Any idea how rehearsals are going?'

'Miss Howarth and Anna assure me that it's all going very well.'

'And I've arranged a small area for the donkey and other farm animals to be kept in whilst they're not performing,' added Sydney, hoping to join in on his contribution.

'Excellent, excellent!' Malcolm enthused.

Once the meeting was over Sydney quickly gathered her things and hurried out into the cold after Nathan. She *had* to catch up with him. She couldn't just let him go. Not like this.

The village had already gone full-force on Christmas decorations. The main street was adorned with fairy lights, criss-crossing from one side to the other, so as people walked along at night it was like being in a sparkly tunnel. Trees were lit and shining bright from people's homes, and some residents had really gone to town, decorating their gardens and trees into small grottos. It didn't hurt her any more to see it.

'Nathan!'

He turned, and when he saw her his face darkened. She saw him glance at the floor.

Standing in front of him, she waited until he looked up and met her gaze. 'Thank you for waiting. I...er...really need to apologise to you. For how I reacted—well, *overreacted* to what you said.'

He stood staring at her, saying nothing.

'I was so in the wrong. I wasn't ready to hear what you said, and I thought you were telling me I needed to be over Olivia's death, and...you weren't. You were telling me to focus on the good times and not the bad, and that was something completely different to saying, *Get over it Sydney!*'

She was wringing her hands, over and over.

'You were trying to help me. Trying to make me see that if I could just try and look at it in another way then it needn't be so painful. So sad. That it was trapping me in the past—'

He reached out and steadied her hands, holding them in his. 'It's okay.'

Relieved that he was talking to her, she had to apologise even more. 'It's not. I behaved abominably. I kicked you out of my house! You *and* Anna! I feel so terrible about that...so inhuman and abysmal and—'

He silenced her with a kiss.

It was so unexpected. One moment she was pouring her heart out, blurting out her apologies, her regrets for her mistake, hoping he would understand, hoping he would forgive her, and the next his lips were on hers. His glorious lips! Warm and tender and so, so forgiving...

She could have cried. The beginnings of tears stung her eyes at first, but then ebbed away as the wondrousness of their kiss continued.

He cradled her face in his hands as he kissed her and

he breathed her in. Sydney moaned—a small noise in the back of her throat as she sank against him. This was… amazing! This was what they could have had the other day if he hadn't thought otherwise and backed off. What they could have had if only she hadn't got angry or scared or whatever it was she had been, so that tricks were playing in her head.

Why had they delayed doing this? They fitted so perfectly!

His tongue was searching out hers as he kissed her deeper and deeper. She almost couldn't breathe. She'd forgotten how to. All she knew right now was that she was so happy he'd forgiven her. He must have done. Or surely he wouldn't be kissing her like this.

And just when she thought she was seeing stars, and that her lungs were about to burst, he broke away from her and stared deeply into her eyes.

She gazed back into his and saw a depth of raw emotion there, a passion that could no longer be bridled. He wanted her.

And she him.

'Drive me home,' she said.

He nodded once and they got into the car.

It didn't take them long to reach her bedroom. Once inside, their giggles faded fast as they stood for a moment, just looking at each other.

Had she ever needed to be with a man this much?

Sydney needed to touch him. Needed to feel his hands upon her. She knew that he would not make the first move unless she showed him that this was what she wanted.

She reached up and, keeping eye contact, began to undo the buttons of his shirt.

He sucked in a breath. 'Sydney…'

'I need you, Nathan.' She pulled his shirt out from his trousers and then her hands found his belt buckle.

Nathan's mouth came down to claim hers, his tongue delicately arousing as he licked and tasted her lips.

She pulled his belt free and tossed it to the floor. She undid the button, unzipped the zipper, and as his trousers fell to the floor he stepped out of them and removed his shirt.

'Now me,' she urged him.

She felt his hands take the hem of her jumper and lift it effortlessly over her head, and then he did the same with her tee shirt, his eyes darkening with desire as her long dark hair spread over her milky-white shoulders. His hands cupped her breasts, his thumbs drifting over her nipples through the lace, and she groaned, arching her back so that her breasts pressed into his hands.

His mouth found her neck, her shoulders, her collarbone, all the while causing sensations on her skin that she had not experienced for a very long time, awakening her body, making her crave his every touch.

He undid her jeans, sliding them down her long legs. His lips kissed their way down her thighs and then came slowly back up to find the lace of her underwear. Then he was breathing in her scent and kissing her once again through the lace.

She almost lost it.

When had she *ever* felt this naked? This vulnerable? And yet…she revelled in it. Gloried in it. She knew she needed to show him her vulnerability, show that despite that she still wanted to be with him. To trust him. After the way she'd treated him the other day, she needed him to know that she couldn't be without him.

'You're so beautiful…' he breathed, and the heat of his breath sent goosebumps along her skin.

His hands were at her sides, going round to her back. He found the clip on her bra and undid it. She shrugged it off easily, groaning at the feel of his hands cupping her breasts, properly this time, at the feel of his mouth, his kisses.

'Nathan...'

She could feel his arousal, hard against her, and she unhooked his boxers, sliding them to the floor.

As he lay back on the bed she looked at him in triumph. This beautiful, magnificent man was all hers. And she'd so very nearly cast him aside!

She groaned as she thought of what she might have lost and lay beside him, wrapping her limbs around him so that they were entwined as their mouths joined together once more.

All he'd ever done was listen to her. Understand her. Give her space and time to be ready to talk to him. Where else would she find a man that patient? That understanding and empathetic?

He rolled her under him and breathed her name as his hands roamed her body, creating sensations that she had forgotten she'd ever felt before. She needed him so much. Longed to be *part* of him.

She pulled him closer, urging him on as he began to make love to her.

This was what life was about! Really living. Being a *part* of life—not merely existing. It was about celebrating a relationship, sharing fears and desires and finding that one person you could do that with. About opening up to another person and being okay about that.

Nathan had shared his own vulnerability, his multiple sclerosis. It must have taken him a great deal of courage. And he had shared Anna with her. Letting her get to know his daughter. He couldn't have known that they would get on like this. Must have been worried that Sydney might reject them both once she got to know them.

I nearly did.

She suddenly understood how much pain he must have felt when she'd kicked him out and she pulled him to her once more, hoping as he cried out and gripped the headboard that he would finally see just how much he'd been right to trust her, after all.

She wrapped him safely in her arms and held on tight.

Afterwards, they lay in bed in each other's arms.

Sydney's head was resting in the crook of Nathan's shoulder and he lay there, lazily stroking the skin on her arms. 'I really missed you, you know...'

She turned and kissed his chest. 'I missed you, too. I hated what I did.'

'I understood. You were lashing out because what I said hurt you. You thought I was asking you to give up even *thinking* about your daughter.' He planted a kiss on the top of her head. 'I gave you the advice someone gave me once.'

She turned, laying her chin upon his chest and staring up into his face. 'What do you mean?'

'When I got my diagnosis I was in complete shock. It was like I was mourning my old life. The life in which I could do anything whenever I wanted, without having to think about muscle weakness or spasms or taking medication every day. I mourned the body that I thought would slowly deteriorate until it was useless, and I couldn't get over that.'

'What happened?'

'Anna was born. I was euphoric about that. But then I started thinking about all the ways I might let her down as a father. What if I missed school shows, or parents' evenings, or birthdays…? And then Gwyneth left, totally appalled by the fact that she'd got involved with someone with this illness, and that made me feel under even more pressure from myself. I *couldn't* let Anna down! She only had me to rely on. I *had* to be well. I *had* to be positive. But something kept pulling me back towards feeling sorry for myself. I'd lost my partner and my health and I couldn't get past that.'

She kissed his chest. 'I'm so sorry.'

'I went to a counselling group. It was led by a really good therapist. She helped me see that I was mourning a loss. I was mourning my future. She told me to look at it in a different way. Not to focus on what I'd lost, but on what I'd gained. I didn't necessarily have a bad life in front of me, that—I had a beautiful baby daughter who loved me unconditionally and I knew what my limits might be. But they weren't necessarily there. I had to celebrate the new me rather than mourn the old me. Does that make sense?'

She nodded, laying her head back down against his beautifully strong chest. 'It does.'

'Gwyneth leaving wasn't about me. It was about her and what *she* could deal with. I couldn't control her reaction, but I could control mine. And that's why I decided to focus on the good that was coming. On what I could learn about myself in the process. Discovering hidden depths of strength.'

'Did you find them?'

'Oh, yes!' He laughed, squeezing her to him. Then he paused for a moment and rolled above her, staring deeply into her grey eyes. 'Have you?'

She nodded silently, feeling tears of joy welling in her eyes.

'I think I'm starting to. Because of you.'

He smiled and kissed her.

CHAPTER EIGHT

It was the afternoon of the Christmas market and nativity and Anna was incredibly excited.

Nathan hadn't been able to get in touch with Sydney yesterday, being busy at work, but at least now he felt better about the direction they were heading in.

It was all going well.

When she'd slammed the door on the two of them and he'd had to walk away it had been the hardest thing he had ever done. Even harder still was the fact that Anna had been full of chatter about the kittens. When could she go and visit them again? Would Sydney mind if they went round every day?

He'd managed to distract her by getting her to read through her lines for her part in the nativity, and he'd been grateful when she'd gone quiet in the back of the car as she read her little script.

But now…? Everything was going well for them. He hoped he would get a moment to talk to Sydney, because he knew that this day would be hard for her.

She'd told him it was the anniversary of Olivia's death. That she'd always faced this day alone in the past. He tried for a moment to imagine what it would be like if he was mourning Anna, but it was too dreadful. He dashed the thought away instantly.

There was so much to do. He'd promised to help out with setting up the marquees and organising the stands, and said he'd be a general dogsbody for anyone who needed him.

Surely Sydney would be there too. She had stalls to organise. The Best Pet show to judge. He hoped he'd get a moment to talk to her, to make sure she was okay.

He parked in the pub car park and walked down to the square that already looked as if it was heaving with people and noise. Right now it seemed like chaos, but he hoped that by the afternoon, and for the nativity in the evening, it would all run smoothly and everyone would be entertained.

He searched for Sydney's familiar long chocolate hair in the crowd, but he couldn't see her amongst all the people bustling about.

This was his and Anna's first Christmas in Silverdale, and he was looking forward to making new connections with people that he'd only ever met as patients. He wanted to let people see him as someone other than a doctor. To let them see that he was a father. A neighbour. A friend.

Tonight was going to go really well. He knew it. And hopefully some of the villagers who didn't know him yet would get the opportunity to meet him and welcome him as a valued member of their community.

'Dr Jones! How good to see you. Are you doing anything at the moment?'

Nathan noticed Miriam, the secretary of the committee, loitering within an empty marquee that had tables set up but nothing else. 'No. How can I help?'

'I'm running the tombola, and all the donated items are in boxes in the van, but I can't lift them with my arthritis. Would you be able to?'

He smiled. This he could do. He was a strong man.

He could lift and carry whatever she asked of him and he would do it. 'A pleasure, Miriam. Where's the van?'

Miriam pointed at a white van parked on the edge of the barriers. 'You are a dear. A real bonus to our committee. We needed some new blood!'

He waved away her compliment. 'I'm sure Dr Preston is hugely missed. I just hope I can fill his shoes.'

Miriam beamed at him. 'You far surpass Richard Preston already, Dr Jones, just by my looking at you!'

Nathan grinned. 'If I was thirty years older, Miriam…'

'Thirty? Oh, you're too kind! *Much* too kind!'

Nathan headed to her van, opened it up and started pulling out boxes. Some were very light, and he assumed they were full of teddy bears and the like. But others were considerably heavier and he struggled to carry one or two.

Whatever were people giving away—boulders?

He lugged the boxes over to the marquee, and just as he set down the last one he heard Sydney's laugh.

Instantly his heart began to pound. She was *laughing.* She was *here.* She was helping out. Same as him. Just as she'd promised she would.

He looked about for her, and once he'd made sure Miriam was okay to empty out the boxes by herself found himself heading over to the pen that Sydney was building along with Mr Bradley from Wicklegate Farm—the owner of Bert the donkey.

'Sydney!'

She turned at the sound of his voice. 'Nathan!'

He kissed her on the lips in greeting—a gesture that earned a wry smile from Mr Bradley.

'How are you doing? I meant to call you earlier—'

'I'm fine!' she answered brightly.

'Really? You don't have to pretend. I know today must be difficult for you. I thought that—'

'Nathan… Honestly. I'm doing great.'

He tried to see if she was just being brave for him, but he couldn't see any deception in her eyes. Perhaps she *was* doing okay? He stood back as she continued to build the pen, fastening some nuts on the final fence with a spanner.

'It's for Bert and the goats and things. What do you think?'

'Erm… I'm no expert on animal holding pens, but these look good to me.'

She kissed him on the cheek. 'I've got lots to do. Off you go! I know you're busy, too. You don't have to hold my hand. I'm doing okay. I've got through this day before.'

He stilled her hands. 'You were on your own before.'

'And I'm not now. I promise if I have a problem, or get upset, I'll come and find you.'

'If you're sure…?'

'I'm sure.' She smiled at him. 'I appreciate your concern. Oh, I almost forgot—I have Olivia's costume for Anna.' She stepped out of the pen and over to her car, opening the boot and bringing back a small bag. 'It should fit. It's all loose robes, and she can tie it tighter with the belt.'

He nodded, accepting the bag. 'Thanks. She nearly had to wear what I'd made her.'

He would just have to trust her. She knew he would be in her corner if she needed him.

'I'm around. Just give me a shout and maybe we can grab a snack later? Before it all kicks off?'

She blew him a kiss. 'I'll come and find you.'

'I'll hold you to it.' He smiled and waved, and then, tearing himself away, headed off to deliver the costume to his daughter.

* * *

Sydney did as she'd promised. A few hours later, when the market was all set up and ready to open to the public, she sought out Nathan, She found him at the bakery tent, manhandling a giant gingerbread grotto scene to place it on a table, and they headed off to sit on the steps around the village Christmas tree.

Nathan paid for a couple of cups of tea for them both and then joined her, wrapping his arm around her shoulders in the cold evening air.

The Christmas market looked picture-postcard-perfect. The marquees were all bedecked with Christmas lighting, carols were being played over the PA system in readiness and—oh, the aromas! The scent of hot dogs, fried onions, candy floss, roasting chestnuts, gingerbread and freshly brewed coffee floated in the air, causing their mouths to water.

'Looks amazing, doesn't it?' she said, looking out at all their hard work. It felt good to be appreciating—finally—the magic of Christmas once again.

'It certainly does. Worth all those meetings we had to sit through.'

She laughed. 'When it all comes together like this it's hard to believe we managed to achieve it.' She paused. 'Did you get the costume to Anna? Did it fit?'

He nodded. 'Perfectly. Thank you.'

They sat in companionable silence for a while, sipping their tea and just enjoying the sensation of *being*. Enjoying the moment. It was nice to sit there together, watching everyone else beavering away.

Nathan took her hand in his and smiled at her as she snuggled into his arms. But then she sat forward, peering into the distance.

'Look! They're letting everyone in. Come on—we

have stations to man!' She tossed her paper teacup into a
nearby bin and headed off to her first job of the evening.

Nathan watched her go.

Was she really as unaffected by this day as she seemed?
He doubted it.

Frowning, he followed after her.

Silverdale was brimming with activity and the centre of
the high street looked amazing. Sydney would have liked
to truly immerse herself in the marvel of the beautiful
fairy lights everywhere. To listen to the carol singers and
their music. To taste the wonderfully aromatic food on
display and talk to all the visitors and customers. Enjoy
the floral displays.

But she couldn't.

She knew she had work to do, but she was beginning
to feel guilty.

Was she really pretending that today wasn't *the day?*
Had she deliberately tried to ignore it because she already
knew how guilty she now felt? She hadn't mourned as
much. She hadn't *remembered* her daughter the way she
usually did today.

She felt bad—even if *'usually'* mostly involved staring
at photographs all day and often ended with her being a
crumpled, sobbing heap.

Her heart felt pained. Just breathing seemed to be ex-
hausting. And yet she had to keep up a steady stream of
false smiles and fake jollity for everyone she met or saw.

Was she lying to Nathan? Or to herself?

The stallholders were doing lively business, and she
could see money changing hands wherever she looked.
People she knew walked their dogs, or pushed buggies,
or stood arm in arm looking in wonder and awe at their
hard-worked-for Christmas Market. And now crowds

were gathering at the main stage for the crowning glory of the evening—the nativity play.

She wandered through the tent with her clipboard, viewing the animals entered for the Best Pet competition. Their owners stood by, looking at her hopefully as she met each one, asked a little about their animal, remembering to remark on their colouring or lovely temperament and scribbling her thoughts on paper.

But she was doing it on automatic pilot.

Until she got to a black rabbit.

Lottie.

Lottie sat in her cage quite calmly, oblivious to all the hubbub going on around her. Her eye had healed quite well, and apart from a slight grey glaze to it no one would be able to guess that she had been attacked and almost blinded.

Sydney stared at the rabbit, her pen poised over her score sheet, remembering the first time Nathan had brought Lottie to her. How hard it had been to fight her feelings for him. How she'd tried to tell herself to stay away from him and not get involved. She hadn't listened to herself. He'd wormed his way into her affections somehow, with those cheeky twinkling eyes of his—*and, my goodness, it had felt so good to lie in his arms. Protected. Coveted. Cherished.*

And he was making her forget. Wasn't he?

No! Not forget. Just deal with it in a different way.

Losing Olivia had hurt like nothing she could ever have imagined. One minute her daughter had been lively, full of life, giggling and happy, and the next she'd wound up in a hospital bed, and Sydney had sat by her bedside for every moment, hoping for a miracle.

She'd felt so helpless. A mother was meant to protect her children—but how on earth were you meant to defend them against things you couldn't see? Bacteria. Viruses. Contagion. They were all sneaky. Taking hold of young, healthy, vital bodies and tearing them asunder. All she'd been able to do was sit. And pray. And talk to her daughter who could no longer hear her. Beg her to fight. Beg her to hold on for a little while longer.

It had all been useless.

She felt a bit sick.

What am I doing here?

'We need the result, Sydney. The nativity is about to start.'

Sydney nodded to Malcolm absently. She wanted to see the nativity. She'd promised Anna she would watch her and cheer her on as she rode in on Bert.

She marked a score for Lottie and then passed her results to Malcolm, who took them over to his small stand in the tent.

Pet owners gathered anxiously—all of them smiling, all of them hopeful for a win. There were some lovely animals, from little mice to Fletcher the Great Dane. Fletcher was a big, lolloping giant of a dog, with the sweetest nature.

Malcolm cleared his throat. 'In third place, with six points, we have Montgomery! A gorgeous example of a golden Syrian hamster.'

Everyone applauded as a little girl stepped forward to receive a purple ribbon for Montgomery.

'In second place, with eight points, we have Jonesy—a beautiful ginger tom.'

Again there was applause, and a young boy came forward to collect his ribbon.

'And in first place, with ten points, we have Lottie the rabbit!'

There were more cheers. More applause.

'Lottie's owner can't be here to collect her prize as she's preparing for her role in the nativity. So perhaps our judge—our fabulous Silverdale veterinary surgeon—would like to give us a few words as to why Lottie has won tonight's contest? Everyone… I give you Sydney Harper!'

Reluctantly, Sydney stepped over to address the crowd—a sea of faces of people she recognised. People she knew from many years of living in this community. There was Miss Howarth, Olivia's schoolteacher. And Cara the lollipop lady, who'd used to help Olivia cross the road outside school. Mr Franklin, who would always talk to Olivia as they walked to school each morning…

'Thank you, Mr Speaker.'

She tried to gather her thoughts as she stood at the microphone. She'd been in a daze for a while. Now it was time to focus. Time to ignore the sickness she could feel building in her stomach.

'There were some amazing entries in this year's competition, and it was great to see such a broad variety of much-loved animals, who all looked fantastic, I'm sure you agree.'

She paused to force a smile.

'I was looking for a certain something this year. I have the honour of knowing a lot of these animals personally. I think I can honestly say I've seen most of them in my surgery, so I know a little about them all. But Lottie won my vote this year because… Well…she's been through a lot. She went through a difficult time and almost lost her life. Instead she lost her eye, but despite that…despite the horror that she has experienced this year, she has stayed strong.'

Her gaze fell upon Nathan, who had appeared at the back of the crowd.

'She fought. And tonight, when I saw her in her cage, looking beautiful in her shiny black coat and with a quiet dignity, I knew I had found my winner. Prizes shouldn't always go to the most attractive, or the most well-behaved, or the most well-groomed. Animals, like people, are more than just their looks. There's something beneath that. A character. A *strength*. And Lottie has that—in bucketloads.'

She nodded and stepped back, indicating that she had finished.

Malcolm led the applause, thanked her, and then urged everyone to make their way to the main stage for the nativity.

Sydney waited for the main crowd to go, and when there was a clearing she walked out of the marquee, feeling a little light-headed.

She felt a hand on her arm. 'Thank you.'

Nathan.

'Oh…it was nothing.'

'Anna will be thrilled Lottie won. She didn't want to miss it, but she's getting ready for the show.'

'Make sure you collect your voucher from Malcolm later.'

'I will.'

'Right. Well…' She wanted to head for the stage. But it seemed Nathan still had something to say.

'You know, you were right just then.'

'Oh…?'

'About people having depths that you can't see. You know, you're a lot like that little rabbit. You have that inner strength.'

She didn't feel like it right now. 'We…er…we need to get going.'

'Wait!' He pulled something from behind his back. 'I got you this.'

He handed over a small parcel, wrapped in shiny paper and tied with an elaborate bow.

'It's for Christmas. Obviously.' He smiled at her. 'But I thought it was important to give it to you today.'

'What is it?'

He laughed. 'I can't tell you that! It's a surprise. Hopefully…a good one. Merry Christmas.'

Suddenly felt this was wrong. Much too wrong! She shouldn't be getting *presents*. Not *today*.

Nathan was wrong.

Today was the worst day to give her his gift.

'I… I don't know what to say.'

'I believe thank you is traditional.'

He smiled and went to kiss her, but she backed off.

'I can't do this,' she muttered.

'Syd? What's the—?'

'You shouldn't give me a gift. Not today. A present? Today? You know what this day is. You know what it means.'

'Of course! Which is why I wanted to give it to you now. To celebrate you moving forward, to give you an incentive to—'

It was too much. Sydney couldn't stand there a moment longer. She had to get away. She had to leave. She—

I promised Anna I'd watch her in the nativity.

Torn, she stood rooted to the spot, angst tearing its way through her as grief and guilt flooded in. This was *not* the way she should be on the anniversary of her daughter's death! She ought to be showing respect. She ought to be remembering her daughter. *Olivia.* Not Anna. Or Nathan. They couldn't be Olivia's replacements. They could never be what her daughter had been to her. Or mean as much.

Could they?

Her heart told her they might, even as the agony of this indecision almost made her cry out.

'Syd…?'

'Nathan, please don't! I can't do this. I can't be with you—'

'Sydney—'

'It's over. Nathan? Do you hear me? I'm done.'

He let go of her arms and stepped back from her as if she'd just slapped him.

She'd never felt more alone.

Nathan just stood there, looking at her, sadness and hurt in his eyes.

'You should remember what you said about Lottie. You're strong, too, you know… You've been through something…*unimaginable* and you're still here. But if you can't see it in yourself…if you can't feel it…believe it…then I need to keep my distance, too. I need to think about Anna. I can't mess her around. If you can't commit to us the way I need you to—'

'I never wanted to hurt you or Anna.'

'I know.' He looked away at the happy crowds. 'But… you did. Please let Anna see you before you leave.'

And he walked away.

Sydney gulped back a grief-racked sob, wondering what the hell she'd just done.

Sydney stood at the front of the crowd, waiting for Anna's big moment. She'd split up from Nathan as he'd headed backstage to give his daughter one last pep talk.

Guilt and shame were filling her. Today was the anniversary of her daughter's death. And she'd kept busy—tried her hardest not to think about her. She hadn't even gone to the cemetery to put down some flowers for her. She hadn't been for so long. Who knew what her daughter's grave looked like now? Mrs C had laid a flower there in November—was it still there? Dead and brittle? Covered by fallen leaves or weeds?

And she was here, waiting to applaud another little girl. What was she *doing*? She'd even given Anna Olivia's old costume. She'd be riding Bert, too. Saying the same lines. It would be too much to bear.

And now she'd hurt Nathan. Played around with that man's heart because she hadn't known whether she was ready to accept it completely.

Feeling sick, she was about to turn and push her way through the crowds when she noticed Bert the donkey come into view, with Anna perched proudly on his back.

Sydney gasped. She'd been expecting to be tormented with memories. But it was *so* clear now. Anna was *nothing* like Olivia. The shape of her face was different. She had her father's jawline, her father's eyes.

If I'd continued with Nathan I wouldn't have been just taking him on, but Anna, too. I'd have let them both down. And now I've broken his heart, and Anna's too...

Overwhelmed by shock and guilt, Sydney stood silently and watched. Suddenly she was smiling with encouragement as Anna's gaze met her own. She felt so proud of Anna. Almost as proud of her as she had been of Olivia, doing the same thing.

How can that be?

As she watched the little girl ride Bert over to his mark by the hay bale, dismount and then take the hand of her Joseph, Sydney felt sadness seize her once more. She could recall Olivia doing that very thing. She'd taken Joseph's hand and been led into the stable too.

'And Joseph and Mary could find nowhere to stay. The only place left to them was with the animals in the stable. And in the place where lambs were born Mary gave birth to baby Jesus…' A small boy at the side of the stage intoned his words into a microphone.

Anna reappeared, this time without her pregnancy bump and holding a doll, swaddled in a thick white blanket, which she lay down into a manger.

Why am I crying?

Sydney blinked a few times and dabbed at her eyes with the back of her hand. Was she being like the innkeeper of Bethlehem? Telling Nathan and Anna there was no room for them in her home? Her heart?

She'd felt there *was* room. It had been there. She'd felt it. Even now she could feel it.

Sydney turned and pushed her way through the crowds, tears streaming freely down her face, unable to look. Unable to face the future she would have had if she'd stayed with Nathan. Unable to believe that she had that inner strength Nathan had said she had!

It was too difficult to move on like this. Accepting Nathan and Anna would be like forgetting her own daughter, and she couldn't have that. Not ever.

Free of the crowds, she strode away from the nativity. She couldn't stay there any longer. She couldn't watch the end. All she wanted at that point was to be at home. To be surrounded by the things that made her feel calm again.

Back at her cottage, she threw her keys onto the table by the door and headed straight for the lounge, casting the still wrapped present from Nathan under the tree. She slumped into her favourite couch, settling her gaze upon her pictures of Olivia, on the one on the mantel of her daughter reaching up for those bubbles, which was now surrounded by Christmas holly and mistletoe.

She stared at it for a moment, and then sat forward and spoke out loud. 'She's not you. She could *never* replace you.'

Despite the heartache he was feeling at Sydney's abrupt departure, Nathan gave Anna a huge hug. She'd acted her part in the nativity brilliantly, and it had gone without a hitch. All those people who said you should never work with children or animals were wrong. Bert had done everything Anna had asked of him, and most importantly of all he had kept her safe.

Scooping her up into his arms, Nathan hitched her onto his hip and kissed her cheek. 'Well done, pumpkin.'

'Thanks, Daddy. Did you see me at the end? With my golden halo?'

'I did! Very impressive.'

'I made it in class.'

'It looked very professional.'

'I saw Sydney.'

He frowned, feeling his stomach plummet with dread. What had Anna seen? That Sydney had looked sick? That she'd run?

He'd almost gone after her. One moment she'd been there, and then the next...

'You did? She got called away, I think, towards the end. But she *did* see you, and she was smiling, so she was very proud.'

Anna beamed. 'I'm hungry, Daddy. Can we get something to eat?'

He nodded. 'Sure. I think the hot dog stand may just have a few left if we're quick.'

Putting her back down on the ground, he walked with her over to the fast food stall. He wasn't hungry. Not at all. All he could see was the look on Sydney's face just before she'd turned and bolted.

He'd been too far away to chase after her. Not that he could have done. He'd needed to be here for Anna, just as he'd promised. But he kept replaying in his mind the change that had come over Sydney's features. The brave smile she'd tried to give to his daughter before her face had fallen and she'd gone.

As they passed them various villagers stopped to compliment them and to tell Anna how well she'd done.

'Hey, guess what?' he said, determined to keep things happy and bright for his daughter.

'What?'

'Lottie won the Best Pet competition!'

'She *did*? Yay!' Anna jumped up and down with glee. 'Can we go and get her?'

'Let's eat these first.' He handed her a hot dog, covered with a healthy dollop of fried onions, ketchup and mustard. 'And then we will. Malcolm's looking after the pets at the moment, so she's not on her own.'

Anna bit into her hot dog and wiped her mouth when a piece of fried onion tried to escape. 'Did she get a ribbon?'

'I think she did.'

'And a prize?'

'I think so. She was very lucky, wasn't she?'

He was finding this difficult. Pretending everything was okay when all he wanted to do was sit alone and allow himself to feel miserable. Had he pushed Sydney too hard by giving her that present? Had he tried to make her accept things she wasn't ready to work through yet?

I should never have got involved! I should have kept my distance!

'We had the judge on our side.' Anna smiled and took another bite.

Did we? Maybe only briefly.

He bit into his own hot dog, but he didn't really want it. The smell of the onions only turned his stomach.

She'd not been gone long, but already he ached for her. Missed her. He'd thought for a moment that they had a future together. He'd pictured waking up in the mornings and seeing her next to him. Her grey eyes twinkling at him from her pillow. He'd imagined them taking country walks together, hand in hand, and having picnics in the summer—Sydney laughing in the warm sun, her hair glinting.

He'd imagined nights watching movies together and sharing a bucket of popcorn. Feeding each other tasty morsels and titbits from the fridge before running upstairs, giggling, as he chased her before they fell into bed. And then moments when they'd just talk. He'd hold her hand. Trace the lines on her palm. He'd imagined them making love. Maybe even having a family of their own together...

They could have had it all.

He'd had his heart broken again, and this time he felt even more distraught.

He'd known Gwyneth was selfish. Had always had to have things her own way. She'd always had the perfect life, and a disabled partner had not been for her. Even the promise of a new family, the child they'd made together, hadn't been enough for her. It had never been enough for her. His diagnosis had just been the last thing she'd needed before she walked away. He'd never expected that she would walk away from her own child, too, but she had.

Sydney was looking out for herself too, but in a different way. Her child—Olivia—had been the centre of her life. Her world. And her world had been taken from her. Her sun had been stolen so that she'd only been living in darkness.

Nathan had thought that he'd brightened that darkness for a while.

'Is Sydney coming to our house on Christmas Day?' Anna asked, finishing off her bun in a final mouthful.

'Er... I really don't know, Anna. She's a bit sad at the moment.'

'Because she doesn't have her little girl any more?'

Nathan looked at his daughter, surprised at her insight. 'Yes. I think that's it.'

But what if it wasn't just that?

'We could go to hers and try to cheer her up. It *is* Christmas, and Miss Howarth says it's the season of goodwill. We learnt that at school for the play.'

How simple it was in a child's world. Everything was so black and white. 'We'll see. You might be busy playing with all your new things.'

'Sydney could come and play with me.'

He sighed. 'I don't know, Anna. Perhaps we need to give her some space for a while.'

'I want to thank her for giving Lottie first prize. Can we go and see her now? Before Christmas Day? Before she gets sad?'

Nathan felt touched by his daughter's compassion. She was doing her best to understand. 'She's already sad. Maybe we'll see her in the village. Come on…let's get Lottie and go home.'

He took her sticky hand in his and together they headed off to the animal tent.

CHAPTER NINE

IT WAS CHRISTMAS MORNING. A day on which Sydney should have been woken by an excited child bouncing on her bed and urging her to go downstairs. Instead, she was woken by the sound of rain against her window, and she lay in bed for a moment, not wanting to move.

Christmas Day.

The house was full of decorations. Encouraged by Nathan, and feeling positive and optimistic, she had adorned the house throughout, sure in the knowledge that this season she would have a reason to celebrate. People she loved to celebrate *with*.

Only it hadn't worked out that way.

She stared at the ceiling and once again asked herself if she was really doing the right thing.

Nathan was a kind-hearted man. Compassionate, caring. And she felt sure he had strong feelings for her. Looking at the pillows beside her, she remembered that night they'd made love. How good he'd made her feel. The brief time that they'd had together had been exquisite. Being made love to, being cherished, being as *treasured* as he had made her feel, had made her realise all that had been missing from her life.

I'm alone.

He'd not come after her after the nativity. He hadn't

shown up in the few days afterwards either. She'd thought that he might, and she'd been prepared not to answer the door. To hide. But he hadn't come.

She'd always believed that by keeping her distance from romantic entanglements she was keeping herself safe—and, yes, she supposed she was. But she was also keeping herself in a prison of loneliness. It was a kind of solitary confinement. All she had was Magic, her cat. Her only interactions were with the people and the animals at work and the friendly faces she saw in the shops. When she returned home all she had left were herself and her memories.

Unless I choose Nathan's way of thinking.

Christmas was a time for family. She could be sharing the day with Nathan. With Anna. Darling, sweet little Anna, whom she also adored. And she was letting fear keep her away. Her fear of being vulnerable again. Of losing Nathan. Losing Anna. Of not being enough for either of them!

'I'm losing you if I do nothing!' she said out loud, angry at herself.

Putting on her slippers and grabbing her robe, she headed downstairs.

The Christmas tree twinkled in the corner, with just a few presents underneath it. There was that gift from Nathan. Something from her parents. A couple of gifts from faithful long-term customers at work. The gift she'd placed there in Olivia's memory.

There could have been more. There could have been something for Nathan. For Anna. There could have been happiness in this house again. The day could have been spent the way Christmas is supposed to be spent.

She could be cooking Christmas breakfast for them

all right now. Scrambled egg and smoked salmon. Maybe a little Bucks Fizz.

She sat by the tree and picked up the parcel from her mum and dad. It was soft and squidgy, and when she half-heartedly tugged at the wrapping she discovered they'd got her a new pair of fleece pyjamas. She smiled at the pattern—little penguins on tiny icebergs. The other gifts were a bottle of wine, some chocolates, a book…

All that was left was the gift from Nathan and the one for her own daughter that would never be opened.

She picked up the gift from Nathan and glanced at the card.

Merry Christmas, Sydney!
Lots of love, Nathan xxx

What would it be? She had no idea. Part of her felt that it would be wrong to open it now. They weren't together any more. He'd made that clear. She hesitated.

He'd wanted her to have it.

Sydney tore at the wrapping and discovered a plain white box. Frowning, she picked at the tape holding the end closed, getting cross when it wouldn't come free and having to use a pen from her side table to pierce it and break the seal. Inside, something was wrapped in bubble wrap.

She slid it out and slowly unwrapped the plastic. It was a picture frame, and taped to the front, was a small white envelope. There was something inside. A memory card…

It's a digital photo frame.

She plugged it into the mains, inserted the memory card and switched it on, wondering what there could be on it…and gasped.

There, right before her eyes, were pictures of Olivia

that she had never even seen before! Some were close-ups, some were group shots, some were of her with other people or children, most she recognised as people from Silverdale.

Olivia in a park on a swing set next to another little boy, who was grinning at the photographer. Olivia at a birthday party with her face all smudged with chocolate cake. Olivia in the front row of the school choir.

She watched in shocked awe as picture after picture of her daughter appeared on the screen.

Where had Nathan got these? They must have come from other people! People in the village who had taken their own photos and captured Olivia in them too. And somehow—amazingly—he had gathered all these pictures together and presented them to her like this!

Tears pricked at her eyes as she gazed at the beautiful images. And then it flicked to another picture, and this one was moving. A video. Of a school play. She remembered it clearly. It had been Olivia's first play and she'd been dressed as a ladybird in a red top that Sydney had spent ages making, sewing on little black dots and then making her a bobble headband for her antennae.

The video showed the last few moments. It captured the applause of the crowd, the kiddies all lining up in a row, taking a bow. A boy near Olivia waved madly at the camera, and then Olivia waved at someone just off to the left of the screen and called out, *'I love you, Mummy!'*

Sydney heard the words and burst into tears, her hands gripping the frame like a lifeline. She'd forgotten that moment. She'd been there. She remembered the play very well; she'd been so proud of Olivia for not forgetting any of her words, and she'd been a true actress, playing her part with aplomb. And at the end she'd seen Sydney in the crowd, and Sydney had waved at her madly and called out to her.

She pressed 'pause'. Then 'rewind'. And watched it again.

Sydney had always believed that she would never get any new photos of Olivia. That her daughter had been frozen in time. But Nathan had given her a gift that she could never have foreseen!

Surely he loved her? What man would do something so thoughtful and as kind as this if he didn't? He would have to know just what this would mean to her.

When the video ended and the frame went back to the beginning of its cycle of photos again, Sydney rushed upstairs to get dressed. She had to see him. She had to... what? Thank him?

'I don't want to thank him. I want to be with him,' she said aloud to Magic, who lay curled on her bed, blinking in irritation at her racing into the bedroom and disturbing her slumber. 'I've been so stupid!'

She yanked off her robe and her pyjamas and kicked off her slippers so hard they flew into the mirror on the wardrobe door.

She pulled on jeans, a tee shirt and a thick fisherman's jumper and twisted her hair up into a rough ponytail. She gave her teeth a quick scrub and splashed her face with some water. Once she'd given it a cursory dry with a towel she raced downstairs and headed for her car, gunning the engine and screeching off down the road.

She hadn't even locked her own front door.

But before she could go to Nathan's house there was somewhere else she needed to go first.

Silverdale Cemetery and Memorial Gardens was a peaceful place. But for a long time it had been somewhere that

Sydney had avoided. It had always hurt too much, and for a long time she hadn't come. She'd not felt she had the inner strength to get through a visit.

But today she felt able to be there.

She *wanted* to be.

Today she felt closer to her daughter than on any other day so far. Perhaps it had something to do with what Nathan had said. Perhaps it was because he had helped lift her guilt. Perhaps it was because he had given her that new way of thinking. But now Sydney felt able to go to the site where her daughter was buried, and she knew that she wouldn't stand there staring down at the earth and thinking of her daughter lying there, cold and alone and dead.

Because Olivia wasn't there any more. She wasn't in the ground, cold and dead.

Olivia was alive in her heart. And in her mind. Sydney's head was full of images long since forgotten. Memories were washing over her with the strength of a tsunami, pounding into her with laughter and delight and warm feelings of a life well-lived and enjoyed.

Olivia had been a happy little girl, and Sydney had forgotten that. Focusing too much on her last day. The day on which she'd been dying. Unconscious. Helpless. In pain.

Now Sydney had a new outlook on her daughter's life. And it was an outlook she knew Olivia would approve of. So the cemetery was no longer a place for her to fear but a place in which she could go and sit quietly for a moment, after laying some flowers. Bright, colourful winter blooms that her daughter had helped her to plant years before.

The headstone was a little dirty, so she cleaned it off with her coat sleeve and made sure her daughter's name was clear and bright. Her eyes closed as she pictured her daughter watering the flowers in the back garden with her pink tin watering can.

'I'm sorry I haven't visited for a while,' she said, her eyes still closed. 'But I got caught up in feeling sorry for myself. You wouldn't have approved.' She laughed slightly and smiled, feeling tears prick at her eyes. 'But I think I'm overcoming that. A new friend—a *good* friend—taught me a valuable lesson. I was stuck, you see, Olivia. Stuck on missing you. Stuck on taking the blame because I felt someone had to.'

She opened her eyes and smiled down at the ground and the headstone.

'I don't have to do that any more. I'm not stuck. I'm free. And because I'm free you are too. I can see you now. In my head. In here…' She tapped her chest, over her heart. 'I can see you so clearly! I can hear you and smell you and feel you in my arms.'

She paused, gathering her breath.

'You'd like Nathan. He's a doctor. He's a good man. And Anna…his daughter…you'd love her too. I know you would. I guess I just wanted to say that I… I *love* you, Olivia. I'm sorry I was gone for a while, but I'm back, and now I have someone looking out for me, and he's given me the ability to get *you* back the way I should have from the beginning.'

She touched the headstone.

'I'll be back more often from now on. And…er… I've put up a tree. I'm celebrating Christmas this year. There's something for you under it. You won't ever be forgotten.'

She sniffed in the cold, crisp December air and looked about her. Two headstones away was the grave of one Alfred Courtauld, and she remembered his wife telling her about how she'd once laid a flower on Olivia's grave.

Sydney picked up a flower from Olivia's bouquet and laid it on Alfred's stone. 'Thanks for looking after Olivia whilst I've been away.'

And then she slowly walked back to her car.

Nathan watched as Anna unwrapped her brand-new bike, her hands ripping off the swathes of reindeer-patterned paper that he'd wrapped it in, smiling warmly at her cries of joy and surprise.

'A *bike!*' she squealed, swinging her leg over the frame and getting onto the seat. 'Can I ride it? Can I take it outside?'

'Course you can.' He helped her take the bike out to the back garden and watched as she eagerly began to pedal, wobbling alarmingly at the beginning, but then soon getting the hang of it.

'Look, Daddy!'

'I'm watching, baby.'

He stood in the doorway, holding his mug of coffee, watching his daughter cycle up and down, but feeling sad that he couldn't give her more. He'd hoped this Christmas to be sharing the day with Sydney. To be opening presents together, giving Anna the feel of a *real* family, so the three of them could enjoy the day together because they were meant to be together.

But Sydney had kept her distance. She'd not dumped him as unceremoniously as Gwyneth had, but she'd still broken his heart.

It wasn't just Christmas he felt sad about. It was all of it. Every day. Christmas was a time for family, but so was the rest of the year. Waking every morning *together*. Listening to each other talk about their day each evening. Laughing. *Living*.

He'd hoped that Sydney could be in their lives, and he

knew that Anna still hoped for that, too. She'd kept going on about it last night before she went to bed.

'Will Sydney be coming tomorrow, Daddy?'

But, sadly, the answer had been no. She would not be coming.

As he headed into the kitchen to make himself a fresh drink he briefly wondered if she had opened his present. It had taken a lot of organising, but Mrs Courtauld had helped—reaching out to people, contacting them on her walks around the village with her greyhound Prince, asking everyone to check their photos and see if any of them had Olivia in them.

He'd dared to hope there would be one or two, but he had been surprised at how many they had got. Fourteen new pictures of Olivia and a video, in which she was saying the exact words he knew would gladden Sydney's heart.

Because that was what he wanted for her most of all. For her to be happy. For her heart to swell once again with love. He'd hoped that her love would include him, but...

His doorbell buzzed. *Who on earth...?*

It was Christmas morning. It couldn't be a door-to-door salesman, or anyone like that. Perhaps someone had been taken ill? Perhaps he was needed as a doctor?

He hurried to the front door, unlocked it and swung it open.

'Sydney?'

She looked out of breath, edgy and anxious. 'Can I come in?'

Did he want her to? Of course he did! He'd missed her terribly. But if she was just here to rehash everything they'd said the other night then he wasn't sure he wanted to hear it.

But something in her eyes—a brightness, a *hope*—made him give her one last audience.

He stepped back. 'Please.'

He watched as she brushed past and then followed her into the kitchen, from where she could see Anna, playing happily in the back garden.

'You got her a bike?'

He smiled as he looked at his daughter, happily pedalling away. 'Yes. It was what she wanted.'

Sydney turned to him. 'And what do *you* want, Nathan? For Christmas?'

Nathan stared at her, trying to gauge the exact reason for her turning up like this on Christmas Day. It wouldn't be a trick or a game. Sydney wasn't like that. *Had she opened his gift to her?*

He couldn't answer her. Couldn't tell her what he *really* wanted. So he changed the subject. 'Did you like your present?'

Tears filled her eyes then and she nodded, the movement of her head causing the tears to run freely down her cheeks. She wiped them away hurriedly. 'I can't believe what you did. How you managed that... I'm...speechless.'

He gave a small smile. 'I wanted to make you happy. Just tell me it didn't make you sad.'

'It didn't.' She took a quick step towards him, then stopped. 'I've come to apologise. I made a mistake.'

Nathan frowned. 'What do you mean?'

'Us. I made the wrong choice.'

He didn't say anything. He didn't want to make this go wrong. He needed to hear what she had to say.

'I got frightened. The day...the evening we were together I...panicked. And then, when I saw Anna on the donkey, I don't know what it was... I started feeling guilty. I felt that if I forgot Olivia on her most important day I would be losing her. But then today—earlier—I realised that it *wasn't* her most important day. The day she died. Her most important day was the day she was born! I can remember Olivia in a different way, just like you said, and by doing so I can also have a future. And so can she. Because my grief was trapping Olivia too. I kept her in pain all that time. Remembering the day she left me...when she was suffering. When I couldn't help her. I kept her there. Trapped in time. But not any more. Not any more,' she said firmly.

He shook his head. 'Love isn't what hurts people, Sydney. *Losing* someone hurts. *Grief* hurts. *Pain* hurts. But love? Love is the greatest thing we can experience.'

'I know. Because I feel love for Olivia. I feel love for...' She paused and stepped closer, laying a hand upon his chest, over his heart. 'For you. I've felt more helpless in the last few days being sat alone at home than I have ever felt. I need to be with you.'

He laid his hand over hers, feeling his heart pound in his ribcage as if it was a wild animal, trying desperately to escape. 'What are you saying?'

'I'm saying I want us to be together. You. Me. Anna. I think we can do it. I think that together we can be strong enough to fight whatever is coming in the future.'

'You mean it?' he asked, hope in his voice.

'I do. I've missed you so much! I've been in pain because I don't have you. I didn't realise what was missing from my life until I met you.'

Nathan smiled and kissed her, meeting her lips with a kiss that burned with fervour. Devouring her, tasting her, enjoying her with a passion that he could barely contain.

She wanted him! She wanted him back and she was willing to take a chance on their future.

It was all he'd ever wanted.

None of them knew what his future would be. How his disease would progress. Whether it would get worse. Just because that happened to a lot of people with MS, it didn't mean it would happen to him. He might be one of the lucky ones. It could stay as relapsing remitting. Who knew?

And even if it did progress he now felt braver about facing it. Because he would have Sydney at his side. And Anna, too. His daughter would not be burdened by carrying the weight of her father's illness all alone on her young shoulders. She would be able to share her worries. With a mother figure. With *Sydney*. And he knew Anna adored Sydney. They could be a perfect family. Or at least they could try!

They broke apart at the sound of his daughter's footsteps running towards the house.

'Sydney!' Anna barrelled into them both, enveloping them with her arms. 'Are you here for Christmas dinner?'

Sydney smiled at Nathan, and he answered. 'She's here for *every* dinner, I think. Aren't you?'

He looked into her grey eyes and saw happiness there. And joy.

'If you'll have me.'

Anna squeezed her tight and beamed.

Nathan pulled her close, so they were both wrapped in his embrace.

'Always.'

* * * * *

LET'S TALK
Romance

For exclusive extracts, competitions
and special offers, find us online:

f facebook.com/millsandboon

🐦 @MillsandBoon

⬡ @MillsandBoonUK

Get in touch on 01413 063232

JOIN US ON SOCIAL MEDIA!

Stay up to date with our latest releases, author news and gossip, special offers and discounts, and all the behind-the-scenes action from Mills & Boon...

 @millsandboon

 @millsandboonuk

 facebook.com/millsandboon

 @millsandboonuk

It might just be true love...

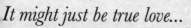

GET YOUR ROMANCE FIX.

Get the latest romance news,
exclusive author interviews, story
extracts and much more!

MILLS & BOON

MODERN

Power and Passion

Prepare to be swept off your feet by sophisticated, sexy and seductive heroes, in some of the world's most glamourous and romantic locations, where power and passion collide.

MILLS & BOON
True Love
Romance from the Heart

Celebrate true love with tender stories of heartfelt romance, from the rush of falling in love to the joy a new baby can bring, and a focus on the emotional heart of a relationship.

MILLS & BOON
MEDICAL
Pulse-Racing Passion

Set your pulse racing with dedicated,
delectable doctors in the high-pressure
world of medicine, where emotions run
high and passion, comfort and love are the
best medicine.